DREAMSCAPES OF DARKNESS

PETER REMEDY

CONTENTS

PROLOGUE

My name is Parker Sage Elway, and I need you to know one thing right now: I am not crazy. Some of the things you're about to read may make it seem like I've completely lost it, and I can't say I haven't questioned my sanity at points, but you must believe me. I am not crazy.

I'm writing this all down because they said it would help. They said that maybe, if I've got it all printed in black and white, I'll remember what really happened, and they'll be able to figure out how to help me. The thing is, I already know what really happened; I've been telling them the story for weeks now. It just sounds so completely ridiculous and insane that they don't believe it.

I probably wouldn't believe it, either, if I hadn't lived through it myself.

Everything that I am about to tell you is absolutely and completely true. This is what happened to me. It's inconceivable and thoroughly terrifying, but I swear that it's true. As you read the story I am about to tell you, I want you to open your mind to the idea that all the things I encountered are completely real. I need you to believe me and not think I'm insane. They think that I am. They think I'm suicidal and delusional and completely out of my mind. And it's not just them, either; it's Logan, it's Juliette—my best friends. They coddle me and pat my head and pretend that I'm okay, even though they really think I'm crazy.

But I'm not.

I'm not crazy.

And I can only hope that by the end of this, you still believe me.

CHAPTER 1

The nightmares began in July.

They sprung from nowhere, twisted horrors spawned from the darkest depths of my imagination to plague me as I slept. They were naught but airy figments, none concrete but each more terrible than the last. They woke me, screaming and sweating, at night's unholiest hours.

They made me fear the darkness.

Because that is what they were: darkness. They all took me to a world of thick, meaty black that was all-powerful and all-consuming, that gouged out my eyes with its completeness. There were no monsters, demons, or any kind of demented creature. What was terrifying, really, was the nothingness. The total lack of shape or matter, the uncertainty of whether or not I existed. And I dealt with these fears night after night without fail, until they had become somewhat of a routine.

For two months, they were the same.

In November, they changed.

I don't know how it happened, exactly. As I remember it, my dream began in the dark place; the horrible, suffocating, aphotic fearscape that claimed my mind when I closed my eyes. I was running, sitting, hiding, screaming—I was everywhere at once, but so was the darkness, and it was choking me. Its tendrils were in my nose, down my throat, clawing into my brain like it was trying to devour me from the inside out. I was dying. It was killing me.

And then I woke up.

Except that I didn't.

I opened my eyes, and it was dark. For a sliver of a heartbeat, I wondered if I was still in my dream—then I saw the outline of my dresser on the wall across from my bed, and knew I was in my room. I thought I was awake.

But I wasn't.

The best way I can describe it is that my brain was conscious, but my body was still trapped in dreamland. I couldn't move. Everything, from my head all the way down to my toes, was pinned to my bed, paralyzing me. I tried to move, to shift, to combat the terror growing in my chest, but my body would not respond.

That's when I realized that the tightening in my lungs was not fear.

And I was struck with the absolute certainty that there was something sitting on top of me. As soon that knowledge registered, the pain instantly doubled. Something dug painfully into the soft spot just below my rib cage—knees, knees, they had to be knees—pressing my lungs into my spine and cutting off my air completely. I could not breathe.

I mostly remember the fear. This fear, it was different from any kind of sensation I had ever felt before. It wasn't like the nightmares, where I knew that the terror would dissipate when I woke. Here I was awake. I was conscious and alert, but I could not move, I could not breathe, and I was seeing strange shadows seething in the air before me. It felt nearly identical to being swallowed by the darkness.

Except that this was real.

How long did it last? One minute, maybe two. But it felt eternal. Panic coursed through my body, not quick and frenzied but slow and thick like molasses, thorough, so that it managed to fill every crack and crevice. I couldn't call for help, because my lips were glued shut, and I didn't have the air to make a sound. It was like drowning and drowning and drowning, but never being able to give in to the blackness.

And in those awful moments, I truly believed that I was going to die.

When the paralysis released me, it was sudden. One moment, I was frozen, crushed beneath the humanoid weight on my chest. The next, I was flying up off my bed, into a sitting position, propelled by all the pent-up energy that had been building in my limbs.

I sat there, gasping, clutching my blankets to my chest and sucking in giant breaths of air. My eyes darted nervously around the room, searching for those misty shadows, but I saw nothing. I wondered, briefly, if it had just been a ghastly new chapter of my nightmare. The more my heart rate slowed and my nerves unwound, the more that seemed possible. I tried to convince myself that it was only a dream, albeit a very realistic one, in hopes that it would lessen my distress.

Regardless, I didn't sleep again that night.

By the time morning rolled around, the strange nightmare had faded into a mildly discomforting thought at the back of my mind. It all seemed so much less terrifying when there was sunlight streaming in through my window, chasing away the darkness.

I dragged myself out of bed at around eight A.M. and shuffled, zombie-like, to the bathroom adjoining my room. The face waiting for me in the mirror was nothing short of horrifying; my brown hair was a frenzied mess, and my eyes were baggy and full of sleep. I brought a hand to my forehead, which seemed to be paler than usual. Sweat came off on my fingertips. I frowned at my reflection for a moment, but quickly attributed my appearance to lack of sleep.

Shivering in the cold bathroom, I padded barefoot across the white tile and turned the shower to its warmest setting, so that steam filled the bathroom and clouded the mirror. Twenty minutes later I was standing in front of my dresser, washed, dressed, and making hideous faces as I put on makeup. My hair hung down my back, damp and wavy. It was annoying, the way it dripped into the hood of my gray jacket, and once I finished my eyeliner, I pulled it up into a sloppy ponytail.

My mother called me before I finished, shouting, "Par-ker! Come down here before breakfast gets cold!" I couldn't see her, but I knew she was at the bottom of the stairs, probably holding a pan full of whatever the hell she was cooking for breakfast.

I caught a whiff of its putrid stench from all the way up in my room.

"Com-ing!" I yelled back, snatching a tube of ruby red lipstick out of my makeup bag and smearing it onto my mouth. I kneaded my lips together as I belly-flopped onto the beige carpet and dug my shoes—a pair of beaten-up, floral Doc Martens—out from beneath my bed.

I threw them over my shoulder, clutching them by their fraying laces, and scooped up my textbook- and laptop-laden backpack. Before leaving the room, I cast one more glimpse into the mirror, silently approving the way my lined eyes and red lips popped out of my thin, angled face. I gave my reflection a staunch nod before moving on, leaving my bed an unmade mess behind me.

My mother did not turn around to acknowledge me as I swept into the kitchen, a tall, ungainly mess of teenage limbs. As I dumped my baggage unceremoniously onto the ground by the doorway, she stayed facing the stove.

"Give the dog food," was all she said.

I sighed at her back, rolling my eyes. But, obligingly, I slipped past her and into the indoor patio, where my dog's empty food bowl lay next to her bright blue bed.

"Zip, food!" I called, shaking a small mountain of kibble into the bowl. At the sound of my voice, there was a yipping response, and a moment later, a white, fluffy ball came bursting into the room via doggy door. Zipper, my three-month-old American Eskimo puppy who really isn't anything but two eyes and a pink tongue buried amidst a sea of albescent fuzz, hurtled past me on four stubby legs and shoved her face in the food pellets.

"Good morning to you, too," I muttered, stuffing my hands into my pockets as I reentered the kitchen.

Breakfast had finished cooking by then, though my mother was nowhere to be seen. A plate was waiting for me on the dining table: mysterious yellow sludge that may or may not have been scrambled eggs. I took one whiff, made a face, and dumped all of it into Zipper's bowl. She scarfed it down without complaint.

My stomach growled as I washed the plate, but I swallowed down the hunger. I'd pick up something from the cafe at school, like always.

When I turned from the sink, my mom was standing right behind me.

I jumped nearly out of my skin, the plate flying out of my hands and clattering against the counter top. The surprised tightening in my chest sparked a memory of the terrible dream, but I shook my head to clear it away. It was, after all, just a dream.

"Sweet Jesus, Mom," I murmured, absently pressing my fingertips to my jugular to feel my rapid heartbeat. "Don't do that."

She scrutinized my face, our identical hazel eyes locked in an unwitting staring contest. Hers narrowed more by the second, and I knew that in her head, she was criticizing my face, my makeup, the way I'd done my hair. She would have said it all out loud, too, if I hadn't told her to shut up the last time she'd tried.

As it was, she merely snapped out a crisp, "Put on your shoes, and hurry up. You're going to be late for school."

Butler County Community College is a pretty little school about fifteen minutes away from my hometown borough of Callery, Pennsylvania. It doesn't have the largest campus, but it's clean and grassy and surrounded by trees. It's also the only conceivable college that my mother would allow me to go after her expedited homeschooling plan had me graduating from high school two years earlier than planned.

She came very close to not letting me attend at all, but I threw a fit and managed to convince her to squeeze six classes a week into my "busy" schedule. That, though, didn't happen without the compromise that I wouldn't pursue my license until I turned eighteen, thereby forcing me to let her drive me to school.

It wasn't the best deal, but I could survive it.

Mom pulled up in front of the main building at approximately nine o'clock; fifteen minutes before my first class was due to start. As I got out of the car, she watched me silently. Her dark chestnut hair was pulled into a severe bun on top of her head, matching perfectly with her intimidating pantsuit.

"You didn't make it, did you?" she demanded as my feet hit pavement, her tone sharp and accusatory.

I raised my eyebrows at her as I shrugged my backpack onto my shoulders. "What?"

"Your bed. You didn't make your bed, did you?"

I heard the danger in her tone; I needed to say yes, because she was explosive. But I hadn't, in fact, made my bed, and she knew that because I never did, and we had that same conversation every single day.

"No, Mom," I said patiently, "I did not make my bed."

Cue the atomic bomb.

"Parker Sage Elway," she began, fisting her hands around the steering wheel, "how many times do I have to tell you to make your bed before you get it through your head? Do you ever listen to anything I say? I swear, young lady, if you continue acting like this, you can forget about ever leaving the house for anything ever again."

"Yeah. Sure. Right. Gonna be late, bye!"

Mom didn't say anything in response, but I could feel her staring daggers into the back of my neck as I strode away. I forced myself to lift my chin and not look back, though I could feel her gaze even once I'd entered the main building with all the other students. She wouldn't leave, I knew, until my first class had begun; she never did.

When people first meet my mother, they sometimes tell me that they're scared of her. And I can understand that. If it's your first encounter with a commanding, obsessive person like her, it can be a little bit disconcerting. But me; I'm used to it.

That was just my mom; Iris Elway: strict business woman, domineering single parent, and absolute control freak who seemed to have gotten the idea into her head that she was a fascist dictator. Were this a movie, I'd go on to say that despite all of those unfavorable qualities, she was actually a kind soul with a wonderful disposition.

But it's not, she wasn't, and if I said that, I'd be lying.

In the hallway between the arts and humanities buildings, two hands clamped onto my shoulders, stopping me in my tracks and pulling me back into a warm, sweater-clad body. Arms wound around me, and I looked up to see a familiar face smirking down at me.

"Morning, Logan," I said, snaking out from his embrace. My best friend returned the greeting, along with a light smack to my ponytail.

"Did you stop at the cafe?" he asked, knowing first hand the horrors of my mom's so-called "healthy cuisine."

I shook my head, grimacing as my stomach grumbled right on cue. I'd passed by the small coffee shop, but the line was so long and I had so little time that I'd decided to skip it.

"Well, then," Logan said, "today's your lucky day. I've brought you breakfast."

With his curly brown locks askew, Logan turned to his backpack and fought with the zipper for a moment before slipping out a paper bag and handing it over to me. His freckled face broke into a dimpled grin as I glanced inside to find two glazed doughnuts; the special, extra-greasy variety that's only sold at the school's cafe.

"Thank you," I cried, mouth already full with half of a doughnut. Logan just laughed shyly, swatting at his ear as we made our way to class a few doors down.

I met Logan Dearborn in a kid's swimming class when we were both five years old. We hit it off instantly, and, although he quit the very next day, stayed best friends for eleven years after. Logan was one of the few people that Mom let me leave the house to see. He's awkward, endearing, and so totally awesome with adults that he even managed to charm my mother, a feat that no one else has been able to accomplish. Like me, he graduated high school at sixteen, and, being that he was enrolled in a real school instead of homeschooled by a nutcase mother, I think his early graduation can be attributed solely to his abnormally high intelligence level.

Logan is very smart.

We walked into our first class of the day a few minutes before the lecture, as the professor was setting up his notes at his infamous stone pedestal. The class was Psych 101, otherwise known as general psychology, and though it met three times a week, it was the only course identical on both of our schedules. Logan's other classes were all art-based, while I was floating around between other psych courses and criminology.

"So, Parker," Logan said casually as we took seats at the front of the hall, "did you sleep okay last night?"

I was in the middle of pulling my laptop out of my backpack, and I froze. My entire body stiffened, and I knew that Logan noticed because he put a steadying hand on my arm. All morning, I had done a fairly good job of erasing the night's terrors with daylight, but a small sliver of fear still lingered in the back of my mind. At Logan's mentioning, I immediately felt it slither down and clutch at my erratically beating heart.

"Parker?" Logan asked carefully. "Are you okay?"

I couldn't move. I couldn't breathe. I couldn't do so much as scream. How could I possibly be okay?

"Parker?" he repeated.

With a big gasp of air, I sat down hard, slamming my laptop onto the desk. My backpack lay open, stuff falling out of it, but I ignored it as I wrapped my arms around myself and shivered.

"I'm okay," I murmured belatedly.

Quietly, Logan sat down beside me and pressed his shoulder to mine. "Was it bad last night?" he whispered.

I nodded silently. At that point, he was the only other person who knew about my nightmares, because he was the only one I could trust not to freak out about them. And unlike most people, he knew how to handle me when I got upset.

"You want to tell me about it?"

He was looking at me, watching my face with evident concern, but I couldn't return his gaze. I whispered, "It's nothing, just weird," and tried to stop myself from shuddering again at the memory.

At that moment, the professor, Dr. Hennessy, cleared his throat at the pedestal and informed us that the lecture was about to begin. I numbly reached over to turn on my computer and start up the voice recorder, but Logan didn't move. He was still staring at me.

"Parker," he said seriously, "are you sure that you're all right?"

Deep breath. Three seconds in, four seconds out. Forget, forget, forget, because it was only a dream.

"Really, Logan, don't worry," I assured him, forcing a smile as I turned to look him in the eye. "I'm perfectly fine."

Chapter 2

Callery, Pennsylvania is asleep by nine P.M. It's a small town, with a whopping population of 398 at the 2011 census, meaning that there aren't nearly enough people to have an active nighttime scene. I hear that in other places, Friday nights are a big deal, with people dressing up and going out on the town for a night of drinking and dancing and who knows what kinds of ungodly things. In Callery, unless you're planning to throw a party at the general supply store, stuff like that just doesn't happen. Apart from the rare occasion when there's a festival or other event in town, the neighborhood streets have been cleared out by nine.

Kids who can be bothered might drive out to Cameo, a club in the heart of the county that doesn't card, or sneak some beer out of their parents' stash and hang out on the bleachers at the high school. But then there's kids like me, who, with strict parents and no car, are forced to spend their Friday nights trapped in the house, lamenting over the fact that they're unable to wander the empty and badly lit streets.

Friday nights, for me, were routine. Juliette Westbury, my neighbor and close friend, would show up at my door at seven in the evening, right after dinner, laden down with a pillow, sleeping bag, and a gargantuan makeup box that was bigger than she was. It was our ritual to paint our faces, style our hair, and dress up like we were going out, only to crash in my room and watch chick flicks and vulgar comedy films until two A.M. She'd sleep over until the next day, but leave before breakfast because my mother's cooking can break down even the kindest spirits.

That night was just like any other before it: Juliette and I were in my bathroom, elbowing each other for space as we applied eyeshadow up to our eyebrows. Juliette's long, copper blonde hair was spun into a braided side ponytail atop her head, pulled back completely so that it exposed her round face and baby blue eyes.

"Parker Sage, will you please pass me the blush?" Juliette asked, holding out a hand without looking at me. I clapped it into her hand, trying to hold back a laugh at the sound of her voice. But Juliette, being the uncannily perspicacious person that she is, noticed my amusement without even looking at me. She lowered the brush from her face and glanced over at me, giving me the same dry stare that I had received so many times before.

"I have known you for six years, sweetheart," she drawled. "It's about time that you get a hold of yourself and stop laughing at my accent every time I speak."

I bit down on my tongue to quell the giggles bubbling up in my throat. "Don't be so touchy about it," I said, rolling my eyes. "I ridicule your voice out of love."

"Oh, I'm really feeling the love," she muttered.

If there's one thing I love about Juliette, it's her accent. She and her family moved in from Louisiana when we were ten, and six years in Pennsylvania hasn't been able to shave off the Southern twang in her voice.

The first thing I ever said to her, when we first met, was, "Your voice is really weird sounding." She took one look at me and the smile fell off her face and she replied, "Your face is really weird lookin'."

I decided I liked her after that.

Juliette was pretty and dainty and careful, and my mother liked her because she said "please" and "thank you" and always called me Parker Sage. But I learned not to be fooled by her faux manners and Southern hospitality; that girl can dole out insults like nobody's business.

"Parker Sage," Juliette said offhandedly, "I do hope you realize that it looks like someone slammed a door on your right eye."

I rest my case.

By midnight, my mom had gone to bed, and Juliette and I were about halfway through Stepbrothers. We'd been sprawled out across my bed in dresses and full makeup for over three hours, watching terribly hilarious comedies from Juliette's bottomless movie collection. I'd all but forgotten about the nightmare by then, as I lay there with my legs crossed and my face in the soft fur of a snoozing Zipper. My eyes were beginning to slip shut, unable to focus on the TV mounted on the wall above my desk.

"Wanna sneak over to Stan's?" Juliette asked as Brennan and Dale were beat up by children and forced to lick dog feces. Stan's was a seedy bar at the edge of town, walking distance from my house, that sold drinks to minors for two dollars over regular price. It was a licentious, illegal rip-off, but if you were a teenager craving alcohol, it was your best bet. The two of us sometimes sneaked over if we knew my mother wouldn't catch us and drank just enough to feel buzzed, but not so much that we'd be hungover the next morning.

After my rough dream the night before, that sounded pretty good—but my limbs were deadweight, and I wasn't sure I had the energy to haul my behind out the window.

"Let's skip it this week," I said, a yawn escaping my lips. "We'll go next Friday."

Juliette shrugged, rubbed at her eye so that her mascara smeared. "Whatever."

I was drifting off into hazy half-consciousness when a frantic buzzing erupted beneath my shoulder, drawing a yelp from Zipper and sending her skittering off the bed. I shook myself awake and pried my phone from beneath my arm to check the caller I.D.

"Who is it?" asked Juliette, her voice muffled by my gray striped comforter.

"Logan," I replied. "I'm gonna take it outside."

She muttered something that might have been anything from "okay" to "I hope you pitch off your balcony and die" as I swung my legs out of bed and padded across my large room to the ornate glass door on the right wall. My room connected to a small, half-circle balcony that looked out onto the street, and I stepped out onto it before accepting the call.

"Hey, what's up?" I said, sliding the door closed behind me. It was chilly outside, just as autumn should be, with a nip in the air that bit at my skin through my sweatshirt.

"Hey," Logan said, his voice sleepy, as I leaned against the white rails and stared down the street punctuated with lights. "You gonna be okay tonight? Should I come over or anything?"

I sighed, rubbing my arm with one hand as my eyes roved over Stella Home's house across the street. "That's tempting," I admitted, "but I think I'll be fine." I smirked slightly. "Unless, of course, you want to come over. Juliette is here, after all."

Through the speaker of my iPhone, I heard him swallow, and imagined that he was blushing at the other end of the line. Since Juliette moved in next door to me, Logan had had a giant crush on her. The three of us were close and hung out often, but that didn't stop him from acting like geek every time Juliette so much as glanced in his direction.

"N-no, um—I trust Juliette to keep you safe."

"Yeah?" I inquired. "Well, who's going to keep her safe?"

An exasperated sigh from his side. "Parker, don't make me hang up on you again."

I allowed myself a private grin at his annoyance. Some might argue that it was cruel of me to tease him about his crush, because Juliette had blatantly rejected him on more than one occasion, but I was pretty sure that being his best friend gave me some kind of right. Besides: Juliette had admitted that she found his advances cute. It's just that she was older than us—seventeen years old, and a senior in high school—and had a strict policy against dating someone younger than her. Personally, I didn't think a year made much of a difference; maybe it was a Southern thing.

I didn't say anything for a moment after that, content to simply listen to Logan's breathing and know that he was there. I leaned my elbows against the railing, resting my chin on the back of my hand as I surveyed the street below. The house across the street, a white paneled two-story, had a deep front yard of overgrown grass and spindly weeds. I knew that from memory—right then, the yard was shrouded in darkness. The moon was just a sliver, so the only light came from a streetlight in the middle of the sidewalk that cast a thin sphere of brightness onto the grass.

I merely scanned over the streetlamp, instead pointing my attention to the darkened sky. Logan's call was still connected, but I couldn't hear his breaths anymore, and figured he must have set the phone down. He did that sometimes. I counted the stars, the clear shining points against a blanket of black velvet, idly connecting them together into their constellations.

A breeze whipped through the air just then, sending an icy finger through my whole body, and I knew that it was time to go inside. Unfortunately for me, I was ridiculously susceptible to sickness. Even ten minutes out in the cold was known to have me in bed with pneumonia. Juliette always claimed that it was because I was too thin—but I digress.

"Hey, Logan," I said quietly, "I think I'm gonna go, okay?"

There was no response—most likely, my best friend had fallen asleep, as was his dorky habit. Shaking my head, I swept my gaze back toward earth, past Stella's white house and weedy lawn that was only partly illuminated, and was just about to turn back into my room when I realized—

There was someone standing under the streetlight.

And they were staring straight at me.

"Oh my God!" I shrieked, jumping back so far that I hit the door. That roused Logan, and his voice immediately came through the speaker, shouting, "What? What? Parker, what happened?"

I was half sitting, half standing against the glass, my eyes squeezed shut and two fingers pressed to my neck. My pulse was hammering.

"Parker?" Logan repeated.

"Holy hell," I hissed. "Logan, there's someone out here, there's someone watching me from across the street, and oh God, Logan, you know that no one comes out this late, but they're there, and they're watching."

I thought I heard him swear before he said, "Parker, who is it? Do you recognize them? Is it a man or a woman?"

"I don't know!" I cried, shaking with surprise and adrenaline and fear. "I'm not looking!"

I pressed my hand to my face, feeling my eyelashes crunch. There was only one thing I remembered about the person, and it was their eyes; their black, black, inkwell eyes, unblinking and staring at me, staring at me still and—

As if of their own accord, my eyes snapped open. I pressed back into the door as I stared across the street, dreading what I would see.

But the sidewalk was empty. There was no one there.

I gasped, eliciting an immediate "What?" from Logan.

"They're gone," I whispered. "There's no one."

Silence.

Crickets.

No one across the street.

"Are you sure they're gone?" Logan asked. Then, after a pause, he added, quieter, "Are you sure they were there?"

Just like with that terrible nightmare, I tried to convince myself that I had just been seeing things, but it didn't work. This time, the scene was cemented in my memory. Maybe I couldn't remember the person's face or what they were wearing, but I knew I had seen those eyes. There was no way that something could be burning a hole in my mind like that and not be real.

"I'm sure," I said with absolute certainty. "They were there. Now they're gone."

I looked up and down the street, squinting at the dark crevices and shadows. I saw no one.

"Well, go inside, okay?" Logan's voice sounded strange, tight. "There's no guarantee that whoever you saw was malicious, but I don't want you to take the chance. Just go inside."

"Right," I mumbled shakily, "inside."

I fumbled with the door, slipping back into my room and locking it again behind me. Juliette was in the bathroom; she had missed the whole episode.

"Are you inside?" Logan questioned.

I nodded, remembered he couldn't see me, and gave an affirmative grunt. My hands were shaking, my body quivering. I slid to the ground, holding onto my phone for dear life, and pulled my curtains forcefully shut. I didn't know who I'd just seen, but they were real. And I didn't want to leave myself in open view.

"I don't know what just happened," I said, feeling the need to say something but not knowing what. "I don't scare easily, Logan; you know that. What was that?"

My best friend blew out a gust of air. "It think it's the nightmares, Parker. It's like the lesson in psych the other day, about how the mind can take a perfectly normal sight and twist it into something completely unlike what it's actually seeing."

I gave a wobbly laugh. "Are you saying I'm hallucinating?"

In the bathroom, the toilet flushed. On the TV screen, Brennan and Dale were arguing. Logan's voice, when he spoke, was very serious.

"No," he said. "I'm saying that your mind is under a lot of stress, and it's reflecting that into reality. The person you saw was probably just a late night jogger—they're rare, but not impossible. The part about them watching you was all in your head."

"Yeah, that's probably all it was," I agreed, just to appease him. "You're right. It's the nightmares."

"Exactly." Logan sounded pleased. "Now go to sleep, okay? You sound like you need it."

I swallowed hard. The prospect of sleep was not sounding great, especially after seeing that person outside. But at Logan's comment, I heaved a giant, arcing yawn.

"I do," I murmured. "I definitely do. 'Night, Logan."

"Goodnight," Logan replied, sounding distinctly relieved. "And remember, Parker—it was just a jogger. I'll see you tomorrow."

As we both hung up, I sauteed those words in my mind. Under a lot of stress. Not impossible. All in your head.

Just a jogger.

But I remembered those eyes, those solid onyx eyes that burned me even from so far away, and I knew (I knew) that whoever that person was—they were no jogger.

It wasn't until nearly three hours later that we finally went to sleep, after we'd exhausted our eyes and turned our brains to sludge with another two movies. My mind was brimming with the schmaltzy sweetness of Cinderella—I'd managed deter Juliette from sneaking in an impromptu showing of Saw II, though only with the promise that we'd watch it the following week—which I would normally loathe, but tonight, the image of twirling blue ballgowns behind my eyelids was bringing me much needed repose.

Once I'd had a few moments to calm down, I'd decided that Logan was probably right: I'd just been messing around with reality. Superstition had never been my style, and as I pondered it further, I really began to realize how ridiculous my fear had been. There was no law in Callery saying that a person couldn't be outside at midnight, and in the darkness an innocent human being had become a ghastly phantom.

I opted not to tell Juliette what I'd seen, because jogger or not, she was the kind of person who'd insist that we go outside with butcher's knives, find the offender, and hack him or her to pieces. And despite being ninety-nine point nine percent certain that what I'd seen was a trick of light, I wasn't particularly eager to go outside at all hours and risk the wrath of my mother. That's what I told myself, anyway—and I wasn't having any trouble believing it.

At two fifty-seven A.M., Cinderella came to a happily ever after ending, and I reached one deadened arm over to turn off the television. It turned out, though, that the remote just happened to be miles away, at the foot of my bed. And as it happens, that's just where Juliette lay sprawled out, having fallen asleep at some point between the ball and the wedding.

At two fifty-nine, I said "screw it" out loud, stifling a yawn as I reached for my pillow. The TV had become a pixelated field of blue and it was buzzing slightly, but I just pressed my face into the sheet and ignored it. It was dark in my room—I'd turned out the light ages ago—but it wasn't frightening just then. The shadows were shadows, but that's all they were and they wouldn't hurt me if I didn't let them.

At exactly three o'clock A.M., I fell asleep and didn't dream. I slept without incident for half an hour.

At three thirty-three, I opened my eyes to darkness.

And that's when the horror began.

Once again, I was frozen. My body was immobilized, anchored in place by some kind of dragging weight. There was pressure on my chest, pressure like when you're at the bottom of the ocean without air and water is flowing into your mouth and the depth is slowly crushing your lungs.

I knew that feeling; I'd been there.

And here, in my room, it was happening again.

My eyes were the only things that could move, and they swept to the left just in time to see the numbers on my digital clock change to three thirty-four. Fear was pulsing through my body, begging it to move. I could, just barely, see my arms and legs splayed out before me, but no command from my brain could make them move. I could feel my chest tightening, fighting, as that bone-crushing tension increased, so heavy now that it should have snapped me in two.

I swear to God, if I hadn't known better, I would have said that someone was sitting on my chest, someone who was invisible and unnaturally heavy and wanted to suck the life out of my soul. What I felt was utter panic like razor-edged butterflies in my stomach, violent and insistent. I longed to press my fingers to my pulse, to make sure I was still alive and not trapped in a terrible hell, but my fingers would not even twitch.

And that's when I noticed something else—the light of the television had dimmed.

With a strange, mounting fear in my stomach, I hurled my gaze to the side before I could hesitate. And there—there—right in front of the still-buzzing TV screen, a figure stood.

It had no face; no features; nothing to identify it by. But it stood beside my bed, tall and shadowed, a calignous being that watched me in my terror. There were no eyes on the vague form of its face, but I felt it staring at me, boring its glare into the center of my forehead.

A thousand panicked thoughts raced through my mind, but none of them had traction and they just kept slipping through in an endless frenzy. I tried to pray, but all the words in my head were sludge, they weren't fast enough, and they weren't enough to save me when the figure moved.

When it slid toward me.

When it reached out something that looked like an arm and brushed it over my face.

A cold breath dusted my cheek, turning my skin to ice. The figure remained there for a moment, its invisible eyes tearing me to pieces, before moving backward, away from me. Without turning, it edged to my door and dissipated into foggy nothingness.

Then air came rushing back into my lungs.

Then my limbs were set free in a twitching delirium.

Briefly, for a few raging heartbeats, I was plunged into an infernal sleep, and the world slipped away for a moment.

When I woke up, I was screaming.

Chapter 3

I screamed until my throat went raw, until spots danced in front of my eyes and sweat poured in torrents down my face. I screamed until my door was thrown open and the lights sparked on and Juliette and my mother appeared in front of me, shouting.

"Parker!" Mom barked, standing stiffly by the side of my bed. "Parker Sage Elway, stop that right now!"

I couldn't stop. I didn't, until my mother's hand shot out and clamped itself over my mouth. Abruptly, my delirious shriek cut off into silence. I stared at my mother, wide-eyed, panting into the cool flesh of her palm. Her touch reminded me of the figure, its icy dark fingertips caressing my cheek, and I had to fight the urge to recoil.

"Juliette," my mother said briskly, "what happened?"

My friend was perched at the edge of my bed, the end of the comforter bunched beneath her chin. I might have laughed at the way her makeup was smeared on one side, except that we were both shaking too much for anything to be funny.

"I-I don't know," Juliette uttered helplessly. "I just woke up and she was howling and I didn't know what to do! I-I'm sorry!"

Through glazed eyes, I watched my mother's sharp face clench, her nose scrunching slightly. Even now, having been roused from sleep, her demeanor was tight and severe. She drew her hand from my mouth very slowly; every move she ever made was deliberate, precise. Her gaze flickered over to me, and she pressed the heels of her hands into her hips.

"Are you done?" she demanded. I nodded emptily. "Then tell me what happened."

I looked my mother in the eye, some of my confidence returning as I straightened up. Even still, I felt the ghost of frosty fingers against my face.

"There was something in my room," I said, my voice as still as I could make it. "It was right there, right in front of the television." I pointed, remembering the inky shadow. "It was this big, black figure, and I couldn't see a face or anything, but it was there. I swear, it was there. I would have screamed or called for help, but I—I couldn't move."

I fisted my hands around the comforter, my bony hands being swallowed by the plush fabric. My hair fell across my eyes, and I knew I looked like a mess. God knows I felt like one.

Juliette, a few feet away, was staring me down with blue-eyed incredulity, her expression conveying complete disbelief.

"Parker Sage," she began gently, "don't you think I would have seen if there was someone in the room? You must have just been dreaming."

I turned on her sharply, glaring, and spat, "I was not dreaming."

My mother didn't even look at Juliette. Her eyes were on me, unblinking, as she calmly stated, "Juliette, maybe you should leave."

"But Ms. Elway!" Juliette protested immediately. "It's nearly four o'clock in the morning, I can't—"

"Juliette," my mother repeated, more forceful this time, "maybe you should leave."

Mom was looking at me, and I was looking at her, but I distinctly heard Juliette gulp down a huge swallow. She knew better than to argue with my mother. No one argued with my mother.

"I'll let you out," Mom stated, calm and stiff. She rose, her firm stare bringing Juliette to her feet as well. My friend grabbed her sweater, raking a hand through her hair. She still looked confused and groggy, but she shuffled over and squeezed me in a one-armed hug, murmuring something about picking up her stuff later.

My mom was waiting by my bedroom door, and she watched me as Juliette made her way out, casting me one more smile before disappearing into the hall. A moment later, I was alone.

I tried to make some kind of sense of what I'd seen—of the paralysis, the dark figure, and the way it simply disappeared. It'd felt so real that this time, it was hard to believe that it was actually just a dream. That was the only way I could think of that could logically explain my experience. Except that I'd been awake; I'd been conscious. And as far as I knew, dreams only happened when you were asleep.

My mother came back a minute later, as I was staring blankly at my reflection in my dresser mirror. She had her hands on her hips, an imposing presence even in her floral print pajamas. We looked at each other for a moment, fierce mother to tired daughter, before she spoke.

"Have you seen things like this before?"

"What?"

"That dream. Has it happened to you before?" I found myself slightly taken aback by her voice; it was like a knife, accusatory and piercing.

Gears whirred in my head, clicking suspiciously. "Who told you it was a dream?"

She blinked. "What else would it be?" she asked, seemingly unfazed. "If it had been real, that figure would be here. Now answer my question, Parker."

I narrowed my eyes. There was something wrong here; my mother was not the type of person to go apeshit over a meager nightmare. She'd freak the hell out over pretty much everything else—but nothing as insubstantial as that.

"Parker Sage Elway," she ground out. "Have you ever had a dream like that before?"

I was too tired to braid the truth into a lie. "Once," I admitted. "Yesterday."

Something flashed in my mother's eye at that—if I didn't know better, I'd have said it was worry. But she didn't get worried. She didn't get anything except angry. And regardless, she composed herself in a heartbeat, pressing her lips together and giving me a curt nod.

"I'm calling the doctor," she declared. "You'll see him tomorrow."

Incredulous, I leapt to my feet. My mother was standing in the same spot the shadow stood, right before it disappeared. For a brief second, the memory of the figure merged with her image, creating a grotesque creature.

I shook my head to clear it.

"Are you kidding me, Mom?" I cried. "You said it yourself; it was just a freaking dream!"

Her hand on the door, my mother rolled back her shoulders and lifted her chin into the air. She regarded me with haughty eyes and said, "I know what I said, Parker. But dreams are powerful things, and the last thing we'd want is for them to begin affecting your reality."

"It's like I've turned to stone. I can't feel my body, and I can't move. And then there's this—this sensation, like there's something sitting on my chest, crushing me. And there was a shadow, a tall, human-looking figure, just standing there staring at me while I lay there, helpless. I couldn't see a face, but I knew it had eyes. I could feel its eyes. And it was—it was terrifying."

Shivering, I focused my gaze on the pale denim fabric of my jeans. My legs hung off the edge of the check-up table, swinging slightly, so that every now and then my beaten-up red Chucks came into view. We were in the hospital—my mother and I—because her insistence had landed us an appointment within hours of the episode. Incidentally, the nurse who had answered the phone at four in morning sounded less than pleased to be speaking with us.

Sitting there on the table, I was beginning to wish that the nurse had simply hung up the phone when my mother told her, quite rudely, that we would be seeing Dr. Pham that day thank you very much, and make sure that he had space for us on his list. Hospitals, in my opinion, were sickly, hollow places, so white and sanitary that they sucked the life out of everyone inside. And everywhere, it smelled like antiseptic, cold and metallic and stinging, mixed with the scrubbed scent of old flesh. Normally, I tried to hold my breath while in the hospital; but with the sensation of suffocation still strong in my chest, every gulp of air felt indescribably precious.

"Well, Parker," said Dr. Pham, once I'd finished my description and he'd typed it into his notes, "I believe I know what's wrong with you." He turned to me, a patronizingly kind smile on his young face. "It appears that you have sleep paralysis."

My mother, in her seat beside the counter, shifted jerkily.

With a learned air, Dr. Pham rose and slid his rolling stool aside, walking over to a poster on his wall. The title read "The Sleep Cycle", and featured a picture of sleeping woman with the stages of sleep outlined above her.

"These are the five stages of sleep," the doctor intoned, sweeping an arm across the image. "During the first four, your body is just beginning to relax, slowing your breathing and preparing your body for sleep. In the fifth stage, dreaming occurs, along with a phenomenon known as rapid eye movement, or REM. You breathe quickly, your muscles go slack, and your brainwaves speed up."

I eyed Dr. Pham carefully, thinking that he was being unnecessarily grandiose in his explanation. He had so much confidence, with his pristine white coat and slicked black hair, that I slumped into my oversized Queen shirt for lack of purpose.

"It's during REM that sleep paralysis occurs," Dr. Pham continued. "Sleep paralysis, by definition, is a transition state between wakefulness and rest characterized by complete muscle atonia, or muscle weakness. Coincidentally, REM can be identified by the same atonic state, because the paralysis prevents dreamers from moving erratically during their dreams. The true cause of sleep paralysis is unknown, but it's plausible that the condition is just an interruption of REM sleep. Your body is still frozen, but you're conscious. It's like having one foot in and one foot out of sleep. Does that make sense, Parker?"

Honestly, I'd been half tuned out during his explanation, but I rocketed back into reality just in time to give an overenthusiastic nod. "Yeah, totally," I chirped.

"Do you have any questions?"

I racked through my memory, trying to recall enough of his speech to formulate a proper query. "Just one," I said eventually. "That shadow I saw—the humanoid figure—what was that? If this can all be accounted for by disrupted rapid eye movement, then where does that fit in?"

Dr. Pham chuckled. "Goodness me, I nearly forgot about that," he said. "It's very common for people with sleep paralysis to experience hallucinations during their episodes, and though it's not clear exactly why that is, a good speculation is that a hyper vigilant state is created in the brain when your body realizes that it's in a vulnerable position. An emergency response is activated and intensified by the helplessness you are feeling, causing the brain to perceive everything it sees as a threat. It creates hallucinations that are very real and very vivid; almost like a parallel between the dream world and reality. Because you are panicking, these shades and shadows take on a menacing presence."

Chewing on my bottom lip, I nodded as Dr. Pham returned to his seat. He fixed me with a reassuring stare and added, "Bottom line is, this condition is nothing to worry about. It happens to half the population at least once, and as scary as it may feel, it won't have any lasting effects. Okay?"

"Okay," I echoed.

From my right, my mother made an disbelieving sound, her penciled eyebrow arching up into the line of her hair. "That's it?" she demanded. "That's all you're going to say? No treatments, no suggestions, nothing to fix it?"

Dr. Pham blinked at her, his face registering confusion and surprise. "Well, there really isn't much we can do, Ms. Elway. Unless the condition intensifies or begins to disrupt Parker's everyday routine, I can't prescribe the drugs that would be suggested for more severe cases. And as there doesn't appear to be any genetic history of narcolepsy or any other sleep disorders in her medical record, we can infer that this is just a one time deal, probably caused by stress or lack of sleep. All that I can recommend is to make sure you get the prescribed amount of sleep for your age group and continue your life as normally as possible. If anything becomes particularly troubling, just schedule another appointment and we'll see what can be done. For now, we'll just watch it. All right?"

"Sure," I replied, speaking before my mother could, "thanks, Dr. Pham."

The man smiled warmly. "Anytime. You folks have a nice day, now. I'll see you later."

As Dr. Pham left the room, I caught sight of Mom's pinched expression. And although she returned his goodbye, I could tell that she was not happy at all.

"Sleep paralysis, huh?"

Logan peered over at me, his face half buried in a thick wool scarf and his freckled nose glowing a wind-bitten red. I could read the worry in his green eyes, boring into mine with concerned intensity.

"Yeah." I shrugged, tugging at Zipper's leash as she sped up in front of me. "Apparently, it's no big deal, just a sleep condition. My mom was flipping out, though, which was weird. I didn't expect her to care."

"She's your mom, Parker," Logan reminded me. "Of course she cares."

I wrinkled my nose. "You only say that because she actually likes you."

My best friend shook his head, his umber curls flying, but said nothing. For a while, we walked in silence, the only sounds around us being the jingle of Zipper's dog tags and the faint whistle of the wind. Logan walked with his hands buried in the pockets of his dark blue jeans, staring down at his feet. It was crisp outside, and the smell of spice and harvest made it clear that autumn was well on its way. Red and gold and orange leaves tumbled down around us from the trees lining the sidewalks.

Walking the dog was one of the few occasions for which my mother allowed me to leave the house, and I'd managed to coax Logan into accompanying me. Call me crazy, but I didn't want to be alone. Along the way, I'd explained to him the doctor's diagnosis, though I'd neglected to fully reiterate the dream.

"Parker," Logan said after a moment, "why do you think your nightmares started? I mean, I've been thinking about it a lot, and it seems like they started so suddenly that I just wondered, you know?"

I managed a small smile. Logan had that habit, of asking a question and then completely diverting you from it by gushing out a bunch of extra words.

"I don't know what started them," I admitted, remembering that first night. I'd woken up drenched in sweat after dreaming that I was falling through an endless darkness. "I just know that they're getting worse."

I saw that vague disquiet flicker over his features, and he moved closer to me protectively. His jaw was set, the way it always was when there was any possibility that I'd be put in harm's way.

"But I'm fine, Logan," I insisted. "They're just dreams; they can't hurt me."

He sighed. "I know, I know. I just worry about you sometimes."

I leaned into him, my head only reaching his shoulder, as we paused to let Zipper leave evidence of her presence on a nearby tree. On the other side of the street, a thin young woman with a stroller waved to us. Stella. We waved back.

"Well, you shouldn't," I chastened. "Hasn't eleven years of friendship taught you that I can take care of myself?"

"Sure it has." He quirked an eyebrow. "I guess I just have a natural hero complex."

He attempted a Superman pose, but his foot caught on a crack in the pavement and he went stumbling forward, sprawling into someone's front lawn. Zipper sniffed at him, her white tail wagging furiously.

"Yeah," I said dryly, as Logan picked himself up off the ground. "My hero."

Logan's ears turned red, and he scratched absently at the back of his neck, a sheepish, lopsided grin on his face.

"Thanks, though," I said genuinely, elbowing him in the side. "You know you're the best."

"How can I forget when you're always reminding me?" he mumbled, but I could tell he was pleased.

We had reached my street by then, Webster Avenue, and stopped in front of my house, the fifth one on the left. I'd always loved my house; it was a deep blue Victorian, regal but simple, with slanted roofs and a paneled exterior. My balcony jutted out gracefully from the second floor, its carved white railing matching the cute picket fence and ivory rosebushes in our front yard.

At the archway leading to my front walk, Logan pulled me into a half hug that was as awkwardly comforting as he was. "You wanna come in?" I asked. "You know my mom won't mind."

"Nah"—he shook his head—"I should be getting home. I don't know how my dad is tonight, but...I don't want to risk it."

I frowned at the shadow that passed over his face and quickly squeezed his hand. Leave it to me, of course, to inadvertently bring up Jack Dearborn, otherwise known as Logan's least favorite subject and the bane of his existence.

"I'm sorry," I murmured, meaning it. "And I love you, you know. Drive safe."

That was a joke between us; Logan always drove his car to my house, but he only lived two streets away.

"I love you too," he replied, hugging me again. Zipper's leash tugged at my wrist as I wrapped my arms around him; she was eager to go inside. "Bye, Parker."

He drew back, and I was just about to go inside when a flashing shadow to my right made me whirl around. I felt an especially cold gust of wind, making my blood chill.

"Parker?" Logan said in confusion, already halfway to his car. "You okay?"

I nodded slowly, shaking my hands to get the blood flowing. I really needed to stop being so jumpy; it wasn't like me at all.

"Fine," I called after him, ignoring the lingering feeling of a presence somewhere behind me. "It was nothing."

Later, in my room, I sat on my bed with my back against the wall, staring at my surroundings but not really registering anything. Like any other teenage girl, my bedroom was my sanctuary, and its décor basically consisted of my personality barfed out into reality.

I was a big classic movie buff, and had posters of all my favorite old films, from Singin' in the Rain to The Birds. Records from all my favorite rock bands had their places on my wall, courtesy of the local Goodwill. They'd never be played, since I was pretty sure my mother had something against good music, but that didn't make them any less attractive against my faded gray-green wallpaper. My favorite part of my set-up, though, was the set of three bare bulbs that hung in a triangle at the center of my room. They were so much more striking than covered lights; not to mention that they made my mother grimace every time she so much as glanced at them.

Frowning slightly, I examined my reflection in the faraway dresser mirror; my kohl-rimmed eyes, my crimson lips. People often told me that I didn't look like my mother, and I think that was my point. If you took off all my makeup, peeled away the band-tees and the combat boots and the skinny jeans, you'd be left with a plain teenage girl who actual bore a distinct resemblance to her mom.

Everyone knew Iris Elway. Everyone knew that she was prudish and obsessive and just generally intimidating; that's what they whispered about behind their hands at the grocery store, because it's a small town and small towns like to gossip. I guess I just didn't want to walk around with a sign on my back proclaiming, "Parker Elway, offspring of the town psycho. Approach with caution." So I dressed like a hipster and acted like a cool kid, and eventually I forgot whether or not that's who I actually was. Sometimes, looking at Juliette's elegance and Logan's innocence, I thought not. But I could never be sure.

The thing about sitting in one place for a long time is that it really makes you think. And after sitting on my bed like a statue for about two hours, my thoughts had managed to make their way back to the subject of the nightmares.

The time for sleep was fast approaching; I'd already eaten dinner and changed into my pajamas, and it was nearing eleven P.M. I knew I had to go to bed soon, because the next day was Sunday and that meant an early, 7 A.M. mass, but I couldn't bring myself to close my eyes. Even though I knew what my nightmares were now, and understood what I was dealing with,

I still shook at the prospect of another night of terror. It wasn't even guaranteed that I'd experience an episode—in fact, the chances were slim to none. But that sliver, that slight chance, scared me more than ever.

Sometime in the past sixty minutes, rain had begun to fall, and now I could hear it pattering against my roof in a steady rhythm. It streamed down my windows (I had two; one to the right of my bed and one a few feet away from the balcony door) in tiny rivulets, masking my view of the darkness outside.

And that was perfectly fine with me; I was in no mood to deal with darkness.

Sighing, I slipped out of bed and shuffled across the carpet to my bookshelf, in hopes that reading would help distract my mind. I scanned the titles, nearly all of them old mysteries, before selecting my favorite Nancy Drew book from when I was younger: number ten, Password to Larkspur Lane. I could have recited its plot in excruciating detail to anyone who cared, but I figured the familiarity would have some kind of calming effect.

As I drew the volume off of my shelf, it snagged on something, sending a tiny cardboard box fluttering silently to the ground. Confused, I retrieved it; the top fell off, and something metallic and glinting slithered out into my palm. I examined it through narrowed eyes for a moment, before realization hit and I understood what I was looking at.

Five years ago, when I was eleven, Logan, Juliette, and I had gone up to the attic of my house, because we'd gotten some idea into our heads that the attic was the place where cool kids went to play. While digging through the forgotten treasures boxed in the dusty storage space, I'd stumbled upon a necklace wedged between two floorboards in a most cliché fashion.

Excited by my find, I'd immediately gone to show my mother—and she'd looked at me as if I'd just brought in a jar of snails and dumped them onto the kitchen counter. She ordered me to get rid of the necklace, but gave no reason why. I had been feeling particularly rebellious that day, so I decided to keep it, shoved into a box at the back of my bookshelf. I hadn't looked at it in ages.

Now, as the tarnished gold chain slipped delicately through my fingertips, I found myself inexplicably drawn to the piece of jewelry. I stared into the pendant, a tiny mirror with an ornate gold frame, seeing my eye reflected back at me. And for some reason, something deep in my gut told me to put the necklace on.

After setting the book aside, I closed the clasp around my neck, liking the way it hung at the center of my collarbone. I looked at my reflection, my face bare now, and swept my hair back over my shoulder. The necklace, a tiny piece, glinted in the bare bulb light.

"Maybe you'll keep away the nightmares," I said to it in a joking whisper. Zipper, at the foot of my bed, perked up her ears. Shaking my head at myself, I grabbed my book and sidled back to bed. Rain poured down outside in a melancholy melody.

And that night, when I slept, I did not dream at all.

CHAPTER 4

Sunday was the day that Edith Hummel accused me of being possessed by the devil.

It was church day; mass was at seven A.M., and I had an obligation that week as lector for the second reading. But that morning, I was late. Apparently, making it through the night unscathed was such a feat that my body decided to keep me asleep for half an hour longer than usual, forcing me to speed through my morning. Which would have gone by much quicker, as I reminded my mother in the car, had I not been obligated to wear a ridiculous dress whose zipper seemed hellbent on getting stuck every time I tugged at it.

At seven-oh-nine, my mother and I entered through the side door. She was fuming at our tardiness, so much so that she practically punched the tub of holy water and sent droplets spewing all over my clothes. By the time we got inside, Blessed Trinity Catholic Church was brimming with people, and the first reading was just about to begin. The lector, a doe-eyed girl named Avery, shook as she walked up to the pedestal. I should have been with her, sitting in one of the stiff-backed wooden chairs that were hidden just out of sight. Biting my lip, I sped up, resisting the urge to let out a stream of expletives as I hurried down the side aisle. Heaven knows the kind of hell my mother would give me for cursing in God's house.

Father Lucas, the main priest of the church, saw me from his perch at the right side of the altar. We made eye contact, and he made a discreet motion with his head toward the back wings of the church. There was an entrance from outside that would take me onto the altar without disrupting mass.

"I'm going around," I whispered to my mom, as Avery began the reading in a quivery voice. My mother nodded curtly, then stepped purposefully into a nearby row of pews.

I hurried out through the back door, tossing a quick wave at Logan as I passed the place where he and his dad were sitting, and had reentered through the back moments later. I passed a white-clad altar server, who smiled at me, before slipping out into the church and hastily making the sign of the cross as I dropped into my seat.

A glance at Father Lucas revealed his bemused smile; no doubt I'd get a lecture for being late later, but for now, it was funny. Though, it appeared, not to Avery, because her entire face was red by the time she finished her reading and sat back down.

"Good lord," she whispered, glaring at me, "do you know how nerve wracking that was? Never do that to me again, Parker Elway!"

I didn't get to respond, because just then, the cantor announced, "Please join in singing number 373 in your Spirit and Song books, Open My Eyes. That's 373 in the Spirit and Song."

Avery and I rose, but I could still feel her dagger-eyes on the side of my face as I mouthed through the song. She swished her blonde bangs from left to right, gray eyes flashing. Avery was a nice girl—a year younger than me, active in community service, avid church attender, blah blah blah—but I swear, sometimes I felt like her babysitter.

When the song drew to a close and the voices of the congregation faded, I smoothed the puffy pink front of my dress, preparing to mount the stone steps of the pedestal. I heard the creak and moan of the old wooden pews as people sat down, and knew that was my cue.

At the top of the stairs I cleared my throat, adjusted the microphone, and glanced down at the sheet of paper before me. I always got nervous before a reading, even though there were only about a hundred people in the church and I knew every single one by name.

Like I said: Callery was a small town. The majority of people were either Catholic or Christian, particularly the former, but only about fifty percent of that group attended church weekly. Those of us who did were either diehard Catholics, fond of a typical Sunday routine, or forced into going by their crazy parents.

I guess you could say that I was a bit of all three.

In the moments before I spoke, I scanned the pews, methodically naming all the faces to calm myself down. Familiarity is a safety blanket—or at least, it was mine, and it was my pre-reading ritual every time I was lector.

Mel McGee, noted my mind, Marcus Ferrait. Theseus Miller. Emily Roswell. Logan. Juliette.

It only took a matter of seconds, too few for anyone to notice my strange habit, and when I was finished, I began.

"'A letter from Saint Paul to the Corinthians,'" I stated, loud and clear into the microphone. "'Brothers and sisters, I have—'"

I didn't get to say anymore. Just as my tongue began to fold over the next word, a desperate wail erupted from the pews. Startled, I stopped in my tracks, my voice swallowed by the sheer volume of the scream.

Throughout the church, people were glancing around, confused and disgruntled, and it was a moment before we all noticed the elderly woman in the first row, sitting in her seat and shrieking one long note at the top of her shriveled lungs.

It was Old Edith Hummel, the ninety-something-year-old woman who had allegedly gone crazy after her daughter left town about twenty years back. She lived in a tiny hole of a house just off the main town center, alone save for an attendant who did everything from cooking her meals to changing her incontinence pads.

Said attendant was now crouching in front of Edith, grabbing the old woman's hands and murmuring what I assumed to be words of comfort. Father Lucas had descended the chancel and joined them, along with a small group of gossip-hungry citizens. I heard someone call for the ushers, but the two suit-clad men were already hurrying down the center aisle.

And through it all, I stood there, Saint Paul and the Corinthians completely forgotten, watching Old Edith as she howled her heart out, her eyes panicked and unfocused. The sound of her screams echoed off the high, vaulted ceilings, and I half believed that it'd blow the stained glass windows into a million little tinted shards and bury us all alive.

"Hey!" shouted one of the ushers. "Paramedics are on their way, they'll be here soon!"

In Callery speak, "soon" meant something along the lines of two and a half minutes. Everyone breathed a sigh of relief.

"All right, Mrs. Hummel," Father Lucas said calmly, "just hold on for a moment, people will be here to help you soon." His voice was amplified by the mic clipped to his robe, but it still barely made a dent in the overwhelming audio of Edith Hummel's screams. Undeterred by her continued noise, he placed a hand on her shoulder, closed his eyes, and murmured a brief prayer that no one could hear.

And immediately, the screaming stopped. Edith Hummel was silent. For a moment, the church reverberated with the emptiness of sound, the buzzing in our ears sharp and sudden. Shocked, the nosy people crowding her moved away, and I was left with a perfect view to see what she did next.

When she raised a bony, wrinkled arm and pointed her finger at me.

"The girl," she intoned, her voice startlingly lucid. "The girl. It is the girl."

I glanced over my shoulder as if there would be some other girl standing there, but Edith's eyes were boring into my skull. Everyone was staring at me now, elevated conspicuously on top of the pedestal, my hands pressed against the long-forgotten reading. My brain wanted to turn and bolt down the steps and behind the altar, but my body decided that we would stay frozen in place.

"Ma'am?" I said, because I felt the need to say something in response. "Are you pointing to me?"

The old woman's eyes went unfocused, and her outstretched hand began to shake. "It is the girl," she repeated. "The girl had been touched."

"Touched by whom, Mrs. Hummel?" Father Lucas asked gently, leaning down to address the woman.

"By...by him." Her arm began to shake violently, and her harried attendant guided it down into her lap.

Father Lucas tilted his head, smiling knowingly. "By God, you mean? Why yes, ma'am, we've all been touched by Him."

Edith Hummel became ramrod straight, her eyes clearing and her voice going level. "Not Him," she snapped, her milky eyes still focused on me. I shifted uncomfortably. "Not Him. Him."

"Who is 'he', Mrs. Hummel?"

The old woman leaned forward, her worn, frail body shrunken in her long dress. "Lucifer," she hissed, her whisper deafening in the silence. "Satan." Her eyes became wrinkled, accusatory slits as she uttered two final words.

"The devil."

Then, in a slumping release, Edith Hummel pitched forward and collapsed into the arms of her attendant. And as I stood there stiffly, melting under the 150 pairs of eyes staring me down, no one made a sound.

The paramedics arrived soon after, and Old Mrs. Hummel was carried away, unconscious, on a stretcher. It happened fast—in heartbeats. And when she and her attendant were gone, the gossipers had returned to their seats, and Father Lucas had mounted the chancel, no one knew what to do.

"I apologize for that interruption," Father Lucas said, clearing his throat, "but let us continue with the second reading." Even the young priest, who was always so collected, was visibly shaken by the ordeal. The deacon, an older man named John, was white as a sheet.

Meanwhile, I stood there, a statue frozen by the blurry gazes of the congregation. They looked confused—my expression must have mirrored theirs. Like everyone else, I knew Edith Hummel, and I had for my entire life. As far back as I remembered, she'd always been the crazy old bat of Callery, the one who kids told stories about and adults looked at with pity. But it was common knowledge that her mind was not all the way here, if you catch my drift, and a clear, straight look from her was an undeniable rarity.

And what was it she had said: about being touched by the devil? I knew she was crazy. I knew that. She was nuts, and I'd just so happened to be in the line of fire during one of her episodes. It meant nothing. So why was there a gnawing, terrible feeling of horror in the pit of my stomach?

"Parker?" Avery hissed from behind me, breaking my reverie. I realized, belatedly, that everyone was waiting for me to begin. I could see the upturned faces of all the snooty mothers in the third row, appraising me silently. As if they actually believed Edith Hummel's proclamation.

Mind reeling, I shakily started the reading again from the beginning. "'A letter from Saint Paul to the Corinthians. Brothers and sisters...'"

Somehow, I managed to get through the whole page without incident, though my throat felt dry and I stumbled over several words. When I'd finished, Avery and I proceeded to the steps, bowed dutifully to the altar, and returned to our seats in the front row of pews. As I sank down onto the soft wood, I felt the needle-prick of all the eyes on the back of my neck.

That was the thing about my town: give them one thing to be suspicious about, and they'll take it and run. You can go ahead and give me the usual crap about stereotypes and small towns, but it's just human nature: when everyone knows one another and there aren't a lot of outlets for frustration, we amuse ourselves by talking about our neighbors. Gossip flows through Callery like rainwater through the sewage system, and I knew for a fact that by the next day, everyone in town would know about the incident.

The idea was far from appealing.

Logan found me as I was sloshing through the still-wet grass after mass on the way to my mother's car. People were crowding the lawn, and he grabbed my wrist as I was ducking beneath the elbow of Mr. Hastings, the general store manager.

"Parker!" he cried, hauling me to a stop. "Dude, are you okay?"

His hand was a refreshing warmth against my chilled skin, but I pulled my arm away. "Of course," I snapped. "Why wouldn't I be?"

Logan sputtered incredulously, his face reddening from the nip in the air—the same nip that was making my fingers feel disconcertingly numb. In my rush to get to church, I'd brilliantly forgotten to snag a jacket.

"Parker," Logan repeated, finally finding his words, "did you hear a word of what Mrs. Hummel said to you?" He gawked at me, his face all rosy cheeks and freckles and viridian eyes.

"Yeah. So?" I demanded. "We both know she's nuts." I shrugged in a feeble attempt to feign nonchalance, but eleven years of friendship had taught Logan to see right through me. He raised a dubious eyebrow and put both hands on my shoulders.

"Questionable sanity aside..." Logan sighed. "Look me in the eye and tell me that what she said didn't bother you."

I squirmed under his gaze; it did bother me, that much was true. Like I said: superstition wasn't my thing. But to have an old woman accuse me of being "touched by the devil" merely days after having a dream that sure as hell seemed like one of those paranormal possession flicks—well, there was no denying how freaky it felt.

Logan, though, was often too empathetic for his own good, and had been known to get himself seriously worked up over things that didn't involve him at all. Like that one time two years back when eight-year-old Terry Cranbrook's dog got run over, and he called their house everyday for two weeks to make sure Terry was all right until Mrs. Cranbrook got fed up and blocked his number. He always had the best intentions, sure, but there was a point when sweetness could become suffocating.

And I was doing quite enough suffocating in my nightmares.

So I lied. Or rather, I tried. I'm generally a fair liar, but thinking about the situation had put an anvil in my gut, and my words came out as garbled nonsense. My best friend eyed me skeptically, his gaze stiff and appraising and just like all those ladies in church who stared me down after Edith Hummel spoke—

My hands began to shake. It wasn't noticeable at first; just a little quiver that could have been attributed to the cold. But it quickly spread up my arms and down my back, a bone-deep chill that sent violent tremors through my entire body.

Logan's arms, still balanced on my shoulders, were thrown off. His expression morphed into one of alarm, and he quickly shed his jacket, pulling it awkwardly off himself, limbs flailing. People were staring now, but he paid them no mind as he flung that sweater around my shoulders, encasing me in the woolen warmth and his arms.

"Oh God, Parker, you're freezing," he murmured, putting a hand to my cheek. "You're definitely not okay."

I tried to shrug him off, but now my teeth were chattering and the action was pretty much impossible. "I'm fine," I ground out. I clenched my jaw, trying to bite back a scream because it felt like my veins were freezing, my blood turning to ice. The cold, wherever it had come from, was more than just skin deep. It wasn't nearly so cold outside—only fifty-five degrees, maybe even sixty—and there was no proper explanation for the shivers. But they just wouldn't go away.

Until they did.

It happened suddenly; one moment, I was shaking like I'd been laying down in the snow; the next, I was collapsing loosely into Logan's chest. A sudden warmth blossomed out from my chest and into my frozen limbs.

"What the hell just happened?" Logan demanded, pulling back to look at me. The minor swear earned him a few disapproving looks from nearby adults, but he ignored them completely. His eyes were on me, boring into my face with unwavering intensity.

"I-I don't know," I breathed. "I have no idea what that was." I pulled his windbreaker tighter around me, hoping to calm my nerves with his familiar scent of wood shavings and Colgate toothpaste. It worked only slightly, but that hardly mattered, because my mother appeared a moment later. And she had no sympathy for anxiety.

"Parker Sage Elway," she snarled, pulling me fiercely from Logan's grasp. "Where have you been? Do you realize that I've been looking for you everywhere? Come with me; we're going home, right now."

"Mom!" I shrieked. There was something wrong. Normally, there would be a cordial hello for Logan, maybe even a smile. That day, she didn't even spare him half a glance. Nor did she acknowledge me when I screamed her name, not until I wrenched my arm away and stumbled back, shooting glares at all the people who stared. Logan was standing a few feet back, looking confused. I began to wriggle out of his jacket, but he held up a hand to stop me.

"Just hold on to it, I'll get it from you later." His expression was twisted, worried. "And call me when you get home, okay?"

I pressed my lips together and nodded at him as his eyebrows knit into a single line. "Yeah, I'll do that. Thanks, Logan."

He tossed a small wave as I spun around. My mother was waiting, tapping her foot impatiently. There was a good five feet of space around her in every direction; no one dared to go any closer. When I was within the danger zone, she recaptured her grip on my arm and began tugging me after her. My black ballet flats squelched in the mud, a sound that normally made her twitch, but she didn't even comment.

It wasn't until we'd nearly reached her silver Maserati that she made a sound, and that was only because she was prompted. Her fingers were on the unlock button of her keys when a voice rang out behind us.

"Iris! Iris, wait up!"

Mom whirled around, eyes ablaze, and I was dragged along with her. Brady Harding, the chief of police, was huffing and puffing as he ran toward us from the direction of the church. He paused when he'd finally gained our attention, his hands on his knees and his gut hanging precariously over his belt.

I could see him eyeing my mother's car with something like jealousy; not many people in this town had the money to afford a Maserati, and of all the people to be driving it, my mother was the last you'd expect. Even I was surprised when she'd rolled into the driveway last year in the sparkling silver sports car. Without a doubt, it was an object of envy for many towns-folk—particularly, it seemed, for Chief Harding. He'd tried to buy it off of her on more than one occasion.

"Iris," he wheezed, "Parker. How are you?"

"In quite a hurry, actually," my mother said blatantly. "What do you need, Brady?"

Chief Harding straightened, pulling his shoulders back in an attempt at an authoritative position. But he wasn't nearly as imposing when wearing a tweed suit instead of his police uniform.

"I wanted to talk to you about Mrs. Hummel," he said, using the deep voice that stops kids from stealing candy from the liquor store. "Do you have a moment?"

Both he and my mother looked at me, then my mother said, "Parker, get in the car."

I raised my eyebrows up into the rim of my bangs. "What?"

"Get. In. The car." Without looking away, she unlocked the Maserati. Her eyes told me to give in; I wasn't going to win anyway, and she wasn't afraid to make a scene in front of the chief.

"Fine," I muttered, crossing my arms in defeat. "It's cold out here, anyway."

I slunk into the passenger seat, glowering, and watched as the two adults moved slightly away from the car. My mother looked irritated, and Chief Harding looked concerned. Narrowing my eyes, I attempted to read the words streaming from their lips, filtering them into a conversation in my head.

"Iris...not...about...Hummel said?" That was the chief, who raked a hand through his comb-over as he spoke.

"Of course not. Why...earth...I be?" My mother, her jaw set.

"Well...you know."

"...don't, actually."

"Iris...all know what...Mary."

"That...years ago."

"But it happened before...same start. Could...again."

"Bullshit."

The last word was spat from my mother's lips, with so much venom that I reeled back from the window. I couldn't hear her, but I could see Chief Harding's shock in the side mirrors. They exchanged a few more words, but it appeared to be more of my mother bearing down on the chief than actual conversation. I hugged my knees to my chest and waited.

A moment later, the driver's door opened, and my mother stormed inside. Her eyes were flashing with anger as she jammed the key into the ignition.

"Feet down, Parker Sage," she snarled. "Your shoes are disgusting."

I obliged silently.

There was a thick whirring as the heat kicked in, and although I began to bake in Logan's thick jacket, I didn't take it off. It was the only thing between my mother and my bare skin, and somehow it felt important to keep it that way.

My mother was a statue as she drove, her jaw clenched, her brows knit, her eyes focused straight ahead. I sneaked glances every now and then, but her expression did not change. Whatever the chief had said to her, it had really set her off. But none of their conversation—at least, what I'd gleaned of it—made any sense. I didn't know what had "happened before," and the only Mary I knew was Mary Home, my neighbor Stella's three-year-old daughter. Surely they weren't talking about her.

As my mom veered sharply into our driveway, I finally mustered up the courage to ask. "Mom, what did Chief Harding say?" My voice was quiet, meek, and pathetic, not at all like it usually sounded.

For a moment, it was so silent in the car that I wondered if my mother had heard me at all. With her hands clenched so tightly around the steering wheel, it looked for all the world like she had turned to stone.

I cleared my throat, tried again. "Mo—"

She cut me off by ripping the keys out and cutting the engine. Her hands were fists as she turned to me.

"Don't ask questions when you know that something is none of your concern," she hissed.

"I didn't even—"

"I don't want to hear it, Parker. I want you inside, right now, and straight up to your room."

I threw up my hands, furious. "Are you kidding me?" I yelled. "You're being ridiculous!"

There was a beat of silence, and my mother leaned closer to me. Then she let loose, shouting, "Oh, you want ridiculous? Fine! You go up to your room, and I don't want to see your face downstairs until tomorrow."

"But—"

"You heard me, young lady. If I so much as hear the creak of your bedroom door, you're grounded for the rest of the week. Is that clear?"

Shocked, I said nothing.

"Is that clear?" she thundered.

Though I was shaking with anger, I managed a curt nod and a squeaky, "Yes, ma'am."

My mother pursed her lips and gave an approving tilt of her head. "Very good." Then, without another word, she stepped daintily out of the car and slammed the door hard behind her.

CHAPTER 5

The thing about my mother that often surprises people is that she doesn't drink.

Ever.

I know plenty of parents in Callery who do drink, and others who are downright alcoholics, but my mother is not one of them. She doesn't even keep alcohol in the house. I discovered that when once, in a fit of rebellious rage, I stormed through the pantry in search of that elusive wine supply that every parent is practically obligated to have, only to find the usual array of crackers and canned soup.

My mother doesn't drink.

I suppose, if she were a good, kindhearted person, I would have been proud of that. It was something she always made very clear in situations where alcohol was involved, even though it vexed nearly every other adult in the vicinity. I always saw them shifting, ducking their heads, wondering what to do with themselves because my mother's piercing gaze made them feel inexplicably guilty.

But that isn't my point—my point is that my mom has no excuse for the way she behaves. I mean, sure, constant drunkenness is hardly a valid excuse, but at least it provides some kind of reasoning for acting like a crazed maniac. With Mom, there was none of that. It was just her personality; it was the way she acted on a daily basis. Her furious outburst had been unprecedented, but it was hardly outside of the norm.

Sending me to my room for over twelve hours, though—that was a little bit different.

As I sat listlessly on my bed, picking at a loose thread on my comforter and watching trees sway out the window, I tried to make sense of it all. My mother got mad a lot, and ninety-nine percent of the time, it was because of me. But I hadn't done anything this time except ask a simple question. A question which, I remembered, I had never received an answer to.

What had Chief Harding said? What words could have possibly escaped his lips that made my mother so angry?

Drawing Logan's jacket closer around my shoulders, I strained my ears to hear my mother clanging around downstairs. I didn't know what she was doing and I didn't dare check, but it was loud as hell.

It had just passed noon; I'd officially been locked in my bedroom for four hours. And since I'd skipped breakfast and hadn't eaten anything but the Eucharist during mass, my stomach was begging for food—loudly. I had half a mind to storm down the stairs right then and there and demand; that would show my mother to exercise her totalitarian authority on me.

But it would also involve effort, and I didn't feel like getting out of bed.

I tried to watch television, but there was nothing good show-ing. Not to mention that I was pretty sure my mom blocked half the channels, leaving me with a pretty scarce array of programs. When I couldn't find anything, I made a feeble attempt to finish the Nancy Drew book I'd fallen asleep on the night before. But I just couldn't seem to focus. My mind would hook onto a sentence for a fraction of a halted exhalation—then moments later, the words would twist and bend and spin out of sight in my head.

It was sunny outside. Burnt orange rays crept in through my curtains, but I felt a world apart from their tranquil brightness. My head was loaded with all kinds of messy, cluttered thoughts, and although I could make no sense of them, I knew they re-volved around a single focus: the nightmares.

I wasn't sure why everything kept circling back around to those terrible dreams, especially now that I knew what they were. Sure, the experience of sleep paralysis was terrifying, but I knew the facts and the fear factor had decreased significantly. Or at least, I thought it had. So why was I sitting here, gnawing on my bottom lip and clutching that old necklace in my hands?

That was another thing that baffled me: the necklace. Since I'd rediscovered it the previous night, I'd had trouble removing it from my grasp. I was half convinced that the only reason things went so crazy at church was because I hadn't had it with me. Now, slung over my fingers in a mess of faded gold chains, it looked so delicate, so fragile. But at the same time, it exuded this—this aura, an aura of refined importance. And I found that I could not put it down.

I gave up on reading eventually, because my thoughts were crowding out the words on the page. I slid the necklace reluctantly between the pages and stood up, trying and failing to ignore the rumbling of my stomach. Just as I was about to give in and risk punishment to scavenge for food, there was a sharp knock on my bedroom door.

I jumped, startled; my mother hadn't made a sound whilst ascending the stairs, but she made plenty as she hammered against my door, nearly shaking it in its frame. Annoyance flooded through me as I shed Logan's jacket and crossed my sweater-sleeved arms over my chest.

"All right, all right," I muttered, padding over to the door. "I'm coming, hold on."

After exhaling my irritation in a silent sigh, I swung it open. My mother stood at the threshold, her hair a surprisingly frizzy mane around her head, with a plate balanced on her hand. The plate, in turn, held a perfectly made grilled cheese sandwich—a rarity, because it was fried and my mother had removed any such foods from our diets. I don't think I'd seen a grilled cheese in months.

But there it was, right in front of me, and the sight of it coupled with its alluring smell was enough to have my weary stomach going crazy. Without really thinking about it, I reached forward, intending to take the plate (which had to have been meant for me) from my mother's hand.

She snatched it away.

"No," she scolded, as if I was Zipper and not her own daughter. "Not yet."

I raised my eyebrows. "What?"

She looked down her nose at me, her hazel eyes razor sharp. "I want two Our Fathers and a Hail Mary. Right now."

"What the hell?" I demanded.

Surprisingly, she didn't even blink at my words. She stood with a weird, rigid determination, her expression flat. "Two Our Fathers. One Hail Mary. Do that, and you get the sandwich."

I didn't know what kind of jacked-up mind game she was trying to play with me, but my stomach was growling too loudly for me to care. Throwing my hands up in defeat, I turned obligingly to the wall beside my bookcase and folded my hand in prayer.

"Our Father who art in heaven," I intoned, feeling my mother's eyes on the side of my neck. "Hallowed be thy name." I finished the prayer, repeated it, all under her scrutinizing gaze.

When I was done with the two Our Fathers, I cleared my throat and began the single Hail Mary. I tried to ignore how weird and random the request was.

"Hail Mary, full of grace, the Lord is with thee. Blessed art thou among women, and blessed is the fruit of thy womb Jesus."

I paused, licked my lips. There was a strange feeling growing in the pit of my stomach.

"Continue," snapped by mother, knifing through the reverent silence.

"Holy Mary, mother of God, pray—sweet Jesus!"

I halted mid-prayer—my entire midsection was suddenly overwhelmed by a feeling equivalent to that of being punched in the stomach by the Hulk. I doubled over, gasping; pain throbbed through my body in a steady, pulsing rhythm. My fingers scrabbled for a place at my jugular, and the pulse I felt was rapid and frantic. It almost seemed to stutter, as if it was just as confused as I was. The invisible wound in my stomach told me that my intestines had just been crushed, but everything seemed intact.

"Well." The single syllable was all that escaped my mother's mouth, but it effectively reminded me of her presence. I looked up quickly, and she was standing just inside my doorway with one hand on her hip. Her face was impassive, but I thought I caught a quick glimmer of something like concern. It was gone in a heartbeat, however, and she stalked into my room as if she hadn't just seen me practically fall over in pain. She set the plate down on my dresser so that it clinked; I heard the jingle of dog tags as Zipper came hurrying up the stairs.

"There you go," she said briskly, turning to go. I watched her dumbly for a moment before remembering my obligatory manners.

"Thank y—" I began, raising a hand to stop her. But if she heard, she made no indication, and my door swung in quietly behind her.

That night, despite the golden necklace tucked in beneath my pillow, I had another dream. It wasn't a nightmare—at least, it didn't begin as one. Then again, dreams never start from the beginning. So basically, whatever middle section of my dream-world that I dived into as I slept did not begin as a nightmare.

In fact, it was almost normal.

When I opened my eyes into my mind's fabricated reality, I was disconcerted. I had become so used to darkness, but tonight, there was none. Tonight, there was only soft, gauzy light, pouring in from all the crevices of the space I was in and momentarily blinding me. I wasn't afraid, though; in fact, if anything I found the strange luminescence calming, because it had a certain fuzzy warmth that enveloped my body.

The light faded away after a few precious seconds, and I found myself in a kitchen. I was sitting on the floor by the refrigerator, and there was something soft and plush in my hands, but I couldn't see what it was. The gauziness hadn't faded away completely, and it created an aura of light around the figure of a girl who was perched at the kitchen table. She sat closer to the stove, facing away from it so that my view of her was in profile. I couldn't see her face; that breathy brightness had settled over her features, obscuring them in a hazy cloud.

I looked up at her, and I felt the warmth of a smile shining from her face-cloud and dancing over to me. Something in the way she swung her thin legs and twirled a pencil in her hand made me think that she was young—twelve, maybe thirteen.

"Come here, lovely," she said sweetly, as I continued to look at her and she smiled back at me. Without meaning to, I pushed myself off the ground, hugging whatever was in my hand to my chest. For some reason, though, I didn't get any taller. The girl still looked impossibly high up from where I stood.

Anxious, I looked down, only to see chubby child fingers clutching a worn teddy bear, and little bare toes scrabbling across the linoleum. Before I could wonder, however, I felt hands under my arms, and then I was being lifted into the air and into the lap of the bigger girl.

"You wanna see what I was drawing?" she asked me, her voice riding ecstatically on air as if sharing a private secret. I felt myself nod, though I'd given my body no consent to do so.

"Here," said the girl, "take a look." She shifted me onto her other leg and lifted a sheet of crisp manilla paper from the contrasting dark wood of the table. I leaned forward as she held it closer to my face.

The picture was a figure, a shadow, really, of a girl in a fluttering dress. She lay at the center of the page, her body a darkened silhouette surrounded by a thin veil of white. All around her, glossed in sooty pencil, was a Cimmerian shade that started thin at the edges and became more and more dense as it neared the girl's prone frame. But the closer I examined the drawing, the more it became apparent that the thorough shading wasn't a single texture. Etched throughout it were shapes, humanoid chassis that mixed and blended with the darkness. They hovered around the figure of the girl, just out of sight, their invisible eyes watching her as she slept.

Suddenly terrified by the image, I began to cry.

As fat tears rolled down my cheeks, the girl squeaked and let the paper slip out of her hands and back onto the table. She brushed my hair out of my face, shushing my hiccuping sobs.

"Sh, sweetie, sh," she murmured, rocking slightly. "It's only a drawing."

From the living room, a doorway apart from the kitchen, a strangely familiar voice rang out. "Is everything all right in there?"

"Fine!" the girl called, bouncing me anxiously on her knee.

An anguished wail escaped my lips. Footsteps came pattering over, and a moment later, a woman was peeking her head into the room. She, too, had a blurry face, one that undulated every time I tried to set eyes on it. She took one glance at me and rushed over, drawing me into her arms.

"What happened?" she asked gently.

I glanced over my shoulder, sweeping the teddy bear over my wet eyes, as the faceless girl turned her picture so that the woman could see it.

"Nothing!" she cried. "I just showed her my drawing, and..." She trailed off suddenly the woman emitted a quiet gasp, shifting me to her hip and simultaneously swiping the drawing off the table and staring at it in horror.

"No," she murmured. "No."

"What?" demanded the girl. "What are you doing?"

"No," the woman repeated blankly, crumpling the paper in her hand. "No, sweetie, no, no, no."

The scene shifted suddenly. One moment, I was in the woman's arms, the next I was in a room, in the dark, cocooned beneath blankets in a twin-sized bed that felt impossibly large. I felt like I was waking up as I blinked my way into the scene, but the shadows of the room were foreign—not mine.

Just then, a quiet whimpering drew my attention from the right. I rolled over carefully, so as not to make a sound, and peeked out through the sheaths of plush comforter. The girl from before was lying in a bed not three feet away, her face in shadows her blanket pulled up to her chin. She was shaking, quivering, staring away at something I couldn't see.

"Get back," I thought I heard her whisper. "Get away from me. You're not real."

Confused, I looked at the air around her, but I couldn't see whomever she was talking to. At first. Because as I narrowed my eyes, focusing on the white beam of moonlight streaming through the window and onto her face, I thought I saw something.

Just a trick of light, I thought—until it appeared again. A tendril of smokey black; a finger of darkness; a thin, ebony ribbon that crossed through the air in sinister waves. It blocked the moonbeam, snaking in to wrap itself around the girl's neck. And as I continued to watch, it solidified; it became a limb, an arm; it grew a hand with fingers that tightened their grip.

The girl was fighting now, flailing, but there was no breath in her lungs to scream. I wanted to do something, but I was frozen in place by the sheer volume of my fear. The girl's face seemed to be darkening—soon, she would be completely out of air. In moments, she would be dead. But in the culminating moment before she lost consciousness, the darkness let go.

She was thrown back onto her bed, gasping, as the onyx arm drew back and returned to its hazy form. Then, it slithered away from the moonbeam, out of my sight, and I was no longer sure if it was still there.

"Oh, God," murmured the girl. "Oh, dear God." Her frantic fingers flashed in the darkness, dusting the sign of the cross onto her skin. She clutched her hands to her chest, folded together in prayer, her ghostly lit lips moving silently and glinting tears tracking paths down her cheeks.

I awoke sometime later in a pool of sweat, my face wet because Zipper was sitting on my chest, licking me. It was still dim outside, but evidently, my mother had already let the dog into the house. The memory of the strange dream was fresh in my mind, crisp like new money, and it only intensified as I caught a whiff of a strong, herbal scent. I couldn't hear any evidence of my mom cooking downstairs—and anyway, nothing she made ever smelled so good. It was piney and spicy, both at once, and it brought back the dream in vivid colors in my mind. And I lay there silently until my mom called me, remembering the image of the faceless girl as she quietly cried herself back to sleep.

"You never called me, you know," Logan said. I jumped slightly at the sound of his voice, looking over to see him snaking his way down the aisle to where I sat. He was carrying too much stuff—his backpack, three textbooks, and two stainless steel coffee mugs. I winced as he stumbled slightly, mentally kicking myself for forgetting.

"I know, I'm sorry," I apologized softly, "my mom grounded me for the rest of the day."

Logan's eyes became saucers as he kicked out the chair beside me and dumped his books onto the desk. "Serious? What for?"

I shrugged. "Don't know. She talked to Chief Hummel and got really peeved, and then freaked out when I asked what it was about. She's crazy."

"Wow," Logan said, shaking his head. "Are you okay, though? Any nightmares?" He set one of the mugs in front of me, sloshing a little bit onto the cap. "I brought you coffee, just in case you aren't."

I smiled, allowing myself a small chuckle at my best friend's anxious face. Coffee was strictly prohibited in my household, and since Logan's coffee was the best in the universe, every time he brought it for me was a special occasion. I patted his arm with one hand and pulled the mug closer with the other, utter a sincere, "Thanks, Logan. I'm fine, really. And I didn't have any nightmares last night." I took a swig of the drink, not minding as it burned my tongue. "You're the best, you know that?"

We chorused on the response: "How can I forget when you keep reminding me?"

His face broke into a relieved smile, and he pulled me in for a one arm hug. "I'm glad you're okay," he said seriously, sliding in beside me. "By the way, did you do the weekend reading?"

"For this class?" I let out a quiet curse. "Shoot, no—I forgot. Wanna give me a recap?"

Logan slurped his coffee and swallowed loudly before answering. "It was actually super interesting," he gushed. "It was all about memory, and how different smells can make you remember certain things. It's because the olfactory nerve is close to amygdala, the part of the brain that deals with emotional memory, and it's close to the hippocampus, too. So when you smell things, your brain connects it to visual stuff that happened at the same time when you once smelled the scent. And if the hippocampus or the amygdala are damaged, it can impair your sense of smell, because you won't have a memory of ever smelling things. Isn't that cool?"

Logan was bouncing in his seat, excited by the topic and probably by the coffee as well. He grinned at me, totally placid, but my mind was whirring.

Memory. Smells. I flashed back to that very morning, and the smell that had filled my room and intensified the dream. Could I have experienced something similar, but in reverse?

"Parker?"

I started as Logan leaned his face in front of me, his expression concerned. "Huh?" I stuttered, drawn abruptly from my thoughts.

"Did you hear what I just said?" he asked.

"Y-yeah," I said, "I did." I smiled, taking a sip of the hot, sweet coffee. "And I agree—that's totally cool."

Somehow, I managed to focus through the entire lecture, taking notes on everything Dr. Hennessy said. Psychology was, by far, my favorite subject to study. I loved delving into the human brain, finding the scientific explanations for general human habits. But most of all, I was fascinated by the mind, all its little quirks and oddities, and the way that every person is different because of what's inside their head.

The lecture was on memory, and although I'd missed the reading, I caught on quickly enough. My fingers flew on the keys of my laptop as I drank in every word that left the professor's lips. He discussed forgetfulness, and how, if one does not revisit a memory often, the memory will decay over time. I loved the way he described it: decay. As if memory is a solid, tangible thing that can rot and molder like an orange left too long on the kitchen counter.

The one-and-a-half hour period finished too quickly, and I lingered for a while as everyone packed up around me. It had occurred to me, at some point during the lecture, that if there was anyone to ask about sleep paralysis, it would be Dr. Hennessy. Despite having already received information about it from Dr. Pham, I wanted something less clinical—something more than a mere definition. So, once I'd finished packing my things, I grabbed a daydreaming Logan by the hand and pulled him after me, down the stairs and to the pulpit of the lecture hall.

"What are you doing?" my best friend hissed, trying and failing to slow me down.

"I just have a question," I replied.

Our footsteps echoed on the cool tile that made up the center floor of the room, but the professor did not look up. He stood at his stone pedestal, shuffling through his notes, pausing every now and then to survey them through bespectacled eyes. It wasn't until I cleared my throat that he even acknowledged us, and even then, all we received was a grunt.

"Excuse me, Mr. Hennessy?" I asked confidently, striding up to the pedestal with my bag slung over one shoulder. He looked up at me, his dark eyes narrowing.

"Don't you have a class to get to?" he asked frigidly, his voice deep and rumbling. I felt Logan shift beside me, but I was unperturbed.

"I have fifteen minutes, sir. I was just wondering if you could answer a quick question for me."

"Hmph," was his response.

"I was wondering," I began, shifting the now-empty coffee mug from hand to hand, "if you know anything about sleep paralysis."

Silence. Dr. Hennessy froze in place, his papers slipping from his calloused hands.

"What is your name?" he asked abruptly, looking up and peering at me sharply.

I stuttered for a moment before answering, "Parker Elway."

He nodded. "Well, Ms. Elway," he intoned, "it appears that today is your lucky day. It just so happens that I wrote my doctorate thesis on sleep paralysis."

"Really?" I asked, intrigued.

"Indeed," said Dr. Hennessy, a rare smile spreading a flash of ivory against his umber skin. "In fact, it's one of my favorite subjects."

"Parker," Logan hissed. I elbowed him in the stomach, smiling at the professor.

"Well, that's convenient." I hefted my backpack higher. "I guess that means you know a ton about it."

The man shrugged, brushing something off the sleeve of his suit. "You could say that. What would you like to know, Ms. Elway?"

I nearly froze, deer-in-headlights style, but at last moment, spat out, "Just anything, really. Some interesting facts, or something."

Dr. Hennessy clapped his hands together, his face lighting up immediately. He bent down and shuffled through some papers at the bottom shelf of his pedestal before retrieving a fairly thick stack of files.

"This," he said, waving the papers, "is the part of the phenomenon that interests me the most: the supernatural element of sleep paralysis."

"Supernatural?" Logan repeated. It was the first thing he'd said, and he sounded blatantly dubious. As was his custom, my best friend was immediately suspicious of anything and everything that bordered on the paranormal.

"Yes, supernatural." The professor pulled out a single page and held it out to us. Printed on the paper in black and white was a strange, grainy image. It was hard to determine what it was at first, but I quickly realized that it was a person lying down, their head hung back and their arms splayed wildly. On their chest was a demonic-looking creature—a gargoyle-like entity with a demented face and powerful wings sprouting from its back. And beside the demon, with her face in shadows, was a barefooted woman in a long white robe. She watched the sleeper silently, the intensity of her gaze obvious, even through the picture.

"What is that?" I demanded, aghast.

"This," Dr. Hennessy stated, "is an ancient interpretation of sleep paralysis. Before modern science and psychology were developed, sleep paralysis was seen in many cultures as an example of demonic activity. Cases were reported as being visitations by malignant creatures, and that is how people depicted it.

"This piece isn't one of his, but in the late eighteenth century, an artist named Henry Fuseli created an oil painting interpretation of sleep paralysis called 'The Nightmare'. It was rather to similar to this one; both have this creature on the chest of the human, which is meant to signify the feeling of pressure that people feel when experiencing sleep paralysis."

I leaned forward, squinting at the picture. "Why that, though? Why such a disgusting-looking...thing?"

The professor chuckled. "Well, it was often believed in many societies that sleep paralysis was caused by an invisible, evil old woman who would sit on people's chests as they slept. Incidentally, it is often called 'old hag syndrome'. But of course, people are people, and we've coined many fascinating terms for sleep paralysis over the years. Some say that experiencing sleep paralysis is being touched by the devil. Many scientists believe that sleep paralysis can account for stories of alien abduction. And then there's the idea of The Intruder, or this woman here, who you can feel watching but can't really see.

"The Intruder, personally, is my favorite, because it is not necessarily connected to sleep paralysis. People often experience the feeling of being watched, or followed—that feeling that they are not alone. And it generally occurs when a person is in a situation that the brain perceives as frightening. A common theory among psychologists, which I personally agree with, is that, because sleep paralysis brings about a feeling of terror, the human mind creates these so-called 'intruders', but whether they are real or not is essentially opinion-based."

"What do you mean?" Logan scoffed. "Obviously these...things aren't real. Stuff like that doesn't exist. Aren't you a scientist? You're not supposed to believe in this kind of thing."

I winced at the cutting sound of his voice, but Dr. Hennessy didn't even blink. His dark, bushy eyebrows raised as he shook his head.

"I never said that I believe in it," he stated. "But the truth is that the phenomenon of sleep paralysis isn't something that science can completely explain. There are still so many blanks; so many unanswered questions that may stay open-ended forever.

"I am a man of science, son. I believe in rational answers whenever they can be provided for me, and if they can't, I am apt to search for them. But in all the years I spent researching sleep paralysis, I was unable to find concrete evidence that every bit of the condition can be demythologized. Many of the things

I studied, in fact, bordered more on parapsychology. That's a science—it's a branch of psychology. But it also includes the study of paranormal phenomena. Basically, while I am more inclined to believe in the more logical part of the subject, I know that there are many people who are not. There are plenty of researchers out there who think that the reality of sleep paralysis is demons and devils, intruders and incubi and old hags. And I have no evidence to prove them wrong."

Dr. Hennessy shrugged lightly, his movement nonchalant. "It's just something to think about," he said lightly. "Science is not necessarily the answer for everything."

A quick glance at Logan told me that he disagreed, but my friend held his tongue. He also refused to look at me, and I sighed internally, realizing that he was mad that I'd brought him along with me here. The thing about Logan was that he was extremely logical, and despite being a regular church attender, he privately refused to believe in anything he couldn't see. And I suppose that I could hardly blame him. His mom, Anna, passed away when he was really young, and even though he'd never say it, I knew he thought that if ghosts and spirits and paranormal beings were real, he would have been able to see her again. And since he hadn't, his views on the supernatural were nothing if not cynical.

"Ms. Elway," our professor continued, jolting me from my thoughts, "if you don't mind me asking, what made you so interested in this subject? It's not a very widely-known study."

"I-I—" Swallowing hard, I racked my brain for an answer that wouldn't involve my having to tell Dr. Hennessy about my condition. "I saw a piece about it on TV," I stuttered out eventually. "It was really interesting, and I wanted to find out more about it."

I dug my nails into my palm, hoping desperately that he wouldn't question further. He didn't. Instead, he scrutinized me thoughtfully, creases forming on the leathery, dark skin of his face.

"Here, take this," he said after a moment, holding out the file full of papers. "There's plenty of great study material in here if you're interested in the subject."

I stared at the stack in his hand. "Are you sure, Dr. Hennessy? I don't want to take all your research and, like, lose it or something terrible."

The professor looked at me down his long, wide nose. "That is why you won't lose it," he said sternly, "correct?" I nodded reflexively, and he let out an emotionless sigh. "And anyway, a good doctor always makes copies of his files. I wouldn't have much success at my job if I didn't have back-ups for everything."

He smiled at me, his demeanor so different from the chilly lecturer that he was during class. "Anyway, I really do want you to take these. You can return them to me whenever you're through reading them, whether that be in a week or three years. I like to see such young, eager blood on the front of psychological studies, and it's my job as a teacher to encourage your academic interests. Enjoy the information, learn from it, and emerge a wiser person at the other end."

My hand was practically shaking as I gently removed the file from my teacher's hand. It was over an inch thick, and so full of papers that it actually weighed my arms down. I grinned down at the package, excited by all the potential learning material stuffed inside of it. What had begun as a simple question about a sleeping disorder had quickly piqued my interest, and I was quickly finding myself become just as interested in sleep paralysis as Dr. Hennessy.

"Thank you, sir," I said, thoroughly awed.

"You're welcome, Ms. Elway," he said. He nodded stiffly, and, as if someone had flipped a switch, his face became impassive again, and he turned back to his notes. Over his shoulder, I saw that more students were filing into the hall; it was nearly time for his next lecture. The clock on the wall told me that my next period was fast approaching as well. I had a good two minutes to run across campus to my 11:15 criminology class, a trek that usually took at least five. Logan, the lucky duck, looked distinctly more relaxed; his watercolors class wouldn't begin for another quarter of an hour.

Swallowing a series of expletives, I beckoned to Logan and took off across the pulpit, trying my best to hurry without looking like I was running. About halfway to the door, Dr. Hennessy's voice stopped me in my tracks.

"Oh, and Ms. Elway?" I glanced over my shoulder, but he hadn't turned from his pedestal. "If you are so inclined, you might consider looking into the parapsychology classes offered here at Butler. I have a feeling that they might interest you."

"Yeah," I replied in a normal tone. "I'll do that, thank you."

Then I turned and skittered over to Logan, who was standing in the doorway and looking very displeased. "I hope you're happy," he snapped, huffing a white puff of breath into the cold morning air.

I rolled my eyes as we sped down the sidewalk, knowing he'd cool off within an hour. "I'm very happy, thanks," I replied dryly.

And I was. I wasn't sure why, exactly, but learning more about the nightmares, though they had only haunted me twice, made me feel like I had some power over them. Not to mention that all the new information was brimming in my brain, easily wiping the memory of the previous night's dream and the strange scent I'd detected upon waking. I found that I couldn't wait to return home and pore over the papers, and I knew that Logan would be soon be interested too.

I was five minutes late to my next class, and I didn't even care.

CHAPTER 6

I was right about Logan—I always was. Because sure enough, by the time I slipped into his car at the end of our three-class day, he was brimming with questions. It took my entire artillery of diversion tactics to keep him from beginning to read the papers in the middle of the highway.

"I still think the parapsychological part is ridiculous," he informed me repeatedly, "but this could be such a cool thing to research. And I bet it would really impress my Oils professor if I told her I know about Fuseli, she loves it when students do extra research and—"

I tuned him out after about a minute of his rambling, because that boy could talk a mile a minute and never run out of air. He babbled for the entirety of our car ride home, and I just smiled and watched his expressions in the rear view mirror. I didn't say a word until we'd gotten off the freeway, when he finally paused for breath.

"You know you're dropping me off at the pool, right?" I asked him, smirking as his eyes went wide and he attempted to stammer out an answer.

"O-of course," he managed, swerving widely around an empty curb. "Headed right over."

I rolled my eyes at his classic dorky mannerisms as he maneuvered his way through the streets. Callery felt strangely deserted, as if everyone had forgotten to wake up that morning.

"We're here," Logan said after a few minutes of driving, pulling his car to a slow stop in front of the indoor community pool. The concrete building hung low and silent in the gray late morning air, devoid of all the children who filled it once school was out.

Sighing, I slipped my gloves onto my hands and began to gather my things. "My stuff's in the backseat," I told Logan as I tried to cram the file into my backpack.

"Oh, and you can't be bothered to get it yourself," he muttered, poking me affectionately.

I swatted him away, nonchalantly replying, "I can, actually. It's just that you're a boy, and that gives you some kind of divine obligation to do things for me."

Logan snorted, an amused light in his eyes. "Is that so?"

"It is." I zipped my bag shut and looked at him expectantly until he gave in, shaking his head. "Oh, you love me," I teased, as he unbuckled his seat belt to dig for my bag of swim supplies.

"You're lucky that I love you," he grumbled.

"And you're lucky that fact doesn't make run away screaming."

He stuck out his tongue at me, and I pulled my knees up to my chest as he began to sift through the mess in his backseat. His car was full of half-used sketchbooks, broken pencils, and dirty erasers that he'd dropped and never retrieved. But it also held a good amount of my stuff, namely my pool bag, because my mother worked on weekdays and Logan was often my only ride. Monday was a ritual, because it was the one day in the week that I specifically designated for swimming.

"What time should I pick you up?" Logan asked, once he'd retrieved my purple tote bag and tossed it into my lap.

I thought about it for a moment, looking at my things and then at the crisp air outside. I lived about two miles from the pool; a half hour walk, at my pace. It wasn't bad, and it would certainly give me an opportunity to clear my head before delving into the world of sleep paralysis.

"Don't," I said eventually. "I'll just walk."

Logan raised an eyebrow. "Are you sure?"

"Certain. My mom won't be home till six, so she won't even know." I smiled, hefting a bag onto each shoulder. "I'll call you once I'm back, though—for sure this time. You can come over, and we'll look over the stuff together, all right?"

It took a moment, but eventually, Logan heaved a reluctant sigh. "Fine," he allowed. "But make sure you really do call me, or I'll tell your mom."

"Yeah, yeah," I dismissed, popping open the door of the car.

"Oh, and Parker?" Logan called, rolling down the window as I mounted the front steps to the pool. I turned around, crossing my arms against a gust of wind. My best friend, who was leaning across the passenger seat, threw me a dopey smile. "Be careful, okay?"

"Will do," I yelled over my shoulder, rolling my eyes but allowing myself a private smile. Sometimes, I swear, Logan was like a second mom.

Within ten minutes, I'd found my way into the dressing room and changed in one of the ice cold stalls, shoving all of my things into one of the many available lockers. I was forced to dance out into the showers, clad only in my horrendously unattractive swimsuit, for the mandatory pre-swim rinse that no one checked for but that everyone got into the habit of doing anyway. But, quite unluckily for me, the hot water was out, so I was stuck hopping from foot to foot in the frigid downpour for a straight minute. After that, a five minute recovery time was practically necessary. I stood for a while with a towel over my shoulders, staring at my reflection in the mirror that we all used to fight over before practice.

Before I finished high school, competitive swimming had been my life. Those toddler classes where I'd met Logan had become weekly practices, then daily, before I'd been invited to join the local swim team at age eight. Swimming was my claim to fame; my magnum opus; the one thing I excelled at that I was actually allowed to do. Sure, my mother had been wary at first—she was suspicious about practically everything I wanted to do—and convincing her had taken the efforts of all three coaches. But once, at a meet, I saw her face after I'd finished in first place, saw the real, genuine smile on her lips, and I figured that she must have been at least kind of proud of me.

But once she agreed to let me go to Butler, I had to make a choice: swim or school. She told me that I wouldn't have time for both, and that I had to pick one or the other. So I chose school, quit the team, and now, my previous life at the pool couldn't have felt farther away. At that point, standing alone in the shower rooms, I'd only been gone for about six months—it felt like years.

Shivering at a sudden chill, I adjusted the straps of my team suit; it was the only one I wore anymore. Even though it was absolutely hideous, bright yellow with three gaudy aqua stripes, I could bring myself to put on anything else. Call me sentimental, but I felt that by wearing it, I was keeping a part of the team with me. I hadn't seen any of the other girls in ages.

When I had finally warmed up enough to move, I tossed my towel onto a bench and proceeded to tuck my hair up into a swim cap, then looped my goggles around my neck. There were thin dark rings under my eyes—though I couldn't tell whether they were from my washed-off makeup or from fatigue. I thought I'd gotten enough sleep the night before, but maybe strange dreams just have the effect of turning your skin purple.

The final thing I did before heading for the water was carefully remove the golden chain necklace. I'd been wearing it all day, tucked into my turtleneck, but I didn't want to risk the effects of chlorine on its already tarnished coloring. As I prepared to put it down on the bench beside my towel, I glanced quickly into its mirrored pendant. The foggy image reflected back at me was the hazel globe of my iris; pale brown streaked with tiny lightning bolts of dusty green. I blinked slowly, following the path of my eyelashes as they descended until I only saw darkness.

When I peeled my eyelids apart again, the eye in the mirror was black.

I shrieked, leaping back and letting the necklace spring from my grasp. With one hand to my heart, I panted heavily. This time, I didn't need to feel my pulse to know I was breathing; I could feel my rapid heartbeat easily enough.

The necklace lay in a coil a few feet away from me, glinting innocently beneath the fluorescent lights. The mirror had landed face down, and when I mustered up the courage to turn it over, I found that a thin, hairline crack had formed on its surface. But in the glass, the slivered of an iris that I saw was my own—no inky pool, no onyx abyss. Just my eye, split in two.

Taking deep breaths to calm my still-frantic heart, I lay the necklace carefully on the bench, lining it up alongside one of the thin gaps in the wood. I was mad at myself now for having dropped it; especially over something as silly as thinking I'd seen another person's eye. This wasn't a scene from Harry Potter, this was my life, and things like that simply did not happen in reality.

"I must be losing my mind," I muttered aloud.

Callery's community pool is arguably the nicest feature of the town: it's indoor, heated, and cleaned twice a day. I entered just as the janitor was leaving, in fact, although I doubt there had been any human filth that morning for him to clean.

"Afternoon, Parker," the man called, tipping his hat in my direction as he pushed the pool cleaning supplies out the door.

"Afternoon, Mr. Kaid," I replied to his retreating back, securing my goggles over my eyes. He sent me a wave over his shoulder.

Once he had gone, the poolroom was empty. The pale blue tiles shone beneath my bare feet, chilly and shining in the natural light of the sun roof. The whole twenty-five meter length of the pool lay out before me, lapping gently against its concrete sides. I stared at it for a moment, shivering from both excitement and the cold, but I had never been the girl who dipped her toes in first.

I took a running start and dived.

My body sliced through the water, stretched fingers and pointed toes knifing a bubbly path to the bottom of the pool. I tapped it with both hands, then used the motion to spin around and propel myself back to the surface. Warm water breezed past me as I cut it with my hands, parting at my silent command until I finally broke into open air.

I emerged, gasping, at the deep end of the pool, my legs beating furiously to keep me afloat. With two simple kicks, I swam to the edge, where the black-and-white depth marker was mounted on the grayish wall. I placed one hand over the thick number eight, preparing to do laps.

Already, I could feel the buzz of breathless exhilaration building in my chest, waking up my brain with quick, invigorating jolts. It was an amazing feeling, not like suffocating but like the sensation of being scared in a horror movie, then realizing that it's all on-screen. That bubbly energy as you laugh it off with your friends, that nervous warmth that tickles at your rib cage.

That was how it felt. And it was wonderful.

I took a big breath, sucking all the air out of the room and into my lungs, before submerging once again. I pushed off from the wall and beat my legs once, twice, mermaid-like, before settling into the steady freestyle rhythm. It was perhaps the simplest stroke, but I'd always been better at it than most of my teammates. I could be fast, when I wanted to be—my average time for the hundred meter free was fifty seconds flat. When I quit competitive, my coach joked that she'd have to cut off my arms and legs and give them to someone else so that the team wouldn't lose their record.

A lot of the other girls, the ones who were good at the butterfly and backstroke and breaststroke, were always asking how I managed to breathe while swimming so quickly. And the truth is: I didn't. In the four lengths that make up one hundred meters, I took about three real breaths. I had lungs of steel, according to Logan, who couldn't go underwater for three seconds without gasping for air. But more likely, I think I was too focused on the pure excitement of being beneath the surface to notice that I was being robbed of breath.

There was, quite simply, something magical about swimming. Gliding through the water was like having wings, like being weightless and airborne—yet not. I loved the way it cut off all sound, encasing me in a submarine palace of ripples and skewered sunbeams. Had it been possible, I would have stayed submerged forever, so I never understood why Ariel had ever wanted to leave the sea. Walking was so painfully middling when swimming was an option.

I don't know how long I swam that day; I had a tendency to lose track of time. But I went through cycle after cycle, a hundred meters of each stroke with a thirty second pause between each. After five repetitions, I got out briefly to get a drink of water, then returned. The center was still empty, the pool silent save for the sound of my body gliding through the middle lane. As I grew tired, my reps took longer, and my breaks extended to a minute. But I kept swimming, kept pushing myself, because the focus on movement took my mind off the chaotic whirlwind of my life.

I was on the seventeenth round when things began to go wrong.

I remember that I had just finished four laps of the butterfly, my worst stroke, and was mentally berating myself for how long it had taken me, when the water suddenly began to get very cold. It was a slow chill, creeping upward as if it had started at the very bottom of the pool. I first felt it at the tips of my toes, like a breath of icy wind, but it quickly wound its way up my legs and torso.

I froze in place, immediately suspicious. The controls for heating the pool were adjacent to the dressing room, but not accessible from within; in order to get to them, you had to go through the main pool room. Even if I had been underwater, I certainly would have noticed someone passing through.

I pushed myself slowly out of the water, careful not to make a sound. Years of watching horror movies taught me that one should never call out when there is a possibility of a potential assailant nearby, so I was silent. I crept warily across the tile, wincing every time a droplet of water left my skin and hit the ground. The control room was sectioned off by a thick glass pane, and I paused at the edge of it, my heart in my throat.

In hindsight, I'm not sure why I was so nervous. It couldn't have been anyone unsavory, after all; the desk attendant never would have let them in. However, the desk attendant was eighty-three, and did have a tendency to doze off at the most inopportune times...

Before my fear could manifest itself, I leapt forward and whirled on the control room, letting out a wild shout. My hands were raised, ready to fend off anyone who might burst through the glass—

And there was no one inside.

I squinted at the dim light, my eyes slits, but the room was empty, the lights off and the seat tucked in beneath the desk. The heating controls lay in their normal position: untouched. My heart was hammering as I backed away, excited by unnecessary adrenaline. Briefly, I entertained the idea that maybe, I had simply imagined the whole thing—but no, that was impossible. My toes felt like icicles, yet the temperature of the pool room was at least seventy degrees.

"My God," I muttered, shaking water out of my ears as I headed back toward the dressing room. Unsurprisingly, I didn't feel like going back in the pool, not if I was at risk of freezing to death. I was feeling that chill again, the same one that had struck at church the day before, except this time, I didn't have Logan's jacket to protect me. I broke into a light jog, bringing my knees up to my chest with each stepped. That warmed me up a little bit, but I still wanted a sweater.

This time, when I went to the showers, the hot water was on full force. I let it scorch my skin, streaming through my hair like hot lava. It effectively melted away all the frost in my system, leaving me warm and happy. By the time I headed back into the dressing room, the freezing pool had been pushed to the back of my mind.

But when I set one foot on the cold floor, something shifted in the air. I swear to you, it was almost visible; it was as if someone had turned on a gas stove beneath the ground, and the thin waves of heat were waving up into the air. Except that this was cold. The temperature dropped again, lower than before, but I didn't shiver; I didn't move.

I couldn't move.

My feet had gone completely numb, the same sensation you feel after sitting on your legs for too long. I knew I could take a step, if I wanted to, but I wasn't about to take the risk. One of the girls on the swim team had once snapped her ankle when trying to run into a dive with numb feet. When you can't feel your limbs, you can bend them completely out of shape without realizing it, because there is no pain. At least, not right away.

Regardless, I didn't move, though a single question was racing circles through my mind at warp speed: what was happening to me?

Eventually, the strange numbness let go, and the air stilled. I thought I felt a gust of wind as I shook the feeling back into my limbs, but perhaps I just imagined it.

I danced across the room on pins and needles, over to the bench where all my things lay. After hurriedly stripping out of my wet swimsuit and drying off, I wriggled into my clothes—jeans and a thick green turtleneck sweater. I had makeup in my bag, but I didn't bother reapplying it; all I wanted to do was get out of that building as soon as possible. There was something weird as hell going on, and I wanted to be as far away from it as possible.

It wasn't until much later, when I got home, that I realized my necklace was gone.

As it turns out, fear and anxiety are the best remedies for lazy feet. With the strange happenings of the pool room lurking over my shoulder, I made ridiculously quick time walking home. I'd made it to the town center within ten minutes, though it usually took at least fifteen.

Checking the time on my iPhone, I saw that it was nearly two-thirty; about an hour and and a half since Logan had dropped me off at the pool and fifteen minutes until all the schools in the area let out. My mother wasn't due home until four, but I didn't linger. The people in town were likely to tell my mother if it seemed like I was loitering around with nothing to do.

As it was, I was on the receiving end of many odd stares from passerby. People I'd know all my life were eyeing me up and down, warily, as if I might lash out and start speaking in tongues. I was able to ignore it without much effort. I knew this particular brand of human like the back of my hand; if you confront them, they will bite, then make their way over to the coffee shop to gab about their ordeal to their fellow big-mouthed neighbors. So I kept my head down, pulled my gloves tight, and managed to make it down Main Street without incident.

Then I reached the general store.

In Callery, just like any other small town in every book you've ever read, the general store is basically the go-to place for all your common needs. Toothbrushes? Got it. Peanut butter? Aisle five. Marlin 336XLR hunting rifle? Well, it's technically not legal, but if you ask in the back and pay a little extra, Jimmy West, the owner, might be willing to part with one of the many guns in his collection.

Point is, the general store has everything and anything you might ever desire. It is also the second home for all of the town's biggest gossips. Everyone goes to the general store, making it the best place to people watch and extract the latest drama from every overheard conversation. So if you ever come to Callery and see a gaggle of middle-aged women in garish clothes watching your every move, try not to be nervous; they're just another part of the scenery.

I passed the usually suspects as I ambled by: Jan McGee, Priscilla Carlson, and Raissa Lerner, sitting at the tables outside the store, their extra-wide behinds spread out on the pewter patio chairs. Ducking even lower, I tried to escape their notice, but though age had deteriorated their figures, it hadn't done squat to their eyesight.

"You, girl!" shouted Jan, just as I thought I was in the clear. I paused, mentally cursing the day that woman was born, and fixed a soppy smile on my face before turning around.

"Hello, ma'am!" I called. "How are you?"

Jan had a cup of tea in her hand, and she swished it around before answering. And when she did answer, it wasn't in response to my question.

"Edith Hummel's inside that store," she informed me. I got the feeling, from the look in her eyes, that she was aiming for a conspiratorial whisper, but that was ruined slightly by the fact that she was shamelessly yelling.

"Oh, that's nice," I said, trying to play off the sudden knot in my stomach with a sweet head tilt. Every muscle in my body was suddenly urging me to run.

"Very nice," Jan agreed. Her hawk eyes bored into my skull. "I heard about what she said to you at mass yesterday. The poor, delusional old hag."

I was torn—half of me wanted to curl into a humiliated ball, and the other half wanted to laugh at Jan McGee's unwitting "old hag syndrome" reference. I ended up doing a little bit of both, wrapping my arms around my torso and spitting out a hysterical little chuckle. My pool bag slipped down to my elbow.

But just as I was opening my mouth to respond with a generic comment, a little hiss of air escaped the woman's mouth. All three women were suddenly looking over my shoulder, their eyes wide. Startled, I turned around, and found myself faced with Old Mrs. Hummel, hobbling out of the general store with her bony hands clutching a walker.

One of the women behind me let out a pitying cluck; Edith didn't seem to notice. She continued moving at a snail's pace, out onto the sidewalk. I was cornered now; behind me were the women, before me was Mrs. Hummel. And either way I went, flat out terror-sprinting would look undeniably suspicious.

As it happened, I was saved the choice, because a moment later, the old woman froze in her tracks. Her head turned toward me, very slowly, her deep-set eyes widening in the planes of her wrinkled face.

"Parker Elway," she stated in that same, strong voice. "The devil's chosen girl."

Behind me, I heard the nasal sound of Raissa Lerner's gasp.

"Hello, Mrs. Hummel," I said, attempting to keep my voice from shaking.

The woman blinked, her milky blue eyes momentarily swallowed by creased folds of loose skin. Her frail body was hunched over, weak, but she sounded very sure as she said, "Oh, sweet girl, you are just like her."

I swallowed hard. "Ma'am?"

"Just like her," Mrs. Hummel repeated in a singsong tone. "Just like the other girl that Satan came to take away. He'll come for you, too, sweet girl. In fact"—she lowered her voice to a harsh whisper—"he's already here. Yes, yes, darling. Already here."

I reeled backward, clutching my hands to my chest. Edith Hummel was repeating those last two words over and over, her gummy lips smacking against each other. She wasn't screaming, not this time—but this was worse.

Just then, from within the general store burst the old woman's attendant, Svana Malone. The poor girl, who had been sent into town by Edith's daughter specifically to take care of her, was a flustered mess, groceries falling from her arms and her wispy blonde hair slipping from its bun.

"Mrs. Hummel!" she shrieked, her Icelandic accent thick with worry. "Mrs. Hummel, you aren't supposed to wander off!"

Edith Hummel opened her mouth and let out a whistling sigh, then said, "He's coming for her, Svana. He's coming for her, and he'll take her away."

As if it wasn't already obvious who the woman was talking about, she raised one sagging arm and pointed at me. Svana glanced over, noticing my presence for the first time, and emitted a horrified little shriek. Her eyes widened at the sight of me, and she ducked her head behind a bag of frozen peas.

"Come, Mrs. Hummel," she hissed. "Let us go to the car, yes?" She urged the little old woman along, but as they stepped into the street, a can of soup fell out of one of the bags.

"Here, let me get that," I offered automatically. My hand was inches away from the can when something cold slapped my wrist.

"No!" cried Svana, her blue eyes in saucers. She had somehow managed to free a hand enough to smack me with it, and now she held it up like a weapon. "I don't need your help. Step away!"

Shocked and disconcerted, I edged back onto the sidewalk. Svana was still watching me, and I could practically feel Jan and co. smirking smugly at my expense. I didn't wait to see anymore; without a word, I turned and bolted, away from the general store and into the alley that separated it from the tailor's. Once I was out of sight, I dug my phone from my pocket and quickly dialed in Logan's number.

"Come on, come on, come on," I begged, hopping from foot to foot as it rang one, two, three times. When his voice answered lazily on the other end, I practically sobbed, "Logan, you've gotta come pick me up right now!"

I was breathing hard; my bags had fallen to the ground at my feet. "Please," I gasped, before he could reply.

"Okay, okay, whoa!" I could hear banging and rusting as he jumped to his feet. "Where are you?"

"Alley between the general store and the tailor," I blurted, "come quickly, okay?"

"Yeah, I'm on my way! Hold tight; I'll be there literally within a minute."

"Okay." I sucked in a breath. "Okay."

Logan hung up on his end, but I stared at his number, still lit on the screen, trying to find some kind of comfort in the familiarity. My head was spinning, my thoughts whirling dizzily as the memory of Edith Hummel's words passed through again and again.

I let out a choked cry, feeling tears building behind my eyes. I couldn't cry. I never cried. This was no time to lose my cool.

"Logan is almost here," I whispered to myself, over and over. "Logan is almost here, Logan is almost here, Logan is almost—"

Quite suddenly, I cut off in the middle of my sentence. I was struck, at the moment, with the overwhelming certainty that there was someone watching me. I could feel their eyes, stiff and unblinking, staring at me just like the creature in my waking nightmare.

I tried to tell myself that it was just like The Intruder; the thing that Dr. Hennessy had described. It wasn't real, but an imaginary manifestation created by my fear. It was just a falsified presence. It couldn't touch me, couldn't hurt me, because it didn't exist. I told that to myself repeatedly, along with the delirious mantra of don't look up.

But in the end, I couldn't help it. I drew my eyes away from the number on my phone and looked up very, very slowly.

There was a man across the street.

I shrieked out an expletive, slamming into the brick wall beside me. I wasn't imagining it this time. This wasn't a midnight jogger turned terrible by my overactive imagination. This was a man, a real, living, breathing man; a man in a crisp penguin suit who watched me with an ugly smirk.

His eyes were black as Christmas coal.

"Oh holy Jesus Christ," I screeched, slamming my finger to the call button on my phone. It rang and rang, too many times, and all the while I couldn't take my eyes off the man, the predatory grin on his young, handsome face, the way he stood beside the lamppost like a statue.

"Parker?" Logan said, when he finally answered.

"Logan, my God, Logan, please please tell me you're almost here."

"I'm just around the corner, I—"

"There's a man, Logan," I hissed, "there's a man across the street, and he's watching me I swear he is, even right now as I'm speaking to you he won't look away dear God please hurry!"

My best friend let out five loud curses (I counted) on the other end of the line before saying, "I'm almost there, Parker, I'm almost there, just stay on the phone with me, scream if the man comes any closer, I'm almost there—"

His words were quickly drowned out by the blood rushing past my ears and into my head, and as the seconds ticked by like hours, like years, the man just stayed there, staring, smiling, looking like he wanted to eat me for dinner. Tiny needles prickled my flesh.

Just as I thought I was going to pass out from terror, the man moved. He drew his feet together, put a hand against his ribcage, and dipped into a low, mocking bow. I was scared out of my mind for a split second, thinking he was going to cross the street and come for me, but he turned to the left, and with measured, militaristic steps, began to walk away.

And, as the terrible man began his retreat, Logan's car came careening in front of the mouth of the alley. I'd never been so happy to see the ratty blue Volkswagen Beetle in my life. The driver's door flew open, and Logan leapt out, taking one look down the alley and breaking into a sprint. I rushed toward him, leaving my bags on the ground behind me, and went flying into his arms. Tears were pouring down my face now, finally having let loose in a geyser down my face. I bawled openly into Logan's sweater as he clutched me to his chest like he hadn't seen me in years. When I finally drew back, red-faced and sniveling, his eyes were a mask of horror and concern.

"Jesus, Parker," he murmured, smoothing my hair back from my face, "what the hell happened?"

I shook my head, a little sob escaping my lips as the world tilted before my eyes.

"I have no idea," I whispered, my voice blank. "I really have no idea at all."

CHAPTER 7

That night, I had a most terrible dream.

I went to bed a fitful, exhausted mess, annoyed because, though I had searched everywhere, I'd been unable to find my necklace. I was asleep before my head hit the pillow. But no sooner had my eyes drifted shut than they flew open again, propelled by an invisible force hidden inside my mind. I'd told myself, during all those hours I'd spent in my room since arriving home, that when the nightmares came, I'd be ready. That I knew what they were, and they couldn't hurt me, and I wouldn't panic when they inevitably appeared.

The reality is, I can lie to myself all I want; but fear will do as fear does, and it has no discretion as to what decisions you have made or what bravery you have tried to muster. And it certainly did not hold back in volume when the shadow creature appeared before me, staring me down with those intrusive, soul-searching eyes.

Frozen in place, unable to breathe, I watched in horror as the dark being that stood at the foot of my bed, the monster with a human shape, moved closer, circling around my bed to move right beside me—just outside of my peripheral vision. I couldn't see it, but I felt it, felt it moving closer, closer, closer, its cold, evil breath brushing against my cheek.

The demonic weight on my chest shifted, digging deeper into my ribs , as the shadow brushed its ghostly hand against my throat. I thought I had braced myself, but nothing could have prepared me for the finger of cold that seeped slowly into my bloodstream and turned my heart to ice.

My mind was screaming, brimming with hot panic, and I swear the monster could hear it because suddenly, it began to laugh. The sound was harsh and metallic, like knives being struck against each other, and it took air right beside my ear. I felt the stagnant heat of rancid breath against my cheek.

An invisible shudder rode a wave down my petrified body. It seemed that the shadow could sense my fear; as I became more terrified, its laughs escalated to hysterical cackles. Yet I still could not see it, at my side and just out of sight.

And somehow, that was even more terrifying.

It's just a dream, I told myself. Just a dream just a dream just a dream.

And I found that, after repeating those words a few dozen times, my eyelids began to drift shut. Somehow, they alone had been freed from the paralysis. The rest of my body was still trapped, that weight seeming to grow heavier by the heartbeat, but I saw only the innocent calignosity of my mind.

I thought I would fall back to sleep, after that. Already, the presence beside me was fading, my body seeming to relax. But just as I was turning over my mind to rest, feeling my breath return, a massive, crushing force came down on my torso. It should have crushed me. Instead, it peeled my eyelids back from my pupils and forced me to watch the scene unfolding before me.

There were phantoms lurking at the edge of my bed.

If it had been possible for me to scream, I would have. I would have emptied my lungs, woken all the neighbors, then sucked in a new breath and begun again. My terror was so tremendous at that moment that I am surprised it didn't simply break me in two.

Just like the monster who had laughed at me, these specters were nothing but shades, dark splotches against the already lightless room. I can't tell you for certain how many there were—four, perhaps five—but they stood in a cluster, surrounding the iron steeples of my footboard with their hulking presence.

As one entity, each the figures raised their right arm (if you could call it an arm), and pointed the wispy limbs at me. And gradually, deliberately, my comforter began to slip off my body.

To begin with, it was pulled up tight to my chin. But as the demon-things beckoned, it slipped off my bed, revealing my pajama-clad form hidden beneath it. They began to laugh, that nails-on-chalkboard screech, as the plush blanket of gray-and-white stripes began to bunch up at the foot of my bed. And all the while, there was this feeling, like a dozen miniscule spiders swarming across my body.

Oh, Jesus, I thought, my mind a whirlwind. Oh dear sweet Jesus someone help me this is just a dream this has to be a dream dear lord—

Suddenly, the horror stopped. The creatures froze their laughter, the comforter stopped its movement, the relentless insects ceased to exist. One by one, with terrible, gut-wrenching moans, the shadows dissipated. The pressure on my chest lessened, just slightly, and my comforter was just beginning to creep back up my legs when all of a sudden, there was an unholy scream and right in front of my eyes, manifesting in thin air—

A face.

Sharp, darkened planes; dark features; sunken, ember eyes. With a mouth wrenched apart in its terrible cry, the face appeared before me for a fraction of a second, spitting icy saliva onto my flesh. Then it was gone, vanished. It dissolved into the same darkness from which it had come. I was thrown up from my mattress in the bundle of nervous energy, my legs tangling in the half-drawn blankets as I literally flew over the edge of my bed. I landed hard on the carpet with a painful thud, my arm twisting beneath me.

It was still dark outside. My curtains were drawn, so my room was still in shadows; perfect for hiding whatever devils lurk in the darkness. But somehow, I was certain that whatever they were, they were gone.

At that moment, curled on the ground in my bedroom in the darkness, the line between dreams and actuality was stretched frighteningly thin. Though all rational thinking insisted that what I'd seen was another, more vivid nightmare, there was that defiant corner of my mind that told me whatever phenomenon had just occurred could not merely be attributed to science. It knew before I did that there was something else at play here, something dark and demonic that barely existed in my sliver of reality.

I'd never felt more helpless in my life.

The thing about the darkness is that once it's gone, all the lurid happenings that define it disappear as well. When there's light, there is safety, security. Knowledge that all the monsters beneath your bed can't touch you anymore. Even if you're possibly being followed by sinister men or haunted by invisible demons, there's something about daytime brightness that chases fear away.

I slept with all the lights on for the rest of the night.

"Find anything interesting yet?" Logan asked, leaning inquisitively over my shoulder. Sighing, I shook my head.

"Oh, I've found plenty of interesting things. I just don't know how to figure out what's important."

I made a frustrated sound at the back of my throat, slapping five new sheets of paper onto the table in front of me. Logan and I had been in my backyard since early afternoon, taking advantage of my mom's working hours to begin sorting through the file Dr. Hennessy had given me. So far, I'd found the same stuff about intruders and old hags, but nothing that could make my situation any more relevant.

"We'll find something eventually," Logan assured, squeezing my arm gently before retreating to the other side of the bench. The papers were spread out on the picnic table before us, held down in stacks by rocks from the garden. I yanked out another stack forcefully, angry at my own inability to figure out what was going on.

"I don't even know what I'm looking for," I admitted. "This, all of this"—I waved my hands to encompass the whole table—"has to have some kind of significance, but I just... I don't know. Maybe I need a break."

Logan nodded in agreement. "I'll second that. There's no way reading about sleep disorders for hours on end can be good for your mental health."

I scoffed. "Yeah, because it's not like my sanity's already under question or anything like that."

"It's not," my best friend said seriously. He looked at me imploringly until I turned to face him, then grabbed my hand and squeezed it tightly. "Parker, no one thinks you're crazy, all right? I don't know what's going on with the people you've been seeing and these nightmares, but we'll figure it out. And I'll be here for you no matter what."

A squeak of relief escaped my lips as Logan pulled me into his arms. He was wearing his jacket, the one I'd borrowed from him on Sunday, but it'd been at my house for two days so now it smelled like my room mixed with his familiar scent.

"So this means we're taking a break, right?" he asked slowly, once he'd released me. "I can go in and make hot chocolate, and we can just watch TV for a while, get your mind off all this.

I nodded vigorously. "Yeah, break. For sure. Let me just put this stuff away so my mom doesn't freak out on me." He was already standing, looking dubious at the idea of me staying outside alone. I flashed him an easy smile. "Seriously, Logan, I'll be inside in a minute."

"Fine," he grumbled, glancing back at me over his shoulder as he made his way back to the house, like he thought I'd disappear at any second. When he opened the screen door, Zipper, who we'd left in the house, came hurtling into the backyard in a stream of fluffy white. She sped over to me, rubbing her face against the hem of my jeans.

"Hey, girl," I cooed, scratching her between the ears. She was only eight months old, still a puppy; we'd gotten her from a woman two streets over whose American Eskimo had given birth to an unnaturally large litter. Zipper was high energy, always a blur of snowy white against the world.

She propped her short front legs onto the bench and tilted her head, her little pink tongue lolling out of her mouth expectantly.

"I have no food for you," I cried, laughing as she licked my hand, hoping for a treat. I gently pushed her paws away. "Go, Zip! Go play, I'm busy."

After whining a bit, Zipper backed up and began her waddling run into the center of the backyard. What I loved about my house, and other houses in the culdesac, was that the forest was literally a stone's throw away. All that separated us from the tree-filled expanse was a low stone fence. When I was little, Logan and I used to play back there all the time, sometimes managing to convince his older sister, Aubrey, to take us down to the small old lake that was hidden back there, beyond the trees.

I watched my dog bullet through the grass as I gathered the papers, slipping them all back into the file. Two hours of reading had done nothing but restate information I already knew, and we weren't even halfway through the pile. It was disheartening, not to mention the fact that I was still extremely groggy from my inability to fall asleep the night before.

I knew that if the night terrors got any worse, I'd have to tell my mother. I was already a mess internally; anything worse and I'd flip out for sure. And, unsurprisingly, I still wasn't able to get over the idea of that man watching me. Maybe I'd imagined it—maybe. But it was so easy to call his face to mind that was was inclined to think he had been real.

Just then, a frantic barking startled me from my thoughts. I looked up quickly to see Zipper, fur on end, standing by the gate that lead out to the forest and growling. Her little tail was ramrod straight, her eyes focused somewhere beyond the fence.

"Zipper," I called, suddenly worried, "what is it, girl?" I followed her gaze, scanning the dimly lit trees, but saw nothing. Yet something had Zipper spooked; I'd never seen her so tense before.

Hugging the stuffed file to my chest, I shouted out a wary, "Come on, Zipper!" before backing away toward the house. Zipper let out one loud bark that bounced off the trees, followed momentarily with a plaintive whimper. She sneezed quietly, a final sound, before running toward me with her tail between her legs.

Once my mother got back from work and Logan had gone home, I retreated to my room with Zipper at my heels, ready to delve back into the papers. I read page after page, information in tiny print scattered across ivory sheets, trying to sort through medical definitions and common cultural legends and real accounts.

It was the latter that I was most interested in; I read countless stories by different people, all of them recounting tales similar to my own. Some were visited by The Intruder; some had seen the shadows; some even claimed to have woken up to an alien perched on their chests. But although a few accounts reported a feeling that their covers were being dragged off their body, none reported that the phenomenon actually happened.

I looked down at my comforter, tucked neatly beneath me. Somehow, last night, it had been drawn all the way down my bed. In the past, I had woken up with my blankets at crazy angles, or even on the floor, and I knew that it was because I'd moved around in my sleep. But I'd watched them move this time. I hadn't been able to move, much less kick my comforter off my bed, but I'd seen its slow progression, peeling away from the mattress at the hands of the dark beings. Even now, staring at my footboard, I could see the entire thing repeating in my head.

"I swear to God, I'm going insane," I muttered.

Zipper, curled up on a pillow beside me, looked up and offered me a consoling tap with her cold nose. She seemed to have recovered from whatever had spooked her in the woods, but she now refused to leave my side.

At around eight-thirty, my mom came into my room uninvited, calling me for dinner. She didn't even seem to notice the mess on my bed, thank goodness. I had a feeling that she'd flip out if she knew what I was researching.

Dinner was bland; unseasoned chicken and brown rice. It definitely beat the health food experiments we'd been having recently, though, so I didn't complain. Zipper had come downstairs with me, much to my mother's annoyance, and was trotting circles around the table as we ate in silence. The only sound in the dining room was that of metal cutlery on china plates, with the occasional clink of a glass being set down on the wooden table.

Halfway through the meal, my mother cleared her throat. "So," she said, trying to be offhand, "have you had anymore of those dreams lately?"

I paused for a split second, my knife halfway into a slice of chicken. It was the penultimate moment, the one that would winnow down all her possible reactions to a single one. If I said no, I'd likely be questioned. If I said yes, I'd never have peace.

"Nope, none," I said, a beat too late. Mom's eyes narrowed.

"Are you lying to me, Parker Sage?"

I masked a gulp by swallowing a bite of food. "Of course not," I retorted indignantly. "Why would I lie about that? I haven't had any more dreams."

My mother didn't blink, nor did she move her gaze from my face as I reached for my glass of water. I was careful to keep my expression impassive, smoothing my feature into a mask of nonchalance until she looked away.

"Good," she stated, and I thought I caught a flash of relief in her eyes. Her jaw clenched as she brought a forkful of food up to her lips. Even when she ate, she did not drop her head. Her chin stayed stiffly raised, like a 1940s movie star. Like an evil queen in a fairy tale.

I returned to my room as soon as humanly possible without looking suspicious, and my mom came in at about ten o'clock to tell me she was going to take Zipper downstairs, then go to sleep.

"What's that you're doing?" she asked before leaving, belatedly noticing the papers scattered across my room.

I resisted the urge to pull them all to my chest, instead saying, "Just some research for school. Nothing big."

Mom sniffed, shrugged, and left the room.

By ten thirty, I had a pounding headache and a lethargic feeling in my limbs. I had school the next morning; it was probably a good idea to go to sleep. I told myself that, yet the seconds ticked by, and I continued staring at the same page for ten minutes. The three bare bulbs that hung from my ceiling swayed slightly from a breeze coming in through my balcony window.

At eleven o'clock, I dragged myself to the bathroom, intending to take a shower and then go to sleep. I was still wearing my t-shirt and hoodie from that afternoon, and my hair was a ratty mess around my hair. Despite my intention to wash up and get ready for bed, I spent several moments, wiping away smears in my makeup and combing my fingers through my hair.

When I emerged from the bathroom soon after, makeup and hair completely redone, I resigned to the fact that I was too afraid to go asleep, and sitting around forcing myself awake was not going to help anything. After taking a quick peek into the hall to make sure the light was out in my mother's room, I snatched my phone off my nightstand and dialed in a number.

"Hello?" Juliette murmured, answering the phone after a few rings.

"Hey, I need to get out of here," I hissed, gathering my papers into a messy pile. "You up for it?"

There was a yawn from Juliette's end, then silence; for a moment, I worried she had fallen back asleep. But after a moment, she muttered, "Parker Sage, it's a school night for both of us. Are you kidding me?"

I bounced on the balls of my feet, making a silent mad dash around my room in search of my shoes. "Pleeeease, J," I whispered, drawing out the syllables. "I'll love you forever."

I heard grumbling and rustling from her side, then a resigned sigh. "God, you're so lucky you have me." She yawned again. "Stan's?"

"Stan's," I confirmed, a grin spreading across my face. "I'll meet you outside."

The good thing about having a balcony outside your room is that it makes sneaking out impossibly easy. All it took was a leg over the rail and a few nervous airborne seconds before I landed in a crouch on the grass of my front lawn. My half-laced combat boots made no sound as I sprinted around back, feeling for all the world like a ninja in an action flick.

When I hopped the fence into the woods behind our houses, Juliette was already waiting with her arms crossed tightly against the nighttime chill. She waved a gloved hand at me as I sprinted over, and we took off into the trees.

Stan's was about half a mile away, but if you took the forest shortcut, it only took about five minutes. We'd learned the route years ago, back when we were going just to spy on the older kids getting wasted, and now traversing it was second nature, even in the dark. We sped through the trees by the light of the moon, the constant movement keeping us warm.

We were about halfway there when Juliette stopped.

"What is it?" I demanded, skidding to a stop. "What's wrong?"

Juliette's eyes were wide white saucers in the darkness, her arms rigid at her sides. "Do you hear that?" she whispered.

I froze completely, straining to listen as the leaves settled around me. I heard nothing.

"No," I replied slowly, "Juliette, what do you hear?"

"Shh!" My friend hushed me violently, her lips trembling. "Listen. It's coming Parker Sage, it's coming closer."

I edged closer, my heart in my throat. "What is, J? What the hell are you talking ab—"

My question was cut off abruptly as Juliette let out at earsplitting shriek, throwing her arm up to point behind me, her face contorted in terror. I automatically screamed as well, hurling myself to the ground as terror pulsed through me, frenzied and untamed, and gasping laughter erupted above me—

Wait, laughter?

"Oh my God, that was the best!" Juliette cried. I dared my eyes open to see her standing a few feet away, one hand against a tree, quaking with laughter.

"You should have seen your face!" she gushed.

I pushed myself to my knees, anger and annoyance flooding through me as I struggled to calm my heartbeat. "Dude!" I shouted. "Not cool! That was not funny!"

Juliette slapped her thigh, cackling. "No, it was freaking hilarious! Oh God, Parker Sage, you're a mess!" She staggered over to me, helping me to my feet and beginning to pull leaves and twigs out of my hair.

"Jesus," I muttered, resisting the urge to smack her hand away as genuine irritation coursed through my veins. "You're such a jerk!"

My friend smiled sweetly, giving me a condescending pat on the head as she said, "Oh, lighten up, hon. After all, you can't have thought that you'd be able to wake me up at eleven at night without having to deal with a few consequences." She winked, and though I was still peeved, she either didn't notice or dutifully ignored it.

"Come on, Parker Sage," she beckoned, "let's go."

At Stan's, we ordered our usual drinks: strawberry daiquiris on the rocks. The first time we'd gotten them, when we were fifteen, it's taken us about two minutes each because we couldn't stop giggling long enough to get the words out. Now, the bartender, Stan, after whom the joint was named, immediately got our orders going the second we came through the door.

Stan was from New Jersey, and he never said much, because a lot of kids would make fun of his accent. Usually, he just made you your drink, took your money (plus the two dollars extra for minors), and left it at that.

But that night, when Juliette and I came in with cheeks pink from the cold, Stan sped right over to us in his apron, towel draped over the crook of his elbow.

"Parker, you got a new boyfriend or something?" he demanded immediately, blatantly skipping any introductions, as was his custom. "'Cause some guy came in 'bout an hour ago, lookin' for ya. He was real nice lookin', too, all fancy clothes and blond hair slicked back—a real playboy type, if ya know what I mean."

I raised an eyebrow, sharing a bemused glance with Juliette. "No, I don't," I replied, shaking my head, "I don't think I know anyone like that."

"Well." The bartender snorted. "Guess you have a secret admirer, then, 'cause he gave me the money to pay for your drink. Knew what you liked and everything, and paid the extra bit."

If it was even possible, my eyebrows arched up even further and my mouth dropped open as I took in what Stan was saying. I tried to rack my brain for whom it might have been, but I didn't know any blond guys who might be interested in me like that. Besides, most of the teenage boys around town were too cheap to spend their own money on a girl.

Seeming not to notice my confusion, Stan continued, "Anyway, you girls go on and sit down. I'll get your drinks stirred up."

"Wait, Stan!" Juliette called after him. "Did anyone come pay for my drink, by any chance?"

Stan just laughed.

"So, a secret admirer," Juliette said, once we'd found our seats at the bar and Stan had given us our drinks. She waggled her eyebrows suggestively. "Scandalous."

I shrugged as I sipped my drink, feeling the gratifying buzz zip through me.

"Probably just a fluke," I said. Music pulsed around us, and in the corner, old men and teenage boys alike shouted at a football game on the television.

"Or maybe," Juliette whispered, "it was Logan. He could have told Stan to keep his identity a secret, so you'd never know it was him." She sighed, her eyes searching the ceiling. "So romantic."

I snorted. "Yeah, right. Because buying a girl a drink at the seediest bar in town is the most romantic thing ever. Call the police, he stole my heart." Rolling my eyes, I fixed Juliette with a dry stare. "And anyway, why Logan, of all people? You know how much he hates bars."

My friend sipped her drink, smirking. "Well sure, I know that. But I also know that the reason why you couldn't sleep tonight is because you were thinking about him. Am I right, or am I right?"

"You're wrong, actually!" I gaped at her, appalled. "Why the hell would that be the reason why?"

"I don't know," she chirped in a singsong tone. "I just haven't seen his hanging around my place so much lately. How is Logan?"

"Deeply in love with you," I ground out.

"Mhm." Juliette didn't sound convinced. "Come on now, Parker Sage. Try and tell me that you don't notice the way he's been doting on you like crazy lately. I mean, he jumped at the chance to give you his jacket at church. And earlier today, when I looked out my window, I saw him hug you, just out of nowhere."

I smacked my friend across the arm, eliciting a tipsy laugh. "You were spying on us?" I spat.

"When you put it like that, it sounds wrong," she pouted. She spread out her hands in front of her, placating. "Anyway, all I'm saying is that Logan hasn't been acting the same with you lately. You'd have to be blind not see it."

"What, so I'm blind now?"

"No, hon, no." Juliette put a dainty hand on my arm, sighing prettily. "I just think that maybe, you don't want to accept the fact that things are changing between you and Logan. It happens all the time, no big deal. All guy-girl best friends go through this phase."

I burrowed my neck into the collar of my jacket, mumbling, "I don't believe you."

Tilting her head, Juliette waved a dismissive hand. "Suit your-self," she trilled. "But just you wait, Parker Sage; I know I'm right."

Taking another sip of the half-drained daiquiri, I shook my head. Juliette had tired of the subject of my and Logan's nonex-istent romance and moved on to a description of a boy in her French class who she thought was totally cute.

"He actually lives in Butler," she told me, "so he has, like, a ton of connections to all these cool parties and stuff. And he has the cutest accent when he speaks in French, it practically melts my heart."

"Mm," I grunted. Juliette, if she noticed my noncommittal response, did not comment. She waved her hands around, telling me about his amazing hair, and I tuned her out. I felt bad, I really did, but there was a pleasant buzzing in my head and it was very distracting.

I glanced over Juliette's shoulder at the football game playing on the TV, a rerun of that night's earlier match for those late workers who had to rely on sleazy bars for their entertainment. A group of men of varying ages were crowded around the dented flat screen, yelling or booing accordingly. I didn't understand a bit of football, but the colorful blur of their jerseys made pretty watercolor streaks.

As I sat there, grinning tipsily at the screen, I became aware of a tugging presence at the corner of my eye. I reluctantly drew my attention away, focusing instead on the blond head of a man—the only man who wasn't flying out of his seat.

Juliette was slightly drunk and still talking, so she didn't no-tice as I leaned forward to get a better look. The instant I noted the penguin suit the man wore, his entire body went completely straight. I inched backward in my stool, suddenly nervous, as very, very slowly, the man turned his head to face me.

And he smiled with his inkwell eyes.

This time, I did not jump or scream. I locked eyes with the man, hazel to jet black, as his teeth glinted in the dim light. There was something mysteriously alluring about his gaze, yet decidedly evil, and I felt a rampant fear course through me at the mere sight of him.

His lips moved. He was speaking to me, silently.

"I hope you liked the drink," he mouthed.

My breath flew out of my lips in a gasp, as if someone had punched me in the stomach.

"Parker Sage?"

I must have blanked out for a moment, because the next thing I knew, Juliette's hands were steadying my shoulders, her blue eyes boring into mine.

"Hon, are you okay?" she asked anxiously.

I couldn't speak for a moment; my mouth was strangely dry. I licked my lips and swallowed, then managed, "Fine. Too much alcohol."

But that wasn't it, not at all. I could down five glasses and not get drunk, and I had never half passed out before. This was something else, something darker, and I was absolutely certain that it had something to do with the mystifying man in the penguin suit, along with his apparent colleague whom I'd seen the day before. My heart hammered in my chest as I realized that these men, and maybe more, were following me, stalking me; I didn't know what they wanted, but they existed, and that was enough to have my fear clawing its way up my esophagus.

For a long, drawn out moment, I didn't dare let my gaze slip from Juliette's face. If she saw the man too, I didn't know what he would do to us. So I waited for thirty seconds, until her eyes glazed over again, and she went back to babbling about the boy from French class. That's when I finally chanced a peek at the booth across the bar, and presently swallowed a gasp.

I hadn't seen him leave, but the man with the onyx eyes was gone.

CHAPTER 8

"Dementia," Dr. Hennessy said, writing the world in big letters on the whiteboard and underlining it with a flourish. "From the Latin root de-, meaning without, and ment, referring to the mind. Its clinical definition is exactly as one would expect it to be: the loss of certain brain functions. Be sure to write that down, it's very important."

My fingers flew across the keyboard of my computer, copying down the definition before the professor could continue. That was our lesson today: dementia. Or, as Dr. Hennessy had put it when we walked into class, "the unholy deterioration of the human mind."

"Dementia in itself is not a disease," the professor intoned, striding measured paces across the pulpit of the lecture hall. "Rather, it is a syndrome, or a set of signs and symptoms, that is caused by a number of other diseases. Many of you, I'm assuming, have heard of Alzheimer's, the most common cause of dementia. A few others would be Parkinson's, multiple sclerosis, and progressive supranuclear palsy. And, generally, dementia does not occur in people under the age of sixty.

"Patients with dementia experience impaired performance in language, perception, and memory, among other functions. If you read last night, you should know that the main concentration of control for language is in Broca's Area. Perception is affected because, as you should all know, it mainly relies on memory, rather than actual sensory nerve signals. When a person's memory goes, so goes their ability to properly perceive the world around them. Some dementia patients may undergo bouts of hallucinations, delusions, and violent behavior as their brain's deterioration begins to interfere with their sense of proper judgment."

My ears perked at that, my fingers freezing mid-type as I processed the professor's words. Edith Hummel had dementia, I was certain of it; I had heard the ladies at church conversing on the subject on more than one occasion. With eyes still focused on the front of the room, I reached over and smacked Logan across the arm with the back of my hand.

"Dude," I hissed, "that's like Mrs. Hummel. She has all those things."

Logan grunted, and I slapped him again, turning this time. He wasn't even listening to the lecture; his head was down, staring intently at the sketchbook in front of him. Sketched on the page was the lightly penciled face of a familiar girl. Squinting, I leaned in closer.

"Is that...me?" I asked, extending a hand toward the page. When Logan realized that he'd drawn my attention, he slammed the book shut with a muffled thump.

"No," he said quickly, quietly, his eyes saucers. "Just my assignment—totally random."

I raised an eyebrow. Since we were much younger, Logan had had a strict policy against drawing people he knew. He always said that he couldn't stand creating art from his life; all of his paintings and drawings were spawned purely from his imagination. In fact, I rarely saw him sketch people at all, but rather strange, hybrid animals and crazy, altered versions of reality. But never simple human beings. And never, ever me.

"All right," I replied, watching his face go from pink to scarlet. I remembered what Juliette had said the night before, about Logan changing his subject of infatuation from her to me. Was it possible that—but no, of course not. Logan was still hopelessly in love with my next door neighbor, because that's how things had always been, and I had accepted years ago that it's how things would always be. So he was drawing a girl who possessed a striking resemblance to me—so what? That was no crime, nor did it mean a single thing. I was just making a big deal out of nothing.

Not to mention seriously over-thinking it.

I shook my head, clearing it, and cast a small glance over at my best friend. His face had returned to its normal color, but he wasn't looking at me and his sketchbook was clutched tightly both of his hands. Like me, he had his laptop open on the desk before us, opened to a Word document for taking notes. His screen was blank, though mine wasn't much better. The shaggy-haired boy in front of me had filled nearly an entire page.

Swallowing down my confusion, I returned to my notes, intending to throw myself into the lesson and be the stellar student that was buried somewhere beneath all my layers of laziness and procrastination. But after a few more minutes of listening to Dr. Hennessy speak, his voice began to get fuzzy.

I tried and failed to stifle a yawn, swiping a hand over my eyes. Juliette and I hadn't returned home until nearly three in the morning, when the bar finally closed. I doubted she was doing much better than me at school at the moment, but she'd had the advantage of getting at least an hour of shuteye before I'd so rudely awakened her. I'd been awake that whole time, and when I climbed back into my room, I was much too busy fretting over the man in the bar to get more than about ninety minutes of fitful sleep. Combine that with the fact that I was in school, learning, early in the morning, and there was really no hope for me. So, I was forced to do the thing that every teenager must do at least once during their educational career: I went to sleep in the middle of class.

And I certainly didn't expect to dream.

In this dream, the girl was back. It had been a few nights since I'd last seen her, but that hadn't stopped her blurry image from remaining tucked away in the back of my mind. I recognized her immediately by the sound of her voice; the melodic, lilting tone that was high like a child but wise like an adult.

The world was blank when I opened my eyes, and bright, bright white. For the first few seconds, all I heard was her voice. But it wasn't her voice, not really; it was the hum of it, smooth and kind but with no words that I could pick out.

As the seconds passed, my vision cleared, and I found myself in a warmly colored living room. Right in front of me was a lit fireplace; beneath my kneeling legs was a coarse brown carpet. I turned around slowly, feeling the heat of the fire against my back. Seated in a chair merely a few feet away from me was none other than Mrs. Hummel.

Something told me that she was younger here, though it was hard to tell. Perhaps her cheeks were a little less gaunt, or her hair a little less gray, but I had some strange gut instinct insisting that this was the way Edith Hummel looked several years ago.

The girl was beside Mrs. Hummel, perched on the edge of a rickety wooden chair. Her brown hair was twisted into a bun, and through the blur masking her features, I thought I detected a smile. The old woman was smiling too, an expression I never thought I'd see on her face, though it seemed to rest there naturally. She was laughing at something the girl had said, her frail hands raising to her cheeks.

I watched their buzzing exchange without hearing their words, mesmerized and confused by the sight before me. The first time I'd seen the girl, I had been a part of the scene. Now, it appeared that the two people in my dream did not see me; I was merely a spectator. And who was this girl? Why did she feel so familiar, sound so familiar, even though I was certain I had never met her?

The longer I stared at the pair conversing, the more I became certain that I was seeing a memory. This had happened somewhere, sometime, maybe long before I was even born. Obviously, it wasn't my memory. And if it wasn't mine, then who did it belong to?

Just then, as I was beginning to puzzle over the idea, a sharp pain skewered through the center of my skull, streaking my vision black. When I blinked away the sensation, I abruptly realized that the conversation—everything Edith and the girl were saying—was suddenly crystal clear. The words flew into my ears, crisp and sharp, seeming to singe my mind as they entered.

"You are such a wonderful girl," Mrs. Hummel was saying, "for coming here and sitting with me. Most of the other children are afraid of me."

The girl laughed, bright and tinkling. "It's no problem, ma'am," she replied. "In fact, I enjoy your company." She lowered her voice conspiratorially. "Most of the other children are afraid of me, too."

A small grin spread across Mrs. Hummel's face, but it disappeared almost instantly. Her mood switched abruptly, her expression slipping into one of quiet despair as she regarded the girl through her sunken eyes.

"Do you sense them in me?" the girl asked softly. The old woman nodded solemnly.

"In you, around you; they are everywhere, darling." She clasped her hands together in her lap. "They are coming, you know, and coming fast. You may not have much time left."

The girl sighed, and when she spoke, her voice was a breathy whisper. "I know."

For a long moment, it was silent. The girl and the woman sat with their heads bowed, and I sat on the carpet and watched them. They both felt so sad. It was if there was an aura of sadness surrounding them, cloaking their bodies in gray light. I didn't know what they were talking about, but whatever it was, it had been powerful enough to reverse their moods completely.

Mrs. Hummel's eyes were closed, but after several stretching seconds, she let them float open. "I'll be here for you, always," she murmured. "They may not let you go so easily, but neither will I."

"Thank you, Mrs. Hummel," the girl said, her arms wrapping around her thin body. "You don't know how much that means to me. But please, don't think that you're responsible. This deal was made long ago, and there was nothing either of us could have done to stop it."

"I know," the old woman said simply. She reached out creakily to pat the girl's knee, then drew back again, seeming to curl into herself. But before another silence could fall upon the room, she looked up very, very slowly. I gave a start, nearly jumping back into the fire, because I swear, she was staring straight into my eyes. Her lips moved in slow motion, but I was being pulled away, away from the blurring room and back into that white, white place, and it was a moment before her words reached me.

"I only wish that I could save you," she said.

"Parker," someone hissed, "Parker, wake up!"

I felt hands on my arm, shaking me, dragging me out of the vivid dream and back into reality. My eyes flew open and I jolted upright, nearly tipping myself back and out of my seat. A strong scent passed across my face, and though it was swept away in an instant, it brought burning tears to my eyes.

"I'm awake!" I announced, much too loudly. Logan was beside me, his hand still on my arm, staring at me in apparent amusement. From down in the pulpit, Dr. Hennessy cleared his throat, the sound echoing through the speakers and bouncing around the room.

"Glad to hear it, Ms. Elway," he boomed, "though it appears that you've managed to miss the entire lesson." Turning back to the rest of the class (most of whom were either snickering at me or glancing over in annoyance), he continued, "Read the rest of chapter seven tonight, and make sure you go over your notes. Next week's midterm is fast approaching."

The majority of the other students had already packed their things, knowing that class was almost over, and they now stood up and began to file out of the aisles. A blonde girl with glasses sitting a few feet away murmured a quiet, "Excuse me," as she slipped behind my seat.

"Can you send me your notes?" I asked Logan, passing a hand over my eyes as I began to pack my things. With every-thing going on, I had completely forgotten about the upcoming midterm. But it was mid-November now, and the exam marking the pinnacle of the semester was merely days away. And between the nightmares and everything else that cluttered my mind, I had done a less than substantial amount of studying.

"Sure," Logan replied quickly, helping me close my notebooks and stuff them into my bag. The room was practically empty now, and I could feel Dr. Hennessy watching me with disap-proving eyes. I think that he thought highly of me, but evidently, falling asleep and then shouting out in class was not something most teachers appreciated. On any other day, I would have been perfectly fine to just stay there, because confrontation never bothered me, and I had no problem arguing with adults—even my professors. But at that moment, with fragments of the dream still fresh in my mind, I wanted nothing more to get out of the lecture hall as soon as possible. I had a lot of things to figure out before my next class, and I couldn't do it under the scrutiny of a teacher.

As I stood up, shouldering my backpack, I was struck with a powerful smell. And, I quickly realized, it was the same odor I had noticed after the last time I dreamt about the girl. I froze in place, sniffing the air suspiciously.

"Logan," I said slowly, "do you smell that?"

My best friend was already heading down the aisle, but he glanced over his shoulder and asked, "Smell what?"

We stared at each other for a second, his green eyes narrowed in confusion, until I anxiously shook my head.

"Never mind," I muttered, kicking in my chair. "I'm just losing it."

Logan stayed close to my side as we left, occasionally glancing over in worry. And maybe there was something else in his gaze, but I wasn't about to rot my brain thinking about it. There was only one clear thought in my mind as we left the hall, something that I knew I had to do, even though the prospect frightened me.

I had to visit Edith Hummel.

"Are you sure you want to do this, Parker?" Logan asked, probably for the twentieth time in the past ten minutes.

I nodded resolutely, ignoring my churning stomach. "Yeah, absolutely," I replied. "I'll never be able to sleep at night if I don't get this devil possession business sorted out right now."

We were parked in front of Mrs. Hummel's home: a small, old, yellow house with stucco exterior and a bright red door. It looked like a faded, abstract interpretation of ketchup and mustard, but surrounded by droopy weeping willows whose boughs bent nearly to the ground.

"I'm picking you up, right?" Logan's hands tapped idly on the steering wheel to the radio's beat, but his brows were furrowed. "I don't want you going anywhere by yourself."

"Yeah, yeah. Pick me up in like thirty minutes, okay? I don't think I'll be long." I shook my head as I got out of the car, as if his concern was ludicrous, but in truth I was half terrified to make the trek from the car to Edith's front door. Logan was already worried enough, and that was without knowing about the man in the bar—my anxiety was about double the amount of his.

But, straightening up, I waved at him over my shoulder and forced myself to take even steps up to the crimson entryway. I knocked confidently, feeling reassured by the sound of Logan's engine idling loudly behind me.

"Come in!" screeched a voice: Mrs. Hummel. "The door is o-pen!"

I pushed against the wood, and sure enough, it slid ajar under the pressure. With some trepidation, I edged inside, shutting the door behind me.

I found myself in a hallway with wood paneled walls that led on for about five feet before branching off into two separate corridors. I paused there, at the threshold, taking in the coat rack and umbrella stand next to me as I waited for some divine directions on where to go.

"Go right," Edith called, her voice looping toward me from the corresponding corridor. I obliged, wincing every time my boots creaked on the hardwood floorboards.

Around the corner, I was struck with a sight that nearly made me fall over, though perhaps it shouldn't have been so surprising. I was in Edith Hummel's living room—the same room that

I'd seen in my sleep. There was the brick fireplace; the Monet painting on the wall; there was Mrs. Hummel, her small body sunken into the same patchwork couch she'd occupied in my dream. When I entered, she turned, her lips pursed.

"You've finally come," she murmured, her eyes distant. "Come, sit; we've been expecting you."

I automatically glanced around, wondering what we she was talking about, but promptly decided that she was referring to the figures in her mind. Smoothing the front of my plaid dress over my thick woolen tights, I strode into the room and took the same seat that the girl had had in my dream.

As soon as my behind made contact with the plush seat cover, I was overcome with an intense feeling of kindness—almost as if the chair itself was welcoming me into the home. It swaddled me like a second skin, and I relaxed instantaneously.

"She always loved that chair," Mrs. Hummel said wistfully, clutching the couch fabric in her fists. "Always told her it was uncomfortable, but she wouldn't sit anywhere else."

"It's lovely," I said, meaning it, and effectively killing the conversation at the same time. I didn't know what to say next, how to ask about the things I wanted to know, but thankfully, Mrs. Hummel spoke first.

"You want to know about him," she stated, not at all like a question.

I shifted in the seat (it was uncomfortable, actually), trying my best to keep my head high. "Actually, no," I contradicted. Chewing on my bottom lip, I tried to phrase my question as best I could without sounding completely ridiculous.

"I-I've been having these dreams," I began. "Well, I've been having a lot of different dreams, actually, but—anyway, that's not the point. I've been having this specific dream, about a specific girl, and I can't see her face, but she seems really familiar. And in the last dream I had about her—just today, actually—she was here. In this room. With you. And I was wondering if, maybe...you could tell me who she is."

Much to my surprise, the old woman let out a mighty gasp. "She reached you. She actually reached you." Those words left her lips again and again, reverently repeated, and Mrs. Hummel began to rock back and forth almost violently.

"Mrs. Hummel?" I squeaked. "Mrs. Hummel, please stop. Are you all right? Mrs. Hummel?"

As suddenly as she had began her fervent movement, the woman stopped. She let out a heavy breath and pressed her hands together.

"Listen to me, girl," she barked, leaning toward me. I bent toward her as well, my heart hammering in my chest.

"Yes?"

"Your mother made a deal with the devil." Edith Hummel began to nod furiously. "She made a deal with the devil, and the devil always follows through. He took her. He took her. And now it's time again, now he needs to take you or the deal will break. But she might be able to save you. She might be able to save you, because you cannot save yourself."

A chill ran from the top my neck all the way to the base of my spine. Old Mrs. Hummel was glancing around the room with crazed eyes, so different from the smiling woman in my dream.

"Mrs. Hummel," I said solemnly, "can you please tell me who the girl is?"

The woman took a big breath, looking for all the world like she was about to tell me. But when she let out the gust of air, she sunk into silence. I waited as the seconds ticked by on the grandfather clock in the corner, but she said nothing.

Just then, I heard the sound of the front door opening and footsteps entering the house. My initial, paranoid reaction was to dive behind the couch, but I froze when I heard Svana's accented voice.

"Hello, Mrs. Hummel!" she called. "I'm back!"

"Yes, hello, Svana!" Mrs. Hummel replied.

"I'm going to start your lunch, then I'll come and help you change, yeah?"

"That sounds lovely, thank you."

Svana did not come into the living room, nor did she react when Mrs. Hummel said, aloud, "Svana is really such a dear." The sound of pots and pans banging came from the kitchen as Svana began to cook. I heard cabinets slam and water begin to run.

I looked to Mrs. Hummel, my mind whirling train tracks over the few words she'd said, but she said no more. And from what she did say, I could glean nothing. Your mother made a deal with the devil. What was that supposed to mean? I was Catholic; I believed in heaven and hell, God and the devil. But I also knew my mother, and as crazy as she was, she would never go against her faith so drastically.

Just I was preparing to ask Mrs. Hummel another question, Svana came hurrying in through the doorway. She took one look at me and her hands flew to her lips, her eyes nearly bugging out of her head.

"Why is she here?" she demanded. "What is the girl doing here?"

Mrs. Hummel tilted her head in confusion. "Svana, she is our guest."

Svana shook her head wildly. "No, no, Mrs. Hummel," she cried, "the girl makes you upset! We are not to let her see you!"

The attendant danced frantically across the room, and before I could protest, had grabbed me by the arm and hauled me to my feet. For someone so petite, she was surprisingly strong.

"You must leave, now, before you upset Mrs. Hummel anymore!"

Glancing at Mrs. Hummel, she didn't seem very upset now, but I knew it would be useless to argue with Svana.

"Goodbye!" the old woman called as I was dragged over the room.

"What's your problem?" I demanded, wrenching my arm out of the young woman's grasp once we entered the hallway. Svana whirled on me, her nostrils flaring.

"You are my problem," she hissed, her accent thick. "Mrs. Hummel is my charge, and I am under strict orders to keep her calm. You upset her. I do not want you anywhere near her."

I opened my mouth to argue, but Svana simply grabbed my arm and began to pull me forward again. "You are leaving now," she snapped.

I didn't get to say anything more, because just then, we reached the fork in the corridor. And as we did, I caught an alarmingly potent whiff of something extremely familiar. It was piney, like a forest. It was that scent: the same one I had smelled after dreaming of the girl on Sunday night, the same one I'd just detected in class a few hours before. It was the same smell, and it was here, in Mrs. Hummel's house.

And it was my one chance to figure out what it was.

"What is that smell?" I demanded, pulling free from Svana as she threw open the front door and pushed me out. She ignored me, her eyes bright with fury.

"Out!" she screeched. "I want you out!"

I snarled at her, grabbing her by both shoulders and shaking them.

"Svana, you need to tell me!" I cried hopelessly. "What the hell is that smell?"

The wild desperation in my eyes must have been evident, because it gave Svana pause. She froze for a moment, carefully peeling each of my hands off of her shoulders and stepping back into the threshold of the house. She regarded me through narrowed eyes as I stood there on the front step, waiting.

"It's rosemary," she said, her voice tilting strangely. "It's Mrs. Hummel's favorite spice."

She gave me a final calculating look, her gaze suspicious, and slammed the door heavily in my face.

CHAPTER 9

Rosemary.

The word pulsed through my mind as I walked across Mrs. Hummel's front lawn, as Logan drove me home, as I unlocked the door to my house and slipped into the empty foyer. It bounced around in my skull as I attempted to read my Psych textbook. It gave me so much grief that eventually, I slammed my book shut and clomped down the stairs to the kitchen.

I wasn't really hungry, but I opened the fridge anyway, staring at its contents: fruits, whole wheat bread, leftover curry and rice. Nothing remotely interesting. The freezer yielded even worse results, and I sighed.

Humming softly to myself, I padded across the tile floor in slippered feet, shivering slightly in the cool air of the kitchen. I let my hand run across the birch cabinets, tracing the wooden edges until my fingers came to a stop at the final door.

Rosemary, Svana's voice echoed in my head. Mrs. Hummel's favorite spice.

Evidently, in my search for an explanation, my subconscious had led me to the one place where I might find something to help me.

My mother's spice cabinet.

I made a racket in opening the door, drawing Zipper from the sun room. Her nails clicked against the floor as she trotted over to me, rubbing her soft fur into the fleece pink fabric of my pants. I nudged her gently with my calf, pushing her back as I stuck my head into the cabinet.

Immediately, my senses were assaulted with the overwhelming scents of many spices mingling together in the stale air. I sneezed twice, wiped my face on the back of my sleeve, and attempted to blink the water out of my eyes.

With breath held, I began to swipe at the containers, reading their labels and shoving them aside. I got the feeling that they were in some kind of order, because basil was lined up before chamomile, but I disregarded that completely. There was a primal hunger gnawing at me: a deep-seated starvation for knowledge that willed me to face the possibility of my mother's wrath.

I went through row after row, shelf after jam-packed shelf, from garlic to mint to thyme, mumbling the names to myself and sometimes knocking the canisters off their perches. Zipper leapt around me, whining, but I just shushed her and continued on. I don't know what I was hoping to find by going through the cabinet, but I needed to and so I did and I didn't stop until I'd gone over every spice and herb twice. Then I checked again, because I was sure that I had missed it.

Rosemary. It should have been right there, between parsley and saffron. But I'd gone through already, and there was nothing. No space between the two to say that we'd run out. Just nothing. Rosemary wasn't there.

"What are you doing?" The incredulous sound of my mother's voice pricked me in the spine, and I whirled around to find her standing in the kitchen doorway, purse in hand. Her mouth was gaping open, aghast, as she regarded the state of the kitchen.

Worry built in the pit of my stomach as I, too, took a look around. Somehow, in my frantic search, I'd upended several containers onto the ground, sending flakes of sage and garlic and who knows what else onto the floor. Other bottles had shattered completely, leaving a mess of glass shards and spices. Zipper, who had accidentally licked up some pepper, was in the corner, coughing.

"Are you going to answer me?" my mother demanded. Her bun was slipping loosely down the side of her head, matching with her deteriorating mood. I frowned at her, not moving from my knees. There was some sort of irrationality in my calmness, a heavy weight in my stomach that made my words solid.

"We don't have rosemary," I stated, staring at her. "I just went through the entire cabinet, and we do not have rosemary."

My tone implied the need for an answer, and looking back, I think I must have sounded crazy. Perhaps that explains the look of horror that passed across my mother's face—at least, that's what I assumed at the time. Because at my words, a flicker of fearful disbelief crossed her features, leaving her expression several degrees more frigid than before.

"We do not cook with rosemary in this house," my mother snapped coolly. "Now go upstairs to your room."

I opened my mouth to protest. "Wha—"

"Now, Parker Sage. I'll clean up this godforsaken mess, just go. And take the dog with you."

Slowly, in the silence, I rose to my feet and began to pick my way over the spilled herbs and glass bits that covered the ground. My mother had left to get a broom, and when she returned, she wouldn't look at me. One hand was pressed against her face, and she used the other to wave me out of the room.

"Come on, Zipper," I murmured. My puppy gave a final hack, then rounded the kitchen table and scrambled over to me. Stooping over, I picked her up and buried my face into her fur as I descended the stairs.

"The Freudian slip," said Dr. Hennessy, "aptly named after Sigmund Freud, a brilliant yet very controversial Austrian neurologist who made countless contributions to the field of psychoanalysis. The idea of the Freudian slip is that it is a mistake in speech or memory that causes people to say things that they do not mean to say or misinterpret words they read or hear. Freud's idea was that these words are normally suppressed within the unconscious, and when a slip occurs, it reveals a person's hidden beliefs, thoughts, and wishes. I assume that many of you have heard the term before, but another common phrase is 'slip of tongue', though that is rather generalized and does not completely cover the entirety of the phenomenon. It's quite an interesting subject, though Mr. Freud was quite a disputed figure during his heyday."

I stifled a yawn at Dr. Hennessy's lecture, typing furiously in hopes of keeping myself awake. It'd been two days since I'd seen Mrs. Hummel, and over the past couple of nights, I hadn't slept any better. Both nights, the paralysis nightmares had returned with a vengeance, bringing not only the demon creatures but a taller, thinner monster who raised its hands at the side of my bed and made it shake violently. Logan kept telling me to tell my mother, but I was hesitant. She and I hadn't been on speaking terms recently, anyway.

I didn't see any strange men for two days, though maybe that's because I never left the house. Thursday was spent with Logan, pouring over the endless papers from Dr. Hennessy in my living room. But apart from a long, occult piece about incubi and succubi, we hadn't found anything new. He didn't ask why my mom was so peeved when she came home, so I said nothing about it. I also hadn't told him about the rosemary incident, because I also hadn't divulged the subject of the strange smell or the girl from my dreams.

I don't know why, exactly, I was being so secretive. Logan was my best friend; I was supposed to spill my mind out to him. I guess I was afraid that the way he thought would not compute what was happening to me. That he would laugh it off the way he did so many other irrational things, passing over the subject because it didn't make sense in his reality. Which was why I was surprised that his art was always so creative and unrealistic; anyone who knew him would have thought that his brain would reflect his logical rigidity onto paper.

I sneaked a glance over at him as I typed, half-listening to Dr. Hennessy's words. He wasn't drawing today, but pecking at his keyboard with his pinkies and pointer fingers; his own weird way of typing that he swore was efficient, no matter how awkward it looked. As my eyes roved over his face in profile, he caught me watching and glanced over with a small smile. I ducked my head, irrationally embarrassed that he'd noticed my stare.

"Just a reminder that your midterm is scheduled for next Monday, the nineteenth." Dr. Hennessy strode around the podium, turning off his projector and killing the PowerPoint of notes projected onto his huge screen. "I haven't quite finished the formatting, but I do know that there will be an essay on a random subject that we've covered so far this year. I do believe that you can can pass, so long as you study. Class is dismissed, have a good weekend!"

For once, Logan and I left class at the same time as everyone else. We trooped outside with the masses and into the chilly Pennsylvanian air, Logan pausing in the middle of the sidewalk to look up at the sky.

"Looks like snow," he observed, glancing at the grayish clouds.

I looked at the sleeves of my sweater with a groan. "Well, damn," I muttered. "I sure hope it isn't; I kind of forgot a jacket."

"Parker Elway, prepared as ever," Logan teased, elbowing me lightly. I ducked away, but he jumped forward and pulled me into a lopsided bear hug that nearly toppled both of us into a nearby rosebush. Squealing, I tried my best to wriggle out of his grasp, but he wouldn't let go. I can't say I minded completely, though, because he was wearing his windbreaker and it was very warm.

"Don't worry," he murmured into my hair, "if you get cold, I'll throw you into an ice drift and make sure you freeze."

I pulled away and slapped him across the arm.

Several hours later, I was cocooned in a castle of cushions, making my first attempt at studying for the midterm. So far, I'd figured that my knowledge would put me at an F level.

"Schizophrenia," I murmured to myself, "is a psychotic disorder in which thinking, emotion, and behavior are severely impaired, often characterized by loss of contact with the environment."

After checking to make sure I'd recited the correct definition, I tossed the purple flashcard onto my bed with all the others. My comforter was covered with them; dozens of color-coded pieces of cardstock labeled with every single one of the 247 vocabulary words we'd covered in the first quarter. In one hour, I'd only managed my way through about a fourth of them, what with having to check for every other word in my textbook.

As I was reaching for the next card, the door to my room was thrown open, rattling the miscellaneous junk in my bookshelf. Zipper, asleep on the end of my bed, jumped onto the carpet and wiggled her way over to the doorway.

My mother stood within it, her hands poised carefully on the waist of her heather gray pantsuit. Sighing internally, I lifted my headphones off my ears, pressing pause on the iPod that lay beside me.

"What?" I demanded, trying and failing to keep the edge out of my voice. Mom and I had been skirting around each other since the rosemary incident, but it seemed like every time I looked at her, she was giving me a look of judging disdain.

It was the same expression that marred her features as she asked, "Parker, have things been all right with you, lately?"

"Uh..." I stuttered for a moment, so taken aback by her uncharacteristic concern that I couldn't form any thoughts. "Fine," I fibbed eventually. "Just studying for midterms." Pressing my lips together, I held up a flashcard as proof.

Mom nodded, her jaw tightening as she appraised me with a frown. "Are you certain? No more bad dreams? Haven't been seeing anything...out of the ordinary?"

She was looking at me funny—almost as if she knew. But that was impossible; the only person who knew about the strange men and continual nightmares was Logan, and he knew me well enough to realize that the subject wasn't one I was eager to discuss with my mother.

For half a second, I considered telling her the truth; then I realized what would happen if I did. No phone, no computer, no school; no leaving my house, maybe not even my room. My mom freaked out about that kind of thing even more than all the other things she freaked out, and that was saying something. She may not have been a loving parent, but she could switch to insanely protective mother bear mode in a heartbeat if the situation called for it.

"Mom, what are you talking about?" I questioned, raising my eyebrows in an attempt to look skeptical. "Nothing's wrong; everything is perfectly all right."

Thankfully, my truth-twisting skills are up to par with my mother's perceptiveness, and she didn't seem to realize that I was lying through my teeth. She nodded slowly, her gaze moving down to Zipper, who hopped expectantly at her feet. I saw her upper lip curl; she'd never liked the idea of getting a dog, and I'd only managed to convince her by the skin of my teeth.

"In that case," she snapped, "take the dog for a walk."

Apparently, in her mind, walking the dog and my mental state were correlated in some way. She did not ask me if I could Zipper around the block, she told me. And that's how things always were with her. Every word she said was law, and everyone was automatically expected to heed her. Most people, though they wouldn't admit it, were at least slightly afraid of her, so they obeyed her orders.

But I wasn't.

So I didn't.

"I can't," I said sharply. "I'm studying."

An eyebrow raised, creeping slowly up her forehead like a thin, plucked caterpillar. "Is that so?" she said frigidly, her hands balanced on her hips. "Well, I guess you'll have to study another time."

"Are you kidding me?" I demanded, my voice shrill.

"I don't believe I look like I'm kidding."

A hiss of anger escaped my lips, and Zipper glanced over at me, her little head tilted in confusion. Fury and fear mingled in my stomach, creating a twisting nausea that crawled up my throat like bile. Disgust at my mother's insistence was only half of it; the idea of going outside where any one of those penguin-suited men might be waiting was even more sickening. But I couldn't tell her that, not without revealing all those other little things that would drive her up the wall.

"You can't make me," I sneered. "I'm not doing it."

My mother threw up her hands, her face contorting in rage. "Just do it, Rose, it's not that hard!"

Rose?

There was silence for a withheld breath as I processed the misnomer and my mother realized her mistake. I saw surprise and worry pass across her face in quick succession, leaving her expression briefly vulnerable.

"What did you just call me?" I asked slowly, the monosyllabic name repeating in my head. Rose Rose Rose Rose Rose Rose.

My mother swallowed, smoothing down the front of her suit as she evened out her features.

"Parker," she murmured. "I called you Parker."

I shook my head, my hair falling into my eyes. "No, no you said—"

"It doesn't matter what I said," she snapped, cutting me off. "This conversation is done, Parker. Take the dog and go outside."

With a final belittling glance, she lifted her chin and stalked out of the room. Zipper glanced between us quickly, fur whipping, before scampering to my bedside and licking my overhanging foot. I didn't even notice; my thoughts were a whirlwind in my head, probably dwelling on that slip of tongue more than they should have.

But what was it that Dr. Hennessy had been talking about in class? A mistake in speech or memory that causes people to say things that they do not mean to say or misinterpret words they read or hear.

Is that what had just happened? Had my mother just made a Freudian slip?

"Zipper, would you hurry up?" I snapped. "I swear to God, you don't have to pee on every single thing we pass." I tugged at her leash, hoping to speed up our procession. But Zipper stayed put, her nose buried in a nearby bush. She snuffled loudly as I stood there, shivering in the cold air.

When the dog finally decided that it was time to move on, I could hardly feel my fingers. Logan had been right; it did look like snow. The clouds overhead hung low and ash-gray, looming over the city like an itch that couldn't be scratched, and there was a icy gale bulleting down from the sky. I thought I'd dressed warmly in my sweats and knit sweater, but they didn't seem to stop my hands from shaking.

Zipper and I hurried down the sidewalk, crossing the deserted street. It was only four o'clock, but the residential part of town was dim and empty. I found myself jumping at every sound, glancing over my shoulder often; and really, can you blame me? I couldn't take a single step without feeling my heart leap to my throat, absolutely certain that I was going to feel that presence, that I would turn around to see those pitch black eyes boring into my face.

On the corner of Mill and Orin, Zipper stopped in her tracks.

Fear is a funny thing: when there is a possibility of finding something to be afraid of, it quickens your step, makes you whirl and then run if you hear or see anything out of place. But when something actually happens that should be frightening, you are suddenly frozen in place by your terror, unable to move even though you should be running, running, running.

"What is it, girl?" I breathed, my voice cracking. Zipper was a few feet away from me, leaning against her leash with her ears perked. She growled, a deep and throaty sound, at something I couldn't see. But I could feel it—oh, I could feel it. The air had suddenly become thin, stretch bare by the overwhelming feeling that someone was watching. Yet my feet were rooted in place. My fear had bottomed out my stomach and plummeted to the soles of my shoes, securing them to the gum-caked sidewalk.

"Zipper?" I squeaked. My dog backed up slowly, coming to stand in front of me as if her fifteen pound body was enough to protect us both. Another growl escaped through her bared teeth, followed by a mighty bark. I scanned my peripherals, expecting to see those men everywhere, surrounding me, but the streets were barren as ever.

So what was that feeling? That overwhelming pressure was in me, on me, around me, everywhere and nowhere all at once. Every muscle in my body was coiled, ready to bolt, and my heart was a jackhammer against my chest. Slowly, swallowing, I raised a hand to press my fingers to my neck, that weird habit I could never break. My pulse jumped erratically against my neck like it was trying to escape.

And as my fingertips touched the soft skin of my throat, the presence began to fade.

It was slow, gradual, an invisible person retreating from a room. Then, like the echoing slam of a door, it disappeared completely, and I was alone.

Zipper slunk forward quietly, whimpering, with her ears pressed flat against against her head. Her little body was quivering, and, I quickly realized, so was mine. I let out the shaky breath that I'd been withholding and watched it stain the air with a frosty white cloud. When no hands reached up to pull me into the gutter, I thought it was safe to take a step. Then another. Then another. Five footfalls, with a disgruntled Zipper creeping along in front of me.

That's when it began to snow.

It, like the appearance and departure of the shapeless watcher, came suddenly. One moment, I was walking down the sidewalk, huddled into my sweater; the next, I was still huddled into my sweater, but now, there were dozens of white flakes skittering down from the sky.

I cursed loudly, kicking at the ground as the snowflakes tumbled into my hair and melted against my skin. Each one was a shocking stab of ice that lanced through my flesh and into my blood. I hopped from foot to foot, glancing wildly around myself in hopes of figuring out somewhere to find shelter, and fast. It might have been the first snow of the year, but I knew from experience that we could end up with a blizzard. I was too far away from my house to get there quickly; but Logan lived two blocks down and around the corner. I could be there in less than a minute if I ran.

"Zipper, let's go!" I shouted, sprinting into the downfall of snow that was rapidly sheeting my vision with blankness. I nearly missed the turnoff, and I would have kept running if I hadn't recognized the ostentatious pink paint job of Gracie Peters' minivan.

My feet slapped loudly against the ground; Zipper's dog tags jingled. I sped up, knowing that Logan's house was at the end of the block. I tried to convince myself that I was only running because I wanted to get out of the storm, but there was still that little sliver in my gut that knew I was driven by fear. Fear of whatever had been watching me back there, that might still be watching me, though the snow, even as I ran and ran—

I arrived at Logan's house a gasping mess, slamming gracelessly into the door and then banging on it, desperately, with both my fists. Zipper, riled up by my desperation, began to bark, her paws scrabbling against the wooden floorboards of Logan's porch. His house, paneled white except for the burgundy rims surrounding the windows, was nearly lost in the storm.

Just as I was beginning to think he wasn't home, the door was thrown open wildly. I tumbled inside, nearly hitting the carpet as my legs tangled in Zipper's leash. Logan, who was standing at the edge at the doorway with his mouth hanging open, was too shocked to catch me.

"Parker, what the hell?" he demanded. I righted myself against the dark chocolate walls, shaking.

"M-my mom m-made me walk t-the dog," I sputtered. "A-and it started s-snowing."

"No kidding!" Logan closed the door with a loud thunk, his expression incredulous. "What was she thinking, sending you out here? Look at you, you're freezing!"

I managed a chattering laugh as I let Zipper's leash slip from my hands. "J-just a little, yeah."

"Well come here, then," he urged, grabbing the arm of my sweater and pulling me into his living room. The switch-on fireplace was blazing, its orange tongues looking invitingly bright. I knelt down in front of it and let the blistering heat wash over me.

"Let me get you something warmer," Logan said, his tone solicitous. I followed his movements with my eyes as he moved toward the stairs.

"Is your dad home?" I called after him.

"No," he called over his shoulder, "thank God. He's at Stan's."

Internally, I let out a sigh of relief. Of course, it never ended well when Jack Dearborn went to Stan's, but him being gone was better than him being in the house, where he could and would wreak havoc on everything that looked at him funny. And I looked at him funny a lot.

Remember how I told you that I know some parents who, unlike my mother, are real, actual alcoholics? Meet the prime example: Logan's dad, Jack Dearborn. The man was never seen without his hand around the neck of a bottle, and I can't remember the last time I saw him with lucid eyes. He'd always liked drinking, but I think he really lost it when Aubrey, Logan's older sister, left for college four years ago. His wife—their mom—died long before, and he'd managed to cope well enough. Then Aubrey went halfway across the country, and he stopped being a father and started being a drunken waste of human space.

It wasn't that he abused Logan, not physically, but he was never there. And when he was, he was either passed out on the couch or so cranky that all he could do was sit drunkenly on his oversized behind and shout obscenities at his son.

"Here," Logan said, drawing me from my thoughts as he pulled a blanket around my shoulders. He sat down next to me, cross-legged, and picked at the carpet. I stared into the waves of heat emanating from the fireplace, not speaking.

"Parker," he said quietly, "are you okay? I mean, I know you're not, but it's just that you've seemed really out of it lately and—and I'm just—I'm worried."

I pulled my knees to my chest and rested my chin on them, chewing thoughtfully on my lip. When my mother asked me the same question, the lie had fallen from my lips without hesitation. But now, I was too spent to fib, especially to someone who I knew would actually care.

"No," I admitted, feeling a weight lift from my chest with the simple word. "I'm not okay. I've been having those nightmares, I've been seeing those people, and I don't even know who they are or where they're from because no one else seems to notice them and I just don't even know what's going on in my head anymore. I feel like I'm going insane, Logan. I feel like I'm completely losing my mind."

For a long, drawn out moment, there was silence. I heard Logan swallow: saw his Adam's apple bob in my peripherals. His expression was at war.

Eventually, with a long exhalation, he reached over and put a hand on my shoulder. "You're not insane, Parker," he said with absolutely conviction. "It's just these nightmares messing with your head. You're sleep deprived, aren't you? Can't people who haven't slept see weird things or something? It makes sense; it's logical. There's nothing wrong with you, I'm sure of it."

I swallowed the urge to let out a laugh. Logan hadn't felt the weird things I felt; he hadn't seen those eyes staring at him; he didn't know what it felt like to have monsters haunting your dreams at midnight. He lived in a rational world, and he didn't know what it was like to feel crazy.

"I'm glad one of us is confident in my sanity," I muttered.

"Parker..." Logan shook his head, pulled back, and pivoted so that he was facing me. "Listen...my sister is coming out this weekend and staying through Thanksgiving. I know you said that you don't want to talk to anyone about this, but Aubrey studies this stuff for a living. If you let her, she might be able to help you."

I pressed my lips together, hugged my knees tighter. Aubrey was a psychology student, studying to obtain a doctorate and pursue a career in psychiatry. I knew her really well; even though she left years ago, she'd hung out with me and Logan when we were way younger, and she came back to visit several times a year. She was one of the people I trusted the most, with every-thing, not to mention that I looked up to her for being strong enough to leave our little dead-end town and not be stuck here her whole life.

"I'll do it," I mumbled.

Logan started up immediately. "Just at least think about it, all right? It's just a suggestion and I—wait, what?"

I peered at him, amused. "I said I'll do it, Logan," I repeated. "Maybe...maybe it'll help."

"Yeah," my best friend said. "Yeah." Then, under his breath, "My God, I can't believe she actually listened to me."

I snorted.

We sat in silence for a while, side by side, listening to the crackling of the fire. Zipper had curled up beneath the coffee table in a pillow of white fur that stood out against the dark green carpet. I tugged absently at the checkered blanket around my shoulders, Logan picked at a loose thread on the sleeve of

his blue- and-gray-striped sweater, and gradually, all my pent
up fear and anxiety began to seep away.

"Parker," Logan said several minutes later, an unreleased
yawn in his voice.

"Mm?"

"You know everything is gonna be okay, right? Like, with you,
and everything?"

"Mm."

"Parker," he said again, disapproving this time.

"Mm?"

"Parker, stop it."

His hand found my arm, peeling it away from my leg and
turning me to face him. His green eyes were clouded with worry,
the freckles on his nose like constellations. I felt the strange
urge to get a pen and play connect the dots on his face, and I
looked down to keep from laughing aloud.

"You're going to be okay," he stated, shifting onto his knees.
"Okay?" When I didn't respond, he grabbed my wrist and shook
it gently. "Okay?"

"Okay," I murmured.

"Parker, look at me." He put two fingers under my chin and
lifted my head so that our eyes met, green to hazel. "Well?"

"Okay," I breathed.

I realized, suddenly, how close we were, our noses nearly
touching. I mean, as best friends, we'd been close—he'd slept at
my house, I'd worn his clothes, we hugged every time we parted.
But this was a different genre of closeness; not an easy, friendly
kind, but a new, intimate variety that made my stomach knot up
because it was such vast, uncharted territory. I could tell that

Logan felt it too, because something shifted in his expression. But neither of us pulled away.

Suddenly, before I had any idea what was happening, he was leaning closer, shrinking the distance between us more and more by the heartbeat. My mind was freaking out, throwing off panic lights behind my eyes. Yet I didn't move.

And then his lips were pressed to mine.

Considering that fact that I'd never had a boyfriend, I didn't have a lot of experience in kissing. The only boy I ever kissed was Barry Bryant in the seventh grade, when a girl from church played spin the bottle at her birthday party and I'd been forced into it. And that just wet and sloppy and awkward.

I knew enough to realize that this was different.

I'm not going to go all teenage girl mode on you and talk about the fireworks and immediate chemistry, because we all know that stuff doesn't happen in real life. But for the few seconds that it lasted, the kiss wasn't bad at all. I felt my eyes drift shut without my consent, my body lifting slightly as I unconsciously leaned in closer. And maybe, possibly, I might have actually enjoyed it.

But the sensation was cut off with a jolt as Logan pulled back sharply, his hands searching for the ground to keep himself from falling. His face was a bright, tomato red, and as we stared at each other, I felt a blush creep over my cheeks as well. I raised one hand slowly to my lips, still feeling the essence of wood and toothpaste on them—the same taste as the way he smelled.

"I'm sorry!" he blurted, slapping a hand over his mouth. "I'm sorry—I didn't mean—I'm sorry—"

"I-It's okay," I said quietly, confusedly. "I—I don't—it's fine."

He shook his head again and again, an odd look of horror in his eyes. But there was no regret there—none at all. Just disbelief at what he had done. I felt that same disbelief, but for me, it was at the fact that I had let him.

"I'll drive you home," he stuttered, standing awkwardly.

I heard the sound of Zipper's dog tags jangling as she looked up, but my eyes were fixated on Logan. In a corner of my mind, I remembered what Juliette had said, about how he was starting to like me instead of her. Unless that kiss had been some kind of fluke, there was now a very distinct possibility that she was right.

And in a strange, nervous way, I didn't think I minded.

CHAPTER 10

"Mom, I'm out!"

I called the words over my shoulder as I shouldered my bag, my feet half-crammed into a pair of hefty boots. As I paused at the hall mirror to pull my beanie lower over my ears, my mother appeared in the hallway.

"And where are you going?" she asked frigidly. She'd been angry at me since the night before, when Logan dropped me off in the middle of a snowstorm that she sent me out into.

"I told you," I sighed. "Aubrey's in town for a week, so we're going to go meet with her."

"Where?"

"Butler. She's staying with a friend over there."

Pensive uncertainty appeared on my mother's face, and she wrung the dishtowel in her hands tightly. "Fine," she said. "I'll be at work in the city until later this evening, but I expect you home by six o'clock, understood?"

I mumbled an unintelligible response, rolling my eyes as I turned away. I felt my mother behind me, hovering, but she didn't speak again until I had already opened the door.

"Say hello to Aubrey for me," she said haltingly, before turning on her heel and striding back into the kitchen. I stared after her, my face contorted in baffled amusement, before shrugging and slipping outside.

The Saturday morning air was chilly as I hurried out to Logan's car, parked right where he said it would be. It had stopped snowing late the night before, leaving the ground covered in the sludgy gray-white aftermath. My neighborhood didn't look much like a winter wonderland, but somewhere more along the lines of the way it would look if a snowman puked all over the sidewalks. And in the midst of it all, Logan's old car, a scuffed bright blue, stuck out like a sore thumb.

"Hey," I said, ducking into the car through the passenger side.

"Hey." Logan's voice was awkward, strained. We eyed each other sideways, stretching for a level of comfort that was out of our reach.

"So...," I began, twiddling my thumbs with downcast eyes. My words petered into a still silence, permeated only by the soft brushstrokes of our breathing. Then Logan keyed the ignition, starting the car with its usual sputter, and I knew we wouldn't be talking about what had happened the evening before.

Noon found me and Logan at a corner Starbucks in the city, the busy cafe where Aubrey had agreed to meet us for a belated breakfast. We walked in at a safe distance apart and merged with the line that twisted through shop and nearly reached the door. I scanned the room for a moment, finally spotting Logan's sister seated at a table toward the back, her eyes glued to the screen of her phone.

After a few seconds of frantic arm-waving and name-shouting that earned me more than a few odd looks from the customers, Aubrey finally looked up, catching my eye and smiling as she rose. She darted lithely through the crowd, her small frame allowing her to duck under elbows and snake past chairs.

"Parker!" she cried, enveloping me in a coconut shampoo-scented hug.

"Hey, I missed you!" I grinned easily, brushing my hair from my eyes. "My mom says hi, by the way."

"Give her a hug for me!" Aubrey smiled, not seeming to notice my grimace at the idea as she turned to her brother. "Hey, short stuff," she said, using her old nickname for him—the one she coined when Logan wasn't a full head taller than her. She reached up, standing on tiptoe to ruffle Logan's hair. The siblings embraced, Logan's expression immediately relaxing.

"'Sup, Bree," he greeted, "long time no see."

Grinning, Aubrey led us to her table, where she'd already placed the food we'd requested before down. I dropped down in front of my croissant and latte, Logan sitting down more fluidly beside me. He was no longer as tense as he had been when we were alone, but it still looked like he was balanced on the edge of his seat and ready to bolt. Aubrey, if she noticed, didn't make a comment.

"So, guys, catch me up. How's school?" she asked, snuggling into her peacoat. Her dusty brown hair was pulled up into a ponytail, secured with a knit headband.

For a while, we made small talk. There was the obvious discussion about our classes, how we were liking college, the usual questions about my mother, and their father. But eventually, our topics thinned, plunging us into a companionable silence (save, of course, for the coffeehouse music and the twitter of conversation around us).

After a moment, Aubrey cleared her throat. "So, Parker," she stated. "Logan says you've been having some, ah, experiences of sleep paralysis and seeing...strange men?"

I nodded. It amazed me, how quickly she dove into her serious, professional mode. In a matter of seconds, she had gone from a smile to a concerned frown, her eyes boring calmly into mine.

"And this started...when?"

"Well, the sleep paralysis itself started last Thursday. But I've been having these suffocation nightmares since around July."

"Right, I remember you telling me about that when I visited in the summer."

"Yeah," I affirmed, and all I could think was how I would give anything to go back to those simple dreams.

"And those men," Aubrey continued, tapping her chin, "describe them to me."

I saw Logan shifting beside me as I gave her a description; every now and then, he would cast a glance in my direction out of the corner of his eye. Half of me wanted to turn and force him to look me full on in the face, but the other half was confused and wanted to just pretend that nothing had happened.

Even though I imagined I could still feel the ghost of his lips against mine.

When I'd finished, Aubrey nodded slowly, her attention wavering as she lost herself in thought. Her brown irises flickered skyward, pondering.

"Well," she said eventually, "I think the sleep paralysis is probably due to something simple, like your late nights and the stress of school. Nothing to worry about, really. And the men...I think they could be any number of things. For instance..."

She began to list a few possibilities, none of them involving the men being real, living creatures. As she was concluding her explanation of hallucinations (a term I'd studied the day before), though, I suddenly became aware of a strong, piercing feeling on the back of my neck.

I froze; Aubrey was still talking, but Logan noticed, and he looked directly at me for the first time that day. His face was taut with worry.

"Aubrey," he said, not taking his eyes off of me. His sister paused mid-sentence, and, catching the look between us, slowly let her voice fade out.

"What it it?" she hissed. "Parker, is something wrong."

I screwed my eyes shut; those two stiletto beams of a staring stranger were driving nails into my flesh. "Look behind me," I hissed, "is there someone there, staring at me?"

With a strange look, Aubrey tipped to the side and glanced discreetly over her shoulder. After a moment of casual scanning, she shook her head.

"No one," she replied softly. "Why? Do you feel something?"

"There's someone watching," I said through gritted teeth. I knew that if I turned around, I'd see that penguin suit, those onyx eyes. Maybe Aubrey didn't see it, and I didn't know why that was but I knew that I would. So I stayed facing forward, my palms pressed flat against the table and my food forgotten.

A moment later—I swear I heard it—a quiet chuckle road a rift of sound waves and traveled straight into my ear. The sound was like nails on a chalkboard, and it sent a quiver down my spine. The sharpness disappeared a moment later, and finally, I was able to release a breath.

When I looked up, both siblings were staring at me in obvious befuddlement; Aubrey especially. She shook her head, eyeing me warily.

"Parker," she muttered, "there was no one there."

"Maybe you didn't feel it, but I did." I glanced between them, my heart racing. "I swear to God, I felt eyes on me." A groan escaped my lips, and I put my head in my hands. "Sweet Jesus, what's wrong with me?"

I heard Aubrey let out a long, whistling sigh; Logan patted my back awkwardly.

"Listen," Aubrey said slowly, "I think you should stay over at my friend's place tonight. She's gone for the weekend, so you won't be a bother, and Logan can come too, if he wants. Will that be okay, or will your mom go all—"

"She'll be fine," I interjected, though I wasn't certain of that at all.

"Good. I want to watch you sleep—God, that sounds so creepy—to try and figure out what's going on. I'm not an expert on this stuff, and you know that, but maybe if I see what happens I'll be able to give you some more help."

Pressing my lips together, I bobbed my head. A night away from home sounded good; maybe if I was sleeping on a couch, it wouldn't shake, and no monsters would bite at my toes. (That had happened the night before, and the horror of it was still fresh in my memory).

"I'll call my mom," I said, "but I'd need to go back and pick up some clothes. What time will we go over to the flat?"

Aubrey checked her phone for the time. "I was thinking soon—like, now. I wanted to ask you some more questions, too. And Logan said you guys have a midterm, if you want some study help. Do you think your mom can drop off stuff, or...?"

"I'll get it," Logan offered quickly, his voice too eager.

"You sure?" I questioned, raising an eyebrow.

"Yeah, totally. I'd need to get my own clothes anyway, so if you give me your key, I'll be in and out in a few. I know what clothes you wear, Parker."

He rolled his eyes at me, the half-smile on his lips looking almost normal. And I knew he knew—he knew me like the back of his hand. But suddenly, the idea of him going through my closet, picking out my pajamas and shirts and underwear, made a blush creep onto my cheeks.

"Text me the directions to the place, Aubrey," he said to his sister, snagging his coat as he got to his feet, coffee in hand.

His sister frowned. "What, you're going right now?"

"Sure, why not? Don't want to waste daylight."

He was acting strangely, and we all knew it. But neither Aubrey nor I protested as he began to wind his way through the maze of people in the cafe.

"Are you guys fighting or something?" Aubrey asked, watching his departure. "He's acting funny."

I swallowed, my mind flashing back to that moment the evening before, when our lips had been so close, then closer, closer...

"No, we're fine," I told her, forcing a placid smile that might have looked slightly nauseous. To avoid further questions, I turned around just in time to see Logan holding the door open for a group of kids a little older than us. Scanning the glass windows of the store front, I saw no ebony-eyed men. But then again, I knew I wouldn't. Whatever they were, they always disappeared as quickly as they came.

And as I watched my best friend hurry a little too quickly toward his car, I wondered if he was thinking that maybe I was crazy, after all.

Aubrey's friend Jessica had an apartment in one of those bustling buildings in the heart of the city, the kind with colorful exteriors and too many dying palm trees. Her flat was on the third floor, room 326, the one with the number plaque that was scratched up and just a little bit crooked.

After Logan left, Aubrey and I had followed suit soon after, arriving at the apartment building at a few minutes past one. I called my mom, and maybe she was busy, because she okay-ed the sleepover with minimal arguments. Aubrey and I hung out in the living room, sprawled out on the mismatched furniture, discussing my problem but mostly just talking: about her, me, and life in general.

Logan arrived at around three—after getting lost several times on the way to the building—laden down with bags of clothes. He turned red when he looked at me. Jessica's apartment had a big TV, and we watched a slew of rom-coms before we all started getting hungry and Aubrey ordered a pizza.

For a while, just hanging out there with my friends, I could pretend that everything was still normal. This was how all of Aubrey's visits were: simple, easy, fun. Even though we didn't talk all that much, I found myself forgetting everything that was going on and almost letting my brain take a break. But too quickly, it was eight o'clock. Then nine. Then ten.

And then it was time.

"So what do you want me to do?" I asked Aubrey, tugging nervously at my black fleece pants. Aubrey had a mountain of blankets and pillows clutched to her chest, and a few of them fell to the rug as she turned to me.

"Just go to sleep like you normally would," she said, dumping her load heavily onto the laid-out futon. Logan, perched at the end of it, slid off gingerly.

"Just go to sleep," I echoed, more for my own benefit. Nodding resolutely, I shuffled across the room and began to lay a comforter onto the futon, all the while feeling the siblings' eyes on my back.

"All right." I swallowed, glancing over my shoulder when I finished. "Goodnight."

As I slipped beneath covers, melting under those twin gazes of my friends, I couldn't shake the feeling of dread that was busy trying to make knots of my stomach. The idea of awakening in that terrible fearscape yet again was endlessly horrifying, and I thought that maybe I'd rather just stay up through the night. But my mind, apparently, had other ideas, because only moments after my head touched the pillow and I let my eyes fall shut, I was plunged into a dream.

I was standing alone in a forest. It was dark out, the trees tinted blue and cast into shadow by a twilit moon. Pines and hemlocks pierced the soil around me and stretched skyward, their boughs shielding me from a gentle white downfall that I quickly realized was snow.

Though clad only in a strange, shifting gray dress, I found that I wasn't cold. Letting out my breath in a puff of white, I began to pad on bare feet across the snow-dusted forest floor. As I ducked beneath a low-hanging branch, a sound from behind me stopped me in my tracks.

A child's bright laugh.

I whirled around, my heart racing, as I peered through the fog of the dreamworld for the culprit.

"Hello?" I called carefully, stepping toward the source of the chuckle.

The sound trickled toward me again, this time from behind me and followed by a whispered, "Follow me."

So I did; I followed it, only because I knew this wasn't real, this couldn't be real. I turned with quiet footsteps, moving toward the sound as it repeated again and again. With each step I took, with each branch I sidestepped, the sound grew louder, until finally, I could have sworn it was right in my ear.

"You found me," murmured the voice.

I jumped, spinning in the air and stumbling through the thicket. When I righted myself, I found that I had reached a clearing in the forest; my feet were no longer enshrouded in prickling pine needles, but muddy water grass. Before me, stretched out in familiar and surprising clarity, was Bear Lake, where Logan and I used to play when we were kids.

Bear Lake was more of an oversized pond, really, considering how small it was, but it went very deep and Aubrey never let us wade in past our ankles. In this dream, the water's surface was dotted with patches of ice, the shards glinting with reflected moonbeams.

And at the edge of the lake, wearing a loose green dress that flew and snapped in an invisible wind, stood the girl.

"Hello, Parker," she said, her voice melodious but tinged with sadness. Another gale whipped past her and fluttered a breeze in my direction. With it came a smell: a familiar, unmistakable smell that was piney and soothing and almost reminded me of this one pizza parlor I visited in Pittsburgh.

Rosemary.

"You can come closer, you know," the girl told me, amusement dancing in her tone. "I won't bite."

Obligingly, I shuffled through the dewy grass until I was a few feet away from the girl. She was looking away, her face shrouded in a pleasant darkness. Up close, she was shorter than me by several inches, and though I still got the feeling that she was fairly young, there was a sage air about the way she held herself, so tall and carefully poised. I thought, in the back of my mind, that she was very much like my mother in that way.

"I visited Mrs. Hummel," I said, in a voice that sounded distant and feathery, "which is what you wanted me to do, isn't it?" The realization hit me with a bolt of certainty, though I think I had known it all along.

The girl laughed. "I guess it was, even though I doubt she actually told you anything worth your time." She shook her head. "Poor Mrs. Hummel. I thought that since she knew I'd be gone, she would be okay. Apparently not, though."

I said nothing. This no longer felt like a dream.

"Anyway," said the girl, "I'm wasting precious time. Listen, Parker, and listen well. There's something coming. I can't really tell you what it is, because explaining it all would take precious time that I don't have. But there's something coming, and it's evil. You need to find a way to stop it."

The devil, I thought. Edith Hummel said the devil.

"Why are you telling me this?"

The girl scoffed. "Because it's coming after you."

My heart hammered wildly in my chest. "But—"

"No time for buts," the girl snapped briskly. "Time for action. There are people who will help you; you only need to find them."

I wanted to hit something; how the hell was that kind of advice supposed to help me? More than likely, I'd end up working myself into a rut.

The girl must have felt my distress, because a sigh left her lips and carried over the soft sound of water lapping against the lake shore. Her brown hair was dusted with snow. I saw her shoulders raise a little, just slightly.

Suddenly, with a herculean breath and six quick steps, she turned around to face me. I gasped; her face, painfully clear amidst the blur of the dream, sent a sharp pang of something stabbing into my gut. I knew this girl—I knew her. And I knew that I knew her with a certainty so absolute that it physically hurt.

"Parker," she stated solemnly, her lips barely moving, "it is extremely crucial that you remember that everything that is happening to you is real. All of it. No one will think so, no one will believe you, and you may very well be alone through much of what is to come. But don't let them tell you that you're crazy."

I stared at her: high cheekbones, dark eyes, wavy chestnut hair; round chin, heart lips, small nose, dimpled cheeks. This girl was so familiar, but I could not put a name to her face. My brain was pulling itself apart, trying.

And behind the girl, I saw dark shapes rising from the lake.

"Uh—" I raised a dead hand to point, but the girl cut me off with a tight-lipped nod.

"I know," she breathed, suddenly sounding weaker, "I wasn't supposed to come here, and I'm almost out of time. I should be going."

She gave me a small smile, an expression that killed me with its familiarity. I felt something, bubbling up deep in my stomach, that tore at my insides with a slow, complete inferno. And it felt a lot like sadness.

That's when I noticed something else: a glint against her neck, a little sparkling orb resting on her sternum. Squinting, I leaned closer—and saw my reflection in the tiny charm of a mirror hung on a golden chain around the girl's neck.

"Who are you?" I breathed, watching the girl through wide eyes as she turned away, toward those growing dark shapes. She looked at me over her shoulder, quietly. Her features were soft, but her lips were turned downward and I could read the sorrow in her eyes.

As she opened her mouth to speak, two arms reached out from the darkness and grabbed her from either side. She did not struggle; did not fight; did not even look back at me. But as the shadows rose from the water to swallow her whole, her small voice came to me in a quiet, disheartened melody:

"I thought you would know by now."

I awoke, spluttering, with the scent of rosemary slipping through my nostrils and filling my senses completely. The blankets were pooled around my feet, leaving me shivering. I sat bolt upright in an overexerted rush and very nearly fell as I leapt from the futon, shouting for Aubrey and Logan and stumbling uselessly through the dim room.

In my blindness, I caught my foot on something and I went sprawling onto the ground. At the same moment, the lights snapped on, and then Aubrey was rushing over, her eyes wide with worry.

"What?" she cried, dropping to her knees on the carpet. "What happened?"

I realized, as I tried to sit up, that I'd tripped over Logan, asleep on the floor, and my legs were tangled with his. He was shouting, asking me if I was okay, and I had no time to be embarrassed because that girl's face was in my mind and I needed it, needed it on paper, needed them to know who it was.

"Logan!" I shrieked. "Sketchbook? Do you have your sketchbook? You need to draw something for me, please, right now, please get it, please!"

"Uh—yeah, I have it, I have it!" Fear flashed through my best friend's eyes as he unsnarled his limbs from mine and dove for his bag, quick extracting his sketchbook and pencil and flipping through his clear page.

"What is it?" he asked, panting.

Aubrey looked on, her jaw unhinged, as I described the girl in as much detail as I could manage. I could see her right there, a clear image behind my closed eyelids. Everything, from her hair to her eyes to that necklace, my necklace, the necklace I hadn't seen in days. Logan sketched as quickly as he could trying to keep up with my relentless tongue, until finally I was out of breath and all the little particularities had been spent.

Then, all was silent in the room.

But in a crevice deep inside my head, I thought I still heard the listless descant of the girl's familiar voice.

"Parker," Logan said strangely, "who is this girl?" His eyes were glued to the paper.

I sped through my brain on race car wheels, each thought an evanescent whisper, searching for a name. And very quickly, quicker than I expected, I knew. As the realization hit me like a freight train, I wondered how I'd been stupid enough to not realize it before.

"Her name is Rosemary," I said confidently, nearly grinning. I expected smiles from my friends, but on Logan's face, there was still a frown. I narrowed my eyes. "Why?" I demanded.

In response, he silently held up the sketchpad, balancing it on his plaid pajama bottoms. Both Aubrey and I let out a disbelieving gasp. The picture he'd drawn was of the girl I'd seen, almost down to a T. And apart from a few little things, I could have been looking at an image of myself in the mirror.

"Because," Logan said quietly, his eyes finding mine, "she looks just like you."

CHAPTER 11

osemary's picture burned a hole in my back pocket as I climbed out of Logan's car and onto the snowy sidewalk in front of Blessed Trinity the next morning. The sun hung low, casting deep forenoon shadows onto the snow-blanketed grass.

"You gonna be all right?" Logan asked, coming up beside me with his hands buried into his pockets. I pressed my lips together, tugging the end of my sweater low over my leggings, and nodded.

"Yeah, I'll be fine," I replied, though I knew the violets blooming under my eyes said otherwise. Even though the dream hadn't been a nightmare, it plagued my thoughts all the same, because I had a deep, gnawing feeling that I knew Rosemary, whoever she was. The girl with my face.

"Are you reading this week, Parker?" Aubrey asked, hopping out of her car to join us. All around us, people in coats and winter boots were tromping the snow, making their way into the chapel.

"Nope." Thankfully, I added mentally. I didn't think I'd be able to make it through an entire reading coherently.

Inside, nearly all the pews were filled, despite it being a quarter of an hour till the beginning of mass. We split up then, because my mother was calling me and Aubrey wanted to say hi to her dad. Mom was oddly calm, considering I hadn't been home since the day before, but her eyes kept darting back to my face when she thought I couldn't see.

The service sped by in a blur of hymns and gospels and prayers, and I felt as if I had merely blinked when Father Lucas dismissed us with the words, "Let us go in peace to love and serve the Lord."

I exited the church with the rest of the congregation, but I felt as if I wasn't actually there. Half of me was in the real world, being towed through the crowd by my mother, but the other half was living and reliving that dream, seeing the girl's face again and again. Rosemary.

My fingers itched to tear the drawing out of my pocket and stare at it until my gaze singed the paper, but I was forced to smile and nod as my mother greeted Aubrey and Logan and Juliette's families, pretending that I wasn't experiencing inner turmoil. Vaguely, I heard the sound of Thanksgiving plans being made between our families—potluck at the Westburys' house—but my attention was elsewhere, and no one except Logan and Aubrey seemed to realize that.

I wasn't pulled from my reverie until the Westburys had already left, leaving only a bleary-eyed Mr. Dearborn swaying between his two children. He didn't seem to be anymore aware than I was, but we were all polite enough not to mention that (even though I really wanted to). Everyone was saying their goodbyes, and I was drawn back into reality by the warmth of Logan's arms wrapping around me.

"I can come over later if you need me to," he said as we parted, though he didn't seem so sure. Not wanting to deal with the awkwardness, I forced a smile and shook my head.

"No, it's fine," I assured him. "I'll see you tomorrow."

The ride home from church—unlike the week before—was uneventful. My mom didn't speak, so neither did I. We hardly acknowledged each other as she unlocked the front door and I brushed past her, heading straight up to my room with Zipper at my heels.

I tried to study—really, I did. With my psych midterm less than twenty-four hours away, that was all I needed to focus on. If I didn't pass my classes, I could kiss school goodbye. But it was impossible. About half an hour into my attempted study session, I'd set my books aside and spread Logan's drawing across their closed covers.

"Who are you, Rosemary?" I wondered aloud. It was a question that had been plaguing me since the morning. When I'd asked the girl the same thing, she thought I knew already. But I didn't. All I knew was that she was there, she existed, and she was trying to help me.

While I'd never been so strict a rationalist as Logan, supernatural explanations had always been beyond my realm of belief. There was a spiritual approach—I could work with that. There was God; there was Jesus, Mary, and the angel Gabriel. I believed in the idea that angels could visit you in your dreams. But that girl hadn't looked like an angel, she looked like a girl. A normal, simple girl who bore an uncanny resemblance to me.

Not to mention that angels didn't have dark shadows sweeping them away into the night.

With the angel theory out of the question, I didn't think to look for some kind of paranormal reasoning. Instead, I thought back to one of the first lessons I'd had in my Psych 101 course: the subconscious.

People who study dreams often find themselves tangled in mysteries of the subconscious, because the two are so closely connected. It's the subconscious that pilots dreams and nightmares, often voicing undiscovered worries or hopes and concerns. In a way, the concept is similar to that of the Freudian slip, except that it happens while you're asleep.

I remembered reading something once, about the phenomenon of "prophetic dreams", in which a person "sees" the future while they're asleep, before it actually happens. The most rational explanation for these is that the subconscious picks up little things in your life that you don't notice yourself, and reflects them into your dreams. Sometimes, those unnoticed details add up to a big picture that we don't often foresee.

Is that what this is? I wondered. A prophetic dream?

But that didn't make sense, did it? If a prophetic dream is comprised of disregarded elements, it wouldn't have created such a clear picture of the girl. And it wouldn't explain the men in suits (who may or may not have been hallucinatory), the vivid sleep paralysis, or the recurring dark nightmares.

Recurring dreams, I knew, exist to call your attention to a matter that your subconscious deems important and/or urgent. They can be triggered by a problem or situation that won't go away, or a weakness that you're unable to face.

If that was the case, though, how did my dreams make sense? There was no kind of visible marker that I could use to decipher a problem, nothing I could see at all. The only thing I saw was crushing darkness.

At some point, when those nightmares first began, I'd looked at a dream dictionary in hopes of figuring out what was going on in my mind. Darkness, it said, could meaning a feeling of insecurity or desperation. Suffocation signified a notion of being oppressed by someone or something in your life. At the time, I'd assumed it all revolved around my mother: because she was suppressing me in practically every way possible, I felt insecure and unsteady in my life. But how could that connect to these new dreams—to the waking nightmares, to the dreams of the girl? There was something else going on, something nagging at my subconscious that I couldn't uncover. And I didn't know what it was.

I didn't even know what I was thinking anymore.

"What am I doing with my life, Zipper?" I asked my dog, who was draped lazily across the pillow beside me. She looked up at me, her big brown eyes so innocent and unconcerned that I envied her. How easy it must have been to be a dog, to not have to worry about anything except peeing and sleeping and eating. I bet that I wouldn't be having nightmares if my life was as easy as a dog's.

Sighing, I looked again to the picture in front of me. The girl's young face stared back at me, wide-eyed and tight-lipped. Her name was Rosemary; I knew that for a fact. And every single part of me insisted that she was a real person, someone who was living or had been living at some point in time. But how could I be dreaming about a person I'd never even met, yet looked just like me?

Supposedly, the people depicted in dreams don't represent themselves, but someone else. Did Rosemary represent me? Or maybe my mother? Or was she someone independent of both of us, yet somehow connected by her resemblance? Perhaps she was a cousin I'd forgotten, an ancestor I'd seen in a picture, or perhaps she was just a vision created entirely from my mind. And maybe the necklace she wore, the one I'd found in the attic all those years before—maybe that was just my mind's way of coping with the fact that it was lost.

If I stretched my brain, I could rationalize the situation; I could think like Logan and rule out every unconventional possibility. And that's what was easy. I knew how to think logically, and a simple situation was familiar to me. Familiarity brought security, and security was what I needed the most when my mind seemed unable to stay still.

Though I was still half-convinced that I was losing my mind.

"Parker?"

I knew something was off when I heard my mother's voice—followed by a knock on the door. She never knocked; usually, all I got was a warning shout before she came barging in uninvited. (And after a particularly awkward incident last year, I'd learned to change in the bathroom).

At the quiet sound of a tap on wood, I looked up, immediately suspicious. Zipper raised her head as well, then let out a soft yip and rolled onto her side.

"Come in," I said belatedly, crumpling up the drawing at last minute and throwing open a textbook at random. I smoothed my hair out of my face and tried as best I could to look completely transfixed on the words swimming before me.

There was a moment of hesitation, then my door was pushed open with surprising gentleness. My mother poked her head in, glancing around for a moment before stepping carefully across the threshold. Was it just me, or did she look a little bit nervous?

"I've just received a—a call, from work," she said haltingly. "I have some business out of town from this evening through to late tomorrow night. It was very sudden, an impromptu transaction with a client."

"Oh?" I raised an eyebrow, frowning. My mother worked for a large local graphic design firm, and trips out of town weren't infrequent for her job. But they never lasted overnight—at most, she might be gone for about five hours for a project in Philadelphia or another in-state big city. And something about her sudden reserve made me wary, if only because normally, I would be getting a lecture about how I'm not allowed to set foot out of the house.

"Where to?" I asked nonchalantly, using two fingers to close my book. The picture of Rosemary was stabbing me in the ankle, and my mother was leaning heavily on one leg. "Philadelphia?" I suggested. "Pittsburgh?"

There was a beat of silence, a moment of still air. And then, the most extraordinary thing happened: my mother did not respond.

Oh, she tried; she stuttered and spluttered and wrung her hands, but she did not say a word. For the first time in probably her entire existence, my mother was speechless.

And so was I.

When her attempt at a response died out, we were left in a thick quiet, staring at each other in mutual disbelief. For once, I caught a note of humanity in my mother's face—that entirely human realization that she had just made a mistake. And unlike usual, she didn't catch herself, freeze her features, or redeem her slip in posture with a debilitating glare. She simply smoothed the front of her suit—the suit that she always, always seemed to wear—and swallowed.

"I've called Aubrey," she said, glossing jerkily over her mistake, "and she agreed to stay with you while I'm gone. But she's out with her dad right now, and they won't be in until about four. Will you be all right here alone for a couple of hours until she's done?"

"I'll be fine," I answered immediately, suddenly willing to forget my mother's odd behavior at the prospect of her leaving. I wasn't so sure I'd feel completely safe alone, nor would I even think about going out of the house by myself, but I needed the time to figure things out.

"All right, then," said my mother, much too softly. "I'll be going. Call me when Aubrey gets here."

Concern. That was concern in my mother's voice; real, genuine concern about me. I knew, at that moment, that there was something very wrong with the situation. That feeling gnawed at my stomach and scratched at my ribcage, propelling me out of bed to follow my mother as she left my room. Zipper trailed silently at my heels.

"Mom," I said, stopping on the last step as she shrugged on a coat and shouldered her purse. "If you're staying overnight, won't you need a bag?"

She whirled to look at me, surprise etching into her features, as if she hadn't realized I'd come after her. This time, though, her response was quick and clipped.

"I already put it in the car," she stated.

With a reason voiced, my mom snapped up her keys with a purpose. Her hand was on the door when I asked my next question.

"Mom," I murmured, "you're not going on a business trip, are you?"

I don't know what told me, but somehow, I just knew. My mother was leaving town for a night and a day, and I didn't know where she was going, but I knew that this was something else.

If I was right, she didn't tell me. All I received in response was a slow blink and a meager shake of the head before she ducked outside and gently closed the door.

My phone rang when I was halfway up the stairs.

I'd stayed put for a while, staring at the space where my mother had been, gripped with confusion and an unprecedented, simmering panic. But I eventually swallowed my emotions and turned around, all the while trying to shake the goosebumps that prickled the back of my neck.

The ring came suddenly, as I was tracing the golden wood of the handrail and Zipper was snuffling at my ankles. The melody—the generic twinkling sound—drifted out my door and into the hallway, spurring my feet into a jog as I hurried to my phone and answered.

"Hello?"

"Hey." It was Juliette. "This is kind of random, but I have midterms this week, and I'm majorly stressed."

I sat down on my bed. "I have them this week too, and I'm pretty much screwed."

"Join the club," she muttered, then sighed. "Look, I know it's Sunday and all, but are you up for a trip to Stan's? I need to get my mind off things."

"I don't know, J. I really need to study."

"Study, schmudy. Parker Sage, don't be a prude. We both know you want to go, and your mother isn't home, so who's gonna stop you?"

I leaned forward incredulously, pressing the cellphone to my cheek. "How do you—" Snorting, I palmed my forehead. "Sweet Jesus, Juliette, you need to learn a thing or two about privacy."

From the other side of the line, I could practically hear her rolling eyes. "Hon," she said, "it's not my fault that your driveway is in perfect view of my bedroom window. And I know plenty about privacy, for your information. I just don't have a problem with violating it. But anyway, that's not what we're talking about. Are we going to Stan's, or aren't we?"

A dusty corner of my brain rationalized that getting our minds off all the things we'd studied wasn't going to help anything, but I couldn't resist the offer. It sounded like it'd be nice not to care for an hour or so—and besides, as Juliette said, who was going to stop me?

"Yeah, we are," I said to her. "Be there in ten."

I hung up the phone, but I'd barely drawn it from my ear when the LED light began to flash bright green, signaling a missed message. Checking my call history, I realized that I had six missed calls from Logan within a span of five minutes; and, in checking the times, I found that he had rung me when I was downstairs with my mother.

Confused—and more than slightly worried—I called him back.

"Parker!" He answered immediately, sounding breathless.

I frowned. "Hey, Logan, I—"

"Where are you right now?" he demanded, cutting me off. "Because wherever you are, you need to leave and get the hell over here."

Logan was speaking in hushed tones, and in the background, I heard the stern cadence of an older voice. Wrapping one arm around my stomach, I stood up and began pacing anxious circles around my carpet.

"I'm at my house," I said, "I've been here since mass, why, where are you? Is something wrong?"

"I," Logan puffed, "am at the library. And you"—he took a breath—"need to get over here, now."

"Logan," I breathed, "is something wrong?"

He let out a frustrated grunt and was immediately shushed. "That's not important right now, okay? Would you just hurry up and get your butt over here? The library closes in an hour and there's something you need to see. And bring the drawing of Rosemary."

My head spun as I hurried to my closet, pulling out a bag and quickly dropping in the necessities. "All right, fine," I told him, kicking my feet into a pair of boots and cramming in the legs of my baggy sweats. "Just keep your pants on, okay? I'm on my way."

Before putting Zipper in the sun room and leaving the house, I shot Juliette a hurried text:

Hey J, change of plans. We're goin 2 the library.

"The library? Parker Sage, are you kidding me right now? I told you I wanted to get away from studying, not be surrounded by it!"

Juliette and I stood outside of the Callery Borough Public Library, the only library in town. It was an old building faced with mottled stone, a design that often horrifies visitors, but that we locals called "quaint."

"I don't know, okay?" I said, drawing my jacket closer as we mounted the wide steps. "Logan just told me to meet him here, and he sounded really upset."

"He probably just wants an excuse to check you out," Juliette muttered.

I snorted. "Oh, yeah, Juliette. Because I am looking so hot in these sweatpants right now." Shaking my head, I spat out a laugh that sounded nervous, even to my ears. I hadn't told Juliette about the kiss yet, knowing the kind of fuss she'd make.

"Whatever, Parker Sage," she said as we pushed open the doors.

The smell inside was familiar: cedar shelves and aged paper. Bookcases lined the space, each one filled with dozens upon dozens of dusty volumes. I scanned the room for Logan, but only saw the old librarian and a few studying teens with vaguely familiar faces.

"Psst, Parker," someone hissed. Glancing over my shoulder, I saw Logan peeking his head out of one of the side rooms, his brown curls tousled. He cast a confused glance at Juliette, but his eyes skidded over her as he beckoned us over.

Juliette and I shared a look, but I shrugged at her and we made our way past a few worktables and over to Logan and the open door. He stepped aside to let us enter, into a dim room with only a chair, a filing cabinet, and a little table with some kind of old viewer in its center.

"Come in, come in," Logan said, clicking the door shut behind us. His movements were jerky, more awkward than usual, a symptom which I knew meant he had something on his mind.

"What's up, Logan?" I asked, at the same time Juliette asked, "The hell is this place?"

Logan licked his lips and ran a hand through his hair. "This," he said, "is the library's microfilm center. It's where they keep records of all the old newspapers and stuff before they started being put on the web. If you want to find out about anything—or anyone—that this town has ever seen, this is the place to go."

Juliette looked confused, and she gave me an exasperated look that I didn't return. I understood what Logan was getting at, and the drawing of the girl folded up in my purse suddenly seemed very important.

"You looked for Rosemary," I murmured, and Logan nodded in confirmation.

"When I realized what I'd drawn, I couldn't get it out of my mind. I knew I had to find out who that girl was, or I was going to drive myself off the wall. So I came here."

"What did you look for?" I asked, my eyes boring into his.

Logan sighed. "Seeing the girl's face," he began, "I knew she had to be an Elway. But the information you gave didn't tell me what era—she could have belonged to any time period since the town formed. So I went back. All the way back, to the year Callery was founded, searching for traces of any Elways. Turns out, your ancestors moved here in 1893, right after that big fire. They were part of a lot of hype for several months, because I guess your great uncle was really rich and funded a lot of the community's reconstruction. I looked for anything about his wife, daughters, nieces—there was no one named Rosemary.

"I would have gone through everything, and you know that, but there are over one hundred years worth of newspapers and I don't have that kind of time. But I realized: hey, the library has Callery's genealogy records, so why don't I just look for her in there?"

Pausing for breath, Logan pushed back the chair and pulled a thick, leather-bound that thumped and shook the table when he set it down. I leaned toward it, immediately drawn by old, worn cover.

"What is that?" Juliette demanded, her nose wrinkling.

Logan flipped open the from cover, exposing the title page. Callery Ancestral Files, it read.

"This has the dates of birth and death for every single person who has lived in Callery since eighteen eighty," he informed us, his eyes lighting up with geeky excitement. "It only goes up to nineteen-ninety, but when I look through, I found out that was enough of a time span."

"This is so cool," I breathed, flipping through the record book. At the very beginning, the paper was brown and crumbling, but the pieces kept getting newer until, by the last pages, they were only slightly tinged with yellow.

"It's really cool," Logan agreed, "especially because it told me who Rosemary Elway was. Date of birth: February third, nineteen eighty-four. No date of death available."

I thought back quickly, doing the math in my head. If Rosemary was still alive, and born in '84, than would make her exactly...

"Twenty-eight," I said promptly. "She would be twenty-eight right now."

Logan nodded grimly. "Yeah, she would be—if she were still alive."

"What do you mean?" I knit my eyebrows, freezing with my hands on a page. "I thought there was no date of death in the book."

"There isn't," Logan said. "But then I found this." He turned away from us for a moment, taking a file off the top of the file cabinet and shaking several flat, transparent sheets onto the table.

"There was something else about Rosemary that really threw me," he continued, "and it was the reason why I called you. It wasn't until after we had hung up that I found the rest."

I swatted at him, dreadfully curious. "Well? What is it?"

Before responding, Logan fitted one of the sheets under the viewing reader, sliding it beneath the lens and focusing the image. He took a glance, then turned back to me.

"Everything you need to know is in that microfiche," he said. "But I think it's something you need to find out for yourself."

I stared at him, and he stared at me, and the silence between us was so anticipatory that I felt its pressure on my skin.

"Would someone please tell me what's going on here?" Juliette demanded, throwing her arms up as I sunk into my seat and lined my eye up to the viewing piece. Behind me, I heard Logan beginning to give Juliette a summarized version of the Rosemary predicament, but that was all tuned out when I began to read.

Magnified before me was an newspaper article from years and years ago; a short piece, nothing more than a notice and obituary. But the few words on the paper meant everything to me.

November 29, 1998

Missing Girl's Body Dredged from Forest Lake

Early this morning, the body of fourteen-year-old Rosemary Elway, missing since Thanksgiving, was found at the bottom of Bear Lake in western Callery. The lake, a small body of water in the forest adjacent to Callery's residential area, was a place frequented by Rosemary, says her mother.

The girl was found by a team of rescue divers, who received a suggestion to check the lake from an anonymous source. She was pronounced dead by way of drowning, though her mother claims that she knew how to swim, and deep lacerations around her wrists and ankles suggest that she was tied up by someone at some point before her death.

Police are still investigating the case, hoping to find the murderer of Rosemary Elway. They ask that if anyone has any information regarding the case, anonymous or otherwise, to please report it to the Callery Police Department, (724)-645-0987.

"My God," I murmured, staring at the blurry, black-and-white photograph of a smiling Rosemary that filled the bottom of the page. I dug the drawing from my pocket and glanced at the two in quick succession. The face was the same.

Goosebumps crawled up and down my arms as I leaned away from the viewer. In my dream, I had seen Rosemary at the edge of Bear Lake; I had seen her being dragged beneath its depths by darkened shadows. And, as it happened, that lake was the very place where she had died.

"So, what do you think?" Logan asked, leaning back on his heels as he regarded my shocked expression. "You okay?"

I laughed a little. "You've been asking me that all day, Logan, and I'm fine," I told him, a sickening suspicion forming in my mind. "I'm just...I'm just confused. Who is Rosemary Elway? My aunt? Cousin? Why don't I know about her?"

For a moment, Logan looked completely befuddled—his head was tilted, his eyebrows knit in consternation. From behind me, Juliette was silent.

"Parker," Logan said gently.

Shaking his head, he put one hand lightly on my shoulder and used the other to flip through the record book. He skimmed over the years, finally stopping in nineteen eighty-four.

Rosemary's entry was near the beginning.

"Look at it," Logan said, not unkindly. I did. I scanned the page, reading the date and place of birth, the ethnicity, the general census information...then I read the names of her parents, and I couldn't help but gasp.

I didn't know my dad; I knew nothing about him apart from his name and the fact that he had died when I was very young. But that was all I needed to know. His name, Joseph Elway, was printed right next to my mother's, both of them situated right above Rosemary's.

"No," I murmured. "No, no, no no no."

Logan cleared his throat. "Look at the dates, Parker," he said quietly, "and look at the record. Rosemary Elway wasn't your grandmother or aunt or even cousin—she was your sister."

CHAPTER 12

It was Juliette who broke the silence.

"You have a sister?" she demanded, striding over to look at the record book for herself.

"She had a sister," Logan corrected, shaking his head. "According to this, Rosemary Elway died when you were two years old."

I stared at my hands, pressed flat against the surface of the table. The coolness of the metal was seeping into the flesh of my palms, but that was about all I could feel. The rest of my body was a numb shell, and even my heart seemed to have stopped beating.

"This can't be right," I murmured, my voice hollow. "If I had a sister, my mother would have told me."

I could feel Logan's hesitation even before he answered.

"I don't know if she really would have, not necessarily," he said. "I mean, you were a baby; you wouldn't remember. Undoubtedly, the death was hard on her, and she wouldn't have wanted to talk about it. And once you were old enough to understand, how would she approach you with it? 'Oh, and by the way, you had a sister named Rosemary who drowned in a lake ten years ago'? It would be hard, and she probably figured that you didn't need to know."

As Logan's words sunk in, I was not consoled but rather angered, and a feeling of fury kindled a flame in the pit of my stomach.

I snorted. "Didn't need to know?" I spat. "Please. This my family we're talking about, Logan. My sister. I deserve to know about it, no matter what happened."

"I know, I know that." Logan held up his hands, looking tired. "You're right. All I was trying to do was give you a logical reason why she might have kept that from you."

I gritted my teeth. Logical. Of course it was logical, because Logan was always logical. And maybe he was right—in fact, he probably was. But I didn't want him to be, not about this. I didn't want to deal with all the possible implications that Rosemary's existence would have.

Hissing out a hot whoosh of air, I let my hands slip into clenched fists in my lap. I took another breath, then another, thinking that it would help release some anger.

It didn't.

Looking back, I don't know why I got so mad. What had he done, really? He was just being himself, being Logan, but I was a fuse burned far too low. Every word he said only served to further ignite my anger, until I swear my skin sparked like hot coals.

"You can't rationalize everything, Logan," I said. "Don't you understand that sometimes, things just don't work that way? I don't want your goddamn logic; I want to talk to my mother and make her tell me what the hell is going on!"

My voice grew consistently louder as I spoke, until I was on my feet and practically shouting into Logan's face. He drew back, freckles popping against blanched skin.

"So why don't you?" he demanded. "Why don't you go ask her and find out that I'm right?"

"Because she's not here!" I shrieked. "Because she left on a random business trip and wouldn't tell me where she's going, and now I won't see her tomorrow night, that's why!"

Logan fell silent immediately.

"An overnight business trip?" he asked slowly. "As in, she's going out of town and leaving you by yourself for an entire night?"

I shook my head. "Aubrey is staying over. But it was totally random—just out of nowhere, she came in and told me that she was leaving. And when I asked her where, she didn't answer. She didn't answer, Logan. She even looked nervous when she was talking to me."

With arms crossed, I watched Logan think that over, the cogs in his brain whirling. Juliette stood between us, her eyes darting back and forth. We had all but forgotten her presence, but she was still there, watching.

Gradually, as the moments passed, I felt all the anger ebb out of me. When it did, my mind was quickly unclouded, and I suddenly began to connect the dots in my brain, using everything that had happened in the past few days to piece together a jigsaw puzzle. The unveiled reality hit me all at once, nearly knocking me off my feet with its sheer intensity.

The first thing was my mother's conversation with Chief Harding. Mary, he'd said. But not Mary; Rosemary. Not only that, but her slip of tongue only a few days before, not to mention her refusal to keep rosemary spices in our house. She'd called me Rose, and who else could that be?

Number two was the necklace in the attic. Rosemary had worn it, and she must have lost it up there at some point, before I found it. My mother had wanted me to get rid of it, and now I understood why: it had belonged to her drowned daughter.

Number three: Edith Hummel. Both Rosemary and I, it seemed, were connected to the old woman. In my dream (Rosemary's memory?), Mrs. Hummel had warned my sister about something that was coming. On more than one occasion, she had said the same thing to me. But what was coming?

I thought back to my first dream about Rosemary, when I still couldn't see her face. If she was my sister, would that make the dreams memories? And would that mean the woman in the kitchen was my mother?

The woman had become upset when she saw the drawing that Rosemary was showing me, the one of the girl in the darkness, surrounded by shadows. And in the latter part of the dream, I'd seen the very same scene happening, but to my sister: the dark tendrils reaching out to her, grabbing her, choking her.

That was years ago. But now, all this time later, the same thing was happening to me.

"Parker," Logan said, breaking my reverie, "do you think your mom's trip has something to do with Rosemary?"

I shook my head, feeling a headache quickly forming. "I don't know," I told him honestly. "I don't know why it would." Running a hand through my hair, I sighed. I stared at him, and he stared at me, our eyes connected in the heavy air. "But I do know one thing," I added, glancing down at the open record book. "There's something going on here that's bigger than any of us know."

It had begun to snow again by the time we left the library, so Logan drove me and Juliette home in the downpour. All I could do, as we maneuvered through the white-frosted streets, was stare at the falling snow and wonder if it had been snowing when Rosemary died.

In truth, I wasn't sure what to think about everything, about the way it all connected, yet left so many gaps at the same time. I knew who Rosemary was, now—my dreams about her were nothing more than dredged up memories. As to what elicited the influx, though, I had no idea.

While mulling over the many things that I had no idea about, I came across a thought of those strange men I had seen. One in front of Stella's house. One across the street from the general store. One leering at me in the bar. Besides the suits, which I'd for sure seen on two of them, all three men had the same distinguishing feature: polished obsidian eyes.

But who were they? Were they even real? I know I'd felt one of them staring at me in that Butler Starbucks, but Aubrey and Logan hadn't seen a thing. And whilst walking Zipper, someone had been watching me—I was certain of it, and Zipper's tenseness backed me up. But I had seen no one. Unless I was being pursued by the Violet from The Incredibles, the penguin-suited men made no sense. However, I didn't think it was a coincidence that they began to appear right after the paralysis dreams began, and right before I first saw my sister. Maybe (probably) it was all in my head, but my subconscious had somehow linked Rosemary Elway to those men.

Just then, the car came to a stop, stalling in a drift between mine and Juliette's houses. Juliette popped the back door and hopped out, letting in an icy gust of air.

"Bye, guys," she said ruefully, pulling her coat tighter. She'd had a wide-eyed look since we'd left the library, and it didn't seem to be going away. "Thanks for the ride, Logan."

"Sure."

Logan and I waved, watching as Juliette mounted her front steps and slipped inside. Neither of her parents were home, judging by her empty driveway, but her two younger brothers were probably holed up inside, playing video games and fighting over controllers.

Sighing, I leaned my head back against the passenger seat, unfastening my seatbelt and letting it dangle back against the side of the car. It was too much, all of it, and I was dead tired. There were midterms tomorrow, exams I'd hardly studied for, and now I had the problem of my sister to infest my mind until my mom came home and I could question her. I'd already tried calling her cellphone twice on the way home, but it went straight to voicemail without a single ring.

"Parker, you getting out?" Logan's voice reached me through exhausted haze, drawing me back to reality with a groan. Some- how, I managed to look him in the eye with a wry smile.

"Are you saying that you want me to leave?" I demanded playfully, though there was more lethargy than jest in my voice.

My best friend didn't laugh, anyway; he just lowered his hands on the steering wheel and gave me a look of concern.

"You can come over, if you want," he said. "When Aubrey gets home, you guys can just drive over to your place."

I had to admit, the offer was tempting. I thought I'd enjoy being alone, but the idea of being in my stone cold, empty house in the middle of snow was sounding worse and worse by the second.

"Or you could hang out here," I suggested, a hopeful look slipping onto my features.

But Logan shook his head. "I can't, I have to study. There's an art history test tomorrow, too, and all my stuff is at home."

"I have to study, too." Letting out a breath, I crossed my arms and pressed my lips together, staring out at my snow-dusted house that looked like something out of the postcard. I caught sight of my reflection in one of the side mirrors; my damp, tangled hair, kohl-rimmed eyes, ruby lips. The girl I saw staring back at me didn't look like Rosemary—she wasn't pure and innocent, just raggedy and rebellious and confused. Yet we were sisters, practically two sides of the same coin.

"Logan, can I ask you something?" I questioned, closing my eyes again and wrapping my arms around my torso.

He paused, sounding hesitant as he replied, "Sure?"

"Well." I licked my lips. "I just wanted to know why you helped me. Why did you go out of your way to find out who Rosemary is when you could have been studying?"

Logan slipped a little laugh, as if the answer to my question should have been obvious.

"For one thing," he said, "I was curious. I looked at that picture of Rosemary and kept seeing your face and I had to know. But mostly, it's just because you're my best friend, Parker. I saw how upset you were, and I thought maybe this would somehow make you feel better."

"Oh!" I injected a note of brightness into my tone, feeling a little warmth growing in my stomach.

He tilted his head and peered at me, forcing my eyes apart to look at him. "You should know that already, though. Why do you sound surprised?"

"Uh..." With my mouth still slightly ajar, I paused. I didn't know why I was surprised. But at the same time, I did. I knew exactly why, and it was more that I was too unsure of myself to say it out loud.

It was a long, daunting moment before I could knit words from the mess in my head.

"Well, see, it's just that"—I swallowed hard—"you really haven't even looked at me since..."

I didn't stop talking on purpose; my mind just went quiet. The words died before leaving my throat, plunging us into a stuttering silence.

"Since what?" Logan asked quietly. His hands were resting on his knees.

I shook my head, pointing my gaze to the dirty car floor. "Nothing, I—"

"Since what, Parker?"

I stared at him, and he stared at me, and I felt a crimson blush creep its way onto my cheeks. And even though I knew this subject was the least important thing right now, I also knew that it was something that we'd eventually have to address, whether I wanted to or not. So as Logan watched me, I let the words fall weakly from my lips.

"Since you kissed me."

I looked back at Logan, and he was frowning, his green eyes wide. "That was a mistake," he whispered immediately. "That wasn't supposed to happen."

Without warning, his words sent a cruel stiletto through my heart. I don't know why I cared, because we were best friends and that sort of thing wasn't supposed to matter. But it did, and that response practically knocked the breath from my lungs.

"Mistake?" I echoed.

He swallowed, nodded, and grumbled, "I didn't mean to. It just...happened."

It just happened.

As in, he didn't mean it? As in, he hadn't wanted to kiss me? I wasn't sure if I had wanted him to, but he did, and that had to mean something. I wasn't sure if I even wanted it to mean something. Because at that moment, my heart was pounding and blood was rushing through my ears in a flood of residual emotion, and I wasn't quite surewhat I wanted at all.

"So you didn't want to kiss me," I said flatly, a note of pain finding its way into my voice.

"No, no, I did, I just—"

"You did?" I mentally berated myself for how curiously hopeful I sounded.

Logan's face flushed scarlet, and he raked a nervous hand through his hair before responding. "Yeah, I did," he murmured gruffly. "I just—I didn't know what you would think, and I didn't want to seem stupid, but you were right there, and I couldn't help it, so I just—"

He took a big gulp of air, and I turned to him with eyebrows raised. Despite myself, despite everything, I felt a small grin slip onto my lips at his familiar, winded distress.

"Look," he said, once he'd composed himself, "I know that with your nightmares and finding out about your sister, this is the last conversation you want to be having. And I know that I'm making this awkward for both of us, especially because you're my best friend, and this isn't something we should be talking about. But—I wanted to kiss you. I didn't mean for it to happen, but it did, and I wanted it to, because for some unexplained reason I have feelings for you. Which is really weird, I know that, and I apologize, but it's the truth."

Silence. When Logan finished, there was silence. He was watching me nervously, and I was watching snow fall onto the front windshield, creating a thick white blanket that darkened the inside of the car. It was getting cold, too. I felt the chill seeping through my sweater.

"You should probably turn on the windshield wipers," I mumbled. Logan looked confused for a second, then gave a little start, quickly twisting the key in the ignition and starting the engine. A moment later, the windshield wipers were clearing snow from the glass. The radio started, too, softly playing a familiar pop song.

I cleared my throat. "I'm glad you told me that," I admitted, rubbing my arms. "I haven't really had time to think about it all, and I'm not really sure what my feelings are, but—I think I liked it."

A pause. "Liked what?"

I hiccuped an anxious laugh. "Kissing you."

The car's interior was getting steadily warmer, but I don't think that was the reason for the heat that rose to both mine and Logan's cheeks. "Oh," he murmured, pulling a hand through his hair. "That's—er—good."

I nodded, but said nothing. Logan tapped his hand against the steering wheel, humming along to the radio. I couldn't decide what to think of the moment. By all logic, the amount of worry I was putting into a silly kiss was ridiculous. Except that it didn't feel like a silly kiss. It felt like new, foreign territory, and I was standing there with one foot in and one foot out, trying to figure out whether to dive in or go running back the way I came.

"I'm sorry," I said belatedly, haltingly. "For putting you on the spot like that."

Logan wrung his hands. "Thanks," he muttered. "And I'm sorry too."

"For what?" I eyed him carefully, crossing my arms across my chest.

"For kissing you again."

Oh. Wait, what?

"But you—"

I didn't get to finish my sentence. Logan was leaning toward me, closing distance faster than I could speak. I was inching closer, too, without meaning to, until our noses were nearly touching. And as an effusive sigh of breath escaped me, our lips brushed oh-so carefully. It was a gentle kiss, cautious and fleeting, but it triggered a foreign rush of fluttering wings against my ribcage.

We pulled away after a heartbeat, and this time I saw the corners of Logan's lips twitch up into a half smile. "Sorry," he repeated, not sounding sorry at all.

I smirked; he had a smear of lipstick across his mouth. "No need to apologize," I said, opening the car door and hopping out onto the snowy ground. "Also." Laughing to myself, I pulled a tissue from the box on Logan's dashboard and smeared it across his face, removing the traces of red. He blushed as I tossed it at him, but I just smiled over my stuttering heartbeat and said, "You're welcome."

As I was mounting the front steps of my house, huddling against the wind, Logan's voice called me back. I turned around, confused, and squinted through the fine, ivory mist to see him in the rolled-down window, holding something in one hand and beckoning me with the other. Wrinkling my nose, I dashed back through the snow on icy toes and stuck my head through the passenger window.

"W-what?" I chattered, my breath clouding in front of me. Logan didn't seem to notice how cold I was; he just held out his clenched fist to me.

"What?" I repeated, this time with growing impatience. It was freezing—I was freezing—and this was not a time to be having a friendly conversation outside.

"I found this in my car the other day," he said, "and I've been meaning to ask you about it but I kept forgetting. Is it yours?"

As I looked at him expectantly, Logan unfurled his fingers. And lying in the palm of his hand, sparkling, gold, and familiar, was Rosemary's mirror necklace.

CHAPTER 13

Three hours later, Aubrey and I sat at my kitchen table amidst an array of flashcards, textbooks, and containers of Chinese takeout. She was helping me study—or at least, trying to—and I was scarfing down a bowl of flat noodles. However, there was considerably more eating going on than studying, and I was interrupting Aubrey between definitions and mouthfuls to explain more about my newly discovered sister.

"So all this time, you never knew about her?" She regarded me with a look of intrigue, shuffling through the flashcards for a new term.

I shook my head. "Nope, nothing. Which is weird, because you'd think I'd have heard something from someone."

Nodding slowly, Aubrey made an affirmative sound. "Ethnocentrism," she said, reading off another lined card.

"Something about....central ethnicity?" I guessed. She sighed.

"'The idea that one's own cultural, national, or religious group is superior to or more deserving than others.'"

"Close enough," I declared, pointing my fork at her.

With a withering glare, Aubrey put down the stack of cards on the table in front of her and reached for her glass of water. I continued eating guiltily, already steeling myself for the lecture that I knew was about to come.

"Parker, have you studied at all?" she demanded. "You've only gotten two right out of twenty cards, and your midterm is to-morrow. How do you expect to pass this if you don't even know the vocabulary terms?"

I shrugged, letting a smirk gloss onto my lips. "With sheer brilliance and my incredible supply of raw talent?" Instead of the laugh I was hoping for, Aubrey fixed me with a dry stare. I let a long breath escape my lips. "Well, I've kind of had a lot on my mind, you know?"

I forked another layer of noodles, driving little holes into the food. It was true; I had had a lot on my mind. Maybe nightmares and creepy men and dead relatives weren't enough to validate failing my exam, but at least it gave me something resembling an excuse.

"At least try to do well, okay?" Aubrey said. "I'm only doing this because I genuinely want you to pass your classes."

"I am trying," I muttered. "I'm trying to finish my dinner."

Aubrey rolled her eyes, releasing a reluctant snort and push-ing her dark bangs out of her eyes. She stood up from the table, grabbing her empty plate and heading for the sink.

"On a scale of one to ten," she said casually, "how badly will your mom kill me for feeding you greasy takeout?"

I thought about it for a moment. "Eleven, probably."

"Then let's not tell her about it, yeah?" She leaned against the counter and began to rinse the evidence off her plate.

"Weeell," I dragged out, biting my lip in mock consideration. "I suppose I could keep my mouth shut...if I get a study break. Which, might I add, is well deserved."

Aubrey turned to me, hands on her hips and eyebrows raised. "You conniving little blackmailer," she gasped, masking a chuckle. "Fine, thirty minutes. But that's it, and no telling."

"Mhm, 'course," I mumbled through a full mouth, "mum's the word."

Thirty minutes, of course, quickly turned into forty-five, which turned into an hour, which eventually turned into me and Aubrey chilling in my room, talking about Rosemary.

"Are you sure you didn't know her?" I asked Aubrey, probably for the hundredth time. The two hadn't been the same age, but they were closer in years than me and Rosemary. I touched the mirror and chain around my neck, staring up at the ceiling.

"Absolutely certain," Aubrey affirmed. "I'd never even heard that name until you told me. And since you and Logan weren't friends back then, I didn't know your mom, either. Maybe my mom did...but I obviously can't ask her that now."

I nodded, chewing absently on my bottom lip as I hung, upside down, off the side of my bed. Something felt off to me about the fact that, in sixteen years, no one had let it slip to me that I had a sister. It was almost as if she was buried, forgotten, and everyone was trying to keep her a secret.

Even from me.

But there was one person who still seemed to remember Rosemary Elway, and she was the one that we all called crazy. Old Edith Hummel, resident town kook. She appeared in my dreams; she cooked with the spice that bore my sister's name. She knew

Rosemary, and she might have been the only person not willing to forget.

"I need to visit Mrs. Hummel," I said, snapping up so quickly that my bed frame shook. Zipper jumped off, looking miffed.

"Mrs. Hummel?" Aubrey said dubiously, peering at me from her perch on my desk chair. "You really think she'd do anything?"

I scrunched my eyebrows together. "I don't know, but she knew my sister. She knew that someone was coming to kill Rosemary, and she warned her."

Aubrey shook her head slowly, disappointment reading in her brown eyes. She ran a hand through her hair as she scooted the rolling seat tediously across the carpet and parked herself at my iron footboard. I gave her an odd look, momentarily confused.

"Parker," she said, "I don't mean to sound like a fart, but you hardly know anything about that woman. Aren't you studying criminology? You don't have to be a mystery buff—which I know you are—to know that little girls being murdered is not something you mess around with. What if, I don't know, Mrs. Hummel is actually in league with whoever killed Rosemary? She warned you about things that she shouldn't know, things that involve you being in danger, according to her.

"Now, I don't think she's right about someone coming to get you. It's hard to get around unnoticed in a town this small, and someone coming implies that the person is from somewhere other than Callery. But that doesn't change the fact that Mrs. Hummel was involved with Rosemary, and the poor girl died. I'm not saying that the same thing will happen to you, and heavens above I hope it doesn't, but you can never be too careful."

Having said her piece, Aubrey leaned back against the chair and regarded me as if daring an argument to fall from my lips. I crossed my legs, then my arms. If things were normal, I know she'd have been right, because Edith Hummel's involvement was suspicious from an outside perspective. If things were normal, I would know that. But they weren't normal, or even anywhere close to it. I didn't know what it was, but there was something going on with me, and with Callery, that was astounding in its complexity. And even though I hated the idea with every rational cell in my body, I couldn't help the word supernatural from slipping into the front of my mind.

It took me too long to respond, and by the time I had an answer on my tongue, Aubrey was speaking again. "Look, it's getting late," she said. "You have a big test tomorrow, and a little sleep would probably do you good. So try to get some rest, okay? I'll be in the guest room if you need me."

Then, like a middle-aged mom trapped in the body of a twenty-two-year-old girl, she sidled and over and ruffled my hair. I made a face.

"Goodnight," Aubrey called.

Zipper barked as I muttered, "'Night."

In the mirror of my closet door, my hair was a frizzy mess.

Zipper slept in my room that night, mostly because she wouldn't budge from her spot on the floor by my bed, and also because I couldn't be bothered to haul ass downstairs and put her in the sun room. Twelve steps and a trek through the kitchen are surprisingly daunting when you're stressed and tired.

All my textbooks lay dormant on my desk, their closed covers imploring me to come and study. I could have. And maybe I should have. But I decided that Aubrey was right, and it was in my best interests to get some shuteye before the midterm slaughtered me in the morning. I didn't once think, what with everything weighing on my mind, that another nightmare would plague me as I slept.

But it did.

And this time, it wasn't just a nightmare.

It began in the usual way: I opened my eyes, I couldn't move, I couldn't breathe, my room was dark. The omnipresent weight was resting heavily on my chest, eating away my air with invisible gulps. But this time, there were no shadows.

In the last few nights that I'd had the waking terrors, the billowy figures had been there unfailingly, standing at the foot of my bed in all their terrible glory. Now, though, as I strained my eyes in their sockets to try and spot them, I realized that my room was devastatingly empty.

That, in a strange way, almost frightened me more than when I could see the creatures. It meant that they could be there, invisible, out of my sight until they saw fit. I knew them. They would shield themselves from me until the moment when they could scare me the most.

Cold panic wracked my body. If I could have moved, I would have been crying, shaking, curled up into a ball in utter horror. I briefly thought of the papers Dr. Hennessy had given me, stacked up neatly on top of my dresser. I wonder if anywhere in them, those researchers had mentioned the fact that a bout of sleep paralysis could make a person die from their fear.

I lay very still for a very long time. It felt like hours; I remembered reading about episodes of paralysis that could last for that long. But maybe it was just minutes, and my shriveled mind was too addled to properly gauge the passing of time.

After some eternal moments of blank perplexity, something in the air before me began to shift. It was barely perceptible at first; just a shimmer in the darkness. But gradually, I realized the air was thickening; certain parts of the darkness where coming together to form a human shape.

A low whine drifted up from the floor. Zipper. I couldn't see her right away, because of her position at my bedside. But after an ephemeral moment, she came into my view. Inch by inch by inch, my dog filled my peripherals, until I caught sight of her whole, snow-white body creeping across the floor.

She was moving.

Zipper had not stood up. She was not walking. In fact, it looked like she was still asleep. But she was moving, head first, as if someone was pulling her away by her collar.

No, I thought. No, no, no. This is not happening, this isn't real, this is just a dream—

My eyes chose that very moment to avert back to the dark figure by my bed, and a silent, airless gasp tore from my lips. The humanoid figure had its hands steepled beneath its chin, its fingers long and spindly. Pianist fingers. Except that it wasn't just a figure anymore.

It was a young man with ebony eyes.

He looked like all the others: penguin suit, cruel smirk, abysmal eyes. He was younger, though, not more than a couple of years older than me, and so devastatingly handsome that, in any other scenario, it would have swept my breath away. But I had no breath, and he was a murderous stranger lurking in my room in the middle of the night.

And my dog had been dragged out my bedroom door.

I wanted to scream, to shriek until my lungs were raw and everyone came running in from the neighborhood. My lips wouldn't even part. The scream was all inside me, bouncing off the inside of my skull in petrifying rhythm.

I heard a thunk, thunk, thunk as Zipper went down the stairs, and the man—the boy—matched it with three heavy footsteps. I heard them; they were real. This was not a dream.

A whispering began in each of my ears, quick and insistent. Parker Elway Parker Sage Elway Parker Elway Elway Sage Parker Elway: my name, playing on repeat in a rough susurration. The boy stepped closer, moving with terpsichorean grace, until I could see the shining peak of his dusty auburn hair.

He paused alongside my bed and I lay there, frozen, vulnerable. His eyes roved over my face, then paused at a spot just below my chin. He was looking at Rosemary's necklace; I knew that for sure. And as he appeared to recognize it, his lips curled into an expression of disgust that made my stomach bottom out in fear.

But no knives flashed in the darkness; no match set my blankets on fire. Instead, the boy shook his head, his auburn hair shivering, and when he stilled, his face was neutral again. He leaned toward me, bending at the waist in a macabre bow. He swept through the darkness, a human pendulum, and rammed his lips to mine.

I didn't have time to react, because his kiss was a weight that pinned me in place more than paralysis ever could. His lips, icy as the snow falling outside my window, sent an intolerable chill flooding into my mouth and through my veins.

And suddenly, I was moving.

Like a beetle taking its last breaths, I flailed wildly, my limbs lashing out at empty air. I was Sleeping Beauty, and the terrible boy had awoken me with a frigid kiss.

This was not a dream. I had known it before, but the reality struck completely when I realized that I was mobile. And there isn't a word for the kind of fear I felt at that moment—an uncharted, clueless fear because I knew that everything was absolutely real.

Just when I was sure that I couldn't take any more, that my lungs would burst from his frozen breath, the boy drew slowly back. His lips peeled away from mine, leaving them feeling bare and used. I slapped a hand to my mouth, springing upright. The boy, leering at me, was still only inches away.

He's going to kill me, I thought. It doesn't matter what I say, I'm dead, I'm dead—

A high-pitched, primal screech from down the stairs cut off my frantic thoughts. Zipper. With a hideous smirk that marred his handsome face, the boy drew back. A glint flashed through his eyes, black as pitch, and a smirk played on his lips, cold as ice. The boy blew me a silent kiss—and then he was gone.

I immediately leapt from my bed, a furious scream erupting from my lips. "ZIPPER!" I cried, charging out of my bedroom on sock-clad feet. My fear was forgotten as the sound of my dog's shrieks resonated in my head. I pounded down the stairs, still shouting, and the sound echoed through the house. Maybe outside, too. Up in the guestroom, I heard Aubrey waking up, calling my name in a sleep-shadowed voice.

I could not respond.

In the living room, I slipped on the hardwood floor and slammed my right arm into a side table. I collapsed to the ground, limb pulsing, but quickly clambered back to my feet and resumed my sprint. Through the kitchen, with the little light above the fridge. Into the sun room. Past Zipper's food, past her bed, and to the patio door that hung slightly ajar.

I threw myself outside without thinking, my body hardly registering the frigid air and biting wind. My eyes darted around deliriously, scanning the white expanse for my dog.

"Zipper!" I screamed.

And there, to my left—a barely audible whimper. I whirled and peeled my socks from the frozen ground to drop down by my dog's side, a gasp tearing itself from my throat. Because there she lay, barely breathing, in a thick pool of blood that seeped scarlet into the snow.

CHAPTER 14

"Is she going to be okay?"

I chattered the fearful question to a white-clad woman who stood, looking tired and exasperated, in the blue-painted hallway of Butler County 24 Hour Pet Hospital. Aubrey was beside me, gnawing pensively on her pinky. There were bags beneath her eyes.

The veterinarian sighed, swiping the back of her hand across her forehead. "Zipper will be perfectly all right," she informed me. "A little beaten up, sure, but nothing stitches can't fix. But it'd probably be best if you leave her here for the night and pick her up tomorrow. We wouldn't want anything more to happen to her, after all." With a barely disguised yawn, the woman led us away from the operating rooms and back to the lobby. She glanced at us over her shoulder as she walked. "It looked to me like she was attacked by something—a raccoon, maybe. You need to keep a better eye on her in the future."

I quickly bit down an attempt to defend myself, remembering what I'd said to them when we first arrived: that the back door had been unlocked, Zipper had sneaked out unnoticed, and I'd found her when she started making noise. The veterinarian hadn't even blinked.

"We'll keep that in mind," Aubrey said, speaking for me. We stepped into the waiting room, our shoes clicking against the pale linoleum. Both of us were still in our pajamas, which probably explained the look of pity on the woman's creased face.

"Great." She flashed a half smile, already beginning to close the door connecting the lobby and the hallway. "You can get pick-up information from the desk."

The man sitting at the desk had disheveled hair and vacant eyes, but he told us that we could pick up Zipper after noon the following day. He then stared at us, hovering across the table, until we took the hint and turned to leave.

A few feet from the door, my cell phone began to buzz. I dug it out from my boot, immediately pressing accept when I realized it was Logan. I'd called him on the way over and left a frantic message, but he hadn't answered his phone.

"Parker?" he gasped, lethargy clouding his words. "My God, are you okay? I just got your message. Where are you?"

Relief swept through me at the sound of his voice. "I'm fine," I replied. "Aubrey's here, and we're at the pet hospital in Butler. If you can meet us here, I'll explain everything."

There was an affirmative sound from the other side, and Logan hissed, "Be there soon," before hanging up the phone.

"He's on his way?" Aubrey asked, watching me stow my phone with her hand on the door handle. I nodded silently, and she pushed open the door.

The snowfall had ceased, making a clear path to Aubrey's car from the building. Unlike when we had arrived, I could actually see air in front of me; it wasn't just sheet of white. It was still cold, though: colder than the cruel boy's frozen lips.

Aubrey silently unlocked her rental truck with a beep that echoed across the parking lot. Her hands, like mine, were buried deep into her sweater pockets. I crunched through the snow en route to the passenger door, pulling my sleeve over my fingers to open the door without freezing to the metal. That, I thought, was the last thing I needed.

Sighing, I slipped into the car, parking my butt on the seat just as Aubrey keyed the ignition and the heat came on at full blast. I tried to focus on the smokey airflow rather that the metallic smell hanging in the air: the scent of iron, the carmine stains on my sweatpants, the blood that rushed from the three claw-like wounds slashed into Zipper's side.

Don't close your eyes, I told myself, or you'll see it all again.

But I couldn't help it. I was tired—exhausted—and the car was so warm that I thought it wouldn't hurt to let by eyes drift shut, just for a moment...

Big mistake.

Immediately, the images lit the blackness of my closed eyelids: dark shadow, moving dog, handsome boy, auburn hair, onyx eyes, icy lips, painful cry, ugly smirk, then running, running, throbbing arm, kitchen light, open door, frozen snow, and blood, red on white on white on white, and red means death, dying, dead—

"Parker."

Aubrey's voice was gentle but firm, and it drew my mind from its state of half awareness. When I opened my eyes, she was peering at me with a look of concern. She had turned off the radio, and the cab was painfully silently.

"Sorry," I said gruffly. I tucked my hair behind my ear, catching sight of my frazzled appearance in the rear view mirror and hardly caring. My mind was not in the right place to be worrying about that, though, not at all. Not when my mother was AWOL, my dog had been attacked, and a person—a living, breathing, human person—had appeared in my bedroom in the middle of the night. This was beyond nightmares; however twisted it might have been, this was reality.

"Parker," Aubrey repeated, resting her palms against the steering wheel, "when you told the vet what happened to Zipper, you were lying." It was a statement, not a question: simple and matter-of-fact. "I think you should tell me what happened for real."

I stared straight ahead, out of the front windshield and into the night. The time flashed green from the dashboard clock: 1:46 AM. Nearly two in the morning, and my test in the morning was suddenly the farthest thing from my mind. Sighing, I ran my tongue over my teeth and tried to formulate a response that would sound the least crazy.

I didn't think there was one.

Eventually, I just went for it, because Aubrey was waiting and I was far beyond caring. "Well," I said dryly, "I'll tell you what happened, but try not to think that I'm insane."

I explained it to her, from the beginning of the dream to the waking end. And Aubrey listened silently, her head constantly bobbing and her lips pressed together in thought. Not once did her features take on the look of incredulity that I expected, and she didn't give me that nervous laugh like she thought I was joking. She didn't speak at all until I'd finished completely, feeling considerably better, though my throat was dry.

For a moment, neither of us spoke. I saw the words processing in Aubrey's mind, the gears whirling in her brain to build a proper answer. Which, I was certain, would contain the words: you are nuts.

But she said no such thing. Rather, with a disbelieving shake of her head, she turned to look me full in the face, her eyes wide and very serious.

"Look," she began, licking her lips. "I believe you. You may not believe yourself, but I believe you. I've done some informal research on parapsychology, met people who discussed it with me. And...I don't know if that has anything to do with what's happening to you, but I know that this isn't normal. You've probably realized that by now." I nodded, and she smiled slightly. "So I get it. I understand, and I don't think you're crazy. But I really can't help you."

I felt my eyes widen, disappointment bubbling up in the pit of my stomach. "What do you mean you can't, you—"

Shaking her head, Aubrey put a finger to her lips. "I mean that I can't. But," she said, "I know someone who can."

The thing about driving through the city to see a psychic medium at two o'clock in the morning is that, with the darkness and the silence and the fatigue behind your eyes, you can trick yourself into believing that the trip is completely normal. Even as your best friend's sister is behind the wheel, explaining how she made a friend in her first year of college who could talk to ghosts and taught her about the the spirit world, you just take in everything and don't question a word.

At least, not until you pull up in front of the so-called paranormal communicator's house. That's about when reality hits.

"Aubrey, what are we doing?" I demanded, staring out the window at the massive white Victorian house that seemed to eat up half the block. "I know that my dream was weird, but you can't be serious about this."

She fixed me with a dry stare. "Don't kid yourself, Parker; that wasn't a dream, and you know it. Just trust me, all right? I know what I'm doing."

"Sure you do," I mumbled.

Aubrey ignored me, instead asking, "Is Logan on his way?"

I nodded. "Last time I checked, he was just getting on the freeway. But I'll call him again." Leaning over, I picked up my phone from the dashboard and dialed his number. It only dialed once before Logan picked up, his voice crackling through the receiver.

"I'm almost there," he said, muffled by his speakerphone. "But Parker, the hell is this place? It looks like some kind of Pennsylvanian Beverly Hills."

I snickered despite myself. "No idea," I admitted. "Some kind of super rich neighborhood, I'm guessing?"

"No kidding." Logan paused, then said, "I just turned the corner, I think I see Aubrey's car." Sure enough, when I glanced out the windshield, I saw two yellow headlight beams slicing cleanly through the night, providing a dim back-light for Logan's car.

"I see you," I said, hanging up the phone. Logan slowed, hugging the curb as he brought his car to a stop behind Aubrey's and cut the headlights.

Aubrey turned to me. "Ready?" She already had a hand on the door, waiting.

I shrugged. "Aw, hell. Why not?" Before I could stop myself, I popped open the door and hopped out into the snow, simultaneously pocketing my phone. Logan approached us on the sidewalk, his skepticism obvious even beneath the dimming streetlights.

"Parker, what's going on? Why are we here?" He toed the ice, kicking up a geyser of ice that dusted over his gray sweats. It appeared that he hadn't changed out of his pajamas either, though his fleece sweatshirt and beanie looked considerably warmer that my skimpy jacket.

I explained quickly, keeping my words blunt. "I had another dream, and Zipper got attacked by...something. Aubrey drove us to the animal hospital, but then she suggested we come here to visit her friend."

"And who is your friend, exactly, dear sister?" Logan asked, raising his eyebrows at the sprawling property. "The president?"

Aubrey didn't bat an eye, though I had to steel myself for Logan's reaction to what she'd say next. "Actually, she's a psychic medium, and she's going to help Parker, because you know those dreams she's been having? They aren't dreams."

Logan's features took on a look of such furious incredulity that I flinched. He fixed me with an open-mouthed glare, spitting out a single word: "What?"

"You heard me," Aubrey said briskly. She turned on her heel, marching down the front walk. Logan looked at me with narrowed eyes.

"You're kidding," he sneered. "Don't tell me you actually believe this bull!"

I put a hand on his arm, chewing nervously on my bottom lip. "Just...try to keep an open mind, all right? Please?"

Logan scoffed, but followed me up to the porch, where Aubrey was waiting. Trying to ignore the tension in the early morning air, I jumped up beside her on the wooden floorboards. They creaked beneath my weight. A dimmed sign in the window read: PSYCHIC: No Appointments Needed.

"Will she even be awake?" I asked dubiously, staring up at the darkened house as Aubrey rang the doorbell. I felt more than a little trepidation at the thought of speaking to this woman—whoever she was.

"She'll be expecting us," was Aubrey's ambiguous reply.

I don't know what I was expecting; maybe a stooped old woman with wild hair and ethnic clothing, or a Professor McGonagall lookalike with a witch's hat atop her head. Instead, when the door was thrown open, I was faced with a bright-eyed young woman in plaid pajamas who couldn't have been much older than me.

"So you did come," she said, brushing her platinum blonde braid over one shoulder. She had a strange, lilting accent, though it was very faint. "Please, come in. She told me you'd be here."

I looked at Aubrey, confused, but she merely shook her head and silently led the way into the house. I hesitated at the threshold, wary of this strange girl and her big, soul-searching eyes.

"Well, come on then." She stared me and Logan down, unblinking, until we both stumbled into the foyer. I glanced at him, and he wore a look of uncertainty that probably mirrored my own.

"Long time no see, Aubrey," said the girl, glancing back at us as we trailed her through a vast and surprisingly modern living room. "I knew you'd come crawling back eventually." Her tone was deadly serious, even mocking, but Aubrey let out a laugh.

"Sure you did, Laury," she said dryly. "Glad to see you, too."

Laury glanced over her shoulder, and there was a wide smile perched on her lips. She stopped abruptly at a door, laying a hand on its handle. We had been led down a corridor, and this door appeared to mark a dead end.

"You're Parker, right?" I nodded, and she smiled warmly. "Your sister has told me tons of great things about you."

I gave a start, leaning away slightly as Laury gazed at me with her big gray eyes. "Wait, what? How did you—"

The girl looked at me, laughing strangely. "It's my job, darling." She then turned to Logan, who hovered just behind me, and the smile slipped slowly off her lips, freezing in a sour half-sneer expression. "And you must be Logan. The skeptic."

"Uh—I—" Logan stuttered, rubbing the back of his neck. "Yes?"

"Mm." Laury gave him a last narrow-eyed look. Her hand was still on the doorknob, and she turned it slowly, moving so that her body blocked the doorway. "This is my sanctuary," she announced seriously. "I ask that you please respect it and treat any visitors we might encounter with utmost respect. Can I count on that?"

Logan and I shared bemused looks, but Aubrey just rolled her eyes and elbowed her way past her friend, disappearing into the room beyond the door. All I could think as I followed her in was: man, this chick is weird.

Laury turned around suddenly, startling me as I slipped through the doorway. She was about my height, and her permanently doe-eyed expression hung parallel to mine. A small smile flirted with her lips as she said, "All of us are weird in this business, darling."

I learned three things about Laury in one minute of standing in her dark and curtained-filled "sanctuary," watching her prepare a table for us to sit.

One: she ended nearly sentence with "darling."

Two: she moved like a marionette.

Three: she never blinked.

I kept close quarters on her face, trying to catch any movement of her eyelids, but there was none. Her eyes stayed open, painfully wide, for the entire duration of our visit. I wasn't quite sure what to think of her.

"Please, sit," Laury said, gesturing to the fold-out plastic table that now sat in the center of the room. She had pulled up four plush arm chairs that had previous lined the bookcase walls and surrounded the table with them. The seats dwarfed it completely.

Awkwardly following Aubrey, I climbed into a chair between the two siblings, directly across from Laury. Neither of the girls had said much to each other, but I could tell from their comfort level around each other that they were good friends. I wondered how they had met; compared to Aubrey, Laury was...oddly eccentric.

And she was staring at me as if she heard everything I thought.

"So, Parker," she said, not breaking her gaze. "I know that we're here because of you. What do you need from me?"

"Uh..." I stared at her, unsure of what, exactly, I did need. I looked to Aubrey, who gave me a reassuring smile.

"Go on, Parker," she urged. "Just tell her everything."

So, nervously, I started at the beginning, explaining my dreams and all the strange things that had been happening since they started. Laury listened to all of it with a frown, her unblinking eyes downcast. At the part about Zipper and the frigid boy, Logan stiffened, and she looked confused. When I finished, she tilted her head, filling her cheeks with air and then blowing it out in a noisy exhalation.

"Well," she said flatly, after a moment, "I can tell you one thing for sure: this isn't what you think it is. Sleep paralysis a real condition, but this is different." She stood up suddenly, darting over to one of the many bookshelves and deftly selecting a thick volume. Heaving it onto the table, she simply let it fall open and pushed the book toward us.

On the paper, stretched across two pages, was an image that looked vaguely familiar. It was a painting of a woman in a white dress lying on a bench, her head lolling off the side. A demented creature sat on her chest, wrinkled and ugly like a gargoyle. And in the shadows, sticking out from a scarlet curtain, was a black horse head with wild red eyes.

"That's The Nightmare," Logan said excitedly, recognizing it immediately. "Remember, Parker? Henry Fuseli's piece? Dr. Hennessy was telling us about it."

I looked closer, quickly realizing that the painting reminded me of the drawing our professor had shown us in class. Both depicted sleep paralysis with the old hag on the sleeper's chest.

Laury glanced down at the painting, the looked around at us. "So," she began, "what do you think?"

I raised an eyebrow. "Um, it's...nice?" I offered.

The girl rolled her eyes. "No, I mean, what do you think about how this relates to your problem?" Under her breath, as if we couldn't hear, she muttered, "Christ, I always forget that these people can't read my mind."

I frowned, glancing closer at the painting and trying to coax my tired mind to piece together an answer. "I don't know," I said eventually, stifling a yawn. "I don't get what you want me to say."

Laury regarded me with careful patience, her smile becoming condescending. I stared back at her with steely eyes and willed myself not to blink. On either side of the table, I felt Aubrey and Logan holding their breath.

"Do you know the Angelic Salutation?" she asked suddenly.

"As in the Hail Mary prayer?" I raised an eyebrow. "Yeah, why?"

Laury still did not blink. Her gaze was giving me goosebum ps."Say it."

I pressed my lips together, feeling my eyes become slits. In the back of my mind, I was remembering the way my mother had demanded the same thing of me, what seemed like an eternity ago.

"Why?" I questioned.

"Just say it."

Silence blanketed the room. My eyes wandered to the sheaths of purple and red and brown fabric hung from the ceiling, then to the candles that rested on the wall in iron sconces.

Might as well, I thought, then began, realizing that Laury knew I would.

"Hail Mary, full of grace"—I paused, immediately feeling a strange tug in my stomach—"the Lord is with thee. Blessed art thou amongst women"—worse now, an actual pain—"and blessed is the fruit of thy womb Je—shoot."

Our of nowhere, my entire abdomen clenched, slashing apart my intestines and caving in at my stomach. I pitched forward, hitting my head hard against the table before falling to the ground. I heard a faint shout, and it sounded like Logan, but there was something trying to eat its way out of my stomach and the voices didn't seem so important right now.

Someone screamed; it might have been me. It felt as if I had vacated my body and been thrown into a foggy astral plane full of moving shadows that looked somewhat like my friends. But the pain was still there; furious and all-consuming, it gnawed and tore at my body. It stung and burned and ached all at once, a combination of every uncomfortable sensation that brought tears to my blurry eyes and made my head pound.

"Parker!" The voice cut through the haze in my mind, dangerously close to my ear. Then there were hands on my shoulders, shaking them, drawing me back into reality. I blinked my way into the room, the dim light suddenly feeling extremely bright.

The initial pain was gone now, leaving deep, rolling waves of nausea in my stomach and a deep throbbing against my skull.

"Parker, what was that? Are you okay?"

That was Aubrey. Both she and Logan were kneeling beside me, their concerned, horrified faces floating into my view. And behind them, standing with her arms crossed and her pale hair falling into her face, was Laury. She wore a twisted, strange smile on her face as she stared down at me, nodding slowly.

"Well, well, well," she said, "it looks like we have an incubus on our hands."

Somehow, we ended up at Laury's kitchen table, sitting in the hard plastic chairs with mugs of tea in our hands in a room that was just as strangely modern as the rest of her house. She hadn't given so much as a breath of explanation, instead hurrying us out of her demode sanctuary because, as she put it, "some things are best discussed over tea."

I couldn't argue with that, especially not when whatever herbal concoction she'd given us was warming me more and more by the second.

Logan, beside me, did not look nearly as placated. He was bouncing his leg, his lips pressed tightly together. The room was silent as Laury swept about, quickly arranging a plate of cookies and pre-cut sandwiches. It was fast approaching three AM, yet it seemed that she had been expecting us.

When at last she sat down, her serious eyes snapped to focus on Logan. He continued fidgeting, staring at the wall as if he didn't notice Laury's gaze. Pressing my lips together, I reached out and tapped his elbow.

"You have something to say," Laury said as Logan jolted back into the present, spluttering. "Well, don't keep it a secret, skeptic. Why don't you explain?"

"I—" My best friend looked around the table, his eyes wide. I was chewing on my sleeve and Aubrey was sipping her tea, but we were both staring at him. "Explain what?" he questioned at last.

"You know. About the incubus."

Logan sighed.

"It's just that I read something," he admitted, "in those notes Dr. Hennessy gave us. Do you remember them, Parker?" He looked up at me, hopeful, as if I could take over explaining for him. "They were about incubi and succubi and the legends behind—no? Okay."

I coughed guiltily; evidently, my expression had given away my confusion. The word incubus sounded undoubtedly familiar, but I still had a headache, and nothing was processing very clearly.

"Why don't you describe what an incubus is, Logan?" Laury prompted, like a school teacher.

He frowned. "C-can't you?"

"Well, sure. But since you know, I thought you might want to tell us."

I saw embarrassment and annoyance pass across Logan's features, the tips of his ears turning pink. He grabbed the handle of his mug, released it, and then clapped his hand behind his neck.

"Incubi," he said eventually, quietly, "are—uh—demons. Supposedly, they're actually, um, angels, but they were cast down from heaven because they were—ah—lusting after women. And according to legend, now that they're on Earth, they lie on sleeping women to, um..."

He trailed off, his freckles standing out in the harsh fluorescent lights. His cheeks were becoming suspiciously red.

"To what, Logan?" Laury demanded gleefully.

"To have, um—to father children," he managed. His words blurred together, making the phrase an ambiguous mush in my ears. But my mind sorted through it, and when I realized what he was saying, I let out a shrieking gasp.

"What?" I slapped the table with one hand and my stomach with the other, suddenly lucid. "I don't—I—tell me he's joking." I turned to Logan, desperate for some kind of consolation, but he merely shook his head.

"But Parker, you know this is ridiculous," he insisted, then looked up at Laury and his silent sister. "This is ridiculous. Incubi don't exist. None of this supernatural bullshit will ever exist in the real world."

Quite suddenly, Laury began to laugh, a hysterical, shattering sound, and finally closed her eyes, just for a moment. Her eyelids were pale and crossed with blueish veins. Then she snapped to attention, her lips curling into a solemn frown.

"Logan," she began, as if nothing had happened, "in your reading, did you come across the five ways to overcome the attacks of an incubus?"

Logan was silent.

"I know you did. Why don't I begin for you? For starters, there's exorcism. Isn't that right?"

He nodded stiffly.

"Then, of course, there's Sacramental Confession, excommunication of the demon, moving the victim to a new location, and the Sign of the Cross. Or, instead of that last one..."

"The Angelic Salutation," Logan murmured gruffly. "The Hail Mary prayer."

Laury smirked. "Correct!" She turned to me then, but I was already putting two and two together. My heart was racing, but I tried to still it long enough to formulate a response. I saw Laury's anticipatory expression; in her weird way, she probably already knew what I was about to say.

"Let's just pretend, for a second, that all this is real," I said slowly. "You just said those five things help to overcome incubus attacks. I'm pretty sure that when I said the prayer, something attacked me. And the boy I saw—the one that appeared in my room. How does that factor in? He wasn't some kind of spirit. He was real." I unconsciously touched my lips, still feeling a ghost of the chill. "He was definitely real."

Laury tutted. "Well, firstly, the demon was trying to fight back. It didn't want you to expel it, or try to, or even to fight against it. Obviously, its first reaction would be to attack." She shook her head, as if that should have been evident. "And secondly, well, I guess haven't been entirely honest with you. I think that what you're dealing with is a form of an incubus. It's a demon and it's certainly evil. But it's not the conventional creature that I'm used to seeing."

I gaped at her. "Then why the hell did you say that it was?"

"Because I don't know what else to call it!" the medium spat, tugging at her hair. "This thing is something that I've never dealt with before, and I don't entirely know what it is. What they are. I don't think I would've ever encountered them if Rose hadn't contacted me."

"Rose?" I blinked slowly, my voice breaking. "Rosemary? My sister?"

She nodded. "Your sister, yes. She approached me because you were in danger, because she knew that Aubrey knew me and figured you would end up here. But she can't say what they are, not completely—they are preventing her."

I felt a shiver trace down my spine. "But...but how?" I breathed. "How does she know who...they are?"

Puzzlement tilted Laurie's head, her doll-like eyes growing wider. "I thought you knew," she whispered, scratching the glass table with one nail. "They are the ones who killed her."

The silence was terrible. I felt it gnawing at me, swallowing all the air in the room. My head was spinning from a sudden lack of oxygen.

Dead. My sister was dead. I knew that. Murdered. I knew that too.

They had never found the killer.

They never found the killer because the killer was in her dreams.

I licked my lips; they were suddenly dry. I could feel everyone staring at me, waiting, but it felt like I had to swim across an ocean before I could make any words leave my mouth.

"So it's not an incubus," I said, trying to focus on my hands in front of me instead of the sterile, white kitchen. The blue polish on my nails was chipping.

"No," Laury affirmed. "Besides the matter of your sister, these men you've been seeing, they—they don't fit in. But they—or it—were affected by that prayer, and that means it's related to the incubi. Not to mention that right now, you positively reek of the thing. I nearly didn't let you in because of the stench, but it appears that your little...friend either can't attack you right now, or isn't trying to."

She peered at me, her laser gaze seeming to bore holes right through me. "But yes, it is certainly there."

I leaned away, feeling intruded upon. My head still felt funny. Discomfort climbed through me as I locked eyes with Laury, infesting my muddled thoughts with poisonous malcontent. This incubus nonsense—it could be real, could it? Logan had to be right. This wasn't a demon. It couldn't be. That was ridiculous.

Yet I remembered Edith Hummel's words.

Your mother made a deal with the devil.

Suddenly, out of nowhere, the young medium bolted upright in her seat. She looked quickly between me and Logan, then clapped a hand over her lips.

"Oh my—oh, my, my. You two have a test tomorrow, don't you? Oh, I'm so sorry, I shouldn't be keeping you." She stood quickly, swiping the mugs and plates off our table. I reached for my half-eaten sandwich, but she was faster. "Go on, shoo," she blustered. "You'll need rest. Keep me posted, and if anything happens, just call this number."

There was suddenly a business card pressed into my hand, but I didn't get to so much as glance at it. In a whirlwind of movement, we were ushered out of the kitchen, through the living room, and back into the foyer. I was confused by the abruptness of it all, and was no longer sure if our visit with Laury had unearthed anything at all. But as she opened the door, sending us back into the snow, I thought once more of Rosemary.

"Laury," I said, reaching out but not touching her. "You—you mentioned earlier that you talked to my sister. I-is she here?" I glanced over her shoulder, as if Rosemary would appear in the foyer behind her.

Laury's expression deteriorated quickly, her entire face seeming to droop in sadness. She took my outstretched hand in her cold grip, genuine regret in her voice as she said, "I'm afraid not, Parker. She tries to get out as much as she can, but their hold on her is very tight. She will try to contact you soon, though, I'm sure. And remember: if you ever need help with any of this, don't hesitate to call me."

I nodded numbly. Laury inspected me with wide, careful eyes, then, after a moment of deliberation, darted forward and enveloped me in a chilly hug. I stood, frozen, unsure of how to react.

"It will be all right," she assured me, her voice muffled by my hair. "It will. And, darling, I think when your mother returns, you should have a nice long chat with her." I froze; I hadn't said anything about my mother leaving. But Laury was wearing that knowing smile, and before I could respond, she said, "Now go—your friends are waiting."

She pulled away, and I began to shuffle toward Aubrey and Logan on unsteady feet. Just as I began to descend the porch steps, however, Laury's voice called me back one more time. When I glanced over my shoulder, there was mischief in the medium's eyes.

"By the way, Parker," she said mysteriously. "The answer is four."

"By the way, Parker," she said mysteriously. "The answer is four."

CHAPTER 15

"I knew seeing that woman was a bad idea," Logan muttered, glancing at me sideways as we dragged ourselves into psych class the next morning. He'd been full of comments like that ever since we'd left Laury's place. Lack of sleep apparently hadn't made him any less crabby about the psychic medium situation. If anything, it probably intensified his annoyance.

"Would you quit it?" I snapped, flashing him a glare as I dropped heavily into a seat. "It's over; it's done. It already happened, so let's move on."

Logan frowned, setting his things down on the table. We both clutched paper cups brimming with extra-strong coffee in our hands. "I don't know. There was just something about Laury that wasn't right."

I threw up my hands. "Well, of course there is! The chick talks to ghosts, for Christ's sake! Do you really think she'd be normal?" My outburst drew several miffed from a few older kids, all of them studying silently at their seats. I shot glares in their directions that drove their eyes back to the textbooks in front of them.

"Does that mean you're sold on the whole 'ghost' deal?" Logan asked, obviously incredulous. "Parker, you've got to be kidding me."

"Logan," I said, quieter now. "My dog was dragged out of my room and attacked—while she was sleeping. I've been having dreams that don't make sense. And last night, a boy appeared in my bedroom out of thin air and kissed me. And I can tell you with absolute certainty that that kiss was real."

My best friend shifted at that, his expression becoming uncomfortable at the word kiss. I knew he was trying not to think about it, but for him, this was a jealousy match. He wasn't understanding the full horror of seeing a stranger in your room, while I was having trouble forgetting it. It seemed like every time I blinked, I saw his eyes, felt the graze of his lips, and realized again and again that whatever was happening to me was not a dream.

"Maybe it was a dream, and you just didn't realize it," Logan tried weakly, but even he knew that the argument was futile.

I raised an eyebrow. "Or maybe some kind of incubus is trying to kill me."

He let out a low breath of air, shaking his curly head vigorously. "Do you know how ridiculous that sounds? That does not happen! This isn't a movie, and you're not that possessed girl in every horror film. I know that there's a reasonable explanation for this, and so do you."

"No, I don't," I hissed. "I don't know anything except that a demon-thing killed my sister and now the goddamned creatures are coming after me."

"You can't be sure!" Logan slammed his drink down, sloshing dark liquid onto the desk. The other kids glared, and this time we both ignored them.

"Maybe I can't, but it seems like the best explanation right now."

"Best explanation—please. Why do you insist on believing this? Do you have some kind of death wish?"

Logan's green eyes were wide, his gloved hands pressed firmly to the top of his head as he attempted to pace back and forth between my chair and his. I watched him from my seat, feeling a strange, contradictory mixture of anger and attraction tickling at my ribcage. And maybe it was the fact that I'd slept for less than an hour and hadn't studied nearly enough to pass my exam, but I was wired and buzzing and my response came out in a confident whip.

"Maybe I do."

Logan was just opening his mouth to reply when there was a tap against the microphone, and Dr. Hennessy cleared his throat. "Good morning," he intoned, addressing us from his podium. "I ask that you all put away your study materials at this time. The midterm is rather long, so we'll begin right away..."

Not two blinks later, there was suddenly a test on my desk, a pencil in my hand, and silence stretching across the lecture hall. I couldn't remember any of it happening, but there I was, staring at a blank scantron and reading the first question over and over again.

How many types of stimuli-response combinations does an individual have?

Did we learn this? I couldn't remember. I couldn't remember much of anything, actually. The answers seemed to swim in front of me, the letters swapping and confusing me even more.

No, come on, no, I begged my brain, please don't do this to me now.

I had to stay awake; passing grade or not, I had to finish my test or risk making a fool of myself in front of people who looked down on me enough as it was. But already, I could feel my eyes beginning to droop shut, betraying me. The room blurred, inviting me to catch up on some much needed sleep, and suddenly a quick nap didn't seem like such a terrible idea. After all, I would only put my head down for a second...

Maybe Logan didn't see me fall asleep, or maybe God just hates me, because nothing woke me up before my cheek hit the table. I fell into a strange sleep, the kind of half-aware variety that you get when you're napping in a public place.

I'd read in one of Dr. Hennessy's papers that sleep paralysis could be prevented by sleeping on something other than your back, because other positions remove the possibility of that chest pressure effect. And I wasn't sleeping on my back; I was scooted back in my chair with my head buried into my arms on top of my untouched test. There was no reason for me to have an episode then, while dozing innocently in class.

Yet I did.

At first, I actually thought that I'd woken up. My eyes peeled open of their own accord, fuzzing for a moment before focusing. That's when I tried to raise my head, only to realize that it was glued to the spot. My entire body was glued to the spot, for that matter, and there was a pressure against my chest that felt like someone squeezing me into a bone-crushing hug from behind.

This episode was different, because usually I was in the dark and this time it was bright, but that didn't make it any less terrifying. I was confined to looking in one direction, to my right, where a girl with carrot ginger hair was sitting.

That is, where she had been sitting. Because now, perched in her sea and wearing an ugly smile, was the blonde man from the bar. The hand was still hers, and it was bubbling in answers, but the man's face smirked at me from atop suit-clad shoulders. And all down the row, and all the other rows that I could see, there were more faces, dozens and dozens of men and even women with eyes the color of obsidian, leering at me from the bodies of my classmates. Terror, now familiar, built inside of me as I watched the figures, half expecting them to converge and take me away right there.

Then it was over, just like that.

Ten seconds, maybe twelve, and the dream released me. Air flooded my lungs, I could move my limbs—and there was a feral shriek ripping from my lips.

My chair went tipping onto its back legs, and were it not for my flailing limbs, I would have pitched straight into the desk behind me. The seat returned to the ground again with a sharp thunk, jarring me enough to bite my tongue and cut me off mid-scream. I pressed my hands to the table, gasping for breath. For a moment, I completely forgot where I was; all I remembered was those grinning faces.

Until I realized that every single person in the lecture hall was staring at me.

"Ms. Elway," said Dr. Hennessy, his eyes bright against his dark skin, "are you all right?"

I nodded vigorously, feeling the stares and wanted to curl into a ball and disappear. Today wasn't a 'stand up and take everything in stride' day; it was messed-up day that was running on espresso and adrenaline. My stomach was roiling, flipping around in my abdomen like waves stirred by a motorboat's fan. I felt Logan's hand on my arm, steadying me as I swayed.

The professor's face showed actual concern as he watched me, frowning. "Everyone, return to your tests," he said. "Parker, will you please come down here?"

Dr. Hennessy was kidding himself if he that thought people would actually continue their exams when there was a crazy girl trying to edge past them in the aisle. They stared at me shamelessly as I made my way down the steps to the pulpit, trying to ignore their gazes.

In my head, I saw the faces.

"Are you sure you're okay, Parker?" Dr. Hennessy asked quietly, once I'd reached his podium.

I felt very small there, standing at the center of the pulpit in the midst of about a hundred other people, but I managed a slight bob of the head.

"I'm fine," I assured, "thank you. I just, uh—" But I stopped right there, because how was I going to explain myself, really?

Dr. Hennessy didn't look convinced. "Would you like to step outside for a few minutes, then? You should still have time to finish."

"Yes, please," I murmured. I dashed outside without another word, because I was dead tired and my mind was full of snippets from the night before and I kept seeing those eyes, those faces, feeling those lips, and it was all bringing my nausea to an alarming cusp.

It wasn't until I felt the morning chill on my face that I abruptly realized the answer to the question I'd struggled on. Four. Four types of stimuli-response combinations. As with everything, Laury had somehow foreseen my problem. Had she foreseen that waking terror? If she did, I wish she'd told me, because I was nauseous and couldn't stop shaking.

I spent the rest of that class in the ladies room, emptying my stomach in the toilet of the handicap stall.

Aubrey stayed over again that night, and this time, Logan came too. I wasn't sure where we stood (we'd spent the morning arguing, after all), but I had to say, I was glad for the company. The idea of spending a night alone in my house after what had happened made my throat clench up in fear.

There was still no news from my mother, either, and it worried me. She called to check up when I ran errands for her. Yet here she was, out of town overnight, and I hadn't received so much as a simple text. Every call I made went straight to voicemail.

Which led me back to the same question I'd been asking since she left: where had she gone?

Having her back was not something I thought I'd ever hope for, not in a million years. But that typical little-kid mentality of "Mommy will save me from the bad guys" had come back in full force, and really, I just wanted my mother to come home.

I thought of calling her firm, but I didn't know what I'd do if they answered and said she hadn't gone on a company trip. She wouldn't just pick up and leave me, right? Not without luggage, not without warning. But something happened, and now she was inexplicably gone. And I was alone.

"Parker, how are you?" Aubrey asked, peering at me over a plate of pizza. I looked up at her over my untouched slice.

"Terrible, actually," I said flatly. I was well aware that I wasn't helping anything, being negative but I didn't care. Everything was a mess, I was a mess, and I couldn't even escape my problems by sleeping.

That was the worst part of it all. With normal life troubles, I could close my eyes and pull up my sheets and have relief for a good eight hours. But this was everywhere; in my dreams, in my head, and in the waking hours of the day. It made me feel completely lost, as if everything was hopeless and fighting was futile—because really, it was.

Beside me, Logan scooted his chair closer and squeezed my shoulder reassuringly. I tried to smile at him, but everything was blurry and faded and only half-there, and all I could manage was a sickly grimace.

I set my pizza down, staring at the wood of the table. In my dream, that very first one, Rosemary had sat right here, a pencil in her hands, drawing. Now Rosemary was buried at the bottom of a hole in a big wooden box.

"I think I'm going to go upstairs," I said, suddenly feeling sick again. "I'm not hungry." Aubrey nodded slowly, her eyes concerned.

"Do you want one of us to come with you?" Logan asked, grabbing my hand gently.

I bit my lip, shook my head, pulled away. "No, it's fine. I think I just need to be alone. But thanks."

With arms crossed and shoulders hunched, I trudged through the kitchen and into the living room, where I saw Zipper, asleep on the couch with her body wrapped in bandages. The sight made my stomach hurt. I mounted the stairs, taking them one at a time, slowly. There was extreme lethargy in my limbs, weighing me down. Several times, I thought I'd just pitch backward and roll back down the stairs.

But I made it to the top, and then I stood in the hallway, swaying, staring into my room. It felt cold in there, and unclean. Just to step inside, I had to hold my breath to keep my teeth from chattering. Twice, I nearly chickened out and ran back downstairs, but I knew that being with Aubrey and Logan, friends though they were, wouldn't make me feel any better.

I turned up my speakers to full volume to drown out that ringing silence, playing an old Fleetwood Mac song that I couldn't help but sing along to under my breath. My room was splayed out before me, looking large and empty and foreboding. Sighing, I scuffed the carpet with my heels, moving toward my bookshelf and selecting a volume at random before tossing myself onto my bed. I glanced at the cover: The Sad Cypress, by Agatha Christie. The book was well-exhausted, as the careworn cover made obvious, but it would make for some kind of distraction.

What time was it? Eight o'clock. It felt like I hadn't moved in ages, but I guess time had been speeding on without me. And that was just fine with me, because I wanted to stay right here, curled up on my bed, and never have to deal with anything ever again.

But I guess it's true what they say: time waits for no one.

It got even colder around ten o'clock, and by then, I only had a few chapters left in the book. Aubrey and Logan had stopped in about thirty minutes before, one after the other, to say goodnight and tell me where they'd be if I needed either of them. Aubrey was in the guest room again; Logan was camping out on the living room couch.

I could tell that they were worrying about me, and really, I was trying to be grateful. But everything was muted and I was numb and scared and I didn't know why. I just hated the idea of being afraid, because there was still that part of me that insisted this is not real, and it was laughing at me for believing in it. Out loud, to Logan, his logic was the enemy. Inside my head, I was a mess.

And maybe outside of it, too.

It was getting colder, though, and I was certain of that much. So I closed my book, drew up my covers, and tried to sleep. I didn't turn off the lights, because I was convinced that they were the only thing keeping the monsters at bay. It was a silly, childish notion: as long as the lights are on, everything will be okay.

What a filthy lie.

For a while, I tossed and turned, lost in that restless state of half-awareness. The light was burning my closed eyelids. Sleep just wasn't coming, and a part of me was okay with that. But, as I suppose I already knew, I didn't have to be asleep for them to reach me.

I felt the presence suddenly; it stabbed at the center of my forehead and jolted me awake. I sat up slowly. An invisible gaze was drilling into my skull, sending a thick shiver down my shoulders and to the base of my spine. Just to make sure, I pinched myself—and I was not dreaming.

I swallowed hard, wrapping my arms around myself. "Hello?" I called softly, stupidly, as if someone would respond. No one did, of course, and there was only silence to answer me.

The bare bulbs hanging from my ceiling suddenly began to sway.

Those look ridiculous, my mother told me, when I was ten and I decided to hang them from my ceiling. You're going to regret that one day.

Today was that day.

There was no wind; my windows and balcony door were firmly shut. But they were swinging back and forth, faster now, clinking lightly against each other. I watched, mesmerized, with my heart trying to fling itself out of my chest. I still felt those eyes staring at me, hidden from my sight. They were in here, I knew it. The bulbs were swaying, clanging, the lights flickering slightly.

And then they floated to a stop.

Just like that, they arranged themselves back into their line, dangling simply from little pegs in my white ceiling. I made the mistake of thinking it was over. A quiet, relieved sigh escaped my lips, thanking everyone upstairs for sparing me from another horror. But that relief only lasted for a moment.

I had my eyes glued to the three bulbs, carefully watching. And as I stared, I saw the light farthest from me begin to quiver slightly. I thought it was my imagination at first, but very quickly, I realized that it wasn't. It definitely wasn't.

A moment later, the bulb shattered.

The room went one shade darker as the soft eruption echoed in my ears. Little bits of glass rained down on the carpet at the foot of my bed.

"Good lord," I hissed, scrabbling back against my headboard.

I barely had time to think; the second bulb had already followed suit, and now tremors were running down its wire and etching hairline cracks into the glass. It, too, exploded in an instant, leaving behind a shimmering trail of reflective shards.

There was only one bulb left. I had my back pressed as close to the wall as I could get it, my comforter tugged up to my nose. In my head, I imagined that I could hear those creatures, their cruel laughter knifing into my ears. But really, there was disgusting silence. All my attention was focused on that single glass orb. The last one. It shivered as if caught in an earthquake, almost imperceptibly.

I braced myself. It shattered louder than the other two, and this time, the shards reached further. One scratched across my arm, slicing skin.

And the room was plunged into darkness.

CHAPTER 16

I got out of bed slowly, carefully, peeling the blankets away from me with extreme precision. The room was like a meat locker, and a shiver edged through my body as soon as my skin touched air. I felt those eyes following me as I tiptoed as quickly as I could across the glassy floor. It was a guessing game, with me trying to catch sight of the shards in the glint of moonlight and skirt my way around them.

Everything felt lighter the second I was out of my room. It was as if someone had given me glasses, and now I could see everything. I suddenly realized that I was shaking violently. When I held my hands up to my face, they were trembling. Despite my sweater and thick fleece pajama pants, I felt a kind of chill that seeped all the way into my blood.

Downstairs, I thought blindly, feeling my way through the dim hallway. I'll go get a drink of water, and everything will be fine.

Funny, how easy it is to lie to yourself when you're scared.

As my foot hit the bottom step of the stairs, I heard something that filled me with both dread and joy, simultaneously. It was the sound of my mom's car, scuffing concrete as it rolled into the driveway. I saw her headlights through the living room window.

I froze in place, feeling my stomach plummet to my knees. She was back; what did that mean? Should I go back to bed and pretend not to see her or confront her right now, in the middle of the night? I didn't have long to decide. Already, I heard her getting out of the car, arming it. The sound of her footsteps kicking up snow and gravel wandered toward me as I stood there, indecisive.

Logan's form made a lump on one of the couches; the longer one, closer to the fireplace. He was fast asleep, and I knew he would stay that way. The boy was practically Sleeping Beauty when he was tired. If I could be quiet, maybe I'd be able to talk to my mother without waking up either of the siblings. It was worth a try, I figured.

It took a moment, but eventually I heard the sound of a key in the lock of my front door. It inched open slowly, and my mom's head appeared around the corner. There were rings beneath her eyes, and her hair was askew. She didn't seem to see me, poised there in the shadows.

She ducked all the way into the foyer, closing the door gently behind her, and I couldn't stifle a gasp. She was still wearing her suit, the one from the night she'd left, but now there were tears in the fabric, and it was stained with something dark and grimy.

Her head whipped around at the sound of my voice, her expression vulnerable, and her eyes found me in the darkness. We stared at each other for a moment, both of us open-mouthed, before I moved from the stair step and onto level ground. My mother's face was completely open, obvious enough for me to read the surprise and fatigue and worry in her eyes.

She spoke first. "Hello, Parker," she said. Already, she was piecing her features back together, smoothing them into that typical soulless line. This time, I didn't react to it at all. My entire body was still shaking, and there was still glass on my floor, but I needed to address this now.

"I think we need to talk," I replied.

We took seats in the sun room, on the two chairs in front of the little wood stove. Aubrey had started it up earlier, because it kept the kitchen warm, but it was just smoldering embers now. Still, it had left a bit of heat in the room.

There we were, mother and daughter, facing each other across a rickety iron table. I wondered if she and Rosemary had sat like this, once upon a time, just holding an innocent conversation because my mother was so lovely back then. I could practically see it: Rose, with her long hair swept into braids, her eyes glowing and a sketchbook in her lap, my mother, smiling, sipping tea and asking her favorite daughter about her day at school. And maybe I was in the picture too, playing with dolls off to the side, forgotten in the moment.

Now, in the present, my mother wasn't smiling or drinking tea, she was just staring at me blankly. Maybe she knew what I was about to ask, but she was so impassive that I couldn't tell. I was just trying to put the words together in my head and not be distracted by what I now saw was blood on her clothing.

"Where is Zipper?" my mom asked abruptly, her eyes darting to the empty dog bed behind me.

"Upstairs," I said quietly, "sleeping in Aubrey's room."

"What? Parker, you know I don't like the dog in the house at night."

I gritted my teeth, sudden anger filling me. She was glaring at me now, so I ignored her words completely, instead leaning back against my seat and crossing my arms.

"Mom," I began slowly, "would you like to tell me about me sister?"

My mother's eyes widened immediately. She licked her lips, then swallowed. "Sister?" An attempt at a laugh. "Parker, don't be silly. You don't have a sister."

I raised an eyebrow. "Oh, really?" From inside the pocket of my pants, I withdrew the many-times folded drawing of the girl and unfolded it, holding it up so that my mother could see. I smiled grimly when she gasped. "Don't even bother, Mom. I know all about her. I believe her name was Rosemary?"

When my mother spoke again, her voice was thinner than I'd ever heard it. "Rosemary," she whispered. "Yes, she was Rosemary. But she passed away long ago, Parker, and I don't want to—"

"Passed away?" I interjected coolly. "Mom, we both know that she didn't 'pass away'. My sister was murdered, wasn't she?"

"No, I—"

"Wasn't she?" I was breathing hard, my grip tightening on that paper. "I read the article in the paper; I'm no idiot. Someone murdered my sister."

My mom leaned forward in her chair, hands clutching the armrests. "How do you know this?" she hissed, evidently frightened.

"Because Rosemary Elway had been visiting my dreams," I stated. "Because she knew I didn't know about her, and she wanted me to. She came to warn me, Mom. Whatever killed her wasn't human, no matter what anyone says. I don't care how crazy I sound, because the same thing that killed Rosemary is after me. I've been seeing men in the streets, following me. I've had dreams about shadows that shake my bed. And last night, a boy appeared in my room, and something dragged Zipper outside and attacked her." I narrowed my eyes. "Something is going on here, and I know that you know all about it. And even if you don't like me nearly as much as you liked her, you owe me a goddamned answer."

To her credit, my mother tried to maintain her composure. I saw her expression at war with itself, slipping between apathetic and twisted. But I had thrown too much at her at one—within seconds, her shoulder slumped, her head dropped, and she looked up at me with very tired eyes.

It was a moment before she spoke.

"Have I ever told you about your father?" she asked.

I shook my head. I'd never thought it strange, but I knew very little about my father. I'd seen a few pictures of him, but my mother never kept them out, and she never talked about him, either. I always assumed that it was just too painful for her, though I'd doubted for a long time that she was even capable of feeling such pain.

"Your dad was a soldier," she said, toying with her hands. "An army lieutenant. We met in high school, way, way back, and fell in love. We got married straight after graduation, because he was planning to enlist and I had college starting in the fall. He rarely came home for longer than a few weeks, but when we were twenty, he was put on leave for a full two years. And that was just perfect, because we were expecting a baby. A daughter. And her name was Rosemary.

"Everything was perfect for those two years, and even after. He stayed safe and visited when he could. Ten years later, he received word that his service time was over. He came home. We were a family again. And then we had another daughter on the way—you—and we were so happy. Rosemary was excited to have a sister, and your father was ready to raise a child...but just after you were born, he received news that he was needed in the army again.

"In mid-ninety-seven, I got a letter," she continued, her breath hitching. "Your father had been among a group of men whose bunker had been bombed. He was in a coma, being sent home, but they didn't know if he would ever wake up. I was devastated, of course. I was desperate, praying constantly that he would wake up and everything would be all right. But for the first time, God didn't help, and I didn't know what to do.

"That's when they found me."

She took a shaky pause, her lips quivering in the silence. I was paralyzed by her sudden change, and could only stare as she tried to compose herself. She had never told me about my dad like this, except to say that he was a good man. But he was never here, so I didn't believe her.

"I don't know how they found me," she went on eventually, "but I guess that doesn't matter. They know who needs them, and they'll find you no matter what. I was driving home from work one night, and one of them was standing there on the side of the rode. It was dark, and all I saw was a polite young man in a suit. He asked for a ride into town, and I didn't think about the fact that I had never seen him in Callery before. So I agreed."

She shook her head, laughing a little. "God, I remember all this like it was yesterday. He didn't speak at all for about five minutes, until suddenly, he said, 'We can help you'. I asked him what he meant, and he started talking about my husband and the coma and how he knew people who could save him. He knew everything, somehow, even though he wasn't from here. He asked me, 'Do you believe in angels?'. And I did, of course. I thought he was one.

"He told me about his 'people', who weren't from here, and how they could help me for a small price. I was so blinded by the idea that you father could be okay that I didn't even think about what it would cost. When he asked me if I wanted their help, I accepted it. I just...I told him that I just needed to see my husband one more time."

A beat of silence followed, and I noticed that my mother's eyes were red around the rims. She murmured, "To this day, I don't know who these people are. But they take their deals very seriously. I said one more time; I got one more time. He came home, woke up for five minutes—and died in my arms. Heart failure, they said, but I knew. And it was too late to take it back; they were already preparing to collect their payment."

It hit me, quite suddenly, what she was talking about, and I felt sick. "Rosemary was the payment," I breathed, my eyes accusatory. My hands clenched into fists. "How could you agree to something like that?"

"I don't know!" A sob escaped my mother's lips. "Parker, these people are evil, but they are very thorough, very official. They have physical contracts and everything. After that first meeting, they never mentioned anything about the payment again. It was only after I'd received my part of the bargain that one of them came to my door, asking when my daughter would be ready to 'depart with them'. They wanted her because she was pure of soul. They take girls like your sister and sacrifice them, then keep their souls trapped in their underworld, whatever it is. I tried everything. Praying, bargaining. But I couldn't fight them; I was one person. And eventually, through her dreams, they reached Rosemary and took her away."

I swallowed. Souls. Underworld. "Incubi," I said, though I knew now that this was not exactly correct. "Dream creatures. I went to see...someone, and she said that's what they are."

My mother shrugged. "Incubus, demon, devil. They're all the same, but I don't know if that's truly what I was dealing with. These creatures were some kind of darker breed, and they don't stop for anyone."

I took an anxious breath. "And now they're coming after me."

My mother did not respond. Her eyes flicked downward, so filled with guilt that I actually felt pain for her. It was warm in the sun room, but there was a chill inside of me. How long would I have, really, before they came for me? I knew they would, and suddenly, the fear was immeasurable.

"Mom," I said after a while, twisting a lock of hair around one finger, "I have another question."

She looked up. "Sure, sweetheart, anything."

She never called me sweetheart before.

I stared at the table, forming my question. "When you went away on Sunday," I said haltingly, "it wasn't a business trip, was it?"

Silence. I heard the wind whistling outside, breathing through the trees. Logan's snores drifted in quietly from the living room. But for a long moment, in the little sun room, it was deadly quiet.

Then my mother heaved a broken sigh, slowly shaking her head.

"No, Parker, I was with them," she whispered. "Bargaining for your life."

Chapter 17

I stared at my mother and she stared back, our anxious gazes tethered by an invisible line of sight. My heartbeat was suddenly very loud, pulsing through my body and echoing in my ears. I was surprised that she couldn't hear it, because the sound was deafening.

"I went back to the place where I had seen that first man," she continued, "some highway strand outside of town. They knew I was coming. They always know."

"And they attacked you," I finished, pulling my legs to my chest. My mom's shoulders were slumped, her head bowed into the palm of her hand.

"Not at first." Her voice was soft. "At first, they greeted me—as if I was actually welcome amongst their kind. They pretended that they didn't know that I knew what they were planning. It wasn't much of a meeting really, in the woods off the side of the road, so one of them, a woman, suggested we talk over dinner. Which was actually ridiculous, because these are demons for God's sake, and they'd just invited me to dinner.

Demons invited me to dinner. Does that sound crazy to you, too?"

I didn't blink. "No."

Mom sighed. "Well, they did. And we went to some Italian place in Butler, three of the...creatures and I." With a shake of her head, her lips curl into a disbelieving smile. "We just sat there, like business partners having a meeting. Except that they didn't order anything, and I don't think the waitress could see them either, because when I asked them if they wanted to order anything, she just stared at me. Christ, I probably seemed out of my mind."

That's how I've been feeling lately, I thought silently. I didn't say it though, and let my mother continue.

"Long story short, after skirting around the topic for all of dinner, I finally told them that they weren't allowed to touch you, that I wouldn't condone it. They just laughed. And then they left. They left money on the table and left. I chased after them, of course, because I wasn't about to let them get away with doing this to you. I threatened them. They weren't happy about that. I was stupid; I should have realized when I'd gone to far. But I was so naively confident that I just kept pushing until finally, they snapped. And that's when they attacked me. I wasn't hurt badly; the injuries were mild enough that I could make my way back to my car. That was my warning, though. I'm not meant to interfere."

A surge of anger jolted through me at the thought of these creatures, these men (and apparently women) in glossy back, beating my mother on the side of the street for having the audacity to try to protect me. But running parallel with the fury was a surprising rush of affection for the woman before me, because I now had confirmation that she really did care about me. The demons and attacks and inevitable doom were still present, but so was the fact that my mother was willing to risk her life to keep me safe.

I didn't want her to do that.

Shifting abruptly, I reached into the pocket of my pajama pants and pulled out the crumpled business card from Laury.

Laury Lincoln, it read. Psychic Medium. No Appointments Necessary, Always On Call.

Following these words was a phone number in sharp blue type. Always On Call. I hoped that always was a solemn promise. I squeezed the card in my hand, then held it out to my mother.

"Aubrey took me to see this girl last night," I said. "She's, um, a medium. She knows about demons and incubi and stuff, and she—well, she's been...in touch with Rosemary. I'm supposed to call her if I ever need help. I think she might know how to get rid of these things."

With quivering fingers, my mother pulled the slip of paper from my hand. She scanned over it, her face gaunt, her lips silently mouthing the words. She seemed to read it several times. After a moment, she set the card down in her lap, looking up at me with eyes full of parental concern.

"It's your choice, Parker," she said. "Do you want to call her?"

I thought about it. I thought about how ridiculous it was, trying to schedule some kind of exorcism with a twenty-two year old psychic. But my situation was far past normal, and at this point, I was going to take any out I could get. This was real. This was happening. I needed help.

"Yeah, I do," I murmured eventually, taking the card back and rubbing it between my fingertips. Somehow, the solid familiarity of the paper made me calmer.

Nodding, my mother reached into her purse beside her and pulled out her shining silver cellphone. After a breath of a pause, she held it out to me, her expression very solemn.

"I'll let you dial."

For the second night in a row, I couldn't sleep. I told my mom I would try to get some rest, that I wouldn't worry about the impending meeting with Laury (or my impending doom). But as soon as she went up to bed around two o'clock in the morning, I realized that there was no way that I would ever be able to go back upstairs to my room. Broken light bulb shards aside, I knew that it would simply be impossible for me to make it through the night up there alone, period.

So I strained for some semblance of normality, and quietly heated up a cup of hot chocolate—low fat, according to the package. I settled into the chair closest to the living room, where I had a clear view of Logan, asleep on the couch. Even in his unconscious state, just seeing evidence of his breath was enough to keep me sane.

Or at least, as sane as I could hope to be.

I didn't realize until after I was situated that there nothing down here to keep me occupied: my books, my iPod, and even my phone were all upstairs, which just so happened to be the last place I was about to go. The only option I had left was to sit there, glassy-eyed, and try not to burn my tongue on sips of scalding cocoa.

It was so quiet; the deadly kind of quiet that sets in just before the demon attack in a horror film. It was that heavy silence that feels as if your ears have been stuffed with cotton and your eyelids pried apart with tweezers. And in that kind of soundless existence, it's impossible to turn off your mind.

Mine whirred at full-speed, all of my thoughts clambering over each other, shouting to be heard amidst the general cacophony. I picked out the memory of Laury's voice among all the straggling sounds, the only words she'd said to me when I'd called her earlier that night: "Expect me in the morning."

There was no greeting from either of us; I hadn't even opened my mouth. She had just known what I was going to ask, the same way she seemed to know everything else: inexplicably. I wasn't sure how, but I knew that come morning, I would find her at my front door. And hopefully, she would bring the solution to my problems.

I sighed, and it was much more than just an exhaled breath. It was a cinematic sigh, laced with worry and confusion and complete, utter exhaustion, exhaustion that I couldn't conquer because sleep wasn't a viable option. Still, I allowed my eyes to flutter shut, knowing that I could sit like this forever and never attain a moment of peace. It was a classic case of mind over matter: my body could feel the fatigue seeping into my bones, but my brain was tactfully ignoring it. Sleep was the enemy, and I knew that well—but that didn't stop me from wishing I could simply forget, even if just for a little while.

With my eyes closed it was dark and silent, and I allowed my mind to wander. I thought I could hear the rustling of movement from somewhere to my right, and imagined that it was the handsome, ink-eyed men, waiting just out of sight for the perfect moment to strike. Was that notion fiction or reality? I could hardly discern between the two anymore. The thought made me tighten my grip on the piping cup of cocoa in front of me, which, though soothing, wasn't proving to be nearly as soporific as I had hoped.

"Trouble sleeping?"

The soft voice crept up from behind me, so sudden and unexpected that I went flailing back from the table, my chair tilting. The yellow mug mimicked my seat, tipping precariously onto its edge and teetering there. It would have fallen, too, if it weren't for the hand that shot out over my shoulder at last second, reaching for the handle and steadying the ceramic cup before its contents were emptied all over my lap.

Logan's sheepish smile came into view as he moved the mug away from the table's edge and dropped into the chair next to mine. His sketchbook, his prized possession, was tucked beneath his arm. He held a hand to his head of sleep-tousled hair, his green eyes meeting mine.

"Sorry?" he ventured, setting his sketchbook on the table. I shook my head, fighting the urge to just drop it into my hands and sleep for days.

"It's fine, you just surprised me," I replied. "What are you doing up?"

"I heard you out here, thought you might need company." He grinned, lopsided and lethargic.

I peered at my best friend out of the corner of my eye, watching him eye my mug of hot chocolate. "There's more on the stove," I told him.

He poured his own cupful and we sat in silence, staring at nothing, occasionally sipping, at a loss for words but certainly not emotions. Those hit the air in excess, like lightning streaks that crackled between our occasionally synergistic gazes.

Just as I was beginning to slip into a half-aware fugue, I felt the soft pressure of fingers against my arm. This time I relaxed, taking comfort in the familiarity of Logan's touch, and didn't open my eyes as I mumbled, "What?"

His response was quick and concerned: "Something's wrong. What is it?"

Nothing was the easy answer. Everything was the moody one. Mine was "Do you want a list?" and preceded by an incredulous snort.

"I mean it, Parker." Logan squeezed my arm gently, and though this was nothing if not normal behavior, I found myself hyper-aware of the feeling. "What's going on?"

I might have told him, if I'd been up for it. And in hindsight, doing so may have saved some things later on. But there were too many words involved in the explanation of the exploding bulbs, my mother's return, and the phone call to Laury, and my tongue was a deadweight in my mouth. This, I decided, could wait until the morning, when I could at least pretend to be alive and coherent.

"It's nothing. I'm just tired," I assured. A fierce yawn escaped my lips, proving my point. I was having trouble forming thoughts, not to mention keeping my eyes open. Staying conscious was growing significantly harder by the second, but idea of sleep made me cold. I felt my body betray me, swaying to the side under the pressure of exhaustion. Were it not for Logan, I would have ended up with a face full of cold linoleum.

As it was, I pitched embarrassingly into my best friend's outstretched arms. Juliette would have insisted that I did it on purpose. I would have been too tired to argue with her. I didn't even want to get up, to move from Logan's makeshift embrace, and it was because of more than just fatigue. It was also that his sweater was warm against my cheek, his heartbeat was steady, and his chin fit easily into place on top of my head.

"You need to sleep, Parker," he murmured, his mouth against my hair.

I groaned. "I can't. Nightmares."

Sighing, Logan shifted me away from him and held my shoulders so that I was forced to meet his eyes. "If you don't get some rest, you're not going to be able to get through another day," he told me sternly. "I know you're scared of the nightmares, but that's all they are. They're dreams. They can't hurt you."

That's all they are. The casual phrase made my ribs itch with imminent laughter. Even after all of this, Logan could still make believe that this was all a crazy dream.

I wished I could be so lucky.

"Parker?"

"I can't," I said, and meant it. The idea of going to sleep, though undeniably appealing, struck a chord of fear in my gut as thoughts of my dreamland visitors materialized. The shaking bed; the shattering bulbs; the dark fingers brushing my face: I couldn't handle it, and I could no longer fool myself into thinking that I could.

"You can't just not sleep," Logan insisted.

I shrugged, fixing him with a halfhearted glare. "Well, I'm not going back upstairs, so...watch me."

I didn't have to say anything more. When you know someone for a long time, they can read all your thoughts through your eyes, through the little micro-expressions that flutter across your face. Logan didn't ask, but his gaze flickered curiously toward the stairs. His hands were still on my shoulders, but he pulled one away to rake it through his hair.

"You believe it, don't you? All of it? Everything that Laury said?"

I hunched over, lifting my shoulders to my ears in a silent shrug. "I can't not," I admitted. "You're my best friend, Logan, but this isn't happening to you. I don't know much more than you do, but I know that you can't give a textbook definition to whatever is happening to me. You need to stop worrying over the fact that this is something you don't understand."

Pressing my lips together, I glanced over Logan's shoulder, at the open doorway to the darkened sun room. Is it possible that only an hour ago, my mother and I sat there and dug up family secrets? And back an hour more, translucent shards of glass rained down from my ceiling? Time, I thought, was finding every way to confound me. It seemed hard to even focus on the here and the now.

But in this present, Logan was looking at me incredulously, a frustrated scoff leaping from his lips. He shook his head, reaching down to grab the base of my chair and pull it toward him, so that we were face to face.

"You think that's what I'm worried about?" he demanded. "Parker, are you even thinking? I realized that I don't understand this ages ago. And I'm still trying, but to be honest, I don't even care about that anymore." He leaned closer, lightly shaking my shoulders. "I'm worried about you, okay? You're been my best friend, and I just want you to be all right."

"I—" I swallowed hard, feeling my heartbeat kick into high gear. I wasn't sure, though, whether that was because of fear, or the close proximity of Logan's face to mine. My eyes darted, searching for a distant focus, but eventually ricocheted back to the pale green orbs right in front of me.

It was another one of those moments, like the one in Logan's living room, where I knew what was about to happen. I knew from the look in Logan's eyes, the hammering of my heart, the shrinking distance between our lips. Warning bells were going off in my head, because it was obvious: he was about to kiss me. Right now, in the middle of my kitchen at two in the morning, in the middle of so many other issues that were vastly larger than this, he was going to do something as painfully simple as pressing his lips against mine.

It couldn't have been too painful though, I suppose, because I found myself kissing him back. And it wasn't hesitant or awkward like the other times; this was the legitimate, sloppy breed of kissing best exhibited in sappy chick-flicks. Logan's hands slipped from my shoulders to rest on the small of my back, and somehow my fingers wound up laced behind his neck.

I didn't know what I was doing, but I suppose it was inevitable; and in some strange way, it felt right. There was still a lingering sense of this is my best friend, think is wrong in the back of my mind, but I managed to push it away long enough to savor the moment. At least, for as long as I could.

My eyes had drifted shut. This, I thought, was natural, because it wouldn't do to be staring at someone as you kissed them. But as I felt the need for air blooming in my lungs, I let them slip open to peer lazily over Logan's shoulder.

The auburn-haired boy was standing in the doorway.

I tore myself away from Logan, a hoarse shriek ripping from my throat as I locked eyes with the boy's ardent glare. His jaw was clenched, his arms crossed. I couldn't hold his gaze for more than a second, though, because my chair tipped, teetering at such an angle that I couldn't stop it from hitting the ground with a wooden clang and dumping me onto the floor. My head smacked painfully against the linoleum, but I was grateful for the subsequent blurring of my vision. I couldn't see the boy any longer—the picture of his onyx eyes was only in my head.

"Parker! Oh God, are you okay?" I couldn't see Logan either, for a moment, until my sight cleared. And when it did, I scrambled onto my knees, swallowing my buzzing fear to check the sun room doorway. The auburn-haired young man had disappeared. Flickering in and out of sight was their specialty, it seemed. They never waited to see the terror left in their wake.

I let Logan help me into a sitting position against the wall beside the refrigerator, trying to make sense of his garbled words through the rushing of blood through my ears. I thought I heard myself say, "I'm fine," a few times, faintly, but it wasn't until Logan pressed his cool palm against my forehead that I jolted back to attention.

"Parker?" he prompted, looking worried. "What was it? What happened?"

I blinked myself back into reality, only barely managing to force out the words, "He was here." Groaning, I pressed the heels of my hands over my eyes and let my head fall back against the wall. Logan rubbed my shoulder, his touch reassuring but not erasing. The disapproving ebony eyes were still burning into my skull.

"Hey," Logan murmured, peeling my fingers away from my face, "what do you need?"

He didn't ask me who I was talking about. He didn't repeatedly ask if I was okay. He just sat there and held my hands and stared at me until I opened my eyes. I let my gaze wander over his face, taking in his dark, messy curls, his freckled face, his virescent eyes. His features were familiar and comforting, and I found myself wishing that I could rewind to when we were kissing, and make it so that I left my eyelids firmly lowered.

Logan stared at me, and I stared back, though the overhead fluorescents were making my eyes water. My fleece-clad legs were pulled up to my chest, but he still held my hands. I wanted to rip them away and cover my face, but at the same time, I didn't want him to ever let go. A part of me was convinced that if either of us moved, even by a mere millimeter, the auburn-haired boy would whisk in and drag me away.

It was entirely too much excitement for a single night.

"Parker, what do you need?" Logan's hushed voice was urgent now, because I had started up that strange shaking again, those tremors that attacked my entire body.

"Talk," I managed finally, through chattering teeth.

"Talk?" His eyebrows raised in confusion.

I bit my lip, stilling myself as much as I could. "Please. Just talk. And keep talking. I can't handle the silence."

He didn't ask. All he did was nod, slowly, and squeezed my hands. "Okay," he said. "Okay. I'll talk. I'm just going to go into the other room for a second to get a blanket, but I'll keep talking." He stood up, leaving my hands cold on my knees. "And I'm still talking." He slipped into the living room. "I'm still here, Parker, I'm just trying to find the—goddamn it, the blanket is stuck. One second, okay? I'm almost done. Just this stupid blanket is caught in the couch, but I'm getting it, I've—there, got it. All right, I'm walking back now, and I have a blanket, a really warm one, it's—"

As Logan slipped back into the light of the kitchen, I interjected, mumbling the words, "You know I love you, right?"

I stared at my feet as he froze there, in the doorway, the blanket in his hands. "How could I forget when you keep reminding me?" he teased gently. His lips curved up into a small grin as he swiped his sketchbook off the kitchen table. As he settled in beside me and pulled the purple quilt over both of our shoulders, he added, "But I love you too, Parker. Obviously."

I nudged him lightly, stretching out my legs as he shook the pencil out of his sketchbook and started talking again. His thoughts meandered and his words blurred the way I'd always know them to, but I was completely all right with listening to the simple cadence of his voice, focusing all the while on the way his socked foot would tap against mine every now and then, or the way our shoulders were pressed together. I tried to simultaneously block out the thoughts that were warning me against my own feelings and tell myself that this meant nothing, but in the end my brain was too tired to maintain any thoughts. Giving up, I let my head loll against Logan's shoulder and closed my eyes. It seemed that tonight, I was actually going to sleep.

Before I drifted off completely, I opened my eyes one last time to take a peek at the newest drawing in his sketchbook. It was a rough, penciled outline of a girl, hands by her side, mirrored necklace resting one her collarbone. Her features were detailed, though incomplete; Logan was still penciling in her hair. Behind her, faint but shaded, was a collection of humanoid, shadowy figures that loomed around her shoulders, menacing even on paper. The girl didn't seem scared, though, just resolute and impassive. I wished I could share her tranquility.

But I could, I suppose, do just that. After all—I knew who this girl was, standing there amidst the shadows. I saw her face every time I looked in the mirror, though she wasn't nearly as fearless in reality. Logan had drawn me as the girl I wished to be, standing calmly by myself and waiting for the darkness to take me away.

Chapter 18

Everything smelled like maple syrup when I opened my eyes. A hazy light filled my vision, momentarily blinding me as I felt behind myself and pushed up into a sitting position. The cushion beneath me was lumpy in all the wrong places, and there was a crick in my neck—most likely the consequence of spending half the night asleep on the kitchen floor. I could hear the faint sounds of conversation drifting casually into my ears: all murmured sounds with no finished words.

As I blinked myself fully awake, I realized that I was no longer in the kitchen, but on the living room couch, a thick quilt draped over my legs. Logan was no longer beside me, most likely having moved me to this more comfortable position at some point during the night. I could hear the low hum of his voice, though, from the other room.

Sighing, I swung my legs over the side of the couch and sat up, staring out the window at the street. It was a sunny day, though snow still caked the sidewalk. A snow plow sputtered past my house, raking up the muddy slush that was beginning to melt into the gutters. I waited until it had disappeared down the street before I coaxed myself to peel off the quilt and stand up, curling my toes into the pale carpet. My socks, it seemed, had fallen off during the night.

"Morning, sleepyhead," Aubrey said as I shuffled into the kitchen, yawning. She offered a wan smirk over her cup of coffee—Logan's coffee, the familiar smell of which was potent in the air. Logan himself was standing at the counter, brewing a fresh pot, and my mom sat next to Aubrey at the table. She, too, was sipping from a steaming mug, and that in itself was enough to stop me in my tracks for several seconds. My mother's aversion to caffeine was practically religious, yet here she was, gulping down the stuff like her life depended on it. And maybe—judging by her pallid complexion and the bags beneath her eyes—it did.

"Uh, hey," I mumbled belatedly, tucking a loose strand of hair behind my ear. My mom looked up and smiled, actually smiled, her lips curling into a tired crescent and her eyes crinkling at the corners. And maybe it was a little stiff, like a pair of new shoes she'd just tried on for size, but it was real and it was something.

"Good morning, Parker," she said softly, nodding at me. "How did you sleep?"

"Fine, thanks." As I said the words, I realized how true they were: the previous night, once I'd settled down for a second time, there were no nightmares, no shadow creatures—nothing to go bump in the night. For one sleep, they'd left my dreams alone.

"Do you want some?" Logan asked, turning to me from the counter and holding up the pot of coffee in his hand.

"Yeah, I'll come and get it." I padded across the room, wincing at the icy shock of cold tile against my bare feet, and pulled a white mug from the cabinet. I set it down beside Logan, leaning lightly into his shoulder as he filled the mug with coffee.

"Why didn't you tell me your mom came back?" he asked quietly, adding in my customary cream and sugar. "She said she's been back since last night."

I turned away, pretending to cough so he couldn't see my eyes. "I guess it just slipped my mind. And thanks." Nudging his elbow with mine, I took the mug from his outstretched hand and brought it up to my lips. Our eyes met briefly over the rim, his slightly narrowed with confusion. He would undoubtedly have some questions for me later, but that was a conversation meant for solitude, especially given the fact that we'd kissed yet again the night before. That, certainly, was something that needed to be addressed, but not until after everything. There were more important matters at hand.

So I just slid into a seat at the table beside my mother, my hands wrapped around the steaming mug. Logan sat down a moment later, his gaze quickly ricocheting off my face. I tilted my head, trying to convey that I would explain it to him later. That is, if Laury kept her word. If she didn't help me, and soon, I wasn't quite certain that there would be a later.

Contrary to popular belief, and the assumption that the voices in their heads would make for frazzled thoughts, psychics are surprisingly punctual. That is, assuming that all psychic mediums are of the same breed at Laury Lincoln, which, considering her individual eccentricity, is rather improbable.

She arrived at nine AM on the dot, about thirty minutes after I woke up. We were all still seated at the table up until then, fresh cups of coffee and Aubrey's pancakes in front of us. We ate in silence, apart from a few casual comments, but even those were only an attempt to pierce the quiet before it swallowed us whole.

"Weather outside is nice today," said Aubrey.

"Sure is," I agreed.

"Great coffee, Logan," said my mother.

"Thanks, Ms. Elway," Logan replied.

Those were the only words that passed between us, and before long, the thick quiet was verging on painful. As we ventured into our second stack of pancakes and the stares between us grew increasingly shifty, a blessing came in the form of a ringing doorbell—and with it, Laury Lincoln: psychic medium extraordinaire.

She pressed the bell several times when she arrived, sending a resounding, staccato echo throughout the house. From upstairs, where she lay recovering, Zipper's soft yips of announcement slid downstairs. No one moved for a moment, each of us caught in a lethargic state of delayed reaction. It was my mother who first blinked herself back into reality, setting her fork down next to her plate and looking at me expectantly.

I cleared my throat. "That must be Laury." Then, before anyone could react, I quickly added, "I'll get it," and stood up, swiftly exiting the room. I tightened my shoulders to ignore the confusion that was left in my wake.

As I hurried into the living room, I saw Laury through the window, standing in the melting snow on my front stoop and looking surprisingly normal. The only thing that was slightly disconcerting was the way her pale lips fluttered, mouthing a silent conversation entirely inside her head. Everything with her, it seemed, was likewise introspective.

I opened the door. "Hey, Laury."

"Oh, Parker!" she said in her lilting accent. She stopped just short of an I didn't see you there, as if she hadn't been the one to approach in the first place. Her eyes widened in brief surprise, but then gears seemed to shift in her head, and her lips formed a knowing smile.

"The skeptic wasn't expecting me, I see."

I stiffened, lowering my voice. "What do you mean? Did you, uh, read his mind?"

"Oh, no, darling," Laury murmured, chuckling. Her gaze slipped over my shoulder. "I can see it on his face."

Startled, I whirled around, my heartbeat stuttering for a moment until I registered the figure behind me as Logan. He stood just inside the door, eyes narrowed and mouth half open, staring past me at a very placid Laury Lincoln.

"What is she doing here?" he demanded.

Laury smirked, raising as eyebrow and stepping through the door without invitation. "I'm helping," she said simply, zipping out of her boots and parka seemingly without moving. Within moments, both articles lay on the hardwood of the foyer, and she stood in socks on the living room carpet.

"Your mother is wondering if she should offer me coffee," she stated, her unblinking eyes flicking toward the kitchen, "and Aubrey is hoping that her skeptical little brother doesn't blow up before I can work my magic." Laury smiled warmly at us, moving her doll-like body toward the kitchen. "If you don't mind, I should meet your mother."

"Of course," I murmured. Bemused, I watched Laury make her way into the kitchen, stepping daintily around Logan, who leaned away from her as if she carried the plague. As soon as she had disappeared through the doorway, he practically dived toward me, grabbing my hand and squeezing it.

"What is she doing here?" he repeated shrilly.

I swallowed, carefully pulling my fingers from his grip and taking a few steps back. "I called her last night. I talked about it with my mom, and we decided to call her. We thought it would be—"

"What, and you decided not to tell me?" he interrupted. "You just happened to forget to mention that some demon-worshiping, incubus-obsessed freak was coming over today? Who are you going to invite over next, Parker? The devil himself?"

An oddly loud giggle pierced the air from the kitchen, and Laury's voice sounded, seemingly in our heads. "Logan, you silly skeptic of a boy. Why invite the devil when he's already here?"

Everything seemed to freeze at that, and Logan and I locked gazes. Our bodies were tense, on edge, ready to spring; I could feel my lengthy nails digging into my palms. I didn't want to fight with Logan, not now, and I knew that he wanted peace as much as me. But when the only other option is fear, all we can do is hold tight to our anger and hope for the best.

Even if the best is, ultimately, the worst.

"She's insane," Logan hissed, finding his voice again. "That woman is completely out of her mind, and you've let her into your house. Do you understand what you've done?"

"Of course I do!" I snarled. "And last time I checked, I don't need your permission to have guests in my own home."

He struck at the air with a frustrated fist. "But I'm your best friend!"

"And I'm my own person!"

I tried to step back again, away from Logan, but my food caught on something and I stumbled on the rug. The object was Logan's overnight bag, and it tipped over, spilling a few of its contents on the floor—namely, his sketchbook, which flipped eerily to the drawing he had been working out the night before.

Whereas last night it had been a mere sketch, now the drawing was detailed and shaded, outlined heavily. I could practically see Logan there in my head, straining his eyes in the dim kitchen light at four in the morning and scribbling so hard that his pencil spat dust from its tip. Scoffing, I snatched up the sketchbook in one quick swoop and took a closer look at the page. The girl was finished now, and though she was still me, the solid resoluteness of her features had disappeared. It was the eyes, I realized: Logan had finished her eyes, and they were nothing more than an abyss of mortal terror. Behind her, dark and menacing, dozens of shadow creatures lurked. At first, I thought they had been created of dark scribbles, but as I brought the pad closer to my face, I realized that their figures were composed of a single word written over and over in a harsh, desperate scrawl.

Soon.

The word spun in an endless spiral, twisting over itself, letters braiding together and stepping on each other to sew themselves into one big, horrifying mass. As I watched, the shadows seemed to move, their lettered eyes shifting and their gaping maws leering. Biting back a shriek, I tossed the sketchbook into the air, stumbling back until I hit a wall. The wall, that was solid: that was real and firm and cold beneath my fingertips. It didn't move, just like that paper didn't move, couldn't have moved, because it wasn't alive.

That was impossible.

Logan fumbled to catch his sketchpad, pulling it quickly to his chest. He looked at the page as I caught my breath, and after his jaw had dropped adequately, I felt steady enough to clear my throat and speak.

"Guess I'm not the only one keeping secrets from their best friend," I snapped, albeit shakily. Logan, meanwhile, was shaking his head, first slowly and then with a sudden fervor, almost mechanically, so that his curls flew.

"No," he breathed. "I don't get it." His Adam's apple bobbed as he swallowed. "Parker"—he looked up at me, his eyes wide—"I didn't draw this. This wasn't me."

I laughed shrilly, hysterically. "Oh, is that so? Well, then, who did, d'you suppose?"

He shook his head, flipping through the other pages but finding nothing more. It was only that one drawing, that one, dark drawing. "I don't know, but—"

"The demons, maybe? The demons that you insist don't exist?" My tone was getting steadily higher-pitched, and I fought the urge to laugh again, to scream, to break down in furious hysterics.

Grunting, Logan lowered his sketchbook to his side. "They don't exist," he said flatly, coolly.

"You still believe that." I scoffed in disbelief. "I thought I'd finally gotten through to you last night, but you're as stubborn as ever."

"They don't exist," he repeated, not taking his eyes off me as he closed the pad and placed it on the ground. His toes curled anxiously into the carpet, an old habit of his. "They're not real, and you'd have to be a fool to believe in them."

I opened my hands at my sides, palms pressing into my fleece pajama pants, and felt my cheeks grow warm with anger as a sudden and unexpected whiff of rosemary hit my nose. She was here. She was real. And if my sister was real, so were they. Logan was wrong.

"I'm no fool," I said, my voice thick with barely-contained rage. "Neither is Laury, neither is Aubrey, and neither is my mother. If anyone is a fool here, it's you, Logan, because you're to damn blind to see what's right in front of your face."

He retorted immediately. "Maybe that's because it's not there to begin with."

"Except it is," I growled, frustration pulsing through me. "And you need to stop telling me that it isn't, because I'm not a helpless child. I can think for myself."

"Can you really?" Logan demanded, his tone bitingly sarcastic. "I guess that's why last night, all you could do was cower pathetically in the corner? Face it, Parker: you act tough, but all you are is scared. You're nothing but the helpless little kid you claim not to be. You're floundering."

Time, for a moment, seemed to come to a standstill. I felt the air around me being sucked into the ground, seeming to pull me with it. The words hurt, probably more than they should have, and the blow was like a wrecking ball to the face. I was frozen there, mouth open, caught in a limbo of gazes and pain as Logan realized just what he'd said.

"God," he murmured. "God, no, I didn't mean that. Parker, you're my best friend, you know I'd never say something like that and mean it, I—"

"But you did say it," I interjected quietly. "You can't take it back." He opened his mouth, but I lifted my hand to stop him and caught his eye. "It's okay, though, because you're right. I've been acting like a little kid, and I can't be that weak right now. I need to grow up, which means I need to stop being so scared and just face this situation head on. But it also means that I need to let go of the things that are dragging me down and figure out who my real friends are: the ones who'll accept me, flaws and all, no matter what."

"Parker—" Logan tried, but the words died in his throat. I felt the rattle of pain as our gazes collided once again, but I ignored it. Gulping down the emotions strewn across my features, I squared my shoulders and marched calmly past Logan, into the kitchen. It was dead silent in there: they had heard everything. Aubrey had her head in her hands, my mother looked shocked, and Laury just stared at me owlishly, a mug of coffee in her hands.

"If you're ready," I said, "I'd like to see what you have in my for taking care of my, ah, problem. I want them gone."

Laury nodded, slowly lowering her drink to the table and getting to her feet. Behind me, I heard the thud of footsteps, the jingle of keys, the slam of the door. I refused to let myself look back.

"Well, come on, then," Laury beckoned, passing me. She gave no destination, but somehow, I knew that we were going upstairs, to my room, where this all began. And somehow, I wasn't afraid. I wasn't anything, really. I was just numb.

We passed through the living room on our way to the stairs, and the echoing door had not lied: Logan was gone, sketchbook and all. But I didn't mind, because soon, I would be fixed. The monsters would be gone. The nightmares would cease to be. Soon, everything would be okay.

Soon.

CHAPTER 19

Aubrey caught my arm as we mounted the stairs, trailing behind Laury and my mother as they made their way up to my room. I tried to pull away, knowing what she was going to say to me, but she held tight. Her eyes bored into the back of my head until finally, sighing, I was forced to turn around.

"What?" I demanded crossly, belatedly yanking my arm away. The sharp movement knocked me off balance, and I had to grab onto the banister to keep myself from toppling down the stairs. Aubrey watched me with concern.

"Are you okay?" she asked, her tone solicitous. Though she said no more than that, it was pretty obvious that she wasn't talking about my near face-plant.

I shrugged. "Never better."

She hesitated. "When I go home, I'll...I'll talk to Logan. You two will be okay."

"I don't care. I'm fine," I snapped, before ducking my head and shuffling away down the hall. Out of the corner of my eye, I caught sight of Aubrey at the top of the stairs, pinching the freckled bridge of her nose.

By the time I got to my room, I'd managed to push the thought of Logan's departure out of my mind—at least momentarily. I tried to pretend that the familiar sound of an old car sputtering out of the culdesac wasn't him, that it was just another passing neighbor. And for some reason, it wasn't that hard; especially once I stepped through the open doorway of my room and found my mother panicking over the state of my floor.

Glass bits were still strewn about, with only the screw caps and support wires of the light bulbs still attached and swinging gently on electrical strings. My mother was stepping gingerly around the pieces in her house slippers, squealing, "Parker Sage, what happened in here?" as she attempted to pluck the shards out of the carpet. Laury, meanwhile, was walking straight into the thick of it, her shoes crunching over the little pieces. Her brows were knit in concentration, her eyes guarded as she scanned the room.

"They were here last night," she stated, and it wasn't a question. I doubted that she even needed to ask me, because it seemed that just by gazing at the aftermath, she could see the twisted events clearly in her mind. Still, I gave an affirmative nod.

I stood at the threshold of my room, staring at the glittering slivers and trying to make sense of the fact that this had happened only the night before. It had merely been hours, but it felt like days.

Aubrey said nothing when she finally came up beside me; her only reaction was a soft exhalation and the whispering rustle of her hair falling into her face. She, too, stayed parked in the doorway, and a moment later, my mom calmed down and stepped back toward the wall to join us. The three of us watched silently as Laury prowled around the room, stopping occasionally to pick up a shard or touch a random piece of furniture.

"I hope you're actually doing something productive," Aubrey said after a moment, raising her eyebrows as Laury dropped to her stomach and peeked beneath the bed.

"Hm? Oh, very much so." Laury grunted as she hauled herself back to her feet. "I'm feeling a very strong source of paranormal energy from somewhere in this room, but I can't seem to place it." Craning her neck, she began to run her hand along the wall. With her big eyes and jerky movements, she looked like a proper supernatural investigator—or whatever title is given to the people with night vision cameras who peruse old buildings at night and assume that every little creak is ghost activity.

"I feel like we're in an episode of Ghostbusters," I joked, before realizing that was something Logan would have said, if he had been there.

"Except that those are fake, darling," Laury said. "This, on the other hand, is quite real." Frowning, she peeled her hand away from the wall; as she did so, her body suddenly went rigid. She was standing next to my vanity, adjacent to my bed, but she immediately dived toward the pillow that rested on my headboard. The pillow didn't stand a chance against her prying hands, and it went flying across the room, hitting the wall with a muffled thump.

"Here," she breathed, lifting something carefully from the surface of the mattress with both hands. "Oh, it's just radiating energy." She smiled at me, her big eyes widening further, if that was even possible. "Clever, is what they are. Immeasurably clever."

Next to me, my mother stepped forward, craning her neck to see what Laury held in her hands. "What is that?" she questioned warily. I was curious too, but had no desire to put my bare feet up against a carpet full of glass. Thankfully, Laury provided the answer a moment later, accompanied by a tenacious smirk.

"It's a necklace." Shaking her head knowingly, she held up the golden chain. At the end of its delicate length spun a pendant, a gold mirror on a chain.

Of course, I thought silently. After Logan had inexplicably found Rosemary's necklace in his car, I'd stowed it under my pillow and completely forgotten about it. All I could think about when I saw it was the pitch black eye I'd seen reflected in the mirror, and though it had once brought me comfort, that necklace became an untouchable omen. I'd shoved it away in hopes of it disappearing, but at the same time, I hadn't wanted it be to far away.

"Wait a minute," my mom said suddenly, tiptoeing around the glass to stop at Laury's side. "I know that necklace. That was Rose's necklace; her father gave it to her. They—they found it on her body when they pulled her up from the lake. But how is it here?"

"I found it years ago," I explained softly. "You told me to get rid of it, but I kept it anyway. I just found it again by accident about a week ago. And I don't know how, but I think it's been protecting me."

At that, Laury let out a sudden bark of laughter. She waggled the charm so that it caught the light and spluttered, "This?

Protecting you? Oh, darling, no. With this under your pillow, you've been drawing those demons to yourself like moths to a flame." She closed one eye and gazed into the mirror. "The gaps between worlds are unbelievably thin, Parker. This necklace is an easy gateway from theirs to ours."

I eyed the necklace, suddenly leery. I'd worn it around my neck; it'd kept the nightmares at bay. Or so I'd thought, at least.

"What do you mean, a gateway?" I said carefully.

"I mean exactly that. It's a passage, a pathway for these creatures to filter into our world. They're not from here; they don't belong here. The only way for them to get here is through charms and trickery."

"Why can't we just destroy it, then?" I asked fervently. "Break the necklace, block the path. Isn't that all we have to do?"

Laury shook her head. "Not quite, I'm afraid. The surface of the mirror has already cracked, and it hasn't put a damper on their strength at all. You have to remember that these creatures are the stuff of nightmares; they don't exist in a physical state as we know it. And so, this necklace doesn't work on a physical level. It's controlled through the subconscious: specifically, your subconscious. Which, like everyone's, is most active when you're asleep. That's why they can come through in such full force in your dreams. They thrive on the inner workings of the human mind, but in truth our brains contain more strength that they could ever imagine."

Her eyes glinting, Laury pinched the mirror between two fingers, casting the reflected morning light onto the wall. "There's power up there," she said solemnly, tapping her head. "Real, formidable power. Psychologically speaking, we are so hopelessly complex that completely understanding our nature is impossible. Which can work to your advantage in undoing this gateway—because I want you to destroy it through your dreams."

"Have you ever heard of lucid dreaming?" Laury was sitting across from me on my bed, her hands pressed together and angled toward me. Aubrey was perched next to her, hugging her knees to her chest.

"Kind of," I replied, chewing on my thumbnail. "Isn't it just when you wake up in a dream and know that you're dreaming?"

"Oh, it's more than that," my mother interjected, looking up from her spot on the floor, where she was meticulously dislodging glass shards from the carpet. "When you're in a lucid dream, you have the ability to control what's happening around you. Everything in the dream is under your command—almost as if you're awake. You become the pilot of your own subconscious mind."

"Precisely," Laury agreed. She pressed her palms against her knees, rocking slightly on the comforter. "It's essentially the twin of sleep paralysis; the yin to its yang. The difference is that in lucid dreams, you control your dreams—in sleep paralysis, your dreams control you."

I fixed my gaze on the wall above my bookshelf, absorbing that. "I could control my dreams," I murmured.

"You easily could. And that, darling, is exactly what I want you to do. I want you to take control of your dreams and obliterate these creatures from the inside out. If we only destroy the necklace, all it will do is slow them down. It won't stop them. But they've rooted a connection deep in your mind, and if you can cut that off, this little thing will be quite useless."

I cast a glance down at the necklace lying between us on the comforter. My fingers itched to pick it up and crush it like sugar glass in my fist, but another part of me felt guilty for wanting to mar it in the first place. The tarnished chain and cracked charm belonged to my sister, and even though their true purpose had been revealed, I couldn't help but feel like this was my last connection to Rosemary; like if it went away, so would she.

I was selfish, though, and when it came down to either preserving or forfeiting my life, my choice was obvious: I would do everything it took to stay alive. After all, there was no sense in relinquishing my existence in favor of trying to maintain the memory of a long dead girl. Rosemary, wherever she was now, seemed to be striving to keep me away from the clutches of the dream creatures. I was no different. And, guilty or not, I was going to stop the nightmares in their tracks.

This, undoubtedly, was the endgame.

"I'll talk you through everything," Laury assured me, swinging herself off my bed. "Just lie back and close your eyes."

I blinked, startled by the medium's fast pace. "Wait a second," I stalled. "Can't you explain anything more? Like, say, how I'm even supposed to know what this 'connection' is? I can't read your mind, Laury. How will I know what to do?"

She stared at me owlishly, tilting her head and tugging at her blonde hair. "Oh, believe me, darling. You'll know." We held gazes for a moment, and I felt a chill pass through me—there was something about Laury's eyes that made me feel as if my thoughts were being plucked out and broadcast to the world. "Now please, lie down," she continued. "You'll be safe."

After a moment of hesitation, I did as she said, letting my eyes drift shut and shrouding my view of the room in black. "I'm trusting you," I reminded her, unable to keep a trace anxiety out of my voice.

"And you might be surprised to find that I'm actually a trustworthy person."

I merely snorted in response as I shifted on my bed, attempting to find a comfortable position. The early sunlight, streaming through my window, was glaring into my eyelids. I felt vulnerable, exposed—not safe. Still, who was I to trust, if not Laury? I had little choice but to place the matter in her presumably capable hands.

"Be careful, sweetheart," my mother said softly, her voice coming from somewhere to my left.

"Mom. I'm taking a nap, not going into battle."

She said nothing.

"All right, Parker," Laury said briskly. "Are you ready?"

I let out a long breath between clenched teeth and curled my bare toes. "Have to be, I guess."

"Good answer."

The sheets rustled near my ear, and I felt something cool and thin encircle my neck. My first reaction was to shrink away, but Laury's voice stopped me. "It's just the necklace," she said. "It needs to be close by."

The chain felt like ice, but I didn't complain.

After a moment, Laury spoke again. "I need you to take deep breaths. Big ones. Six seconds in, six seconds out. And you need to keep breathing like that until you absolutely can't any longer. Okay?"

In response, I sucked in a lungful of air, holding it for a moment before breathing it all out. Then another inhalation; then another. Deep breath in, deep breath out.

"Next thing." Laury's voice sounded farther away now. "Try to count your breaths. Focus on them completely, and number them in your head as you take them."

One...two...three.

"Block out every sound around you, even my voice. Concentrate only on your breaths, and try to become acquainted with your mind. As you approach sleep, try to discern between whether or not you are in a dream."

She might have said something after that, but I can't be sure; I did what she said and tuned out her voice. It was an odd feeling, as if rather than plunging straight into sleep, I was approaching it up staircase, all the while being completely aware of my ascension . Each footfall was a new breath; each breath was another number. And as the numbers grew, my connection with reality grew ever thinner.

Time seemed to stop working as I lay there, and though I was still counting my breaths, I wasn't sure of the number, nor was I aware of whether or not I was actually still breathing. I had entered the fugue state between consciousness and reality, and even that was fading fast. I tried to keep up a steady count, but a moment later, I spiraled into sleep.

I must have lost several seconds to darkness, as is customary before waking into a dream, but when I regained some sort of spatial awareness, I found that there was still no light anywhere around me. It wasn't that it was dark; it was more like my eyes were closed. Except that, wherever I was, I didn't seem to have eyes.

Then, suddenly, with a jolting shock, all the feeling rushed back into my limbs. My eyes flew open, and I found myself lying on my back, looking up at something gray and hazy. I sat up slowly, stuck out an arm and wiggled my fingers. They moved on command, but were blurry around the edges. And, like every other part of me, they seemed weightless. It was akin to how they say it feels to be on the moon: how gravity is gone, and with it, every ounce of mass that your body held on earth. It seemed to me that if I were to jump, I'd simply float away.

I knew where I was; it was obvious, judging by my slightly distorted vision and the strange dull tinge to the foggy air around me. Yet at the same time, it felt so much more real than what it was, so much more lucid. I stood carefully, deliberately placing my feet and marveling at their compliance. This was a dream, and I knew that. Somewhere, a million miles up, my body lay asleep. But here I was, in the heart of my subconscious, inside my head, and I was wide awake.

This was a dream.

And I was in control.

CHAPTER 20

Everything was gray. All that I could see was a dense, heavy fog that crept stealthily into my vision and hid any figures that might have been lurking in the vicinity. I was rooted to the spot in the midst of all that filmy nothingness, adjusting my blurry vision every few seconds and trying to remind myself that this was not real life. Because no matter how hard I drilled that fact into my mind, there was still a lingering fear of my odd blindness, and a solid conviction that wherever I was, I was not safe.

Though I was completely stationary, everything around me seemed to be in motion, swirling and shifting and distorting my senses until directions became nonexistent. The only thing I was certain of was that there was something solid beneath my feet, but the fog was so thick that I couldn't see my shoes, if I was even wearing any. I had arms, I had legs—I could feel them—but when I reached out, they were concealed in gray mist. And in my head, everything felt not quite there, a little dizzy, as if I'd stomached a few too many loop-d-loops on a theme park roller coaster. Thus, when I began to hear faint whispers in the back of my mind, I told myself that it was simply my spinning subconscious in action.

Until they got louder.

Focus, Parker, urged the whisper. This is your dream—your rules.

I squeezed my eyes shut and brought up my hand to pinch the bridge of my nose. That little guiding voice is generally supposed to know best, so I trusted its murmured words and, behind drooped lids, imagined that the fog was thinning.

Good, Parker, very good.

I peeled my eyes open very slowly, suddenly feeling incredibly exposed. It was that sensation of being watched, that pressure drifting over your shoulders that doesn't exist. I felt it deep in the rush of my bloodstream—the unmistakable feeling of eyes on me. It was an itch I couldn't scratch, and when I looked up to see nothing but gray again, its faint tickle spurred me to turn on my heel and greet the watcher behind me.

I found people and a voice.

The people registered first, because they were evidently visible. Blurry on the edges, sure, but still people nonetheless. It was a great crowd, dozens of bodies thick, just hundreds of humans milling around. Their destination seemed to be nonexistent; they wandered as one being, but with the listless steps of individuals.

The voice came back as I watched these people from some kind of elevated vantage point. It begun as low buzzing in the back of my head, like static on a radio, before almost seeming to tune itself until the electric feedback became words.

Can you hear me, Parker?

I glanced over my shoulder automatically, thinking that I was being addressed from somewhere behind me. But even as I whirled, I knew that I would find nothing—I knew that the voice was inside my head. And I knew, instinctively, whom it belonged to.

"Yeah. Hey, Laury," I said, though I neither felt my lips move nor heard any audible trace of my voice. In comparison to the situation, my words sounded pedestrian and lame, but the fact that I was communicating with someone someone in the waking world made me slightly less concerned about being profound.

You're on a hill, observed Laury—or rather, her disembodied voice. You need to get off of it. Whatever you're looking for, it's down.

"You can see where I am." It wasn't a question, and I didn't move from my place. "How?"

I'm inside your head, at the pit of your consciousness. I have, essentially, infiltrated your dreaming mind. Whatever you see, I see.

I blinked at that, slightly disconcerted by the idea of another person borrowing my eyes. I felt the sudden need to touch my face, just to make sure I was real. My skin felt slightly filmy, like gauze, but it was there. Maybe it was only the faux senses of a dreamer, but it was convincing enough.

Please tell me you're not just going to stand there and admire yourself, Laury snapped after a moment. We haven't got all day.

"Right." I shook my head. "I'm on it."

With light footfalls, I began to make my way down the hill. Each step seemed to hover a little bit off the ground, and though I knew that I was traveling down an incline, it felt for all the world like I was strolling across a completely flat surface. The only indication that I was actually moving was the fact that I was obviously getting closer to the crowd. Every time my feet met with the cloudy ground, I was one step lower, one step nearer, one little step closer to ending it all.

Remember, Parker, that this is all you, Laury said as I reached the people. Everything in this place is of your own creation, and you can control it as will.

Her words washed over me, and I made some sort of affirmative sound in the back of my throat as I merged with the crowd. Almost immediately, I felt a hundred pairs of eyes swivel toward me and rest on my face, blankly appraising this newcomer to their world.

My world, I corrected. This was my world, my dream—it didn't even exist. So, if I didn't want these people to look at me, all I had to do was wish their attention away.

Blink.

Just like that, all the endless bodies were strolling along again, their focus diverted in a fraction of a second. I thought I heard Laury mumbling some word of praise, but her voice was so quiet that I shelved it in the back of my mind and just kept walking.

As I ducked and elbowed my way through the fuzzy group, I once again became increasingly aware of a stare drilling into the back of my neck. I swallowed hard and willed it away, but the unseen gaze did not waver.

"Laury," I mumbled, slowing down, "there's someone watching me."

The medium swallowed—and odd sound to hear inside one's head—and replied, Turn around, then.

With some trepidation, I did as she said, cringing prematurely in anticipation of the worst. But rather than a deformed creature from the depths of my nightmares, I found that staring back at me was none other than Logan Dearborn.

"Laury," I hissed.

This Logan was a dream creation too—I had to remind myself of that. Yet despite the soft light around his figure and the lack of recognition in his eyes, there was something more alive about him, as if he had been given another layer of solidity.

"Laury, why is he following me?" I asked clearly, not daring to break eye contact with the pale green eyes of this imaginary Logan.

It happens sometimes, Laury said, sounding frustrated, perplexed, and awed simultaneously. You're in control, but only because you've managed to put a leash on your subconscious. It still has some leeway, and occasionally it'll materialize the people and things that you need or want most.

"But I don't get it," I replied, beginning to feel seriously uncomfortable with this confrontation. "I wasn't even thinking about him."

The medium laughed brightly. Oh, but darling, this is your subconscious. It knows you better than you know yourself.

I chewed on my bottom lip, staring at the recreation of my best friend. That this wasn't the Logan who was furious with me, who had stormed out of my house less than an hour before; this was an illusion. But that was hard to fathom, especially when I saw the tips of his sneakers lifting as his toes curled in that old habit, or as I imagined that I could smell a whiff of his familiar toothpaste.

"What do I do?" I was aware that, though no words had actually left my lips, my voice sounded desperate. I took a step back, only to have a blank-faced Logan take a step forward. I shuffled backwards again, and we repeated this awkward dance until Laury broke the silence.

You need to keep going, Parker, Laury said. Do your best to ignore him and just find what you're looking for.

"Sure," I said shakily, walking backwards and nervously licking my lips. To distract myself, I asked, "Just wondering, though, what exactly am I looking for?"

I could hear the smirk in Laury's voice. Oh, trust me, darling. You'll know.

I kept walking. Logan kept following. I wound my way through the crowd and tried to ignore the feeling of his eyes on the back of my neck. After a while, I began to recognize random faces in the throng of people. Dr. Hennessy, girls from my old swim team, Stella from across the street. Every now and then they'd find their way into my vision, their gazes sweeping impassively over my features.

Time in dreams is always strangely distorted, sometimes freezing and sometimes catapulting forward at light speed. There were moments when I would blink and feel my consciousness fold around me, trying to pry the control of the dream out of my hands. Time would come to an infinitesimal standstill, and my legs would quiver like I'd just stepped aboard a rocking boat. It was a game of tug-of-war between two parts of my mind; a silent battle over lucidity. And all the while, as chaos filled my head and faces shimmered around me, Logan remained at my heels, a fact in the midst of all the unreality.

When I stepped, he stepped. When I froze, he did the same. It was in equal parts chilling and fascinating; reassuring and unnerving; eerie and completely unsurprising. A few times, quite abruptly, I felt this pull from behind me, some kind of magnetic attraction that begged me to turn around, run back to the completely imagined figure of my best friend. When that happened, Laury would murmur something in my head about continuing, and I'd sever the connection and trudge on.

That worked for a while—until out of the blue, everything began to fade. My vision became hazy and discolored, nearly blinding me, and the fog returned so completely that it blurred and muffled everything. All I knew was that Logan was still behind me, still standing there, still endlessly staring and driving me mad.

I didn't know where he was, where anything was, but I whirled around and around, a strange anger building in my chest. I heard Laury's distressed voice, demanding to know what I was doing, but I was hardly sure myself. I could only strike out blindly, furiously, and try to steal back the power that had been wrested away from me and was suddenly being used to turn my dream into a nightmare.

And then it went away.

Just like that: the fog, the fury, the fear; they all disappeared as quickly as they had come and left me there, standing not in the endlessly gray, crowded prison of before, but in a section of the woods behind my house. I knew this place well—everything down to the woodsy smells had been perfectly recreated in my mind.

I was facing a tree. Its bark and leaves were surprisingly clear, but I still knew it was a dream because of the way its gnarled trunk twisted and rose into infinity. That, and the omnipresent feeling of Logan's gaze, which seemed to have become a permanent fixture in this dreamland.

I sighed inwardly, staring down at my hands. From somewhere that seemed farther than before, Laury's faint voice trilled, Parker? What just happened? Where did you go?

"I didn't do anything," I replied, annoyed. "It just happened. Can't you see me?"

I can't see anything, and I can hardly hear you. You've practically disappeared.

Those words made me straighten slightly, as all of a sudden, I felt the gazes on my back multiply. I heard a sharp intake of breath leave my lips, and Laury called my name.

Turn around, uttered a voice, this one different, foreign. Turn around.

Slowly, fearfully, I turned around, praying that the only figure I'd find behind me would be the same, emotionless Logan. But even as my feet shuffled across fallen pine needles, I knew it wouldn't be him. Not here, in this scene. When I made it all the way around, my suspicions were confirmed: no Logan. Instead, before me lay an endless expanse of shark-like grins, penguin suits, and a million pairs of ebony eyes.

"Laury," I whispered, hardly daring to breathe. "They're here."

They leered at me.

I heard a muttered expletive from Laury's end, then a long, calming breath. They're all in your head, Parker, she reminded me. This is imaginary. No matter how real it feels, it's your dream, your control.

My dream, my control.

I took a shaky breath, staring at the mass head on. These were the men from my nightmares, the ones who had haunted me day and night, taking it upon themselves to make my life hell. But here, for once, they weren't real. They were products of my imagination, and I had power over them all. So if I were to move my hand just there...

Let the little girl pretend she's in control.

I jumped back, having been assaulted once again by that smooth, low, unfamiliar voice. My fingers flew to the side of my neck, a habit even in my dreams, and I was imagined that there was a pulse. My heartbeat—strong and real even though it wasn't, a steady drumbeat that slowly, slowly calmed me down.

Deep breath in, deep breath out, and the monsters began to move. As I had previously intended, they began to spread apart, separating at the center to create a pathway between them. And while they moved, their bodies began to shift, morphing from humanoid figures into tall, looming shadows.

Another huge, gulping breath (these were becoming second nature), and I took a step forward, then another, scuffing the uneven ground with the heels of my shoes. Laury asked what I was doing and I told her, quietly, all the while keeping my eye on the shadows.

They parted like the Red Sea to Moses' staff, and I tried to forget that though they had spread, the figures were still here, encasing me in a semi-transparent tunnel. It's just a dream, I told myself again and again, as fear struck like lightning. I went so far as to close my eyes and wish that Logan would once again appear behind me. My thoughts were so shaky, though, that nothing happened.

At the end of the dense tunnel, the creatures had congealed to form a solid, dark wall. The beginnings of panic clawed at my throat and tinted my vision red with fear. I glanced behind me, anxious, to see that they were closing in behind me, trapping me. The already dim light became nearly pitch black, and my breath came in quick, terrified pants as the darkness shrunk and shrunk.

But there was a voice that spoke to me from the tiny niche in my brain that wasn't breaking down. Maybe it was Laury; maybe it was of my own creation. It reminded me calmly that this was just a dream, that this nightmare was my invention, and was therefore subject to my destruction. And it told me, in a firm, irrefusable tone, that all I needed to do was run.

It seemed to almost pilot my movements, because a second later, I was leaping forward, straight into the center of the unearthly barrier. A shriek tore from my lips as a heartbreaking chill rushed into my bones. I pressed my hands over my eyes until I hit the ground again with a yelp. Thankfully, I had enough sense to mentally soften the earth beneath me.

For a moment I simply lay there, contained in a self-inflicted darkness, catching my breath. It's a strange thing, to have your eyes closed in a dream: you can see everything inside your head, all the swirling thoughts and emotions, connected by a glistening channel that stretches between sleep and reality.

But I had to get up eventually, and when I did, I found myself alone. I was still in the woods, bathed in its dim light, but the shadows had dispersed. All that was left of them was a residual chill in the air.

I lifted my head and saw, mounted on a tree at eye level, an oval mirror that matched the one Rose's necklace. It was tarnished on the edges and the reflection was slightly distorted from grime, so I had to look closer to see myself. Except it wasn't my image that I saw, staring out from the glass; it was that of Rosemary, my long dead sister, matching my movements to a T. She wore the mirrored charm around her neck.

"I found it," I breathed to Laury, tilting my head and watching my sister mimic the action. It was her, most definitely. I stared straight at her eyes to see if there was any recognition, but she remained stoic, as if she was only a projection.

What is it? Laury questioned, still unable to see.

"A mirror." I reached out to touch the flaking gold paint on the sides, losing sight of my sister to inspect it more carefully. "The mirror, actually," I amended, and scratched at the surface until dry paint got under my nails. "What do I do with it?"

Destroy it, was the medium's immediate answer. Find something heavy and break it into pieces. It needs to be completely obliterated.

I swallowed hard, trying not to think of shattering Rosemary's face. "Right," I said. "Not a problem. Let me just find—"

I froze mid-sentence, because suddenly, another icy wave swept through me. I felt utter fear—not the panicky kind, but the kind that seeped in so slowly that it shocked me into placidity. With slow, measured breaths, I leaned back and returned my focus to the mirror. Now, instead of Rosemary, it was in fact my impassive face that filled the mirror. But over my left shoulder, close enough to touch, stood another figure. A familiar, chilling, unmistakable figure.

It was the auburn-haired boy, spun from nothingness and without my consent. He lingered there, in my dream, a supposed figure of my imagination. He wasn't meant to be real, not here, where everything was under my control. Yet although I willed him to disappeared, he stayed in place, unmoving. A fact, not a pawn.

His abysmal eyes met mine in the mirror, their pull almost magnetic in nature. The darkness, though repulsive, seemed to draw me in effortlessly. From somewhere that I could no longer fathom, I heard Laury shouting my name. A shiver of dread snaked up my spine.

And the monster smiled.

CHAPTER 21

I didn't dare turn around.

The auburn-haired boy, the handsome demon with midnight eyes, was mere inches behind me, so close that his frosty breath brushed against my neck. His grin was cruel and sharp—like everything else about him—and the sight of it rooted me to my place in fear.

Yet it was not only my immobility that stopped me from turning. When I stood and stared at him in the mirror, I could still entertain the notion that he was not real, that he was yet another subconscious imagining. A figure in a looking glass.

Except that he was wasn't. There was another layer of reality about him, more than even Logan's projection had had. He was solid and fixed, and I was certain that if I held my ragged breaths, I'd be able to hear his mind crowding into mine.

This, certainly, was a dream.

He wasn't.

Parker, you need to stay calm. Laury's voice resumed suddenly in my head, louder now. Don't look at him.

"Can you see?" I breathed, not taking my eyes off the boy. As long as I watched him, I was paralyzed, but if I had stopped, he would have been out of my sight. I preferred stillness to being blindsided.

"Laury?" I murmured, when she didn't reply right away.

Yes, I can.

The monster cocked his head, still smirking.

"The boy," I whispered. "Dream, or real?"

Laury hesitated for a moment, that beat of silence giving away her answer before she even spoke it.

Real.

I let out a long, long breath and pressed my palms against my thighs. The boy's eyes wanted to swallow me whole.

He's not stopping you, Parker, Laury said quietly. He's just watching. He isn't doing anything, even though he could do plenty. He could kill you in this dream, really kill you, and you'd never wake up. But he isn't.

"Thanks for the reassurance," I said, keeping my voice sharp to counteract the fear that was coursing through me. As terrifying as this was, Laury was right: the boy wasn't doing anything. He was simply standing there, albeit far too close, and watching me. If he was aiming to cause any damage, he would have done so by now. But he was as motionless as me.

This changes nothing, the medium said forcefully, her voice bouncing around in my skull. You still need to get rid of that mirror.

I took a deep breath and squinted at the mirror; it's gilded edges seemed to be flaking paint even as I watched. For a split second, I took my eyes off the young man behind me, and focused entirely on my own reflection. It wasn't Rosemary anymore: it was me. Stringy brown hair, big eyes, smeared eye makeup and fading red lipstick. Disheveled, maybe, but it was still me. And looking into the eyes of my reflection, I felt a boost of sudden confidence, a steady conviction that I could do this, monsters or not.

I blinked slowly, looked up, and much to my surprise, it seemed that demon-boy was getting out of my way. With slow steps, he was retreating, his hands clasped behind his back and a knowing smile still ghosting upon his lips. I turned around without thinking—but in those few moments that he was out of sight, the boy disappeared. There was nothing left but the mere whisper of his presence, and even that was beginning to melt into the blurring forest.

Parker, you need to hurry, Laury urged. You're starting to lose control.

I didn't even realize it, but Laury was right. The scene around me was shifting and tunneling, becoming more like a normal dream. As I became of aware of it, the changes became more drastic: people began to appear around me, speaking in loud voices, the sound of it vibrating and shuddering. I began to feel myself separating from the dream; my brain was beginning its transition back into reality.

Parker!

I didn't trust myself to respond. Every movement was a risk, and to call back would pull me back up too quickly. Instead, focusing, grounding myself, I turned back to face the mirror. My reflection had disappeared, as had any other reflection, and the mirror was clouded with a dusty blackness. I ignored this, instead gritting my teeth and kneeling on the floor, focusing my energy into materializing a rock on the forest floor. It appeared in my hand, and I imagined that I had enough strength to pick it up, to carry it, to drag it a few feet back.

The people still swirled around me, nothing more than a blur of colors that might have been human figures. I wasn't even sure if I was still in the forest; it was hard to be sure. It was as if I'd spun around and around until I could no longer stand, and now the world was tilting off its axis and threatening to dump me to the ground.

I was waking up.

But not yet; I had one last thing to do.

With a fluid motion that could only be accomplished in a dream, I hefted the stone above my head and brought it down upon the face of the mirror. My movements were governed by another, my consciousness already vacating my dream body.

I watched the mirror shake. Shatter. Shards of glass scattered, some of them slicing my skin. I felt nothing. I stood there as, in near slow motion, the looking glass came tumbling down. Destroyed. Gone. And I thought I caught something out of the corner of my eye; nothing more than a darting shadow, really, and a breath of icy breeze. I tried to turn my head, but my movements were too sluggish now. Everything was fading back. The last thing I felt was a cool fingertip, tracing gently down my cheek.

I shivered.

I woke up.

My eyes opened slowly, as if they were being carefully pried apart. I saw Laury straightaway, then my mother, then Aubrey, but the sunlight from the window made their faces hazy. My stomach was churning. My body was drenched in cold sweat.

I didn't feel fixed. I just felt sick.

Distantly, I heard Laury's command to give me space; my ears felt like they were stuffed with cotton. My senses, still dull, were gradually returning. The sensation of ice against my face lingered. I raised a hand to my cheek as I sat up, trying to blink myself back. Everything felt muffled. Against Laury's command, my mother dived forward and embraced me.

"Thank God," she breathed. "It's over."

I saw Laury sigh in relief, and Aubrey crack a smile. The chain around my neck broke and crumbled into my lap: the mirror in the charm had disappeared. Gone as well, like its twin in my dream. My mother's relief was glaring and tearful, and she kept repeating that last word. Over over over over.

Funny thing, though. It didn't feel like it was over.

CHAPTER 22

I t was Saturday.

Eleven days had passed since I'd had nightmares. Eleven days since Laury had gotten rid of the incubi. Eleven days since Logan had so much as looked at me.

Thanksgiving had passed in a blur of food and cooking and greeting all the friends and neighbors who my mother invited to dinner. Logan wasn't speaking to me, of course, and I wasn't speaking to him—but I was trying to ignore that. Juliette thought we were having problems in our "secret relationship," and I was too tired to convince her of anything else.

Aubrey left on the Friday after Thanksgiving, and by then, everything felt like it had gone back to normal—but a better normal. Zipper was getting healthier, my mother and I were getting along, and Dr. Hennessy had called and graciously scheduled a makeup date for the midterm, which I studied for properly and took without a problem. Everything that had gone wrong was slowly piecing itself back together.

Except that something didn't feel right.

In the grand scheme of things, ending this had been astound-ingly easy. But when I thought about the amount of grief that the nightmares had been giving me, that didn't seem plausible. I should have had to fight so much more to banish the monsters from my head; they should have tried to stop me. They hadn't, though. They had let me win.

And that was the problem.

I was at the pool on Saturday, and it was so empty and so quiet that my mind was almost forcibly compelled to think. The last time I had been here was the day of the necklace incident, and though I had no plans to relive that event, I couldn't stop the feeling that something, somehow, was going to go wrong.

As I cut silently through the water, eyes burning with chlo-rine, I remembered the auburn-haired boy's appearance in my lucid dream and thought, with a slight rush of dread, that he had just been toying with me. He had been there, inches away, a single aspect of my dream that wasn't under my control. I saw his black eyes clearly in my head—his ebony pupils so dilated that they left no white, no veins, nothing to vouch for humanity, because in him, humanity didn't exist.

It couldn't have been so easy. They were messing with me, taunting me, letting me believe that I had achieved normality, raising me to a pinnacle of relief just to rip every shred of imagined comfort right out from beneath my feet. They were cruel, and they wouldn't be turned away so easily.

I was convinced that I was not safe, not really, not yet, and the lingering fear made every breath of air I took harsh and desperate. It had been eleven days of silence in my head and in my dreams, but that meant nothing. The most terrifying monsters were the ones who knew patience.

The air was cold when I left the pool, and it stung my skin until I found my towel and pulled it tightly around my shoulders. Everything felt strange and not quite real: the air, the water, the smooth tile underneath me. It was if everything was taking a deep breath. The calm before the storm, I thought, and shivered.

My phone buzzed as I was leaving the recreation center, but by the time I managed to dig it out of my bag, I was on the front steps and the call had gone to voicemail. I paused against the railing, shuddering as heavy gust of wind blew my damp hair across my face, and played the message.

It was Laury.

"Parker, it's me," she said, her lilting voice urgent and strained. "I made a mistake. When you broke the connection in the dream, I"—she swallowed—"I thought they were gone for good. But I was wrong, and I'm so, so sorry. I don't know when you'll hear this message, but I can only hope that it's soon. Listen to me, Parker: I need you to stay inside your house. Stay indoors and don't leave; that's the safest place for you right now. I'm on my way this very second and I'll be there to explain as soon as I can, but please, stay in your house. Don't let anyone in, no matter who they are. They aren't gone, and I—"

The message ended.

I held the phone numbly to my ear as the automated voice gave me my options—save, delete, call back. I hung up. As I lowered my hand, the late afternoon shadows around me suddenly seemed to take shape, shifting into figures that were a whisper away from human, lurking in the shadows of buildings and creeping behind trees and bushes. The snow-speckled streets were eerily empty, and the more I stared, the more the shadows built, and the more the terror sank in.

Walking home in the encroaching evening darkness wasn't sounding like such a good idea anymore. But my mom was still at work, Juliette didn't have a car, and Aubrey had been back at school for a week. The only person left was Logan, and he and I weren't exactly on the best of terms. Still, as I weighed my options—a few minutes of awkwardness in the car versus braving the monsters alone—I decided that I was willing to take the leap.

I dialed his number, edging back against the wall of the recreation center so that I had a full view of my surroundings and nothing could sneak up on me. The phone rang for so long that for a moment I was afraid that he wouldn't pick up. But after a short eternity, he did, and answered with a terse, "What?"

His dispassionate tone hurt, but I forced myself to ignore it. My eyes darted left and right as I choked out the two syllables of his name. "Logan," I breathed, my pulse racing beneath my fingertips. Even to my ears, I sounded terrified, and, fighting or not, he'd spent ten years of friendship learning how to tell when something was wrong.

"Where are you?" was all he said.

"The rec center."

There was a pause, the sound of keys jangling. "Stay right there," he ordered. "I'm on my way."

He hung up, and I let gravity take over, dragging my body to the ground. No one passed; no one saw me; no one was there to witness the shadows. But they were there, waiting, and I knew this in the same way I knew that they had never really gone.

I tried to call back Laury's number, but there was no answer and I didn't leave a message. In the pit of my stomach, I was fearing the worst: that these creatures, whoever they were, had gotten to her and taken her away. And then I had a horrible, unbidden thought that sent a shock of guilt through my stomach as soon as it surfaced—that maybe, if they had her, they wouldn't come after me.

I slapped my hand over my mouth as if I'd spoken it aloud, but it didn't matter either way, because the only ones to hear were the shadows. So I just sat there, phone in my hand, fingers over my mouth, staring out into the street until the streetlights came on and Logan's car came wheeling around the corner.

I thought of the last time he'd come to pick me up like this, when it had only been one man lurking across the street. Now, they were everywhere, and even Logan's presence didn't scare them off. They were crouched in the corners of my vision, just out of full sight. If I moved at all, I was certain that they would amass, immerse me in their darkness and swallow me whole.

But I didn't have to even stand, because Logan leapt out of his car and around the front of it, looking around until his eyes found mine. There was a pained look on his face, and his body was shaking, but he did not hesitate to run up the front steps and kneel in front of me.

"Parker," he said loudly, his warm hands finding the sides of my face. "Parker, what's wrong? What do you need?"

"I need to go home," I murmured, and I felt his worry, his confusion, his need to protect me. His eyes roved over my face for a moment, looking for answers, but he didn't ask.

"Come on, then," he said, and gathered me into his arms. I felt like a child as he lifted me off the ground, but his warmth was safe and solid and real. I buried my face into his shirt and breathed in his familiar scent, curling up against his chest and wishing the shadows away.

They didn't leave, of course, but they were held off long enough for us to get to the car. Logan set me gently on the passenger seat, swim bag and all, then returned to the driver's side and revved the engine. The shadows were not gone, and they were watching, but I kept my eyes shut and focused on my breathing and Logan's breathing and the smell of his car and the way the loose sketchbooks under my feet shifted as he turned the corner.

Neither of us spoke during the short ride, until Logan pulled up in front of my house. He cleared his throat and said, "We're here," and I opened my eyes. Looking out the window, I still saw the shadows, but I got the feeling that Logan didn't. They only wanted me; I was the only one who had to see them.

"Okay," I said, then repeated, "Okay. Thanks."

I made myself open the door, just like that, and Logan looked alarmed. "Are you okay, Parker?" he asked. "Do you—do you need me to come in, or?"

I looked into his green eyes and shook my head. "It's fine," I assured him. "I'll be fine."

As I began to step out, though, he grabbed my hand. Bewilderment was written across his face, but he still didn't ask, and only said, "When I came to get you, I—I felt something. Like someone was watching."

I looked at him, with his hand over mine, then at the walk to my front door, polluted with darkness. Logan squeezed my fingers.

"I know," I said, my voice breaking in fear as I looked back at him. "I'm so sorry."

And I pulled away, shutting the door before Logan could speak and racing the shadows inside.

I waited for hours. I sat there on my bed, back against the wall, knees pulled tightly to my chest, and waited. Laury never came—but then again, I had realized early on that she wasn't going to. Something had happened to her, and I didn't know what. I didn't know what would happen to me, either.

I could only wait.

My mother called at around seven to tell me that she would be home late: "Will you be okay for dinner?" she asked. I said yes. I couldn't say anything else.

And then I waited some more, because that's all there was to do. Wait. Something was coming, something that had scared Laury so much that she had tried to drive here, and I didn't know what it was, much less how to stop it. I couldn't do anything but marinate in my own fear.

I was too afraid to leave my room—I was too afraid to stay. My stomach growled and my hair was matted with chlorine, but I couldn't move. I was scared of staying awake, but I was terrified of falling asleep. It'd gone back to that: the fear of what lay behind my closed eyes.

The darkness was closing in. The light bulbs on my ceiling had been replaced, but the switch was across the room, and in my haste to get inside, I'd forgotten to turn it on. Now it was too late, too far away, and I had to make do with the dim lamp at my bedside. Its illumination was meager at best, but I huddled up next to it and tried to ignore the way the shadows were shifting.

Zipper came upstairs at one point, but she stopped at the threshold of my room, barked, and ran back downstairs. She could feel them too. She knew they were here.

It was a stalemate. Here we were, face to amorphous face, but they weren't pushing forward, and I wasn't pushing back. We were frozen here indefinitely, waiting. Counting seconds until someone's patience ran out.

And the shadows grew.

At around ten, it began to rain. I heard the water hitting the roof, the claps of thunder echoing through the street; I saw the flashes of bright white lightning outside my window. It was a storm, here to wash away the remaining snow. As the sounds of it all climbed into my head and the tense air crawled down my throat, the shadows continued to shift and move and grow.

"Just do something, already!" I shouted at them, tears springing to my eyes. "What are you waiting for?"

But I knew. Oh, I certainly knew. They were waiting for the fear to build, for me to become so petrified that I couldn't breathe, because they reveled in the quiet, debilitating phenomenon of human terror. To them, this was nothing but a game, and time belonged to them.

I sat there until eleven, until I was stewing in my own fright. I became my fear; it boiled in my blood and lit on my face. It seeped in slowly, gradually, and then it took control.

At eleven on the dot, there was a particularly bright flash of lightning from outside my window. It cracked the sky and spat white daggers into my eyes, so that for a moment—a sliver of a moment, really—I was blinded. When I could see again, there was someone on the balcony.

A strangled, sobbing shriek escaped my lips, and I slapped a hand over my eyes as if that would make it go away. But even behind my closed lids, I saw those familiar black eyes, that head of auburn air.

"You're imagining things," I murmured to myself, still im-mersed in that self-inflicted darkness. I knew I wasn't, though, and I didn't know why I was pretending. It's a very human reaction, I suppose: denial.

They're gone, I told myself. They're right here. Laury said they'd be gone. Laury was probably dead. She'd done what was supposed to be done, and I was supposed to be left alone. Except that I wasn't alone, was I? The cruel boy was not on my balcony, because he simply couldn't be.

I was entirely unconvinced, but I willed myself to open my eyes.

The auburn-haired boy was leering right in my face.

I struck out instinctively with a blind fist, my body poised for attack even as my mind was reeling in horror. I swung my arms again, again, again, but they only met empty air. My room was empty; the man was gone.

I scanned my bedroom, picking out every corner and crevice to make sure that he wasn't simply hiding from me. Not only was he not there, but there was no evidence of his presence to speak of. Here and then gone, all in a blink. It was only the shadows and me, alone again.

But he was the shadows, wasn't he? He was them, and they were him. His heart and soul were as black as his eyes, fueled by the same umbrageous force that lent the obtruding shadows their movement. And I had the very pointless thought that these creatures knew humans well: they knew how completely we feared the dark.

I pressed a finger to my neck to feel my rapid heartbeat and tried to remind myself to breathe. My head was a flurry of utter panic because if the boy was back, that meant that they were all coming. I'd wanted to badly for something to happen, but now I just wanted it to all go away.

"Please," I murmured. "Leave me alone."

I swear, the shadows laughed.

I didn't take my eyes off them, but I stuck out an arm and felt around until my fingers closed around my cellphone. Logan's number flashed onto the screen the moment I began to type it in, and I called, sensing the way the shadows pressed in closer in protest. I rocked back and forth as it rang, and begged him to pick up, because I needed him, and he never ignored that.

"Please, please, please," I mumbled, my thumbnail between my teeth. The phone trilled six, seven, eight times, then paused. For a moment, I thought he had answered, but it was just his voicemail message telling callers to leave a message so that he could get back to them later.

Beep.

"Logan," I said desperately, "they're back. When you felt something at the rec center, it was them. They're back, and even if you don't believe in them please just believe in me, you have to—" My sentence was cut off abruptly as something very strange happened: something gripped my body, snaking in as if someone else was stepping into my skin. I felt shoved aside, as if I was no longer in control of my own movements. I felt a tug on my arm, trying to tear my phone away from my face. I resisted, gritting my teeth to keep the cellphone at my ear so that I could hiss out two final words.

"Find me."

My body let go with a bone-deep shudder, and the phone was flung out of my hands. It slammed into my mirror with a resounding crack, and the glass shattered. That hardly even registered, though, because the shadows were coming closer, edging in around me until I could feel their icy touch on my skin. Tears flowed freely down my face, but I was hardly feeling them anymore: I felt only an aching lethargy tugging at my limbs and calling me to slumber. Black tendrils crept steadily into my vision, filling it, and before I even knew what was happening I was falling, falling, falling into a deep and solid sleep.

CHAPTER 23

In my dream, I was in my room. A kind of bone-deep darkness hung in the air, but it wasn't complete; suspended above it, almost as a second layer of atmosphere, was a strange, gauzy glow. Colored streaks lived at the edges of my vision, the way that teen prevention movies show the world through the eyes of kids on hallucinogenic drugs.

But in this dream, the lights didn't seem strange—they were pretty, and I got out of bed to chase them out of my peripherals. My feet seemed to have other ideas, though, because they marched me across my room and to the door, which hung slightly ajar. I thought I felt a prickling on the pads of my feet, but the sensation fled quickly as I ducked into the hallway, which was bathed in the same fuzzy light, and sidled easily down the stairs.

There were shadows all around me, guiding me through the living room and kitchen with icy fingers, but I was not afraid. This was only a dream, after all; they couldn't hurt me.

I waltzed into the sun room on floating feet, past the sleeping form of dream-Zipper. The outer door was streaked with water; it was raining hard. Still, I did not hesitate to push it open and step out into the downpour. It should have been cold, and I knew that, but I didn't feel the chill, even as I strode through the muddy grass on my bare feet, leaving the door ajar behind me.

The wind whistled; I felt the pellets of rain bearing down on my scalp, but the sensation was muted. Everything was still hazy, reminding me with every step that this was not real. I wondered if somehow, I'd unlocked a lucid dream all on my own; but no, that couldn't be right, could it? If that were the case, I would be in control, and I wasn't. There was a force in my feet that guided my steps through the dirt.

At the fence I stopped, placing two hands on its slick surface and hauling myself up to sit atop it. I paused for a moment at that vantage point, looking first to the right, at my blurry blue house, then to the left, at the forest. Ahead of me lay a mystery, all of those trees there that were just begging me to get lost in their mazes. So, with a sigh that had no cause, I leapt to the ground and padded calmly into the dark.

I followed my own footsteps into the woods, walking in a careful rhythm as the howling gale threw leaves into my hair and hair into my face. A small branch flew by, scratching my cheek, but I paid it no mind; I hardly even felt it. I had a destination, and though I didn't know what it was, I knew that I needed to get there.

Step, step, step, said my brain, counting the soft squelches of my feet against the sopping ground. In my mind, the woods were alive with sound. Branches bending, creaking, their wooden limbs crying out in pain; birds, tucked away in their nests, chirping as they tried to protect their homes from the rain;

animal footsteps, darting in and out of bushes, just out of my sight. Everyone had come out to see the show, and I guess that was where I was going, too.

Eventually, after a hazy eternity of walking, I found myself approaching a familiar clearing: the little crescent of space just before Bear Lake came into view. That is where my feet stopped, planting me right in the clearing's center. The wind whipped around me and rain poured in a frenzied tempest, but I just stood there and smiled a little and let myself be lifted slightly off the ground. It was a strange sensation; I felt as if I was detached, not quite tethered to reality and at the mercy of the wind.

"So, she is here."

The voice came from nowhere, yet everywhere; it wandered into the air with a sudden rush of smoothness. I felt it crawl through the clearing like a living creature and slip lithely into my ear.

"I said she would be, did I not?"

While the first voice had been male, the second was female. Where the other had been smooth and accented, like melting molasses, this one was sharp and harsh. The woman's voice grated; the man's voice purred.

"You did," acknowledged the first voice. It paused, then called, "Turn around, please."

Again, my feet acted of their own accord, twirling me around in a gentle pirouette. I squinted against the rain, scanning the treeline for the speakers. After a moment my eyes landed on a pair of shadows, nothing more than a dark assemblage of tinted air.

"Hello!" I called blithely.

I heard a scoff as, right before my eyes, the humanoid shapes began to materialize into flesh. It was like watching a flickering image appear on a projector; they took form gradually, become real creatures with bodies and limbs and faces. They were clad in misty black, their clothing shuddering into solidity like a dredged up memory. Suits. Both of them wore suits. It began to dawn on my as I stood there, still as stone, but nothing sunk in until one of them looked up and fixed me with a familiar smile.

"Hello, Parker," said the cruel, cruel boy.

And my dream was suddenly imagined into a terrifying reality.

They were everywhere: shifting shadows with icy edges, pouring from the forest in a wave of ebony. They gathered behind those first two, the cruel boy and the sharp woman, and took solid form, so that I could see their unfathomable eyes.

I felt the cold now; I felt everything. I felt the rain as it pricked my flesh, the wind as it stung my face. I felt completely soaked through, and my teeth chattered as I lifted my stinging feet in a quick march, trying my best not to sink into the mud.

This was not a dream.

It never had been.

After a short eternity of traded gazes, the cruel boy stepped forward from the pack, crossing the clearing with those measured steps until he was only a few feet away from me. He didn't seem bothered by the weather in the least, and he merely tilted his head and let his lips curl up into an ugly smirk.

"Are you cold?" he asked me.

I tried to stand up straight, but my entire body was shaking. Still, I shook my head. "No," I snapped. He was close; too close. If he had been three miles away, he would have been too close.

I wanted to run away, to release my fear in an endless scream, but I forced myself to stand my ground.

"That's too bad," he murmured, his eyes drifting over my shoulder. "But I suppose it doesn't matter. You'll be easy to subdue, regardless." He snapped at something above my head, and I suddenly felt the pressure of twin grips on either of my arms.

"What are you doing?" I demanded.

The boy tilted his head. "Subduing you."

I looked over my should to see two of those shadows, their wispy arms somehow pinning my arms to my side. Their touch was like ice, and the sensation of it overpowered even the rain. I threw myself against their grip, struggling furiously, but they whipped me back so quickly that it knocked the wind from my lungs.

The creatures laughed as one.

"Who are you?" I spat, though I guess, deep down, I already knew. "What the hell are you trying to do with me?"

"I hope this doesn't sound too crass," said the boy, his accent smooth and old, "but we're going to kill you. I don't quite think it matters who we are."

"I don't care what you think," I chattered, rainwater flowing into my eyes. "If you're going to kill me anyway, why can't you just tell me?"

He looked at the woman, who shrugged, her face impassive. The boy nodded.

"We don't have a name," he said simply, "but your kind have called us many things. The shadows, the nightmares, the devil, God; we've heard it all, in a million tongues and voices. Really, though, we are nothing but deal-makers. We will help anyone who needs us, and all we want is a small gift in return."

"A gift." I tried to scoff, but shivered instead. "Like my sister?"

That gave the boy a moment of pause, and he regarded me through those soulless eyes. "Your sister," he said softly, "Rosemary." With a few slow, deliberate steps, he shrunk the distance between us and put the back of his hand beneath my chin. "You are even prettier than she was."

I reeled away from his icy touch, but only backed into the shadows. "What does that even matter?"

"We collect beautiful things," said the boy, rocking back on his heels. "Treasures. It is our entire purpose: to gather all the lovely things in your world and bring them back to ours. And the most precious treasure, by far, is souls. It used to be easy, finding an untarnished soul. But your kind is rotting, and we have to look hard now, just to find someone whose soul is clean." He frowned, looking me up in down. "You're not spotless," he added, "but you'll do."

I leaned against my captors, fighting the urge to dissolve into hysterical laughter. I was drenched in ice water and being held captive by shadow monsters in the middle of a forest, and they wanted my soul. Things like this happened in movies, not my life.

"Souls," I murmured, a crying laugh slipping from my mouth. "Why? Why do you need souls?"

The boy looked at me as if that should been obvious, and when I didn't react, he sighed. His hand snaked up to the collar of his suit, and he pulled it away slightly to reveal a small, opaque sphere.

"We wear them," he said, "and they keep us alive."

I stared at the boy, and the little charm pinned within his clothes. "I-I don't—"

"You don't understand what you're worth," he snapped. "When you humans think of souls, you think of that little wisp of smoke that floats off to your imagined heaven. But they are so much more than that. Your souls are the very core of your life, and when we take them, we take everything you are, everything you were, and everything you ever will be."

"But—but that's not fair," I breathed, my voice a quiet plea.

"Hasn't anyone ever told you that life isn't fair? We need this to survive. There are six billion of your species; there are mere hundreds of mine. What is one human life to preserve an entire race?" He pinched the sphere between his fingers, smiling faintly, reminiscently. "This belongs to your sister," he said. "It's running low. But after tonight, I'll have a replacement."

I tried not to shudder as he smiled at me, shark-like.

"You won't," I said, with as much force as I could muster. "Human life is worth more than monsters like you could ever understand, and I won't let you take it away."

The boy laughed, the sound sharp and painful, like squealing metal. He leaned near to me, very close, too close and narrowed his eyes. "You think you matter," he spat. "You think people care about you. But really, who does? Your mother? You were never her favorite. Your neighbor? She'll have no trouble finding a new friend. That boy you care for so much? Oh, Parker, he'll move on so quickly. You have no one to miss you. No one to care. You are just as insignificant as every other miniscule human being on this planet. We're the ones who make you matter. We're the ones who take your souls and make them into something great. And we are so much more deserving of your pointless existence."

I lifted my chin in an attempt at defiance; my lips quivered. "That's not true," I said lamely, but I felt every one of his words like stabs in the pit of my heart. The brutal smirk on the boy's lips curved up contemptuously as he brought a chilly hand to the side of my face. Rain beat down on us from all sides, but while I shook, he remained stoic, calm, complete unaware.

"Maybe it isn't," he agreed, his palm against my cheek. "But maybe it is. Either way, Parker"—his frost-tipped nose touched mine—"how do you intend to stop me?"

I thought he would try to kiss me; I steeled myself for the frigid iron of his lips. But he pulled away, shaking his head. "You have no idea. Of course you don't, you foolish human being with nothing to live for." He looked over his shoulder abruptly, turning to the masses of shadows that lurked in the forest behind him. "Bring out her friend," he called.

My stomach hit my rib cage, churning in dread at the word "friend." Images flashed through my mind, of Logan, Juliette, Aubrey, stolen from their beds at midnight and dragged out into the darkness. But they were not the ones who stumbled out into the open from behind the suited creatures. They were not the ones who fell to their knees, thin hands in the dirt—and looked up at me with a very placid smile.

"Oh, hello, Parker," said Laury, her blonde hair falling over her eyes. "Fancy seeing you here."

CHAPTER 24

Laury smiled at me, her back to the mass of shadows that lined the clearing. Confusion lived in my veins, fueling my rapid heartbeat and making my head spin. I was vaguely aware of my teeth chattering, but the cold was forgotten as I tried to make sense of the medium's sudden appearance.

"She was coming to warn you," the cruel boy hissed, and I could feel his breath on my ear. "We stopped her." To Laury, he barked, "Get up."

It was only after a moment that Laury attempted to rise, and even then, it was with considerable effort. Now, as she struggled to her feet, I could see that her bare, drenched arms were darkened with bruises and smeared blood; her bottom lip was swollen, too, and she couldn't stand all the way up.

"What have you done to her?" I breathed, afraid to look at her but too fixated to turn away.

The boy simply chuckled. "We dealt with her."

As if on cue, a thousand twisted voices rose with his in a sick symphony of laughter, shuddering through the air and stabbing my ears with its discordance. Never before had I stood somewhere and felt such evil around me—this, I thought, was every tale of the devil ever penned, suddenly manifested into being. And right now, I was being slowly lowered into the depths of hell; though for what sins, I didn't know.

Forcing myself to breathe, I looked back at Laury, only to find that she was staring right back at me. Except now, rather than a smile, her eyes were brimming with an unspoken apology.

"I should have known," she murmured, her whisper carrying in the wind. "Oh, Parker, I shouldn't have let them fool me."

Looking at her sent a pang through my chest, and my knees buckled beneath me. Were it not for the monsters still clutching my arms, I would have crumpled to the ground. Laury's words brought me back to her hurried message on the phone, cut off before she could finish her sentence. The reason for that was now clear, and though my friend was certainly not okay, I found myself thanking God that she was, at the very least, alive.

"You wouldn't have had a chance against us, regardless," said the boy, still beside me. "You're only human."

Laury's eyes were still strained, but her mouth opened to bark out a harsh laugh. "If you're using the words 'only' and 'human' in that context, you clearly don't know this species as well as you think you do. You feel so superior to us, yet all you are is a nightmare that we make up in our heads. We don't believe in you—not really. You are nothing here."

"We are trying to survive." His voice was sharpened metal.

"The survival of one species is not worth the death of another," Laury stated coolly.

"Do you hear yourself, medium? One human death, just one, and an entire species can survive just a little bit longer. And really, your kind die by the thousands everyday. Every time you blink, a person takes their last breath. So what does it matter, in the grand scheme of things, if we borrow one more life?"

Borrow, he said; I snorted dizzily. I was beginning to lose feeling to everything around me: the cold, the shadows, the implications of the cruel boy's words—all of it began to blur and spin. Darkness crept into my vision quite suddenly, and I felt myself begin to slip into unconsciousness.

I jolted awake.

But not from a dream: I was still in the clearing, swaying beneath the rain as the shadows pinned my arms back and the boy lurked at my side. His auburn hair glinted in the frosty moonlight, and he looked straight ahead, not seeming to notice the way I jumped beside him. I was certain that I had just woken up, yet I was still in the same place I had been before.

Across the clearing, Laury was watching me.

Her eyes, large and unblinking, met with mine, even as she answered to words the boy had spoken an eternity ago. "A life is not something to be borrowed," she said evenly, "especially not from a girl who has barely lived the one she has been given. Once you take a person's soul, you sever them from any possibility of truly living—and you can't give it back."

Her lips moved, and letters spilled out, but all the while, her gaze was resting on me. Shivers crept up and down my spine; though whether from the cold, the creatures, or Laury's intensity, I couldn't tell.

The boy was saying something, but it was meaningless, trivial, because Laury's eyes were words in themselves and as I glanced back at her again and again, I felt myself spinning, spiraling—

I took a deep breath, as if emerging from underwater, and a sharp pain crammed itself into my head. The rain was pouring, and my thoughts were pouring too, out through my ears and mouth and nose, seeping into the air so that there was nothing but blankness in my mind.

Pulse.

A streak of white, and for an instant—and only that—my eyes were not my own. I was smaller, my skin feeling foreign, but I stood in the same place in the same rain with the same shadows everywhere.

Slash.

A resounding crash in my head brought me back to reality a mere millisecond later, bringing with it a white-hot agony that thrashed my skull to bits and unraveled every conscious though I tried to fathom. Yet I didn't grab my ears, didn't scream, didn't collapse; I simply stood there in the cold and felt my brain be slowly torn apart.

My mind was at war with itself, and no one seemed to know it.

Except, perhaps, Laury, whose focus on me was hardening into curiosity. She narrowed her eyes, just for a heartbeat, then turned quite suddenly back to the auburn-haired boy. For a split second I felt the sensation of playing tug-of-war when the person on the other side suddenly lets go, and flailed mentally until I could blink myself back to reality.

Again, I'd woken up.

"Why Parker?" Laury was asking, when I tuned back into real time. My head still hurt, but now, it was nothing more than a dull throbbing in an unreachable crevice. "Why choose her out of the billions of other girls on this planet? If I'm correct, your species isn't the kind to reuse that same toys twice; and after Rosemary, Parker isn't fresh blood."

That, for the first time, seemed to give the creature pause. As I looked at him hazily, I saw something that looked almost like confusion etched across his handsome, calm features. For a moment, the clearing was still; even the rain seemed to hold its breath for that little, pointless moment.

"She has a strong mind," the boy said eventually, but his voice carried none of the pompous superiority that he had exhibited before. "We need souls, yes, but the mind is key."

I leaned forward, my body seeming to act of its own accord; I felt my lips pull back into a broken snarl. Without meaning to, I let a stream of words fall from my lips. "It's because you travel through dreams," I intoned, my voice dead. "It's all inside our heads. You thrive by poisoning my mind."

Both Laury and the boy glanced over at me sharply, surprise clear on their faces. But while Laury's expression quickly became thoughtful, the boy masked his disruption with a cunning twitch of his lips.

"And you can bear it," he said, reaching out to touch my cheek with an icy palm.

His fingers trailed down to rest beneath my chin, and I held myself rigid against his touch. Every time he looked at me, I felt as if I were a lab specimen, placed under a microscope, burning beneath a bright white light. His eyes had no expression, no shape, only endless depth, and they hurt—they sawed crudely at my insides and sliced apart my heart.

Meanwhile, Laury was appraising me as well, but with the cool, calculated determination of a chess player. "She has a very strong mind," she said, after a moment. "So strong, in fact, that you could be threatened by it."

The boy barked out a sharp sound that might have been a laugh. "No one is a threat to us—especially not her. Look at her! Does she look like anything dangerous?"

A flash of indignation sparked through me, and I pressed my lips tightly together to keep the retaliation locked inside. Laury merely tilted her head at his words, a pitying smile flickering quickly across her mouth. "Assuming that nothing threatens you is the easiest way to be beaten."

"Ah, but it is just as bad to assume that you can beat those who threaten you."

"I assume nothing."

It was still pouring rain, but that seemed arbitrary as Laury and the boy faced off across the clearing. The shadows outnumbered her a thousand to one, yet she stood as tall as her broken body would let her and did not allow the ferocity to drop from her eyes.

"I do know something, however," Laury said. "I know that you—all of you—are not nearly as terrifying as you wish you could be. You're just scary shadows, the things that go bump in the night; but if you didn't exist in our heads, you wouldn't exist at all."

"You don't know what you're saying." The boy's eyes flashed eerily in the darkness.

Laury chuckled. "I know exactly what I'm saying, and I know that I'm right. If I were wrong, you wouldn't look so frightened right now." She lifted her chin, tapping one calculating finger against her lips. "That is fear in your eyes, is it not? But not fear of me, no. You're afraid of her."

A thousand pairs of pitch black eyes turned to me; hundreds upon hundreds of gazes crawling along my skin. The shadows behind me loosened their vise-like grips on my arms, and that was probably because they knew the stares alone could root me to my place.

Laury believed that these creatures were scared of me, but if anything, it was the other way around. They petrified me; they ignited a fear in me that was so deep, I couldn't help but think it'd become ingrained on a cellular level. And fear, you know, is a funny thing. It makes you act as an alien to your normal self; it forces rash decisions into your brain and convinces you that they are okay. And when you are put into a situation that is either fight or flight—it often makes you run.

I ran. The terror built up inside me and I hurled myself forward, into the clearing, my bare feet burning as they scraped against bark and rocks. Mud caked my ankles, but that didn't matter as I ran straight for the flimsy wall of shadows. My breath came in heavy pants, water flowed into my eyes, and my entire body shook with the effort. I heard a shout, then several, but I was too far, too far for them to catch me, and just when I thought I'd made it—

I wasn't fast enough.

Because suddenly, I was airborne. An invisible force slammed into my back and sent me hurtling skyward, to a dizzying height. As I plummeted back down, I heard Laury scream my name. Then I hit the muddy earth, landing on my right arm with a sickening crack that reverberated through my entire body. I curled into the ground, my face in the dirt, I bit my tongue to ward off the agony. Darkness filled my mind, consuming me for a single freeing moment.

"Where do you think you're going?" a furious voice bellowed, jolting me back to consciousness. I opened my eyes blearily to find myself staring up at the boy. He was livid. His eyes were narrow slits, and his face burned with anger. He glared down at me, his foot poised as if to kick me in the stomach.

He didn't.

Instead, with a cold, strong hand, he gripped the collar of my shirt and hauled me to my feet. Rain streamed through my hair, spilling clods of soil into my eyes and onto my tongue. He shook me, sending sharp pain through my arm, and I cried out.

"Does that hurt?" he asked, his voice heavy with cruel glee.

I tried to choke out a "No," but the sound was pitiful. Soulless joy filled the boy's eyes, so close to mine, and he took my limp, throbbing arm between his fingers. His grip was gentle at first, but only for a moment—because seconds later, he was squeezing my arm like it was the only thing left to anchor him to the ground. It hurt so much that I scream tore itself from my lips, the white hot pain rushing through my nerves and into my head and building up a strange lucidity that somehow resulted in anger.

"Don't touch me!" I shrieked, and arched back as far as I could, flinging myself out of his grip and back onto the ground. As I scrambled to my feet, I swear I could see the air between us simmering.

The boy stared at me for a moment, his jaw set, his eyes on fire, his pale lips pressed so tightly together that they were almost white. For a moment, all that existed was him, me, and the curtain of rain pouring down between us. The forest, the lake, and the shadows all disappeared, leaving only the two of us skirting around each other. He edged toward me, and I backed away, and this game continued until, before I knew it, my feet were digging into the coarse sand at the very edge of the lake.

"Watch out, Parker," said the boy. "Wouldn't want to fall in; especially not in weather like this."

My teeth chattering, I risked a glance over my shoulder at the lake. The boy was right: it was overflowing, the rain causing it to spill onto the banks and the heavy wind making the water rise in waves. Without thinking about it, I took a step forward, only to crash right into the boy's solid frame. He laughed at me as I stumbled away, and his voice tread air like razor sharp wings. His eyes drifted briefly shut, and for that miniscule moment, I looked at him and could almost believe that he was normal; a teenager just like me; a handsome boy standing in the rain. But when he lifted his gaze and fixed me again with those bottomless irises, I knew that normal was the word least apt to describe him.

The boy was a monster, and nothing more.

CHAPTER 25

My arm throbbed, pulsing white hot pain through every nerve ending. The boy shook his head at me, pursing his lips delicately in an expression that managed both pity and spite.

"I'd have thought that by now, you'd know not to cross me," he breathed. "It seems as if your spirit will be harder to break that your dear sister's was. She was so easy."

At the mention of Rosemary, wings shuddered through my mind once again, and for a moment, I felt as if I was surveying the scene through another person's eyes; smaller, younger eyes that were even more frightened than I was. The pain in my arm subsided, and as the boy smiled at me, the whimper of fear that escaped my lips was not in my voice. I realized suddenly that this was a memory—a memory that wasn't mine, but that I was reliving with so much clarity that it was as if I had been there there...or as if someone who was there was inside my head.

And with all that had happened to me, that notion was far from surprising.

I came back to the present with a jolt, blinking rain out of my eyes. The lake water was lapping up against my muddy ankles, warning me with every icy slap that its consuming waves were only inches away. The boy was still staring at me, his eyes expectant, so I straightened my shoulders and forced myself to meet his gaze head on.

"You don't scare me," I said, and the words were both the biggest and best lie I had ever told.

He saw right through it, of course, and laughed. "Yes I do. We all do. Look at you: you're terrified. It's pathetic."

"It's human," I countered. "In other words, everything you can never be, no matter how hard you try."

Anger flashed in his eyes, and I sensed that finally, I had struck a chord. "We're not trying," he hissed. "The last thing we want to do is be like you."

I clenched my fists, ignoring the pain in my arm, as if I kept them tight enough I would be able to hold onto the small sliver of confidence that had crept up within me. Before I could grind out another response, however, the boy spoke again, murmuring, "There is far too much talking going on right now. This needs to be finished before you are missed."

As the boy placed a chilly hand on each of my arms, I couldn't help but worry about just what he meant by "finished." By the sinister gleam in his eyes as he leaned closer, and the way the surrounding shadows seemed to cluster in, I didn't think that it could be anything good.

"This won't hurt," lied the cruel boy, his lips curled into a perpetual sneer.

"Yes it will," I replied. My voice was stronger than it felt. I wondered briefly how, at this moment, seconds from having the very center of my being vacuumed into the soulless pit of a monster, I was finding a sense of tranquility.

It was the calm before the storm.

"Yes," he agreed, a moment too late. "It will."

I shuddered as a breaking wind snapped over us, bending the boughs of a low-hanging willow to brush the surface of the lake. As if in response, the water splashed into the air.

"What are you going to do?" I asked softly, staring into the trees.

The boy was silent for a moment. I wasn't looking at him, but my gaze was forced in his direction as he placed two fingers beneath my chin and turned my head with a surprisingly gentle touch. He studied me with his eyes, and thought I couldn't read the look in them, I quickly realized what was about to happen.

"I'm ever so sorry," he said, not sounding sorry at all, as he leaned forward and pressed his lips to mine.

The cruel boy had kissed me once before; once, as I waded in and out of sleep, when I was still unsure of what was real and what wasn't. This time, every sensation was intensified, and every shred of fear was blown into maximum proportions. His lips, cold to the touch, burned icicles against mine. His fingers, wrapped around my wrists, sent pain shooting up my arms. It quickly became very clear that this was far more than just a simple kiss in the rain.

I felt it inside of me, something that started like the gentle flutter of moth wings and morphed into the slicing blades of a propeller. It turned my blood to ice and then set it on fire; the flames burned behind my eyelids. My eyes were squeezed shut in terror, and any hope of a scream was trapped in my throat. And though I wanted to struggle—though every part of me was demanding that I fight back—the spell of the boy's insistent lips left me rooted to the spot.

Having one's soul forcibly removed from their body feels exactly as it should: as if something is being ripped out of you, being clawed away so savagely that it turns you inside out. The pain was sharp and thrumming, like a heartburn that was everywhere all at once, and it hurt. It really hurt. I felt the tears on my face and the sweat on my brow, and I felt the complete and utter hopelessness of my situation. Because at this point, I thought, there was no chance. I could wish a thousand times over for everything to disappear, and to wake up in my bed in a cold sweat with the realization that everything had just been a bad dream, but it wasn't going to happen. There were no whispered prayers or lucid dreams that could save me.

There was only a spunky psychic with an uncanny amount of resolve.

I had all but forgotten about Laury in the midst of accepting my imminent death, but she clearly had not forgotten me. Even now, I wonder how she did it: how she tore herself away from the shadows and ran, broken body and all, faster than they could catch her. I wonder how she was brave enough to barrel straight into me, screaming, "Don't touch her!" and sending me flying off balance.

But she did it. One moment the boy's lips were crushed against mine, and the next I was being shoved away from him, somehow catching air and lingering there for a split second. The lake was below me, tossing fitfully, and the boy was reaching his slender fingers toward Laury's neck.

I heard a scream as I hit the water, but I'm not sure whether it was hers or mine.

Have you ever nearly drowned?

I had once before, at a swimming practice back when I was seven. I dived a little bit too enthusiastically into the deep end, it my head on the bottom of the pool, and forgotten which way was up. I remember my mom telling the coach that the safety standards needed a major boost, and almost made me quit the team. She had already lost one daughter to drowning, I guess—and that was one too many.

That's what I was thinking about as I plunged into the ice cold water: swimming practice all those years ago. Swimming practice, where there were parents and coaches and lifeguards. Not here, in the middle of a freezing lake at midnight with a potentially broken arm. I didn't have time to be confused as to why Laury had shoved me into the lake, or what was going to happen to her now. The most imminent problem was the matter of how I was going to get out.

At first, as I sunk into that murky abyss, I wasn't very afraid. My air supply would last for a minute at least. The water rushed around me, and though it was dark and cold, it blocked out all the sound, cocooning me in a tight, familiar embrace.

But the deeper I got, the more panicked I became. I was start-ing to feel the strain on my lungs, and as fear set in, I began to kick and flail against gravity's insistent tug. If anything, though, that only made me sink faster. This was a new position for me: as a swimmer, I was used to having complete control over all my limbs, and knowing where I was in the water at all times. I was only one appendage shorter, but now I found myself unable to go anywhere but down.

My air was going fast.

I knew what was going to happen. My lungs were going to scream for air, and choke when they couldn't get any of it. My head would start to throb, and my eyes would drift slowly shut. A burning sensation would arise in my chest and spread through my blood like wildfire. Inch by inch, my body would shut down, my movements becoming heavy and weak. Then my mouth would open in a last attempt to breathe, sending a flow of water into my throat. Eventually, my heart would stop.

But I wasn't there quite yet. And until I got to that last point of complete immobility, I wasn't about to stop fighting.

I was slipping downward, looking up, kicking fiercely and sweeping my one good arm in an attempt to change directions. Something was slowing me down, however, besides the obvious injury, and I realized that it was my fleece pajama pants, billowing out around my legs and filling with water. They had to go. Using my toes and a hell of a lot of willpower, I managed to inch them off my body and send them floating upward: in other words, the very direction I needed to swim. The lack of cover made my bare skin sting with the cold, but I ignored the feeling as I swam as fast as I could after the streak of pink fabric.

My hurt arm was shrieking in pain, but I didn't hesitate to use it as best I could, even if all it could do was flap uselessly at my side. I followed the pants on their diagonal, ascending path until finally, they stopped rising. They'd hit the surface about five meters away, and soon, I would too.

At least, I thought I would. What I had forgotten while swimming for my life was that their were hundreds upon hundreds of monsters waiting along the shore of the lake, wanting to kill me with every fiber of their being. And what I hadn't counted on was the fact that they would follow me down in the form of a thousand shadows collecting on the water's surface.

There had been a sheen of moonlight against the water, but as I watched, every glimpse of light was slowly blotted out by a massive shade. They brought in the night piece by piece, filling in a jigsaw puzzle that left me immersed in darkness. I tread water and watched, breathlessly, as everything disappeared.

Time had lost all meaning by that point, and it didn't matter so much about how long I'd been underwater, but how much longer I'd be able to hold my breath for. I couldn't see, but I got the sense that the shadows were converging—and if that was the case, I would have nowhere to turn. My lungs ached, and I felt my lips strain to open, but I pressed them together and clenched my teeth. If I gave in to that one need, everything would be over.

Cold water stung my eyes as I squinted at the surface, trying to assess the situation in the few milliseconds of air I had left. And as I stared up at the black water and my limbs began to go limp, I decided that I only had one choice: I had to keep going up.

Not allowing myself a chance to hesitate, I gave one final kick that sent me spiraling skyward. I tried to tell myself that this was just another swim meet: I was streaking through the final leg to hit the wall before my opponents. This thought set a familiar seed of determination in my mind, and with all else forgotten except the need to make it to the end, I plunged through the shadows and into the open air. My instincts took over immediately, and I gulped in a heaving breath, tipping my head back against the waves. My eyes darted from left to right, and I quickly realized that there was no sign of the shadows. There was, however, a thick layer of ink spread out over the lake like frigid oil. Still, I knew that my focus had to be on getting to shore. So I paddled my arms and kicked my numb legs, ignoring the water that splashed against my face and the fact that it was very hard to stay afloat.

As it turned out, staying afloat wasn't on my agenda.

I had barely been swimming for a second when a hand seemingly appeared from nowhere, landing on my head and pressing me back beneath the water. I wasn't prepared; I had no time to take a breath before I went down. I struggled, panic racing through my veins, but the arm that held me in place seemed to have infinite strength. At the same time, all those melting shadows crept toward me through the water, surrounding my flailing body and encasing me in a frigid embrace.

Without thinking, I tried to scream; by the time I realized my mistake, it was too late to take it back. Water flowed into my mouth and down my throat, choking me. The darkness melded with my skin and turned my flesh to ice. And in that next moment, that single second before I lost consciousness, I looked up and saw the cruel boy's face, distorted by the water, smiling as he watched me drown.

In the darkness, I heard a familiar voice.

It wasn't quite words, though, that traveled into my ears and slipped like molasses into my head. It was more like the idea of them, the faint echo of something spoken and not understood.

I wondered briefly, automatically, if I was dead, and if this was the part where I was informed that I was going straight to hell. It was too dark to tell.

But there was that voice again—and now, as my brain cleared, I was almost certain that it was saying my name. Those quiet, whispered breaths were saying Parker, Parker. Parker.

I opened my eyes.

The first thing I noticed was that the ground beneath me was uncomfortably damp; the wetness seeped into my clothes. However, it wasn't raining wherever I was, and that was a slight improvement. And, I realized as I flexed my fingers, my arm was no longer broken.

As my surrounding registered, I noted that I was still at Bear Lake, lying on the shore of clear, calm waters. It was late at night, same as before, and the moon above cast a spotlight on the familiar figure standing over me.

My sister.

"Parker," she said again, peering at me through hazel eyes.

"Rosemary?" I mumbled groggily, blinking as I slowly sat up. My sister knelt down at my side, the knees of her jeans burrowing into the mud.

She looked much the same as she had in every dream, photograph, and memory I'd ever witnessed: she looked just like me. She was my older sister, preserved forever at age fourteen, and somehow, she was here.

"Hey, sis," she said, filling the space with a bittersweet smile.

"Hey?" I lifted a muddy hand to rub my temple. "Where am I?"

"Bear Lake."

"I figured out that much, thanks. But I was just drowning five seconds ago. Where am I?"

Rosemary bit her lip and tapped her palms against her thighs. "You're dreaming," she admitted. "This is a dream. You're actually floating somewhere in the middle of the lake, and demon boy is probably removing your soul from your body as we speak."

I raised an eyebrow.

"Sorry," Rose amended. "That was blunt."

"No kidding."

She sighed. "But it doesn't matter anyway, because he's not going to get very far." She looked over at the lake, her eyes narrowed as if she saw something more than just the silver reflection of the moon.

"I don't—"

"They're not getting away with this, Parker," Rosemary said, her tone steely as she returned her focus to my face. "Not again. I didn't get to grow up, but you will. I'm not letting Mom lose another daughter to these monsters."

I stared at my sister in disbelief, leaning forward to study her features. She was serious, without a doubt, but I couldn't help but think that she was also just a little bit out of her mind.

"Rose, are you listening to yourself?" I demanded. "These things, they—they killed you! They're trying to kill me. There's no way that we have any chance against them. Not us."

"Who, then?" She glared at me. "Who is there to stop them but us? Who else can stop them from killing, once and for all? There's only us, Parker, and I know it's not a lot, but we're all we have."

I was silent.

She said nothing for a moment, and instead opted for picking at the her bare pinky toe. Finally, she sighed and murmured, "Laury said you were strong."

"What?" I said.

"She said you were strong—or at least, that your mind is. And that's why they need you; that's why they're afraid of you. And they are, Parker. I hear them all the time. You terrify them. And I think that makes you the only person who can stop them."

I swallowed hard. We met eyes, sister to sister, and hers were filled with steady determination. I ignored the twisting anxiety in my stomach and tried to channel some of the hardheadedness that I knew we both shared.

"How?"

My sister smiled. "Do you remembered the mirror?" she asked.

"The mirror?"

"Yeah, the one in your dream. Laury made you break a mirror, thinking it was connecting you to them. What she didn't know was that the mirror was actually a gateway for the monsters to come fully into our world. The real connection isn't a real thing, an object; it's just inside your head."

"So, what then?" I frowned. "I break the connection and I'm free?"

She hesitated; just for a moment, but long enough to make me nervous. "Almost."

"Almost?"

"It's not—it's not them you have to sever the connection with," she said. "It's me. I'm the one who's been keeping them alive. My soul has been sustaining them for all these years, and they can't go away until I do."

"What do you mean 'go away'?"

"I mean I have to disappear. I have to extinguish. It means no more talking to you in your dreams, no more sisterly guidance. It means I go to where I should have gone when I died in the first place."

There was a cold look in Rosemary's eyes as she gazed into the trees, her mouth falling into a straight, white line. I felt a shiver run down my back as the implications of her words hit me full force.

"No, okay?" I said, slowly understanding. "There has to be some other solution besides extinguishing you."

"Yeah, well, there's not," she snapped.

I didn't respond. My head was hurting all of a sudden, and it was from more than just the cold. When I looked at my sister, she seemed real—but she had been dead for years, and this was just what was left of her. A dream. A memory trapped inside my head. I had to let her go.

"That's the only way to stop them?" I asked meekly.

"They're nightmares, Parker," Rosemary replied, her voice gentle again. "I'm a nightmare. We're in your head. You dream us into reality."

"But all this time, you've—"

"Only existed because you let us," she finished. "The monsters came in and planted the seed; you gave them water and sunlight and let the plant grow."

I swallowed hard, wrapping my arms around myself. "Then how do I stop them—you?"

"The same way you stop any other bad dream." My sister smirked sadly. "You wake up."

I blinked at her, not quite sure that I was understanding. "I wake up," I echoed. "That's it? No dramatic chases or magic spells or epic battles?"

She chuckled. "Don't go thinking it's going to be easy, little sis. They're in your head, right now. They're keeping you locked inside this dream until they're done with you. But you need to do the same thing to them. You're going to have to fight your way out, because once you do, they'll be the ones trapped in here, you'll be alive, and I'll be on my way to...wherever."

I pursed my lips, playing her words back in my head. "But trapped, you said. That means they're always going to be here, in my head, forever."

My sister's face sobered as she affirmed, "Yeah. They'll always be there. As long as they can't get into your dreams, they won't come back. But you're going to have to live with them, Parker. They'll be there for the rest of your life."

I stared at my legs, somehow once again cocooned in dry, pink fleece. "And if I don't do this?"

"You die, and end up trapped in the dreamworld. Like me."

I looked up, and Rosemary was fixing me with an expression of pleading. I could read it all in her eyes: how she wasn't afraid to disappear, how she thought this could really work—how badly she wanted me to live. This was my sister, my flesh and blood, and if I couldn't trust her at this very moment, I couldn't trust anyone.

"All right," I said. "Now or never."

A smile of relief fell onto her lips, and Rose pulled me into a tight hug that felt very real, considering. When she pulled away, her hands slipped to the back of her neck, tugging off something that glinted and shone in the moonlight.

Her mirror necklace.

"Something to remember me by," she said, clipping it around my neck.

I nodded and touched the cold glass, but said nothing. There was nothing that really needed to be said, not anymore. I took one last look around me, at the calm, quiet lake of my dreams, knowing that when I awoke, it would be to chaos and rain and struggling. And I spared a final glance at my sister, so similar in looks that she could have been my twin. This, I knew, was the last time we would speak. Soon, all I would have left of her would be fading memories in the corner of my mind.

"What do I do?" I asked, forcing myself back to the present, to this dream.

"Lie down and close your eyes," Rosemary instructed. "You'll start to fall asleep, and when you do...well, you'll know what to do."

"Are you sure?"

"Of course I'm sure, Parker." She smiled. "You're my sister, after all. It's in your blood."

I nodded, took a deep breath, and lay back into the mud before I could hesitate. Rosemary grabbed my hand, squeezing it in a tight, comforting grip. I looked up at her for the last time, and slowly, slowly closed my eyes.

"I love you, Parker," she said, as darkness filled my vision.

My voice was already gone, but I thought the words, and knew she could hear them.

I love you too, sis.

I was rushing up through darkness, swimming through an endless vat of ink. My limbs were lost in it, but something was propelling me forward, forward, out of my head. I could feel the shadows grouping around me, touching me with cold tentacles, trying to hold me back. Everything was a blur as I evaded their grasps, speeding away, away, away. It was like the lake all over again; as I swam, I could see the surface coming up fast. Somehow, in all the black nothingness, there was a little sliver of brightness. I drove myself toward that, and finally, when I was close enough, threw myself straight into it.

As I tumbled into the light, I felt my mind reasserting its power over my body. I also felt, though, at the same time, a cord in my head being severed, like an electrical plug ripped from its socket. I screamed at the pain, only to realize that I was, in fact, back in the lake, lost in its murky depths. Water rush into my mouth and down my throat, and I knew I didn't have long. I'd stopped the monsters, but with my head filled with pain and my senses a mess, I had no idea how I would be able to save myself.. Because I was still sinking, sinking, sinking, slipping into the lake bed and back into my unconscious mind.

And then—the air began to shimmer before me. In my dazed state, I couldn't fathom quite what it was. It was a person, surely: a glittery, filmy, person who wasn't quite there. I could have been imagining it, for all I know, and maybe it was because of my inebriated state that when the figure reached out a hand, I took it.

But my eyes were already closing, the water was everywhere, closing in on me, staining my vision black. Maybe this was an angel sent to take me to heaven—or the devil here to drag me down to hell. Maybe I wouldn't survive, but maybe, wherever I went, I'd find my sister.

That is what I hoped as once again, everything went dark.

I don't know when they found me, and I don't know where. But I know that at some point, I drifted back to consciousness long enough to hear a familiar voice calling my name.

"Parker! Oh my God, Parker."

It was Logan. And then there were hands on my arms, on my legs, pulling me out of the lake and into the mud. There were more voices too, in tones I couldn't make out. I thought I heard my mother somewhere in the mix, and maybe Juliette. I felt hands, pumping my stomach and forcing water out of my mouth. And lips, pressed to mine, familiar lips; Logan's lips. But not kissing me: giving me breath.

Then more voices.

It was altogether entirely too much. Nothing had quite registered yet: the fact that I was safe, that the monsters were gone, that Logan was there. That would all come later. At that moment, I was shivering, wearing nothing but a t-shirt and my underwear, and had been completely soaked to the bone. A blanket was draped around my shoulders, and I smelled that familiar scent of toothpaste as Logan pulled me into his arms, rocking me back and forth.

"She's breathing," I heard him say, his lips against my hair. "Thank God, she's breathing."

I couldn't respond, of course. I didn't need to. Everything would sort itself out, but I was there and I was alive and even though I wasn't quite sure how, I wasn't about to take it for granted. Taking a small, grateful breath, I pressed my cheek deeper into Logan's sweater—and let myself realize that finally, I didn't have to be afraid to close my eyes.

CHAPTER 26

According to everyone that mattered, I had attempted to kill myself.

It was the grief, they said. After finding out I'd had an older sister who'd been murdered years before, the belated sadness was enough to drive me over the edge. Some unexpected streak of madness had possessed me to trek through the forest in the middle of a rainstorm and go for a swim with a broken arm—broken, they said, by a fall I could no longer remember.

All things considered, they told me I was lucky. The impacted fracture in my forearm was a doozy, but it would heal. There was also glass to be pulled out of both my feet and some stitches needed on my forehead where I'd somehow bashed it underwater, but those, too, would get better with time. It was just that on top of all of that, my stint in the lake had left me with a particularly nasty case of hypothermia. They told me that I should feel blessed to have been rushed to the hospital so quickly, because, as my nurse had so gently put it, "If you hadn't gotten immediate care, you'd be lying in a coffin right now, not a hospital bed."

As much as I hated the hospital, suffocating under six inches of blankets was infinitely better than six feet of dirt.

So many words were said in those first few days, as I drifted in and out of consciousness and learned to live off of much-needed painkillers, but none of them were the truth. The true story of what had happened that night was one that the doctors and nurses could never hear, and would never believe. The official story left me tangled in a million lies; lies to physicians and therapists, lies to police officers, lies to the countless busybodies who drove an half an hour into Butler just to nose around in my dramatic and anguished life.

My mother was a frequent visitor, of course; she practically lived at my beside for most of the time. Father Lucas made a trip up too, telling me that the town was keeping me in their prayers. Aubrey called from Boston to give her get-wells, and made me promise to give her the full breakdown of what had happened that night when she came down for Christmas. Even Mrs. Hummel made a trip up with Svana to hear the whole story, and she cried when I told her about my sister. (This threw Svana into a fit, so our visit didn't last very long).

The one person I didn't see during those few days of recuperation was the very boy who'd made sure that I was alive to even wonder about him. Logan never showed up, never called, and never returned a single text. When I asked my mom and his sister, they both said they hadn't heard from him. Spending all day in a hospital room staring at the wall leaves a lot of time for thinking, and I found myself worrying in every spare moment, trying to think of what I could have possibly done to warrant his completely ignoring me.

It was driving me just a little bit mad.

By my fourth and final day in the hospital, everything had been mended and all the questions had been asked, and I had all but given up hope of Logan coming to see me. My mother was at work, so I was trapped in my room, flipping through the most useless selection of channels I had ever had the misfortune of seeing. The television on the wall barely had enough connection to manage a visible picture, though, so perhaps I wasn't missing out on much. All I wanted was to get out of the suffocating hospital and saw the uncomfortable gown off of my body so that I could go back home and be miserable in peace.

"Parker." One of the nurses poked her head into my room as I was trying to determine whether the fuzz on the screen was Toddlers in Tiaras or Keeping Up With the Kardashians. She was speaking to me in that soft, pitying voice reserved for puppies and babies: the tone that had become the soundtrack of my days ever since I arrived. "You have a visitor," she continued, smiling slightly.

"Mm," I mumbled, hardly paying attention to her. Odds were, it was nosy Jan from back home, in for another fresh wave of inpatient gossip. But the voice that thanked the nurse as she pushed open the door was immediately recognizable as very much not Jan—and not even a woman, for that matter. It beckoned my attention immediately, and I turned my head, my suspicions were immediately confirmed. Logan was standing in the doorway, one hand in his pocket and the other crushing the stems of a colorful daisy bouquet.

"Hey," he said, his eyes skimming the white tiles.

I swallowed and hoarsely replied, "Hey."

As Logan shifted from foot to foot, radiating about triple his usual amount of awkwardness, I carefully used my one good arm to hoist myself into a sitting position. I was suddenly conscious of the fact that four days of immobility couldn't have done me any good: I had no makeup on, and my hair was ages overdue for a serious brushing. And while those things had never quite bothered me, the way Logan was studying my face made me hyper-attuned to the fact that I was looking significantly less attractive than normal.

"I, um, I brought you some flowers," Logan said eventually, haltingly, dissolving the silence that had cropped up between us. He took a few tentative steps forward, his sneakers scuffing softly against the floor, before coming to a stop a few feet from the side of my bed and looking at me expectantly.

"Right." I glanced quickly around the room, as if the sparse white-and-gray furniture was somehow going to sprout a vase. When nothing appeared, I coughed and sheepishly slipped the glass of water across the table beside my bed.

"You can go ahead and put them in here," I said, ducking my head. Logan raised his eyebrows, his lips twitching in a quarter of a smile, before leaning over and carefully arranging the bright flowers in the small glass. Once they were situated, he hesitated for a moment—then, as if on impulse, strode forward and sat down on the edge of my bed, facing me. His green eyes searched mine, filled with an emotion that I couldn't quite place, and he fiddled with the loose end of a blanket.

"How's the arm?" he asked after a while, his voice low.

I shrugged. "Broken. But healing."

"It doesn't hurt, does it?"

"No, thankfully. My feet, though, on the other hand—let's just say walking isn't really high on my to-do list at the moment."

Logan tried to laugh, but it sounded forced and hollow, and when it petered off, the silence remained. I had known Logan for nearly three quarters of my life, but at that moment, I couldn't figure him out. He was here visiting on my very last day in the hospital, but the simple act of opening his mouth seemed to physically pain him.

And he was being far too quiet.

"I guess I really should be thanking you," I remarked eventually, just to fill the space.

Logan looked up quickly, his expression flustered. "What, for the flowers? It's fine, really, I just thought it'd be nice to—"

"For saving my life," I murmured.

After a moment, he cleared his throat.

"Oh, that. It's not a big deal."

"Not a big deal?" I scoffed. "The doctor said if you hadn't gotten there when you did, I would be dead."

A shadow flitted across Logan's features, and he mumbled a few unintelligible syllables. I tilted my head, peering at him through narrowed eyes, keeping my focus trained on his face until he finally look my way. When he did, I immediately taken aback by his wide, fearful eyes.

"You could have died." His words were quiet and strained, as if it took an unimaginable effort to drag them from his lips.

"But I didn't," I said softly, wringing my hands.

"But you could have. Jesus, Parker, you were so close. Even after I pulled you out of the water, you just looked so—so broken, I didn't know how you could possibly survive."

"I did, though." Tentatively, I reached for his hand and brushed it with mine. "I'm right here, and I'm perfectly fine."

Logan shook his head, continuing as if he hadn't heard me. "And I keep thinking about how if I'd insisted on going inside with you when I dropped you off that night or insisted you come over, none of this would have happened."

"Logan." Hating the self-loathing in his voice, I grabbed his hand in my good one and squeezed until he was looking at me again. "Maybe that's true, okay? Maybe if you'd gone in with me and stayed until my mom came home, none of this would have happened. But the point is that it did happen, and you can't undo that. And at the end of the day, you're the only reason I'm alive right now. So can you please stop feeling guilty and just realize that I literally owe you my life?"

In spite of Logan's regrets, my words sufficed to make him smile, even if just the slightly bit. I let my lips curve up a bit in response, and used my good arm to brush my knotted hair out of my face. The moment didn't last, though, because within seconds the vaguely happy expression was slipping from my best friend's features. He pointed his gaze away from me once again, shaking his head.

"I just." He took a deep breath. "I don't understand. Why you did it, I mean. Why you didn't call me and try to talk things out."

I wrinkled my nose, confused. "I did call you, though. Isn't that why you came to the lake?"

"Yeah, after you had thrown yourself in. I know you were going through a lot with Rosemary and your mom and everything, but I would have listened to you. You know that, right?"

Something about Logan's tone—the slow, therapist-like edge—and the condescending expression on his face set off warning bells in my head. I looked at him carefully, his hand still in mine, trying to figure out what he was thinking.

"I don't understand," I said belatedly. "What are you trying to say?"

Frustration clouded Logan's features, and he pulled his free hand through his hair. "I'm trying to ask you why the hell you attempted suicide when I was only a phone call away."

My jaw dropped along with my stomach: I took in the torment in my best friend's irises and suddenly felt as if I was going to be sick. It made sense, of course, because not only had no one been in touch with Logan, but he hadn't believed in the demons in the first place. There was no easy way to describe it to him concisely, and there was sure as hell no way to make sure he believed me. All I could do was hope for the best as I met his eyes, took a breath, and tried to explain.

"Logan, please," I said, my voice firm. I tried to squeeze his hand, but he pulled away, and I sighed. He wouldn't look at me, but I kept talking. "I wasn't trying to kill myself. I would never do that to you. I wasn't even trying to go to the lake, and that's why I called you. I was scared, because somehow those...crea tures found a way to crawl inside my head and control me. I thought I was dreaming, but then suddenly I was by the lake, and everything was real, and—and they were all there. Everything out of my nightmares was just lined up there in the forest, and that boy, the one who kissed me—he was at the center of it all. He killed my sister, Logan, and he was going to kill me. But Laury was there, and she—"

"Laury?" Logan interjected, confusion spiking his eyebrows as he turned back to me abruptly. "Laury was there? But the police said that she...well, they found...you heard about it, right?"

I nodded solemnly; they'd told me everything, and I'd pretended to be surprised. "Yeah, I heard. They found her car totaled in a ravine off the side of the road, but she was nowhere to be found. They think she must have survived the crash and dragged herself off somewhere, but officers with rescue dogs have combed the area and there's nothing. No body, no clothing, no blood."

Logan made an affirmative noise, then shook his head. "Parker, how could Laury get from the scene of the accident to Bear Lake alive? They said her car was in pieces."

"I don't know, okay? It wasn't her, it was them. They ran her off the road and dragged her with them to meet me at the lake. She was on her way to warn me about them—she called just before you picked me up from the pool. But she never made it; they got to her first."

The tiny room was silent for a moment save for the low hum of the television as Logan mulled over that. "Then where is she now?" he asked eventually, a frown curling his lips.

"I don't know," I mumbled, shrugging. "She's the one who pushed me into the lake, actually. Not that she was, um, trying to hurt me, or anything. She was trying to stop the boy from hurting me, and I kind of fell in. If she hadn't shoved me, I probably wouldn't be here right now. But"—I shook my head—"I have no idea what happened to her. I'm alive, but she's just...gone."

Logan studied my face, his eyes so intense that I had to look away. Finally, he pursed his lips and breathed, "I'm glad you're alive."

"Yeah, so am I."

The atmosphere in the room had become significantly less tense, but it was still a far cry from the companionable silence I was accustomed to having with Logan. Chewing on my bottom lip, I tugged absently at the unbroken pendant around my neck—it was my sister's somehow in pristine condition, as if it had truly become solid in the transition from dream to reality.

Logan seemed to notice it, because he leaned down and squinted at the glimmering mirror. "That necklace," he said. "That's the one I found in my car. I thought it was broken; when did you fix it?"

I cleared my throat, dropping the charm back against my collarbone. "I didn't. This is going to sound crazy, but my sister gave it to me. In a...a dream, or something, at the lake. Something to remember her by."

"You're right," Logan affirmed, shaking his head. "That does sound pretty crazy."

"But do you believe it?" I asked after a moment, tilting my head. "The monsters, the nightmares, Laury—or do you still think I'm crazy?"

"I never thought you were crazy, Parker. I just thought that—I don't even know what I thought, at this point. But I didn't think you could be right."

"And now?"

He let out a breathy snort. "Now? I'm more confused than ever. I'm not sure what I believe"

I looked up at Logan out of the corner of my eye and, with as little fuss as possible, swung my legs over the side of the bed. He edged over to make room for me, and I settled into place beside him.

"Just a thought," I said, clenching and releasing the sheets in my fists. "You might consider maybe believing me."

"I—" He swallowed. "It's weird, because now that everything has happened, I think I'm beginning to. I can see in your eyes that you're telling the truth, so either you're completely hallucinatory, I'm being pranked, or all of this has been completely real."

I chuckled. "The last answer is the winner."

He didn't speak, just nodded, and it was quiet for a while. I looked around the sparse room that had been my home for the past few days, and my eyes were drawn to the vibrant shock of Logan's daisies sitting in my glass of water. As I studied their bright colors, I felt a tickling in my head: almost like something was scratching against a door up there. I tried to ignore it; I'd been getting the feeling since I got to the hospital, but I figured it was simply paranoia. There was no use in getting worked up over a pointless stray thought.

"God," Logan said just then, providing a much-needed distraction. He seemed to be thinking to himself, but I still asked, "What?" as he scrunched up his face.

"I'm just thinking," he said, closing his eyes briefly. "You really could have died out there, Parker. All these weeks, you could have died, and I've just been here telling you that you don't know what you're talking about. Jesus Christ, do you know how close I was to losing you?"

He was looking at me now, his eyes wide. I eyed him carefully.

"You didn't," I reminded him.

"But I was this close. And I just keep wondering what I would have done without you and realizing that the answer is absolutely nothing because I really just think everything would be pointless if I didn't have you. I know I don't understand everything that's going on, and maybe you'll explain that to me sometime, but I don't even care right now, Parker, honestly. The monsters could have just been under your bed or they could have been flesh and blood, but I don't care at all because you're here, and you're alive, and you're okay. I could have lost you, and I think that's made me realize how much I actually I—"

I kissed him. I didn't know why, at the time. Now, I tell myself it's because I wanted to shut him up. But really, I think it's because I knew what he was about to say, and I wanted to beat him to it. And the best way to achieve that at the time didn't seem to be with words, but with a surprisingly simple action.

At any rate, it was a good kiss. It was the kind you get lost in: the kind that makes you forget the clouds over your head and the skeletons in your closet because all you can do is focus on the moment. My hand that wasn't encased in plaster mysteriously wound up tangled in Logan's hair; his found their way to my lower back, pulling me closer to him as if even a grain of space between us was far too much.

We had definitely gotten better at this.

If it was up to me, those few seconds would have stretched on for hours. I didn't want to think about anything else; not the whispers in my head, nor the prospect of going home. I'd almost forgotten that those things existed, and perhaps that was because I was so eager for them to go away.

As it turned out, even my silent wishing for more time was not enough to draw out the moment. We were still very much occupied when the nurse came in, coughing awkwardly and rapping on the door until we had the decency to pull apart for air.

"Pain medication," she said, her voice stiff and squeaky. "And, um, visiting hours are over, young man."

I felt a blush rise to my cheeks. "Do you think you could leave the meds on the table?" I asked casually, just a little bit breakfast. "And can he just stay for one more minute so we can finish our, uh, chat?"

I thought I heard the nurse scoff a little bit at the word chat, but she left the pills on the table beside me and marched dutifully out of the room.

"Wow," Logan said, once she was gone.

"I, um"—I cleared my throat—"I didn't mean for that to happen. I just kind of just went with my gut."

Logan snorted. "You are officially welcome to do that anytime."

I smiled, leaning my shoulder into his and letting my head fall against him. I didn't say anything about anything that hurt, because that was all behind us now. The monsters were gone, the nightmares had ceased, and I was free to start over and pretend none of it had ever happened. Even Laury's disappearance wasn't painful; although that might have been simply because I was refusing to think about it for more than a heartbeat.

"Is it your last night here?" Logan asked, breaking into my thoughts.

I nodded. "Yeah, and thank God, too. I can't wait to go home. The hospital is so cold."

"No kidding."

Logan's arm had absently found its way around my shoulders, and now he calmly fiddled with strands of my hair. I chewed on my lip and inhaled the smell of his t-shirt.

"Will you call me?" I questioned, tipping my head to look up at him. "When I get back?"

He gave me an odd look. "Parker Sage Elway, I am your best friend. I will be the very first one to greet you when you step onto the curb, whether you like it or not."

I smiled softly. "Trust me, I won't mind."

Shaking his head, Logan squeezed my shoulder a final time and got to his feet. I tipped my head back expectantly, without really thinking about it, but he leaned forward and gently pressed his lips against mine once more. A soft smirk jumped at the edges of his mouth as he headed out.

Just as he reached the door, though, Logan paused. He glanced at me over his shoulder, something like concern altering his features. "Parker," he said slowly. "The...monsters. Are they gone? You never said."

I swallowed hard, feeling that niggling scratch once again in the back of my mind. "They've been taken care of," I assured him with a smile.

He still looked worried. "Where are they?"

Where? I could hardly answer that. I pressed my lips together, then parted them again to repeat my answer more firmly: "They've been taken care of."

Logan didn't seem entirely convinced, but it was enough to earn a nod. He was still nodding as he murmured a shy, "I love you," as he slithered out into the hall.

"I love you too," I said aloud to the closing door, the familiar words somehow feeling different on my tongue. I didn't question it. I simply reached over for my meds, scooping the little pills out of their cups only to realize that my only glass of water was being occupied by a bouquet of effulgent flowers. Smirking to myself, I pressed the little button on my TV remote that called the nurses' station and asked for a new cup.

As I waited for my nurse to come, I shook the pills around in my palm. There were three: one in bright red, one a dull blue, and one as black as the cruel boy's eyes. It was so easy to compare the color to him now, to them; I figured it always would be. They personified the darkness that had haunted me for so long. Sometimes when I closed my eyes, I still saw those of a handsome, auburn-haired young man staring back at me, reminding me that he hadn't disappeared completely.

He was still there. He would always be there, lingering. He was there, always trapped inside a dream I could never have, and my sister and Laury were gone. But I was here. I was sitting in an itchy gown in a lumpy hospital bed, but I was very much here. The monsters under my bed had turned out to be just that: monsters. They were nothing more than silly little creatures that I made real by believing in them. They were in my head now: my mind, my rules. They weren't going to hurt me or anyone else ever again, because I no longer lived under their maleficent shadow.

And I wasn't afraid of the dark anymore.

I never ended up going home.

As it turns out, the hospital has a special care plan for patients who have attempted suicide. And since that's the story I went with, I was forced to follow their rules. They thought that I was a danger to myself, so they took me out of Callery and moved me to a rehab center in Philly. They said that it would help me, and anyway, my friends could visit whenever they wanted.

It just made things worse.

I hardly ever sleep anymore. Those little whispers in my head have gotten louder, so that now sometimes it's like the monsters are screaming inside my head. It didn't take long for that to become too much, and that's why I'm still here. Because one day, in yet another one of those countless therapy sessions, the psychiatrist had asked me what was wrong and I'd broken down and told her the truth.

Or, as she called it, the "falsified reality."

She didn't believe me, of course. Who would? I've given up on trying to convince them of my sanity. Every week, they ask me what happened, and I tell them the same thing each time: the truth. Now they all think they've lost my mind along with my will to live.

I know they whisper about me back in town. When I close my eyes, I can practically see Jan and Raissa parked in front of the general store, discussing my mental state behind their hands when my mother walks past. Logan tells me about it, too, how all around the streets they talk about the girl who lost her mind.

But I'll be released soon, or so the nurses tell me. They've been preparing me, gently, for the day when I go home, when I'll no longer have these white walls to protect me. They think I'm excited; I guess, usually, people can't wait to get out of this place. I don't particularly mind it here, though. I don't think I'm ready to face the reality waiting for me outside these doors. I'm not ready to be labeled as insane.

And I'm not ready to be out in the open, where the monsters can find me again.

I know where they are: I know that they're inside my head, and they're trapped there. But I also know that it only takes one bad dream to bring them all back. The constant fear of a nightmare has turned me into an insomniac; I can barely close my eyes anymore without automatically jolting awake. The bruising bags beneath my eyes have become permanent installments. I thought the fear was over, but it's slowly been seeping back in and taking over my life.

My friends come in sometimes. Juliette pops by on the weekends with cookies and a confused little smile; she doesn't know the whole story. Logan stays for hours on the days when he doesn't have school, just sitting and talking to keep boredom at bay. He brings me homework from Dr. Hennessy's psych class, because the professor was so kind as to let me stay on top of my studies while I'm locked in the nuthouse. My mother drives up every single day without fail, and our relationship is better than ever.

But I'm still afraid to leave. It's been four months, and they've been long, but I get food and a television and my room has a nice view. I feel safe here. I don't trust myself to be safe anywhere else.

I'll manage, I guess. Somehow.

You know, though, they were right: writing this down has helped me, though not in the way they hoped. It's made me realize that all of this has really happened to me, and that no matter what they say, I'm not insane. When most people look at me, they feel sorry; I can see it in their eyes. Every doctor and nurse and shrink has pity lingering in their eyes. They shouldn't feel sorry. I'm not broken. I've just been stuck here for a while, because they think I'm broken inside my mind.

They think I'm crazy. But I'm not crazy.

You believe me, right?